Absolutely Perfect

The Author

John Martin was born of Anglo-Irish parentage in London where he was brought up. He is a graduate in Economics of the London School of Economics where he specialised in International History. A financial and business consultant, he has managed companies in Britain, Germany, Japan and the USA, and is the author of a number of books on management and consumer affairs. His first novel, *A Land Without Heroes*, was published in 2002.

He is married to Larisa Kleymenova, and lives and works in Norwich.

Also by John Martin:

A Land Without Heroes

'The events are startling.... *A Land Without Heroes* tackles racial hatred, religious tolerance, wartime romance ... courage in the face of great moral challenge.'

Eastern Daily Press

'This is the first book written in English about the impact of the last world war on Polish Silesia ... surprisingly written by an Anglo-Irish writer from a country where the embers of intolerance still glow ... and deals with political, economic and religious issues as well as the survival of a Polish family under occupation. The book shows love and goodness can survive the stupidities and follies of war.'

Polish Daily

A Land Without Heroes recounts the tale of a young Polish boy as his world crumbles around him ... it is a well-written book with a laudable depth of background research. The sparse and understated prose fittingly accentuates the bleakness of the subject. One simply cannot help but be moved by this tale of triumph over incomprehensible evil and suffering.'

Norfolk Journal

ABSOLUTELY PERFECT

by

JOHN MARTIN

ANGLIAN
PUBLISHING

First published in the United Kingdom
in softback form by
Anglian Publishing,
Sackville Place, 44–48 Magdalen Street,
Norwich, NR3 1JU

First Edition: October 2003

ISBN: 0–9543172–1–1

Typeset by Curran Publishing Services, Norwich
Printed and bound in the United Kingdom by
Antony Rowe Ltd., Chippenham, Wilts

A Work of Fiction

DEDICATION

For Larisa

What is a woman? I assure you, I don't know.
I do not believe that you know.

Virginia Woolf
The Pargiters
(London, 1977)
Talk to professional women in 1931

CHAPTER 1

IT WAS A bright sunny morning in October 1990. One of those wonderfully deceptive and stolen London mornings when the palest of golden light, broken by the last of the pale-green leaves of the giant plane trees, filtered through his lace curtains which, fluttering in a fresh morning breeze, summoned him to another and reprieved summer day.

For some weeks now David Droylsden, stirring in his comfortable bed in his fashionable flat in one of London's up and coming locations, had wanted to get up in the morning. Gone were the dog days which had reduced him to despair and to his bed: a time during which he lacked employment, position and prestige, and when his wealth – and most importantly his cash – was in steady decline. He said to himself that thanks to his cunning and shrewdness he was now back in the saddle: in control of a substantial public company and without the investment of a single penny.

He laughed at the sheer joy of it – but only to himself. How had he achieved it? It had proved to be very simple. He had befriended the chairman and chief executive of a company needing new capital and had beguiled him into believing that he, David Droylsden, with his reputation and contacts in the City, could enable the company to raise the much needed funds. He had wooed the existing directors and persuaded them to the view that he alone stood between them and failure, and that he would invest with others to save their jobs and future careers. He had dangled the prospects of capital gains before them, for 'if the circumstances were right,' he had said, 'then they could have part of the action'.

At the right moment he had switched sides. The new merchant bank had made it clear it would only proceed if the chairman stood down and he, David, took his place. The directors voted the chairman out and were persuaded to put the company into administration, when it could be bought by a new consortium free of debt. Some directors never made it: they were fired. The remainder of them, together with senior staff, were given non-voting shares in a new company formed to take over the old business. There you were. As easy as falling off a log.

But today he couldn't stir. The headache and sore throat of yesterday had turned into a thoroughgoing flu: his head throbbed and his limbs ached and he stretched out his legs for relief. The sheets – the very best linen – symbolised for him the change in his circumstances: they were newly bought and collected, laundered and returned weekly by the very best bespoke dry-cleaner. In mid-week his wife Esther turned the sheets following the practice of her mother and her mother before her. It had not been like this for some time, but now all sorts of things were possible.

What did he say to himself? Was he sorry for the fallen chairman who had mortgaged his properties and his life to grow a successful enterprise? Was he concerned that good people had been deceived into believing that only by breaking the ties of friendship established over many years, and in good times and bad, could the company be saved, then to find that they had lost their jobs, capital and self-respect? Was he disappointed for the creditors who, trusting the company, had lost their money? He thought nothing of these things. He believed in the law of the jungle: in a capitalism 'red in tooth and claw': in the survival of the fittest – synonymous with his own self-interest. He admired Machiavelli, although he had not read him; he thought Nietzsche's attack on Christian ethics to be right, although he was hazy on the details; and he believed that much could be said for a new type of European superman, which included himself, which was odd really as, being Jewish, he was aware of what had been done by Germans in the name of a super race. And on his bookshelf he had his father's copy – now quite valuable – of Dostoevsky's *Notes from the Underground*, which he had read time and time again, which he admired for its demonic energy and advocacy of free spirit and free will, and from which he quoted spontaneously.

Above all he believed in his family: his immediate nuclear family; and then his mother alone in the world; and farther, his kith and kin; and farther still, the wider family of all those who like his parents, and in living memory, had found themselves to be alienated from a new and often hostile world, and who by their own energies and the mutual help and respect of others, like themselves, had made something of it.

It had not been easy for his family. His father had been born Jacob Liebermann and into an Estonian family rooted there for only two generations; the only member of his Jewish family to survive the last world war. Jacob had been incarcerated in a concentration camp in Riga where he had met David's mother Judith. Following the war these two made their way to England where they determined to make a success of the opportunity for a new life. Jacob believed in racial and religious integration and was determined to lose his Jewish identity and find a new one. Finding himself in Droylsden, a suburb of Manchester, he renamed himself in its image. In that simple act the family redefined itself: place, locality and identity became one, and existence became concrete and believable – and not Jewish.

But Judith had other ideas, and Jewishness seeped back into family life like the tide, inch by inch, inlet by inlet. There was the synagogue and the Hebrew lessons; the choice of friends; and the remembrance and practice of religious ritual and festivals. There was, when he was thirteen years old, a bar mitzvah and his entry through ritual into the large and flourishing Jewish community in Manchester. And then there was a reaching out to distant family and friends wherever they could be found and recovered – to the lost, the fractured and distraught.

Now, although he did not welcome it, and could not conceive for what reason or by what process it occurred, in the early hours of the morning these childhood memories ground through his dreams in unpleasant repetition, denying him the pleasure of rest: rarely so intense and frightening as to wake him, but disturbing enough to deny him peace.

In the small kitchen, for the two-bedroom flat lacked space and all the rooms were mean in size, Esther sought the weather forecast, to find that showers and lower temperatures were expected for later in the day. Vexatious. Never to know quite what to wear. Always this problem for women, with men not realising how lucky they were, wearing as they were prone to the same suits regardless of the temperature, with the only decision being whether to wear a topcoat, and if so which one. There was also the importance of things. They were significant to her, carrying as they did the discriminatory power of recognition and place. But on limited means keeping up presented difficulties of placing and matching; taxing and difficult decisions had to be made, rendered more difficult by changeable weather.

The need to make these decisions troubled and upset her this morning because she had become fearful of what she must do, without being able to understand the causes of her confusion and the justifications for her solutions. For many nights now she had slept badly. An inquietude had stolen upon her, shrouding her, wrapping her around, even while she remained snug and warm in her bed. Her heart weighed heavily upon her as a cold and impenetrable stone. She lay on her back to avoid what she feared she might feel if she were to lurch upon her side. What Esther knew was that she disliked the way he did things. But there was nothing new in that. Always sailing so close to the wind. Whether it was legal, she thought not always, and even if so, was it ethical? Usually she tried to avoid these considerations but this morning she could not: for she liked Roger Greer. He had worked so hard to establish his business and now things must be desperate for him and his family. David had made so many enemies and he didn't care a damn. She thought of Ivor. She really liked Ivor. And what did David say? Oh, yes, 'A man who did things always made enemies, and you should judge him not by their existence or number but by their quality.'

'Very clever, I don't think.' She spoke aloud.

The necessity to maintain control of her appearance became of greater importance as her influence over the home diminished. The flat was rented and there were many things she could not do, the lease being restrictive in its terms, and other things that she might have done she chose not to do because in the long term she would not benefit from them. Not that there was nothing she could do, and she had prettied it up – you could see that – but for the most part the colours, materials and textures were not her own: the furniture was not of her choosing, and while bland and inoffensive she had in some respects come to find it hateful. While there were personal objects in the flat, many of which had memories, once treasured, and which had attachments to her and she supposed to him, they had lost their immediate association and power to charm; and to be frank, had become baleful to her.

It seemed to her this morning – and it had grown on her – that marriage, and she had had twenty-five years of it, was a very strange institution whatever her mother might say about it. *Perhaps the most strange thing that had happened to her.* She thought that she had been weakened by marriage. Did it always weaken women, she wondered, or only her?

Appearances mattered to Esther this morning. She looked in the wardrobe mirror and liked what she saw: she remained slim and nicely proportioned and her glossy black hair was fashionably cut in the latest Vidal Sassoon style. She had always liked her appearance but the face she saw now was not the sassy girl of twenty-five years ago. Of course, the passage of time had wreaked its own effects. But it wasn't that. Suddenly it was clear to her: she had lost the 'I' and had become a 'We'. Very often she listened to herself speak and she was always a 'We'. Sometimes, when very angry or moved, and she could be by even the most superficial or sentimental of matters, she would ask herself whether she was really feeling the emotion for herself or whether it was a collective experience. Was it a 'We'? She had tried several times, and always tremulously, to tell David about her confusion. Did he listen? Did he hear? She could not be certain. And how did he comment about this upsettedness? Something to the effect that 'the tears we weep are always for ourselves'. She hesitated for a moment in her panic of herself and hoped he was not right, for since her marriage she had never sought to live wholly for herself.

As she looked she could still see the art student he had married. She was still there somewhere. But what had happened to the girl with bright green hair and brass rings in odd places who had smoked pot late into the night and then slept with boys she had never met before and whom she would never meet again: the unattached and unaligned social revolutionary who believed that the world could be changed for the better if people like her could be heard? Not that it was all like that. There were other memories. Foreign holidays on the cheap. Crossing the Alps in a very old car with a radiator which boiled over every two hundred metres; and sleeping under canvas, under the stars and waking shivering with the cold and exhilarated beyond measure. A world with very few rules or personal boundaries.

You couldn't go back. All her women friends said this, yearning for lost moments or people. What did they mean? Should not? Not physically possible? Incapable of being recaptured? 'A lost country from which no traveller can return.' There is a popular song for any emotion, no matter how banal. Esther thought of *Salad Days*, seen many times. How did it go? 'If I start looking behind me and begin retracing my steps, you must remind me to remind you, we said we'd never look back.'

Esther believed that the study of art had given her a philosophy to live by and that at this time art had equipped her for the life she was leading. She thought of the concept of the 'golden section', that magical focus of all pictures described by the ancient Greeks with mathematical precision and found in Neolithic cave paintings without any mathematics to guide their composition; arriving there – and it must be so – by human intuition alone, by and through which she had lived her life and now by which she defined her boundaries. She envisioned it as a 'golden circle' and within it was all that was important to her: family, friends, beliefs and possessions. Whenever she could, David was pulled in, held down, cajoled to stay and to abide by the rules; and sometimes he did and more usually he didn't. She tried to ensure that the world of his work and his deals – of money – was excluded or placed in quarantine at the end of the day and at weekends; and in this way the 'golden circle', although not hermetically sealed, had survived.

Now seated in the kitchen playing with her breakfast, she trembled. She ran her hands up and down her arms as if to warm them – to revitalise them. Why was she shaking? It had been better. The last few weeks of struggle and difficulty for him had been solace for *her*. She had drawn him in. He had been at home more. He had needed her. He had wanted to talk, seeking contact and comfort and, she hoped, the possibility of compromise. Now this precious delicacy, mediation, the precursor to happiness, had been partaken and was at an end. He would go back into the other world – the 'real' world. His mother had said that when David was a small boy she would ask him, 'David, where are you going, what are you going to do, and when will you be back?' And he would reply, 'I'm going to conquer the world.'

'Not today and not without help, and not this morning, it's likely to rain,' had been her response. It was a ritual.

Her mother had said that the 'real' world was a pleasant place to visit but not to inhabit.

She took him in a cup of tea together with some pills for his headache, but seeing him asleep she put them on the bedside table, and sat carefully on the edge of the bed so as not to wake him. There he was, her little Napoleon, brought to a halt by natural forces beyond his control. Inert and relatively harmless; lacking his usual energy and drive in the absence of his usual focus and intensity. She loved him for that – his intensity; and when the focus had been on her, she had been swept away and totally convinced by his sensitivity and imagination. It was just too wonderful for words. She sighed.

David, half-asleep, heard the weather forecast. He saw himself – and the moment was captured in a photograph in his mother's possession – at the garden gate in Droylsden: thirteen years old and the only boy in his class with short trousers! He remembered his entreaties, which had fallen on deaf ears, and felt the painful pink chaps on his legs caused by exposure to slanting Manchester rain and winter cold. She had wanted to keep him in childhood for as long as possible even when she knew it to be absurd and hurtful to him. What sort of mother was that?

He associated his mother – whom he loved unquestionably, blindly, above all others – with the hurts and slights of his life: the pressures to conform to his Jewishness and to religion which separated him out from his friends and circumscribed and limited the things he could do with them. When he tried to avoid the special Jewish prayers at school, which absented the Jewish boys from part of the morning assembly, it was his mother who found out and insisted that he attend. Half-way through the assembly they would reach this point – the awful moment – when the head teacher would instruct the Jewish children to fall out and they would troop in line to the back of the hall as condemned and humiliated black sheep. These Jewish boys would chant the *shema*, their thin and mumbling voices echoing in a sparsely furnished and empty classroom. But later, although he disliked this visibility, he allowed himself to be drawn into what he experienced as a 'secret society'. He would not admit it, especially to his mother, but he hugged to his heart and welcomed with all his soul the notion that he was initiated into a special world of the chosen: he had found kinship, and a certainty that there existed for him an indefinable bond with others he did not know; that there would be for him some form of social recognition; and that ultimately there would be a refuge if it were needed.

His childhood family memories were almost all of his mother, for when young he had seen very little of his father. Jacob was a taxi driver who was willing to work all the hours God gave him to support in some reasonable comfort his one-child family. During the day he touched home base. Occasionally, when David found himself free for some reason from school attendance, he found his father at home: but he worked in the evenings and at the weekends and then David saw nothing of him. And then suddenly he was not there at all. His father had a brain seizure while driving his taxi down a busy main road. The taxi free-wheeled for some distance before mounting the kerb, colliding with a street lamp, and coming to rest. It happened in the morning and a school friend drew his attention to it as a story in the evening paper before anyone in authority had told him.

A post mortem established the cause of death. The coroner, expressing his regrets, said that unfortunately there was a pronounced risk of coronary failure whenever excessive hours were spent at the wheel of a public service vehicle. David thought how stupid it all was. The very least you could expect of a father was that he would have the good sense to stay alive for a decent period of time.

Now life was very different. It was the beginning for him. The defining moment of his entry to adult life. He was on his own in at best an indifferent and in all probability, a hostile world. He carried out an inventory of his assets and liabilities and was cheered by the notion that he was in surplus. While he was not clever, in the academic sense, he was bright and quick with a good sense of number; fit and energetic, smart and persuasive.

He decided he could and should ignore his mother's wishes about higher education and get started in the world of work and dealing; but he conceded to her pleadings by taking a part-time accountancy course in the belief that it would be useful.

At fifteen David became a second-hand car dealer, cheating about his age and the possession of a legal vehicle licence, and never looked back. From the beginning he made money – sometimes a lot of money. He showed remarkable determination and became legendary in his neighbourhood. At one time when repossessing cars – or so it was rumoured – and experiencing difficulty in recovering a particular vehicle, he tracked it down to a garage in a run-down suburb of Manchester. The garage was part of a row of temporary structures built like metal containers, with frames which were secured by metal joints to a base. He hired a small crane and, after levering the garage off its joints, lifted it from its base and deposited it in the roadway in one sure movement. The exposed car was driven away and the owner charged with the costs. Actions such as these established his reputation. In 'the business' he became a legend and a man not to be trifled with: and one good thing followed another.

In those early years David learnt valuable lessons, the first and most important of which was to hold on to what you possessed, and the second to trust no one who was not in some sense one of you. When game-playing he developed these skills. When playing monopoly he bought the high-value properties and clung to them, exploiting them for income, and eschewing all minor opportunities for capital gain. The effect of his moves rendered his position impregnable and tended to prolong the game – even if, as a result, he could not win it himself. Some players muttered about him – 'typical Jew, what more can you expect?' Others, while not sharing these emotions, thought it a pity that one would not be willing to lose a game by striving to win it; for that was all it was really – a game. These playing tactics made him very unpopular; but unpopularity was a price he was willing to pay.

He learnt that business was amoral and the law a hindrance (perhaps life itself was like this?) although on the whole there was no point in getting yourself into trouble by being arrested and charged with some avoidable offence, and indeed it was foolish because it spoilt your reputation and capacity to deal. But you were entirely justified in devising your own rules and game plans.

He believed that most of your opponents would prove to be – when put to the test – foolish, vain and weak characters, and that it was almost your duty to do them down so that the assets they commanded could be placed in more capable hands. His own hands. That after all was how capitalism worked. He was fond of saying, 'Well, of course, communism rests on a more justifiable set of human values than capitalism, depending as capitalism does for its success on human avarice and greed: but in the ultimate it is greed and self-interest that makes the world go round. Isn't that true?' Who could deny him – and anyway he would have stopped listening even if you had tried.

But as he lay restless in his bed, he knew that he was more than the sum of these parts. He had a presentiment of something better within him, which while not a conscience as such, for it lacked shape and certainty, pointed him outwards of himself. It pleased him to play with these emotions and sometimes to act upon them, so that he could refer to these acts as self-certifying proof absolute of his ethical awareness of others and his good intentions towards them.

Esther had come to look at him, turning him over and straightening him out.

Back in the kitchen, Esther, whose mind and emotions were elsewhere, had to cope with her son Garth. At that time, on that sunny morning, Garth was staying at the flat, his wife being away with the children at her mother's. Esther had forgotten how much space he occupied: a grown up puppy dog of a man, yelping and following you around and demanding your attention. Of course, she loved him, but now she preferred to do this at a distance. How like him to turn up demanding a place. A more self-sufficient and confident man would have got on with things in his own home, welcoming a chance to have some time of his own: to catch up with himself.

She looked at her watch. Did she have the right time? This damn watch always gained time, but she continued to use it. Should she wind it back to the correct time? Sometimes she did but usually she didn't. Not being sure that the winding mechanism permitted it – that is, without damage – she would most times wind it forward to the right time. It was a sort of compromise with fate: you might wind it back a few times for it was quicker, but not always, and if only occasionally, this backward motion might not be disastrous. She was annoyed with herself for complicating even the most simple of tasks.

What she disliked most about the way the two children related to them was their expectation that David was a never-ending stream of largesse. Of course, every parent wanted to help their children financially and emotionally. She did. But these children acted as if their lives had been set up as requiring their very own personal gravy train. David was the gravy train. He had appointed himself the quartermaster of it, so he and they had only themselves to blame. But while these children waited on him, their own prospects – their gravy trains – lay neglected in remote sidings. They had even forgotten where they lay.

Garth was excited this morning. Yet again his father had come up trumps for him and not a moment too soon. His time had come again. New doors were being opened and soon he would be able to hold his own again at the dining tables of his friends. And his mother remained so good and helpful. Putting him up at a moment's notice, feeding and watering him so well. He had been given a job at the new company, and on this morning he was going into the office for the first time. He asked for her help. 'Mum, Dad's car keys and parking pass. Where are they? Can you get them for me?'

She demurred. She didn't think David would like his new car to be driven by Garth. The car was brand new and Garth was a poor and even reckless driver. Best kept away from other men's toys, she thought.

Garth looked out of the sunny window at the shining green Jaguar XJ6 on the free standing below. He longed for it. It seemed to symbolise all he desired and strained after: success, prestige and recognition.

'Please mum, be a sport. Get them for me.'

Still she hesitated, while observing his expectancy. But time was pressing and she wanted him out of the house.

'All right, I'll find them for you', she said, knowing where they were from the start and giving them to him without the necessity of search.

'But if he asks me, I shall blame you. Is that understood?'

'Of course mum, understood.' He kissed and hugged her. 'You're a star.'

Through the open bedroom door David overheard this conversation. He didn't like it, but being too ill to argue, turned over in the bed to capture the cool of the unoccupied position.

The explosion when it came blew in the windows and shattered glass over the bed as if in a sudden storm. A giant black smoke-filled cloud rose beyond their second-floor window, blowing all before it across the room. From the kitchen David heard Esther's agonised screams, which were to scar his memory forever. Unhurt, he scrambled out of the bed and found her, cutting his feet on the thousands of glass fragments scattered across the bedroom floor and into the hallway. He clutched her and hung on and when the shrieking stopped there was a silence which seemed to last for a very long time; to be broken by shouts, the tumult from the road below; and the sound of sirens, and then of high-velocity water; and of kindly firemen, and later policemen, blundering their well-meaning way in.

There are moments in life when the motion of the Earth is arrested; it stays still on its axis. When movement is resumed no person or object is in the same place and their relationships are changed for ever. In these moments the normal mediations of life, the strategies, tactics and devices by which we compromise ourselves and others, are of no use to us. They have failed. They had failed. A vast black hole had been created and it seemed that all their hopes and fears, all their necessary hesitations, had been sucked into a screaming abyss and then into eternal silence.

CHAPTER 2

BOB CHURCHILL-JONES tidied his flat. Not that it needed it, for his cleaner Mrs Frost came in twice a week on Mondays and Thursdays to 'do' for him, and this being a Friday the flat was impressively clean and shining with everything in its place, so that he had to invent things to do. Mrs Frost shopped for him once a week, and she had left him her usual note complaining that although the flat might be thought fine for him, for her it was a real inconvenience, being remote from any decent supermarket with only expensive chi-chi shops within reach. How could she be expected to provide for him in such unpromising surroundings? She cooked him pies and cakes to make up for the deficiencies, as she thought of them, of his circumstances.

He knew that Mrs Frost enjoyed complaining, and he tut-tutted and agreed with her. It was hard having a household help, and he would not have employed one at all but for his sister's solicitude. When his sister had discovered that his wife Gloria had left him she had found him assistance, and he had been too weak to turn it down. Every evening before a cleaning day he felt obliged to make the flat spick and span for fear of letting himself down: tidying things had now become an obsession.

The flat was fine for him, and one of the perks of being a policeman in central London – at least for a senior one. The Metropolitan Police owned all sorts of properties in London, of which this pleasant red-bricked, four-storied block in High Street, Marylebone was one. It was Edwardian, and built to spacious and satisfying proportions with outstandingly good light. Being a tall man he welcomed the high ceilings; and being a person of discernment, if not of extended education, he loved the original features: the cornices, central roses and fireplaces so lovingly and well preserved.

He had lived on his own in this flat for two years, and loved both it and its surroundings. The area was very prosperous with good pubs, bars and restaurants catering for a good class of trade – what in other times might have been described as carriage trade – and it was his practice to frequent them whenever he could in the evenings and at the weekends. Being so well known and recognisable, he had became something of a local celebrity: perfect strangers would come up to him in the street and in bars and engage him in long discourse as if they had always known him. Little did they know that their matiness, and his resulting attempt to live up to their expectations, would result in his downfall.

For Bob Churchill-Jones was a detective chief inspector specialising in anti-terrorism. When IRA bomb outrages were visited on London it was Bob who fronted the scene and gave the public the police side of things. A large television audience was disarmed by this tall, handsome and well-spoken policeman with his well-articulated reassurances. His pinstriped dark suits and colourful ties were beamed into every sitting room in the land at moments of national anxiety. But for some in Scotland Yard the pinstripes were a little too wide, the ties a little too florid, and the tones not well modulated enough. Might there not also have been a jealousy at the Yard? A belief that public recognition had been gained too easily by him, and had not been received at all by other well-deserving, earnest, educated people like themselves?

At this moment of professional doubt, Bob made mistakes. He began to relax in his new role and even – albeit unconsciously – to play to his gallery: his public explanations of these disasters grew in rhetoric and in their oratorical qualities. It became his eccentricity to wear a fresh carnation in his lapel every day – provided by the flower seller at his nearest underground station – and on one occasion, when attending a particularly nasty outrage, he forgot to remove it before the cameras zoomed in. It seemed wrong to many viewers, who complained about what they described as a lack of sensitivity to the dead and the dying.

His enemies at the Yard took their chance and pounced. Bob lost his job and joined the plenitude of experienced detectives out of the rat race. Bob was replaced by not one, but several media managers: a new species of policeman trained and skilled in denying the public any meaningful information at all.

Bob was moved without protest to less high-profile cases, where his immense experience held him in good stead and his knowledge of terrorism could be used. For a while, and until the circus had moved on, he became a kind of case history. 'Poor Bob,' they would say, 'now his mistake was…'; and then they would give you their theory.

Bob looked out on the familiar street below, aware of how much he liked it. Many of these scurrying figures in the street, and the shopkeepers dressing their windows or stalls, were known to him, or at least recognised. They were busily ensconced in their own tasks and you could set your watch by the timing of the performance of their daily routines. He liked the reassurance that they would be there at these times tomorrow, give or take a few minutes. And the strangers were interesting too, whether browsing or passing through. They made a sort of mosaic or kaleidoscope. He had always liked that as a child. He used to get kaleidoscopes as Christmas presents.

He hoped Alec would not be late. He had always hated being late or kept waiting. Very often the tension of waiting was so great that he had to walk away. People would say, 'Good God, man, I was only thirty minutes late. This is London. Everyone's late. You can't help being late.' Of course you could help it. They regarded punctuality in another way – their way – and they were right to do so. But no one had told his nervous system about the change in values. While he waited, and looked, he eased his weight onto the balls of his feet, lifting his heels and rocking gently to and fro. It was a recent mannerism of which he was entirely unaware.

But Alec wasn't late. Bob, having made the journey to Norfolk many times, was prepared for it with thermos flask, sandwiches and a rug. He insisted on the rug. Alec, his bright and chirpy Hendon College trained detective sergeant, packing these objects into the boot of the car, was curious. 'You're well prepared, boss. It's only Norfolk.'

'There speaks the voice of the innocent. Trust me', was the reply.

He made the journey to Norfolk regularly, and knew that it would be an age before the crawl through London traffic would spill them out onto the M25, and then an eternity before they could edge their way further to the M11, a motorway without service stations. And even if the sun was shining, and when you were deep within the county, there would be a niggling wind blowing in off the North Sea, originating somewhere in Siberia, and clearly lost, but destined for you. It was best to be prepared.

'Bungay,' said Alec, 'where exactly is that?'

'It's difficult to explain. Well, you know what they say about Norwich not being the end of the world, but that you can see the end of the world from Norwich.'

Alec laughed.

'Bungay is nearer the end. Anyway, that's where our suspect lives, and that's where we seek him.'

While they negotiated London traffic, they reviewed the case. Obviously the bomb had been intended for the father and not the son. Forensic research had identified the detonator as being a type used by the IRA, but there had been no warning. So far no reason could be deduced why the IRA would have had it in for David Droylsden. The detonator had been an old type, and as the IRA vehemently denied involvement it was thought a rogue element could be involved.

'So then,' said Alec, 'what do you think?'

'We don't think, at least not yet. Look, we're working together for the first time and I'll spell it out for you how I work. I'm an evidence man, usually gained the hard way by painstaking inquiry. It may be a much slower method than is fashionable today, but it's the only sure-fire route to the truth – whatever that might be. And I can tell you now that the current passion for quick fixes to satisfy the politicians and a public clamouring for retribution will lead to no good.'

'What do you mean?'

'What I mean is trumped-up charges, dodgy confessions and when you get to court your witnesses being as untruthful as theirs. That's what I mean, and thank God I'm not a part of it now.'

There was silence for a while. Alec continued, 'Well, we're on safe ground in thinking that a man like David Droylsden had a lot of enemies. He says so and so does his wife.'

'How many names do you have?'

'Twenty-one.'

'Good God. And who gave them to you?'

'Four chaps from him, seven from his wife, five from the directors of this company he's involved in and the rest from his old associates in Manchester. There's overlap, of course: seven people named the fellow we're going to see – what's his name, Roger Greer. Strange really because almost everyone seems to like him. He's the loser, of course, and from all accounts this bloke Droylsden did him down.'

'And what did you make of him, David Droylsden?'

'Impressive. Intelligent, energetic and resourceful. I pity the poor bugger who did it were he to get his hands on him.' He paused. 'Very boastful, going on about this achievement and then the other. Boring, that. And did you see the framed letter on the wall of his living room of all places?'

'No.'

'A letter from Robert Maxwell stating that he considered him an outstanding businessman. Who needs enemies with friends like that?'

'Any criminal record?'

'No.'

'And what about the wife? I noticed that you implied the masculine gender when talking about the perpetrator.'

'Well, quite dishy. I rather liked her.'

There was another silence, broken by the older man.

' I've been involved in a lot of murder cases, Alec. A very abnormal and horrible thing, murder – or manslaughter, as it is in this case – and in my experience most of it committed by very ordinary, even decent, people. Caught out by something very terrible happening to them and not being able to deal with it. Like war, really. You know, the continuation of negotiation by other, violent, means – when the options run out. A failure of mediation, you see. No other way open to them. Yes, yes, I know there are some real monsters, they make the headlines, but most murderers aren't like that. The public doesn't understand it but we do.'

'Well,' said Alec, not caring to follow him, 'perhaps this Roger fellow's our man then.'

' Don't rush in. I've warned you about that. Sometimes, when people suffer a hurt, a deep injury to their psyche – so to speak – they break and react immediately; but with others … it sort of festers, lies there not dormant exactly, but buried. And then something happens – it can be something very slight, and not related at all, or apparently not, to the earlier hurt – and the dam bursts. Tragic. It really is tragic. In all probability they wouldn't hurt a fly for the rest of their life. But it's too late, they did it and must suffer the consequences.'

'So you're saying that there may be someone out there on our list – or not – who's been bearing a grievance of long standing,' said Alec.

'It's possible. Evidence, evidence and more evidence, that's what we need.' He spoke with rising emphasis, and then laughed at himself: it was a mistake to take yourself too seriously.

Ivor Bowen had waited patiently for over an hour before he left the bar. Usually he didn't like to hang about in bars, but this time it was not a hardship for him. This bar was one of those lush and discreet places to be found in the backstreets of Mayfair. It was a place of real leather upholstery and brass fittings, and the dim lighting and discreet Victorian alcoves guaranteed privacy. You paid more for your food and drink to secure these advantages, but it was money well spent and rarely begrudged. Then there was the anticipation. There can be few assignations more pleasurable than waiting in such a place for a desirable woman.

When she didn't come, he recovered his car from the underground car park and drove to the area where she lived, parking the car at the first available meter. As he approached, he saw that the roads leading to the block were screened off by police cordons. In front of the block there were the remains of burnt-out cars. Fire engines were still at work, dealing with the smouldering wreckage. The fire had affected the building itself, and many of the windows had been blown in. It was scene of some confusion, and he walked away from it with painful foreboding and fearing the worst. Later he tried to contact her, knowing he should not have done so, to find that there was no answer.

There was no need for the rug. Close to Bungay they found a good pub. There was a cold north-easterly blowing, however, and they were glad of the log fire. They relaxed in its warmth and glow, and began the process of getting to know each other better.

'Are you married, Alec?' inquired his senior.

'No, not married, but I do have a settled partner. A girl called Sandra. It works out well.'

'Oh, good. Doesn't she want to get married – security and all that?'

'No, not really. If there were children, as I suppose there might be one day, we might change our minds.' He paused, uncertain whether to go on. 'It's an open relationship. We both have difficult jobs with awkward hours that take us away from home. We don't ask too many questions.' He paused again, uncertain of the response, before gauging it to be friendly. 'To be frank, when she has an adventure of some kind it works to enliven our relationship. I'm not judging her – nor her me – so she can bring back whatever she's gained to us with a renewed confidence. And vice versa, of course.'

'Well, you are modern about these things. Good for you.'

'And you, boss? I hear you're separated.'

'Yes, you hear right. We separated two years ago, and now my wife seems to have gained a new partner. I'm rather sad about it but not without hope. Things are improving. She lives near Bungay.' He downed a good part of his pint before continuing, and Alec, seeing that he was drinking heavily, decided to call a halt himself.

'Since you've been so forthcoming I'll tell you something exceptional. My ex-wife and I remain remarkably good friends. Yes, we do.'

Alec saw that Bob had had too much to drink and tried to head him off before he said something that, when sober, he might regret having uttered. Bob waved him away. 'She seems to live with someone – a funny-looking fellow who owns the pub she works in – but it makes no difference.' He rubbed the forefinger of his right hand along his nose, winked suggestively, and nodded his head knowingly.

'You mean that you and your wife continue to have … a relationship?' He couldn't get the usual word out.

'Yes. Enough said, for the moment. Judge not that ye be not be judged.'

'Yes, quite so. I should think so. I'll get us some coffees.'

Once back in the car Bob was back to his usual professional self.

'Remember, I ask the questions and you take the notes. You say nothing unless I give you the nod.'

'Right, you're the boss.'

They approached Bungay on the long straight road from Diss. On either side rough pasture, reclaimed from marsh, stretched as far as the eye could see. Heavy rain had caused the road to be edged with water, and the spray created eddies that were now threatening to wash back onto the highway from the swollen fields. Near to the town, the road from Diss, and most of its traffic, swept away around the settlements, while the road to the centre snaked downwards, as if in sympathy with the river which silted before the town. Hesitant and arrested in its flow, the river, and thus the town, was denied the onward passage of holiday-makers cavorting in their boats higher up the river reaches and on the Broads. The new houses on the outskirts faced them as they approached, appealingly, as if seeking the uplands from which the travellers had come. In the town they saw many fine seventeenth-century buildings standing out from other humbler dwellings from more recent and meaner times: but all were mud-strewn and uncared for as if the trials they experienced, both natural and man-made, were too much for them. The town seemed, on that day at least, to be little more than a heap of mud, which is what in origin its name had denoted.

Neither visitor was impressed by Roger's semi-detached, red-brick workman's cottage in a small road abutting the market place. There were no compensatory satisfactions to be found there. 'Poor sod,' thought Alec, 'if this is to where he has sunk.' But inside the cottage the freshly painted walls and sparsely furnished rooms were pleasant enough. Roger greeted them politely, offering them coffee and cake, and settling them down at the far end of an oak trestle table in his back room. Alec, the least active of the three, studied him: middle-aged and of medium height, an academic looking man with a big head and glasses, but with an unexpected smile which redeemed the severity of his usual demeanour. And then direct and amusing in his speech. A toff, yes, but by inclination and not by birth or schooling. And then something else which Alec couldn't make out.

Bob explained that the reason for their visit was that they were conducting a police inquiry into a young man's unfortunate death, and he, Roger, was being invited to help the police with this inquiry. It was all quite informal at this stage.

'Quite so,' Roger responded. 'But you two distinguished policeman have come a long way to see me, and I can imagine that a number of people might have cast the finger of suspicion at me.' He pushed a small but expensive-looking tape recorder across the table towards them and clicked it on. 'It's my invariable practice to tape all important conversations. I'm sure you understand.'

They objected, complained that it was unnecessary, and expressed their surprise that he was so hostile. Roger laughed. 'Gentlemen, I'm surprised at you. You do this type of thing all the time. Come, come. I must insist. You can have a copy if you wish. Please speak your names, and I shall name myself and the time and place, so they can be recorded.' The seriousness of the moment was impressed upon them all.

Bob and Roger looked at each other more closely as the result of this brusque exchange. They shared a moment when they liked each other, recognising things in common, although it was not clear to either of them at that moment what it amounted to: perhaps, a similar view of the world and their place in it, or some commonality of experience or conclusions about it. Bob spoke. 'Would you tell us, please, where you were on the evening of 8th October and on the following day, 9th October?'

Roger consulted his diary. 'I had a business meeting with my solicitors on the 9th, at ten o'clock, so travelled down in the late evening to London where I stayed with my friend Sylvia – Sylvia Clark.' He gave them names and addresses and the precise times.

'Thank you. I assume that your solicitors and Ms Clark can confirm these times?'

'Of course.'

Bob continued, 'Roger, tell us what are your feelings about Mr Droylsden.' Then, realising the inappropriateness of his wording, 'I imagine they …' He halted. 'And what's going on between you.'

'Well, I'll do my best to show restraint, but you must understand that this is a man responsible for my ruin, who set out to do so for his personal gain. Oh, yes, it wasn't an accident you know. Some unintentional happening or act of fate. Here I stand now with my capital – the result of twenty years' hard labour – and my living, gone, my family rendered homeless, my marriage on the rocks, and hopelessly in debt. What do you think my feelings are, as you put it? But if you think I'd want him dead, you'd be quite wrong. There are other things I can do to hit back.' He explained to them: the complaint he had lodged with the Department of Trade and Industry, the legal action he was considering, and whether he might trade in competition with his old – that was, his reconstituted – company.

'And do you think you might be successful in any of these actions?' Bob interrupted him.

Roger paused. He was conscious that he was telling them too much. He was too impassioned. The words he spoke had a life of their own. He had tried – he did try – to hold them back, to limit the flow. But he knew now as he listened to them, the words he used, that they were fripperies, and useless to him. The events he described had actually happened. That clock could not be turned back. The old instincts and reactions that had served him so well could not help him now. Would not help him survive.

'No, I don't think so.' The answer surprised him. Had he let go of the wreckage? Was he already swimming away from it, and to where?' He went on, 'I might be wasting time and money to pursue them. The best I can hope for is to embarrass him.'

They changed the subject. Had he any Irish connections? He seemed prepared for the question. 'I am Irish. I have an Irish passport. My mother was Irish, you see, which gave me an entitlement, which I exercised.'

And he told them more: that he had owned a small consultancy business in Dublin for six to seven years. But that had been a long time ago. He had not visited Ireland in the last ten years. They pressed him on this. Where he stayed when he visited Dublin, the names and addresses of his former colleagues and people who knew him there. He had forgotten most of it, and even why he had bothered to have a business there in the first place. Of course an Irish passport was always helpful. Very few countries around the world had hard things to say about the Irish – the mainstream of many a UN peacekeeping force – but most had reservations about the British. And you never knew when you might need another identity. But that was not something you could tell them.

They wanted his cooperation in making his bank accounts available to them. He knew that they could get hold of them through the courts, but it would take them time, and without his cooperation they could not be sure that they had secured the vital accounts, the ones that really mattered.

'No, gentlemen.' He was firm on the matter. 'I won't help you there. You're wasting your time with me. Turn your attention to other people.'

They were nice to him then. It appeared that the more he cooperated with them, the quicker he could be taken out of the frame. A decent and responsible citizen would want to help the police in so serious a matter. They expressed their surprise that he was unwilling to do so. Roger laughed and wished them a pleasant journey home.

They said nothing until back in the car. Alec was to drop Bob off at the Ship Inn in Billingham where his wife Gloria had found him his usual room, and he was to travel back by train early on the Monday. Bob seemed to have lost interest, his thoughts turning to other matters. 'Plenty to check up on there, Alec. Get going as soon as you can.' Bob waved him away. He had already said much too much about Gloria, and Alec was not welcome at the inn.

When they were gone, Roger recognised that the need for bravado had lapsed. He poured himself an early whisky and drank it slowly while remaining at the kitchen table. He wept slowly. The tears trickling down his cheeks tickled him, but he left them to course slowly down until, tasting them, and suddenly feeling stupid, he wiped his face. It was still raining but he decided to take his usual walk across the marshes. There was a need to steady himself ahead of the evening. He used an outside telephone box. The children were not available to him, being out, he was told. Sylvia listened carefully to his account and asked a number of telling questions, which were no less than he expected of her. It was raining gently, and although well protected, he was going to get wet. Although encroached upon, the marshes remained open to walkers, and the eye carried across gorse and scrub to a distant column of trees guarding the river flowing beyond them, and suddenly vulnerable to him in its gentle flow. Early in the morning, before human disturbance, rare birds could be spotted from the river banks. Otters had returned and could be found if you were quiet and still. He had heard the plaintive cry of a curlew lost too far down the river for the succour that awaited it on the mud banks of the estuary. He quickened his pace, becoming firmer in his resolution, and despising himself just a little for his self-pity.

Gloria was very pleased to see her husband, kissing him gently before showing him to his room. On their return she seated him in a protected area of the bar and provided him with his starting drink. She asked him who he had been seeing in Bungay, and without revealing everything, he told her.

'Called Roger,' he said. Roger the lodger, Roger the dodger, he thought. 'In his fifties, well educated, lives in a small cottage, a nice chap down on his luck.'

'Roger Greer, you mean', said Gloria.

'Goodness, do you know him? Tell me what you know', said the astonished Bob.

Gloria kissed him again, as if, he thought, to appease. And then she told him.

CHAPTER 3

GLORIA LOVED HER husband. She had never had any doubt about that. It had come as a very great shock to her, as well as to him, when she had left home. It was not a precipitate act which when she would think about it, and when she judged herself, as she was much too wont to do, she would think badly of. It had come to her over a passage of time, starting with the thought that she could if she wished take control of her own life. She might get a job and train for something better, live on her own for a while, pay her own way and sleep in her own bed. After a while these thoughts excited her, and she began to think how it might be done, finding the practical steps difficult and daunting until by accident, at her hairdresser's, she read an advertisement for a barmaid in a seventeenth-century coaching inn in Norfolk with accommodation provided if needed. The magazine was old, but she rang, was given an interview by a unobjectionable man called Fred, lied about her work experience, got her friends to supply false references without questions being asked, and got the job.

When Bob returned to their flat late one evening, tired and a little the worse for drink, he found her note telling him she had gone, with the request that he should not try to find her. She had emptied the wardrobe of her clothes and had taken some of her personal possessions but that was all, as far he could remember. What he could recall, and with a pain that always engulfed him, was that the wardrobe was not quite empty. There! Still in its wrapping which had protected it for many years, and carefully hung on a good wooden coat-hanger, with the fashionable high-heeled white shoes that she had worn on the day set out neatly beneath it: there was her white wedding dress. What did it mean? Was it merely that she did not have any further use for it? Perhaps she did not care to be reminded of what it meant or what it had stood for, while not having the courage to discard or abandon this 'it'? Was it, as he hoped it might be, that she was inviting him to take care of 'it' in her absence?

Being a man, he thought that the act of leaving him could not have been perpetrated without there being another man somewhere in the background primed to replace him; but in this he was wrong. Being an outstandingly good detective he found her without difficulty, and then studied what he had found, quietly and dispassionately. He did nothing, nothing at all for many months, knowing that he did not want to lose her: for he had concluded, after weighing the evidence of his senses, that his only chance of winning her back was first to let her go.

After a while Gloria stopped missing him or even thinking about him, at least not very much. She had a room of her own. With Fred's help she painted the walls white. The floor was stripped and polished. Fred searched a dusty storeroom and retrieved for her several antique pieces of furniture which gave her room a certain solidity and permanence. Her favourite rug covered the bed, and pictures of her loved ones and a few precious paintings adorned some of the blank places on the walls, and a Victorian bookcase had welcomed her books. She thought it a very nice room, and all that at that time she really needed – and it pleased her that it was truly a room of her own. Gloria's room had a view of its own. It faced backwards from the road and over hedgeless farmland to the rear of the inn. As she looked the land sloped gently to a distant horizon to where sky, in its manifold hues and moods, encountered land, which in summer sunshine flared in golds and yellows, and in winter rain rose up in hues of brown and green; where large skies imitated sunnier climes or changed before you, in drifting, driving, baffling shapes and tones of grey.

As Gloria looked she wished the inn to be taller and to be on the top floor, for there beyond the land before her, within walking distance, and then from high land, was the sea. Here you could see a horizon where land was welded to sea; and where on some nights, the pathway to it was luminous. Throughout time the red-sailed Norfolk ketches had butted round the Norfolk coast and up its rivers. When the tides were right some had felt the twitch of the horizon, as if magnetised, and had felt called to seek the unknown beyond it; and in answer, they had changed direction towards it, in search of plunder and riches beyond their imagination.

Gloria did not think of herself as an ascetic, and the Ship Inn would not have been the place for being one: but the sparseness of her room pleased her as she lay on her bed, arms folded behind her head, propped up by a large and extravagantly embroidered cushion. As she looked, there was not a single object she did not value or wish to be there, and in its place, the right place; and all the flotsam and jetsam, the detritus of a long life with others, had been swept away.

At this time Fred, the boon of Gloria's new life, was in the bar of this pleasant inn polishing glasses. It was the start of a morning routine, which placed everything afresh, which polished and wiped and tidied. There were helping hands but he followed them, unobtrusively, without stricture or friction, to ensure that everything was perfect and commensurate with his own high standards of excellence. This was part of the charm of this popular and intensively used hostelry: it was always clean and shining, its colours fresh but warming, so that even the rough and boisterous quietened themselves and learnt to respect it, but without in any way being intimidated or put off. Cigarettes were dutifully extinguished in the car park; beer was not spilt on or food trodden into the expensively carpeted floor; voices were modulated; and laughter, although common, was rarely raucous. In short it was a real pleasure for anyone to be there.

Fred had recognised in Gloria what he believed to be a kindred spirit, and while not believing her story, and unconvinced by her references, had not had the slightest hesitation in employing her. In some ways his impressions of her were right and in others hopelessly wrong; but none of this was of any real significance and they became firm friends, and in time, business partners. Fred Chateris was in his thirties and retired from the Royal Air Force where he had reached the rank of flight sergeant, responsible as an electrician for keeping complex equipment in good and serviceable working order and planes in the air. Fred was a careful and highly practical person, economical in his ways and in his practices. In eschewing personal risk he had avoided marriage and what he considered to be dalliance with the other sex. He thought about these things, sexual things, but in the end he was not interested, finding them confusing and even troublesome, if his observation of others was to be regarded as anything to go by. His mates ribbed him about his reasons for not joining in. Was he gay? He thought not, although as he considered the possibility, his sense of identity weakened. He preferred not to think about these matters at all; and he concluded, and thought perhaps it was a pity, that it might in some circumstances have been different, that he was under-sexed in an over-sexed world.

Fred could see that Gloria was a highly attractive person who caused heads to turn whenever she was in the bar, and really much more than that, who occasioned advances and propositions: all of which she deflected and disarmed with great charm and skill. Gloria was naturally fair-haired and of pale complexion, of medium height and trim. Her features were perfectly formed but of no great character in themselves, but Gloria herself, when she shone through, was irresistibly pleasant and kind. She engaged and was even curious – and about you. She dressed very carefully, in a feminine and gently revealing manner, resting just short of being fashionable, and slightly too young for her age, the late thirties. Her hairstyles, while in the mode, were of the sort that required attention and regular attendance at a salon, being short and wavy and taken back from her face. She moved very well, erect and composed, purposeful but considerate, and even gentle – which is how she really was.

Fred saw these qualities but was not moved by them. He recognised competence and good order, which was also there, and he gave her more and more to do; and as she did these things with precision, and even flair, he began to think of her as a partner and to encourage her ideas. It was because of Gloria that a new restaurant service was conceived. Gloria designed and supervised its building and then managed it with great aplomb. The inn and its restaurant began to be listed in the tourist guide books, its reputation spread by word of mouth, and it became a common experience and necessity that to eat there required you to book your table weeks in advance. And all this while, Gloria became more relaxed and confident of herself, and although Fred was not to notice it, more desirable. She took a business course at a local college, met other women in a businesswomen's support group, and was listened to with respect. This is what Fred noticed most: she was a considerable asset to the business.

Some of the women in her group became good contacts and brought their family and friends to the inn while others, busily networking, referred business to her, valuable group bookings for the restaurant. Gloria was certainly one of them, and as she became successful, she became accepted within a circle that pleased her. Making true friends was another matter, and took time. Then one day, when business was slack, she was invited by a friendly group of women who were eating in the restaurant and then drinking in the bar to join them; local women, confident and smart, who seemed to do interesting things together; visiting art galleries and country houses, sometimes with their children but often on jolly picnics without them. She was invited to an outing, when the sun shone, the girls wore summer frocks, and there was rather too much white wine for safety driving home. These women were mostly married but with husbands who were often abroad or working in London or, for one of them, on an oil rig. They had money and time on their hands, and they were determined to enjoy themselves. It was all great fun – these country jaunts – and something she had read about, rather than experienced in her homespun upbringing. She would arrive back at the inn flushed and exhilarated by the outside world, by sunshine, sea breezes and laughter.

And then Rachel, whom she thought quite the nicest of them all, invited her to lunch at her house, a converted barn deep in the country and not far from the coast and swimming. Two of the same girls were there, and they really became quite free with each other. Rachel was a tall girl in her thirties with natural red-gold hair which she enlivened with streaks. At first glance she seemed a little way out, at least for Gloria, but a closer look revealed a much classier and conservative girl: the hair, while wayward, was on examination seen to be immaculately cut; the jeans were designer label; and the top, although casual, was a top name, and not to be bought locally. Her house was beautifully furnished with a mix of traditional and smart modern, and as she saw Gloria look, she was quick to be modest about these pieces and to ascribe them to Daddy. Rachel said, 'Don't get the wrong idea, Gloria. A little money, well I suppose quite a lot, yes: but a life which is quite hard for me really. Two former husbands, and three children to care for, the two girls with me, and my son Fergus with his father. I miss Fergus, it hurts.'

'But you all get on so very well together, don't you? I've seen you all. The children are wonderful and seem very happy to me. You must be so proud of them.' Gloria was certain of it.

'Yes, we do, but when you know us better you'll see the joins and the children coping, managing their disappointments and unhappiness as best they can.' She smiled, wanting to move on. 'We must find time to talk properly, but not at the moment, I think.'

Over coffee, when Gloria was helping in the kitchen, Lucy discussed her with Rachel. 'What do you think? Is she up for it?'

'Behave yourself. Gloria's a very nice girl and I value her and don't wish to lose her. It's more important than any of that.'

'Come, come, you can't pay the prude with me. Anyway, my guess is if you're not interested someone else will step in.' Lucy looked mischievous.

'You wouldn't dare.' Rachel was emphatic.

' Watch me,' said Lucy.

And sure enough Lucy, an athletic, lively and engaging girl, invited Gloria to play tennis on the all-weather court so generously paid for by Daddy. It was no real match: Lucy, carefully coached, played well and produced her winning forehand punch, running round it so as to avoid her weaker backhand, which at the pace generated by Gloria she had time to do: and Gloria was well out of practice, but improving when Lucy let her into the game. The end came quickly, and an exhausted Gloria called quits. But she was pleased to be playing at all, and with Lucy whom she saw as a sophisticated, witty girl and pleasing in every way. And then as they leant on the net laughing, Lucy put her hand into Gloria's and with the other hand began to gently caress her arm.

Gloria, surprised and then alarmed, did not know what to do. She did not wish to offend by abruptly withdrawing, but on the other hand the advance was not welcome. She glanced down at

the hand enfolding her own: brown and firm and beautifully
shaped, with fingers slightly too long to be proportionate, and
nails that owed their colour and smooth rounding to the regular
care of others; and she remembered, with a shock, a painting of
a Portuguese princess she had seen in the National Gallery, and
the princess's hands as they rested on a chair, and the princess's
enigmatic smile, which she knew was for her, and her thought,
how lucky the chair, and how she had laughed at the absurdity of
such a reaction and her amusement that the comment had come
seemingly from nowhere. She looked at Lucy, who stared boldly
at her, smiling, and saw for the first time that Lucy had violet
eyes, deeply hued and bright. Gloria had never seen anyone with
violet eyes. Gloria withdrew her hand, laughing a little, and toss-
ing her head as if to say no, although she said nothing at all as
she strode across the carefully mown lawn towards the terrace
and laughter ahead.

Rachel told Lucy on the telephone that evening to 'cut it out'
but Lucy would have none of it.

Gloria decided to see less of this crowd. Life was very busy for
her now, and fun had to find its proper place. Seeing Lucy once
by accident, when shopping, she had cut her, crossing the street
quickly and pretending she had not seen her at all. Gloria told
herself that she had been freed, she had freed herself, from that
sort of thing to pursue the serious things of life, and that preoc-
cupation with fleshly things was grossly overrated. 'Why,' her
mother had said to her once apropos of nothing, as an aside, in
the garden, 'I get more pleasure from the first appearance in
spring of a crocus than by anything your father can do for me.'
Her mother had thought that novelists always got this sort of
thing wrong, filling their pages with a false romanticism and the
'goings on' of their characters, whereas in real life there was no
time for this; real people, she had continued, spent their time
working as hard as they could to pay their bills, and when they
had paid them they started all over again. 'Like painting the
Forth Bridge', were her words. Gloria had responded by saying
that man could not live by bread alone, and had got a clip round
the ear for her impudence.

Gloria, in leaving Bob, had hoped to escape from the sheer
attrition of having to consider others. In some way, which she

felt but could not articulate, she had been worn down by the effort to relate: her 'outer skin', by which she sieved out her impressions, had become worn out and porous and she was vulnerable to any emotion and to anyone; just about anything could overwhelm her natural defences and cause devastation. But at least marriage, she realised now with a certain wryness, had built up these defences in the first place: marriage gave you something to hide behind, to withdraw within, whereas now she was prey to almost anything. It was worse than this, for she was conscious of giving off something in the way she looked or the way she behaved, moved and responded, which signalled availability. She couldn't help it, she didn't want it, but in some way – she sighed – it happened.

One morning she woke early to find a body in the bed and occupying her space. Her arm had lurched sideways to encounter Fred, who she was to discover had made his way to her room at some time in the night and curled up beside her. She shrieked, shouted and pushed at him in the effort to drive him out; and red with embarrassment, he withdrew. She clutched at the duvet to cover herself, being naked at the time, and he gathered himself awkwardly and stammered his inadequate response. Gloria demanded her privacy and guarantees that he would never attempt it again. And then she laughed, at the farce of it, at the sheer absurdity of the scene being enacted and her part in it; and then he laughed, removing himself, if not with dignity, in the knowledge that no harm had been done.

Later Gloria put her arm around him and it became understood between them that if he was distressed he could come to her so long as nothing was expected. And he never did it again. This bizarre event drew them closer together, so that he felt that he could talk to her about some of the deep things which lurched within him from time to time – which is all he wanted – and she was willing to listen and give advice on these personal matters, and to give and receive hugs. And then, she thought, that if it went on like this she would become impossibly good and better off in a convent.

In all the confusions of the marriage rupture, Gloria had been able to remain good friends with her daughter Susan, who had happily taken up a place to study English at the University of

East Anglia in Norwich. They saw each other from time to time for a meal or the theatre. On some weekends and in vacations, Susan stayed at the inn and they walked together along the north Norfolk coast with binoculars to spot the birds and windcheaters to rebut the wind and rain. It was immensely to Susan's credit that she remained good friends with both her parents, whatever the difficulties. At the outset she had steadfastly refused to discuss the affairs of either parent with the other; and though she had been deeply distressed and upset by the marriage rupture she kept this disaster within a robust fortress of her own making, with the gateway firmly shut.

What Gloria felt she did not need at this time, the time of her walking out, was the reappearance of a contrite, even reformed, husband; but when, almost a year to the day of their separation, he entered the inn, she was very pleased to see him, as obviously he was moved to be there. Not that Gloria was entirely uninformed about him, because although Susan had said nothing, she had followed his television exploits, amused by his newly learnt media technique, which while oblivious no doubt to many, was obvious to her.

He had approached her tentatively, uncertain of his reception, but she wanted him to kiss her, offered herself, and was embraced. It was as if in all the important ways nothing distressing had happened between them. Gloria was able to take him to an alcove and to hold his hand while she questioned him, but he had no question other than one, 'Are you all right?', which always elicited a laugh and sometimes an objection from her. He had always said it, and what could you say in answer? It had irritated her so much, the repetition of it and the need to answer. But, oh, how desirable now.

And she responded, 'Of course, I am. Can't you tell?' She lifted her head for his admiration.

'Well. I don't know what's happening to you. You look so confident, and I fear the worst. But to be honest, you look quite wonderful', was his reply. It was obviously genuine, this response, and a true test of her feelings towards him. For she knew that the most wonderful compliment from a man you cared little for was nothing, mere seed on barren ground; and a suggestion of regard, no matter how slight, from someone close to your heart was as manna from heaven. She was very pleased. She was more than pleased. But being wonderful now had nothing to do with him, although it might in the future; she had done it, almost all of it, herself and for herself.

This encounter had happened a year ago, and since then they had grown closer: but the gap between them had never closed. What she had not been able to tell him, although she had tried, was that resuming a relationship with him in the fullest sense was impossible. The very thought horrified her. Not only was she building a new life for herself, which she could respect, but his life was truly terrifying. As she watched him on television, mouthing acceptable responses to unspeakable acts of horror, she knew that at any time he might become the next target, or anyone close to him – it might be her or Susan. And when he laughed and said that there was no risk, or hardly any risk, which might be true, she didn't – couldn't – believe him. It was pathetic, of course, but that was how it was. It was not the whole truth of her feelings about him, but what it was not was more difficult for her to articulate.

Lucy was not easily denied. She was persistent, gentle and amusing with her calls and messages; but although flattered, and who would not be, by Lucy's close attentions, Gloria was firm in her rejection. With the spurning of the offer was lost, denied to her, almost as if in a punishment, her newly found group of friends. Then one evening, when she was checking up on the restaurant, she saw Rachel dining with her daughter and a handsome dark-haired young man. They were seated at a pink-covered table in the bow of a window. The lighting was soft and the rays from the lamp were thrown across the soft green lawn beyond it. They were celebrating and had dressed up for the occasion. At that moment, if a frame had been placed around the scene, one would have encompassed a charming and appealing picture of family life.

Gloria hesitated, uncertain, but as she had been seen she approached, and they all turned towards her with shining happy faces and with a pleasure which embraced her. Fiona, a demure and serious young girl of thirteen, squealed with delight and jumping up, claimed her, pleading with her to join them, which she did. And Rachel, restrained and very beautiful, in what seemed to Gloria to be an entirely normal way, just looked and looked, and smiled and smiled, and murmured her delight, her pleasure, to have found Gloria again.

The young man was Rachel's brother, down from Cambridge, and celebrating his birthday. It was all so pleasant, so convivial, so without edge and expectation, other than the assumption that they were all jolly nice people and unencumbered friends. From that moment Rachel was forgiven for the company she kept, and a tacit understanding was reached that Rachel and Gloria were friends and would spend time together; and that it would be better, for the time being, if this time excluded others outside her family. They went for walks together. Gloria learnt how to horse ride and in time, as her savings and confidence grew, she bought a horse, which Rachel stabled. Rachel's two girls were competitive, Fiona with her riding and Sophie with several musical instruments, and Gloria became a necessary supernumerary at shows and concerts and a loved extension of the family.

The advent of Bob's disgrace and demotion within the Metropolitan Police was a moment of quiet rejoicing for Gloria, for now she saw that the dark menacing clouds of terror could be lifted. Bob would think of other things he might do outside the police force. His life could be changed and she might, just might, be a part of it; or preferably, he might be a part of what she could create. She had let him back into her bed. And what a sweet man he is, she thought, a real gentleman. He had got himself fitter and had lost his paunch. He said he had stopped drinking. She was not so sure of that claim, while willing to give him the benefit of the doubt. And then he had done something remarkable: he had undergone an operation, at his own expense, to stop snoring. There were no more roars, snorts and whistles rattling the bed frame: he lay there sleeping quietly as a babe.

But as she lay there, enjoying his hard-earned docility, she had another thought, and it quickened her pulse, so that she heard and felt the fluttering of her heart. How much more pleasant might it be to have the finely sculpted, rounded concavities and exotic presence of Rachel in the bed beside her? It perturbed her, and she got up and sought to control herself while he slept quietly on. It would be more pleasant, it would be most devoutly to be desired: affection without claim, and possession without dominance. All this will pass with the night, she thought, and in daylight we shall laugh at it. But it didn't pass. So Gloria came to the conclusion that nothing could move, and nothing could change, until she knew what Rachel meant, and in relationship to this what she felt.

In the meantime she took things further with Bob. She enjoyed Bob. When in the early hours they made love, it was Gloria who took the initiative, on top and imaginative. Bob, breathless, joyous and impressed, experienced the freedom of her passion as a need for him, whereas the face that Gloria saw and the body she embraced was something entirely other.

On Sunday afternoon Bob had a call from Alec. It was bad news. A former director of Roger Greer's company, an American, had been shot dead in Detroit; and one of the British directors had reported his car and car port being set on fire. It was a lucky escape for the family, apparently, because a neighbour had spotted the fire in its early stages and had raised the alarm. David Droylsden had friends in high places in the Metropolitan Police. He had complained to them, to all of them, that nothing was being done to catch his son's killer. Now the other directors were up in arms and seeking protection for their families and a prompt arrest; for they were all in no doubt whatsoever that the perpetrator was Roger Greer. Alec said, and Bob thought he detected a certain relish in the saying of it, that the Commissioner's message was, 'Tell him to get his arse into gear and back here pronto, where he should be.'

Bob was to take the next train back to London, and Gloria drove him to the station, disappointed at the abrupt ending of his stay, but used to this type of regret. She decided to warn him. 'Don't expect too much, Bob. I'm glad we're friends again but you mustn't assume some coming together. While I'm not ruling it out, and I hope you're not, I'm not ruling it in either. We must be gentle with each other and see what develops.'

'Oh, quite, I understand. My view too, entirely.' He kissed her quickly on the cheek. He had already decided that he would wait forever.

There was a pause. She should have left it at that but she didn't. It burst out.

'It sounds awful I know and it's not all that I feel, but I think I've done too much caring, for you and your family and that dreadful police force. Those awful social occasions with half the wives punch drunk with it all and the other half yet to discover the realities of police life, although it was dawning on them. You know I've never liked police life. All those lies and personal tragedies.'

He glanced at her but said nothing. Gloria continued, having some difficulty with words. 'The place I occupy in my emotions isn't comfortable. I have no balance or resting place. This place moves, I shift, as if I'm swimming. Moving towards something, which excites and daunts me at the same time.'

He glanced at her again, seeing her upset.

She continued, 'It must sound nonsense to you, and I'm sorry, but until I stop moving and know where I've reached, I can do nothing for you.'

His voice when he spoke remained even. 'Gloria, I want to understand, I really do. As for the past I must have been mistaken. I thought I was working hard for all those years to look after my family; and that I did well. We had pleasant times. Didn't we have happy times? Don't you remember any more: good holidays, lots of laughter? And I told you then – and I meant it – that you could do anything you liked with your life and I'd support you in it. It's quite a lot to be mistaken about.'

The muskets had been fired and they sat quietly together until the fog cleared. Bob had tears in his eyes while Gloria, although upset and pale, looked very determined.

CHAPTER 4

BOB HAD LEARNT the first rule of politics: you can't afford to be absent. On Monday morning he was about early in seek of amends, and by seven o'clock he had entered his office building. For the last few months entry had been a time of perturbation and expectancy, that he might find his office locked or occupied, with its contents, the tools and records of his trade, disposed of in plastic bags neatly lined up in the corridor. This morning entry was unimpeded. He started to catch up. Soon the place was buzzing and Alec, quick off the mark, was updating him on the day. There was to be a briefing meeting at eight-thirty to bring the newcomers up to date, for the team had miraculously increased from three to ten; followed by something of a deputation, for the directors of the new company had insisted, successfully as it had turned out, on being heard.

Bob listened to the echo of his own voice. 'And we remain in charge?'

Alec smiled at the plural. 'Yes. But, to echo Wellington, it was a damn fine run thing. We're on probation. Action is required – and results. And his highness, Jenkins, wants to see you right away.'

The Assistant Commissioner was brief and to the point. The investigation had become political. There had to be progress – and quickly. Bob would be given two weeks to show that it was being made. It was understood.

Bob recapitulated for his new team. 'As you know, Garth Droylsden was blown up by a car bomb which we are certain, fairly certain, was intended for his father. The IRA have denied involvement, and although the device has their hallmark we're inclined to believe them. I say fairly certain, because we're going to check out Garth's background a little more thoroughly. We know he has a police record. Alec –.'

'He has two minor offences for possession of drugs going back to his student days, five years ago, but nothing since. Probably nothing.'

'Thank you, Alec.' Bob took over again. 'Most of you know something about my methods. I'm an evidence man.' He paused, and there were some sniggers and yawns behind hands. 'And at this stage of our inquiries there's very little evidence. David Droylsden had a lot of enemies. We have a starting field of twenty-one but we'll find others. Alec, how many of these have made witness statements?'

'Six. Only six.'

'That's slow progress. We must have them all completed by the end of the week, and I need to see them as they become available. Anything untoward and we'll throw the whole book at them: searches, bank statements, their associates and so on.'

'Guv, excuse me.' He was interrupted. 'Isn't it all rather obvious? Everyone seems certain that it must be this chap Roger Greer. Shouldn't we get him in here and put the pressure on?' Eyes were focused on Bob.

'The main difficulty with that advice is that we've no evidence to support an arrest. On the face of it I don't see how Roger Greer could be shooting a man in Detroit and burning down a house in Surrey at the same time, especially as he was talking to me in Norfolk around the time he was supposed to be doing these things.' He played his confidence card. 'But I do have warrants to search his premises, his matrimonial home and his girlfriend's flat; the Garda are assisting us in checking the Irish connections; and we're sending his personal records to the cleaners. Dave – it is Dave, isn't it? – let me tell you this. Roger Greer's a smart chap. Any wrongful arrest will be uncomfortable for us. He'll come at us. Is that clear? Good. OK, let's get going. Divide it all up, Alec.'

There were only two of the directors of Roger's old company left, with two being fired and one shot in Detroit. They were here because of fright. David Droylsden had brought them here, had arranged it, because of his determination to nail Roger Greer. He said his piece, stated his demands for effective action, his conviction that Roger Greer was the man, and his grounds for maintaining that there was sufficient justification for his arrest. He stopped, waiting for a response, so that he could weigh up what he should do. Should he rely on them at all or should he seek his own retribution? He was not impressed. These police-men didn't fill him with confidence. The other directors bleated on, concerned by the personal safety of their families, and getting assurances but no action. The anger rose within him like a tidal wave with no shore to crash on. He thought of his mother and the journey back to Manchester after the funeral, and what she had said, what she had always said to him, about the impor-tance of reaction, retaliation, and that for a Jew turning the other cheek was never an option. It was not just a matter of religious belief, 'an eye for an eye and a tooth for a tooth', but a lesson of history, of their history. She looked to him to do the right thing while staying within the law. He must be strong. And then this policeman had the nerve to warn them about not taking the law into their own hands, together with the importance of not jump-ing to conclusions, urging them to trust the police and what he called due process. When he asked himself what they had gained, he found himself without an answer, or rather the answer that was always there, that it was up to him.

The damage caused by the explosion had been difficult to contain, it had been widespread, and try as they might the pieces could not be put together again. Esther had gone to stay with her sister, and then the two of them had departed for France. David had stayed at the flat, which emergency repairs had made habit-able, but empty, and he had gone quickly back to work, shrugging off the half-hearted attempts of his new colleagues and backers to persuade him to stop and grieve for a while. The ripples had caught up Sylvia, alarmed by the possible consequences for Roger, who had in turn drawn closer, in mutual horror and vulnerability, to his wife Melissa, who was at this time performing at Convent Garden and worrying about the children.

Roger spent weekends with Sylvia, who had in her own way been kind to him. The relationship was six months old, and at the stage when both had to consider whether it was going anywhere, and if so, where, and what energy and hope might be invested in it.

Almost everyone would have considered, on first reflection, that Sylvia was a good catch for Roger. At thirty-eight she was much younger than him. A successful City lawyer, she was entirely self-sufficient, with a comfortable Kensington flat and money in the bank. And to cap it all, she had looks reminiscent of a model, and an easy elegance even at those moments when the rest of humanity would prefer you to look away. Sylvia was highly analytical and an ideal person to whom to bring a complex problem, which was, of course, the reason for her well-being and the source of her comfortable income.

And yet, perhaps, all was not quite perfect. The question was beginning to be asked, and indeed she asked it of herself, why there had not been any serious relationships before Roger; and at work it seemed that her career had reached a plateau. Murmurings among her colleagues could be heard that in some subtle way Sylvia lacked 'get up and go' and that as a consequence she had lost her way; while others were of the view that Sylvia was not a risk taker. 'No risk, no gain', they muttered. Roger was not risk free, and much though she thought she loved him, the necessary time at which she would lay all before him might well have passed. And Roger could not think of such a time at all, although he thought it would come, bound up as he was in the moments of ruin and threats to the remaining tatters of his well-being. And, perhaps, then, if this could not be her moment, there never would be one: for she would have become aware that there would always be reasons for drawing back, and that in the ultimate, these reasons would be compelling to her.

Roger was overwhelmingly grateful to Sylvia. She had taken him in and given him a key. She had started to offer herself to him in such a discreet and considered way. She listened and gave good advice, albeit most of it, given that his circumstances were dire, was entirely useless as he could not act on it. Sylvia took him to the theatre, looking her best, which made him for a short time an object of male envy and not, as he habitually thought now, of contempt and ridicule.

His disgrace was signified by his post. Each day brought threats from his creditors and demands, sometimes angry, from those who had gained most by his efforts in the past. All those loans with which he had bought his shares, with the eager consent of clearing and merchant banks, were now secured on worthless share certificates. As he struggled unsuccessfully to pay the huge mortgage on the family home, the risks for his family becoming homeless became real and imminent: and in the effort to keep them afloat a host of smaller creditors, left unpaid, snapped at him daily.

He felt his losses keenly. Whatever he might have thought of himself to be in the past, now he felt an abject failure, perhaps worse. Perhaps dishonest, a rogue, a person not to be respected. Who could blame them, for he could not respect himself? Above all he wished to retain the love of his children, and, perhaps, if it were possible, not too late, of his wife. Each day, he would say to himself, '*Courage, mon brave*', and up he would get to charge the windmills.

Since it was a Saturday morning Roger was off to see his two children, and to wander in a desultory fashion with them in the local park or anywhere else that seemed important to them at the time. It was his habit afterwards to spend time with Melissa in the kitchen, where the embers of their relationship seemed to flicker briefly. In his pocket he had two letters: one indicated the beginning of bankruptcy proceedings against him, and the other was from Melissa's solicitors, seeking to ascertain whether he would facilitate a divorce.

These postal missives lay heavy in his inside pocket as significant despatches from the front, and their simultaneous arrival he thought significant. He thought of Borodino and Napoleon's pyrrhic victory. He knew it was necessary sometimes to fight a battle with heavy losses in order to win a campaign. He was going to lose many a battle, and in all probability the campaign itself, but it would all be worthwhile if he could save his family. Whatever had happened in the past, surely Melissa would see that he couldn't fight this losing campaign at all unless something worthwhile could be obtained from the ashes of defeat. He decided that honesty, if not the only policy, was still his best option.

Melissa had sought counselling assistance in order to deal with her distress. This seemed to him, innocently, to indicate a concern for the truth. He could offer to share this approach. If she were willing to share her insights about the past, the things that had worried her, he would do the same: if she would answer his questions he would be able to be honest with her.

His entry had been inauspicious: stumbling on the steps and grazing a knee and tearing a trouser leg, then knocking his cup of coffee off the kitchen table. But at last he made it. They sat together across a kitchen table drinking coffee and eating cake. She continued to be as fresh as the Viennese pastry before her, and as delicious as the arias she sang so melodiously. He had always loved the way she presented herself, picturing herself as part of a scene, and always sure of the words and tones and the necessary movements about the stage. He was conscious that he was not always as certain of his part, his words, and where he was on her stage.

This scene was carefully choreographed. It was such a pleasing little kitchen, with everything carefully in its place, but like her, comely, colourful and extravagant in an understated way. The immortal words, 'speak up and don't bump into people', flashed before him. He realised in his embarrassment that his performances over the years must have disappointed her, and he became suddenly anxious to please; but while she was dressed for the part, glossy and neat, with her wonderful brown hair tied neatly in a fashionable bun, he was in need of some grooming, and with clothes that needed a good dry cleaner or at least a visit to the washing machine. He had known her for nearly twenty years and for most of these he had adored her, been besotted by her. He could not look at her for all the happy images of passion and joy which threatened to crowd her out as she looked straight at him. He was confused, seeing the past as a series of cut-outs kaleidoscoped together, rendering him dizzy as he tried in vain to focus on what was before him now. He swallowed hard. She was amicable and he tried her out.

She said hesitantly, 'I'm not sure that's a good idea. These exchanges with the counsellor are confidential. If I'd thought I'd become answerable to you for my revelations I wouldn't have volunteered them. And anyway what good can it do, raking over the past?'

'For me, a great deal of good. I have to live with myself. This is the second time it has happened to me. I need to understand my mistakes and learn to live with them.' He paused, and then while he had not thought of it in advance he offered her a deal. 'If you can answer my questions' –seeing her face – 'as best you can, when we've done this, if you still want a divorce, I'll facilitate it.'

She laughed. 'Maybe it'll be you wanting the divorce if I do that.'

'I'll take my chance.'

'OK, how shall we start?'

'Chronologically, that's how I think of it? But first let me give you an example of what I mean, what I want us to be frank about.'

She nodded, waiting for him.

'There came a point in my first marriage when Marion began to ring me at work. She'd ask me to hurry home to start the meal, as she'd been delayed at her office. It was always awkward. I always agreed. After all, her work was as important to her as mine was to me, we shared a common responsibility to look after things, and so on.... I was a modern, caring husband.' He looked at her and she gestured, showing her impatience. He always did this: speeches, and too long. And never responding to a straight question with a straight answer.

'Well, to hurry it on. After the marriage came to an end she told me that on these occasions she'd been carrying on an affair with one of her colleagues. Quite a serious affair, apparently, and he was willing to take her in and have children with her and she'd considered doing it. And then she told me exactly the moment she'd decided not to do this.'

'Where is this leading?' Melissa was anxious to know when her lines would begin.

' I wondered whether, unconsciously, I knew that this was going on, and made some deep decision of my own to say nothing about it to myself. What I mean is that when we're cheated on we always know, really, that something's going on, and that alters the way we behave. Do you see what I mean? And if we'd known, if it had been explicit, we might have behaved differently. It can drive you mad, not knowing for certain.'

Melissa said that she did know.

'With us I have to go back sixteen years to the time, just after our marriage, when you left me for three months. You described it as a kind of breakdown but we both knew there was someone else, and we chose to skate over it, not to make an issue of it.'

'Are you sure you want to discuss this?' Melissa looked sad. 'You'll regret it afterwards.'

'Yes.'

'You know that between engagements I had a temporary job I hated. As I told you, a senior international executive there, with a flat in the West End and a wife in Amsterdam, took a shine to me. I was flattered, feeling very low at the time, not about you in particular but about not singing, not really working and time passing me by, and we started something together. I'd go to his flat, and once as a consequence I was very late in meeting you, and I had to try to explain myself to you, and I knew I couldn't, and I didn't want to stop and so I left.'

'Then why did you return?'

'I shouldn't have done. I realise now that although I cared for you it wasn't a mature love, but I needed someone. This new relationship wasn't going to work out, so I returned. This makes it sound more calculating than it really was. I was genuine and I did want us to work out.'

'And did it end there?'

' No, not quite, there were a number of other occasions, but then he was posted to Brussels and it stopped.'

'And then on one or two other occasions you went away for short breaks, sending me loving cards from hotels in seaside resorts. You told me that in order to recover from the exhaustion of performances you needed short breaks, and that without them there was a risk you'd have a further breakdown.'

'That was true, I did need to recover, but I wasn't on my own. I should explain something to you, which you know really. Being on a stage, when the whole of your being's laid bare to an audience, is a demoralising experience. When the curtain and lights go down you're in desperate need of reassurance. Performers give this to each other. Everyone knows the rules, and when the show comes to an end life gets back to normal. It has no other meaning. But I knew this was unacceptable to you, so it had to be kept secret. Some of these relationships rolled on a little because deep emotions aren't easily halted, but hardly ever for long. And then there are stage door johnnies. I'd tell you about some of these from time to time.'

'But not about them all, apparently', he retorted, not being able to stop himself.

She was angry. 'The trouble about this type of account of the past is that it gives a false picture. I was always committed to you, and after the children came along and I was at home more these problems largely disappeared.'

'Largely?'

'I'm being completely honest here, as you want me to be. As you became more successful you travelled abroad a lot and sometimes people, not very often, and then as time passed hardly ever, would ring me up. I didn't seek it but I got anxious when you were away. It was usually nothing, a drink or a meal and a good laugh.' She saw him crestfallen. 'Not such a good idea, after all?' She was willing to stop.

But he continued. 'Tell me about the abortion.'

Melissa hesitated, and for the first time she lost her composure. 'Are you sure?'

He nodded.

'You remember, at that time I stopped using the pill because we wanted to start a family, and then out of the blue came the opportunity of appearing at the Sydney Opera House. There are rare chances in a stage career, which if you don't take you blame yourself for the rest of your time.' She spoke defiantly, just hating it.

He expressed his dissent.

'Well, the director, and I don't want to remind you of his name, had other things on his mind, other conditions. Not only would I need to be perfect in the roles, of course I would be, I'd be absolutely perfect – but then so would many other people – but I had to be pliant in other ways. So when I became pregnant I didn't know whether it was his or yours, and I couldn't take the chance. You're sorry now, aren't you? Not such a good idea, eh?'

He cried out. And she shouted at him, showing her resentment and dislike not only of the discussion but of him, or so he imagined it. It had been agonising for him, all this fair-mindedness. He remembered at a Parliamentary election he'd fought being approached by the pro-life campaigners with their questionnaires and the way he had answered their careful questions in his committee room. He had replied that while he was not dealing in absolutes, he personally was not in favour of abortion. He approved of the law as it stood as a justifiable balance between different rights: whatever his personal opinion, he defended the right of a woman to decide for herself. But when it had come to the crunch, he had felt as sick as a dog; listening to her, not seeking to turn aside specious reasoning; taking her part, collecting her from the clinic, hearing the whispers that it was so small, this foetus, that no one could be sure of its very existence; and feeling it to be an indecent assault on their very being, their future.

She got up and busied herself, waiting for him to continue.

'And when you were in Sydney? I know this was a difficult time for you.'

Melissa abandoned all reticence. 'Not what you think. The attentions of a kind stage hand, a nice young chap, from time to time. Someone who could understand what was happening to me, night after night, and was simple about it.' She counter-attacked now, her mood quite different. 'And all this time you were as good as a little angel, I don't think.'

She needed to hear his lines again. He said them. He had rehearsed his words many times.

'As for me, for much of this time I was completely faithful to you. It wasn't difficult, for I was hopelessly in love with you and the children were pure joy. But then when you were away, and you were away for very long times, or I was under some particular pressure, there were people, one-night stands of no importance at all to me.' He wanted to tell her, but he didn't, that he had been a latchkey child, arriving home from the school with the probability of no one being there and pulling the doorkey through the letter box on its string and an entering a cold empty house: and that ever since he had problems in dealing with separation. It sounded so pathetic. He swallowed hard and took a deep breath.

'With one exception. At the end of the seventies I was picked up by a young Jewish girl on a plane to the States who'd read some Erika Jong and was determined to get off with me. But although this was how it started, it wasn't how it continued. She became a very good friend. She was anxious not to disturb her family and I was desperate to keep mine. It lasted for seven years. The friendship was very helpful to me and I was sorry to lose it. It's my belief that if I hadn't let this relationship come to an end the company wouldn't have gone under.'

'Goodness, what a little deceiver. And I knew nothing of it', she said bitterly. She withdrew from him. 'This conversation was a bad idea, don't you think? Confirmed you in your belief that I was a bad egg, when in truth I loved and cared for you and your children over so many years. Now, if you've finished, and I have nothing more to say, can I have my divorce, now, as you promised? Thank you.'

'One more thing.' He needed to say it even though it was redundant now and he had no hope in it. 'Two into one won't go. My financial circumstances are very difficult now. I desperately want to look after you and the children, and I can do it best if we're together in some way, perhaps under the same roof. Could we manage it – if it has to be contrived?'

He was pleading with her. She stamped on it, showing her contempt. She needed to be brutal. 'No. Everyone I speak to tells me that you're a busted flush and if you cling on to me I'll drown too. I have to stay afloat not only for myself but for the children.'

She had always intended it to say this. It crushed him, as she knew it would. But still he looked at her. He was still there. So she went on.

'A performer's a kind of athlete. You have a limited number of years to get to the top, and what's the point of it all if you can't be there, singing the leading roles with the very best, being the very best? And I could have been the very best, I know I could. Success requires all your time and energy. It was a mistake for me to have this family life and to be sucked up in the lives of others.'

It was done now.

Over that weekend Sylvia found Roger very cast down, and there was no joy in him. On the Monday her senior partner called her into his office for a fatherly chat. He had heard about the police search of her flat and she gave him her best explanation. He warned her in a kindly way about the inadvisability of getting involved with a married man with serious financial and emotional problems which would dog him for many years, and if she was not careful, would ruin her life also. She listened very carefully and thought about what he had said for two days. Then on the Wednesday she wrote a short note to Roger bringing their relationship to an end.

At five-thirty on a Tuesday morning two police vans drew up outside Roger Greer's cottage in Bungay, and five policemen got out and began to hammer on his back door, waking not only Roger but his neighbours. They produced a warrant and, pushing him to one side, began a search of his premises and its outbuildings which lasted six hours. He observed then what he was to find on other occasions. They were excited, much as a group of football fans arriving at the ground of a rival team, and aggressive. They were up for it. He had to wait around while they searched through his things, what they chose to examine, before selecting and bagging up his life, or such a part of it as they thought useful to them. Inconveniently they took his computer, the essential tool of his present trade, and if he had not dissuaded them they would have taken his car. That, they told him, would need to be the subject of a forensic examination, but they gave him four hours to find a substitute. He tried to remember what William James had said about possessions. Something to the effect that man was the sum of them: his farm, his livestock, his land, his wife and children: they were indissoluble. Now, what was left was disappearing through his door in bags in the hands of men wearing white plastic gloves.

Outside a small group of people had gathered, and he asked them as nicely as he could to go away, to get lost. He felt incapacitated in dealing with the whole incident, by the very same reasonableness that characterised him and kept him afloat. He had always possessed the ability to see the other person's point of view, all sides of the question, whereas what he needed to do now was to scream at someone, anyone. It was a small town and already rumours were beginning to take hold. Over the coming weeks the locals would be viewing him differently, and the journalists would be gathering in the hope of some raw meat, and shouting at them would not do him any good.

As he thought these things the telephone rang, and a pleasant voice introduced itself. It was someone called Rachel. 'A friend of Gloria's. The barmaid at the Ship Inn?'

'Oh yes, Gloria.'

'I hope you don't mind, it's a cheek really. But I saw you talking to Gloria at the bar, and she gave me your name. I'm having a party soon to mark the completion of my barn conversion, and we're short of eligible males. Would you come if I asked you?'

' I'm flattered. It's some time since anyone called me an eligible male.' He paused. 'But...'

'Good, that's settled. I'll send you a formal invitation.'

'How did you get my number?'

'The phone book.' They laughed at the absurdity of his question.

The conversation was short; but Rachel being there had warmed him. He felt that she had washed over him.

CHAPTER 5

I N THE PROLONGED absence of his wife Esther, David
Droylsden took a train to Manchester every Friday to visit
his mother. As work was never far from his mind, he occupied a first-class seat, spreading his papers and positioning his
portable computer before him. On this Friday he took from his
briefcase a report he had commissioned from a firm of private
investigators into the life and times of Roger Greer. It was apparent from his demeanour, a concentrated focus, that this report
was of compulsive interest to him, and he read slowly and took
notes which he typed up as a written record. He did not think it
would be difficult to help Roger Greer into the gutter, for only a
nudge was needed, but he worked out to his own satisfaction
what he could do. Then there was the related issue of bringing
this man to justice for the death of his son, a matter that could not
be left to the mercies of a played-out policeman. There were
good lines of enquiry suggested in the report, and he highlighted
some for a further commission.

Important matters attended to, he leant back, closed his eyes
and thought of Esther. It did not concern him that she had not
returned home after her two-week holiday, or to discover that his
wife had moved on to Florence and then to other places. He
received enigmatic postcards from Esther from diverse dots on
the map, and his reading of them inclined him to the conclusion
that he should not worry about her. They told him little else,
other than a record of the names of the art galleries and museums
she had visited. She seemed to be embarked on the modern
equivalent of the Grand Tour, although the selection of the places

and works of art visited seemed somewhat quixotic and inexplicable. Nor did it seem entirely incongruous to him to have received a card from New York, where they had relatives and friends, although his eyebrows rose and twitched a little on the news. He knew she would return in her own time, and he was content to let her do so. Not wanting to have her run out of money, he had dipped further into his savings and without telling her had transferred quite a large sum, more than he thought prudent, into her bank account.

As for his mother, he had isolated in his mind a number of things he needed to do for her that weekend, practical tasks about the flat, things that needed attention, some of which she had noticed and complained about, and others of which she was not aware. He had to be careful about what he did: she remained his mother. One weekend with the help of a friend who was a plumber he had plumbed in an entirely new kitchen, but although she liked the new units, and they had agreed on them, the change was too precipitate and upset her; having been a highly practical woman for all of her adult life she disliked the thought that she had not done the entire job herself. Nowadays he concentrated on smaller matters which were subject to due consideration and even mediation. Not that there were any larger matters to be discussed, because over many years he had already done everything he could think of to modernise her small flat. He had failed to persuade her to shift out of her reliance on the council into more recent and desirable accommodation which he could buy for her. Her place of abode remained an ugly post-war grey block: a place of distinguishable noises and smells, raised and abrasive voices, and graffiti and syringes on the stairwell. When he spoke to her about these things she told him they were getting better. She resisted him, knowing he was seeking to uproot her, to move her on. But the time had not come for that; perhaps it never would. She was weaker now, and sensing and knowing it, he did less, and said very little, while watching her, which pleased her. He was a good boy.

For Fiona it was very different, curled up on her own straw bed in a commodious, and what was to her a sweet-smelling, stable; for early on a Saturday morning there was no other place she wished to be. Rachel had discovered that her daughter had been staying awake, while pretending to be asleep in her own pretty bedroom, then when the others were asleep shifting out to the stables. Rachel had come looking and found her firmly established there. A mother's prerogative had been exercised and it was agreed that she would not do that any more. But Fiona was a sophisticated thirteen year old, or so she thought, and exceptions had been negotiated: weekends, when there were no staying friends or relatives, and when a horse was sick. Their health had seemed to deteriorate from that point, and then Rachel made sure that the straw was always clean and the sleeping bag and blankets were sufficient to keep her daughter warm.

Fiona knew all these horses very well. She thought them more reliable than humans, although she would be among the first to admit that there was more to it than that. Grown-ups were a mystery. Some of them were reliable in some ways, for example her mother; but most were inscrutable and their ways could be highly damaging. The horses played games with you and could be tricky, but horses were easy to decipher. When you told horses enough was enough they usually stopped it, whatever it was; but adults were opaque and resistible.

Today was to be special and to belong to Sophie, her sister, and one year her junior. It was the day of the school concert, when Sophie was to play the Mendelssohn violin concerto, and when an important person from London was to come and listen to her and to decide her musical future. Today, she thought, Sophie would bound ahead of her in one sure leap – over the hedge and far away. She would be pleased for her, of course. It would be wonderful to have a famous sister. She could reflect in her glory. It was no more than Sophie deserved. Everyone would say it. But she was jealous, feeling it unfair that a younger sister should overleap an older and have her future decided first.

The concert complicated the day. There were to be visitors: her granny, Rachel's mother Janet, whom she liked and who was always giving her money, and who had bought her first pony; Fergus, her younger brother, who was good fun, but who always pinched her hard so it hurt, with his father Ralph, who was not her own – her and Sophie's father being dead – and his new wife Chloe. Fergus would bring his dog, an excitable red setter, like Fergus, and it would run around and around in circles jumping up at people. They were all to have lunch at the house and then tea out, so as not to make Sophie nervous by hanging around in a pointless sort of way. It was foolish, really, because Sophie took after her mother – everyone said so – and her mother was never nervous. Then Gloria would be there, but too late to go riding with her. She liked having people over on special occasions because it was good fun. There would be more men around, which she preferred to her mother's week-day gatherings: after all half the population were men, and they were different from women, and she would have to do things with them as well.

But people complicated things, and if she was to get her pony ride into the day she would have to start early before they were around to interfere. She left a note on the stable door and disap-peared across the fields before anyone could stop her, and stayed away for the whole morning. Her mother was always good about these migrations, not asking any questions and only insisting on a hot bath to eliminate horsey smells, which was a pity, she thought, for they were her favourites. Ralph said she scrubbed up well, and the other adults laughed. She didn't like this sort of remark but no one could stop Ralph, especially after a glass or two. Sophie had disappeared into the studio where she continued to practise although it was obvious that she was perfect; that is, as perfect as you could be at twelve.

Gloria walked her into the garden and down to the pond. Gloria seemed to know a lot about ponds and the life in them, which was really interesting. She had noticed that Gloria was unexpected: she knew nothing at all about some subjects, even when they were easy-peasy and everyone else did know; and heaps about others, when almost everyone, except experts, knew hardly anything about them at all, although they pretended that they did. Really interesting things, not only about ponds and rivers and animals, but about writers and painters and the lives they lived, and what had happened to ordinary people in the past, and how the things around them had come into being. Rachel had said to her that Gloria had underperformed in her life, and that her capacities for doing astonishing things were much greater than she or other people in her life could imagine.

Fiona was surrounded by clever people with intellectual capacities, so she had not learnt to value these other qualities. It seemed to her now that Gloria had much more exciting gifts than mummy's clever friends: a feeling for life, and emotions and thoughts not always governed by reason and caution. Gloria was intuitive, with the gift of knowing instinctively how things were or might be, without a lot of boring ifs and buts and maybes. And Gloria was inquisitive in the nicest possible way, asking natural questions about things you were really interested in and then, unlike other grown-ups, listening to your answers. She had become a good and loyal friend, and not only to her mother; Fiona felt that she could talk about anything to Gloria and Gloria could talk to her.

Rachel had organised tea in a tearoom in a village near their rather nice fee-paying school for respectable girls like them, and they piled in and around a trestle table specially prepared for their party. As the school had thrived, so had the teashop. It had grown, pushing out into its adjacent neighbour, a general store, and gentrifying itself. The pinafored waitresses now bustled between white-linened round tables, and their voices needed to be raised to counter the distinctive bray of the classes on display. Some of these visitors knew each other, and Rachel was greeted cheerily by several, but Fiona thought her mother not to be one of them.

Rachel had positioned the party carefully. Fergus was stuck in a corner under Granny's tutelage, where he could do least harm, but it did not prevent him flicking bits of bread roll at her and making faces. She admired her Granny, who was very well turned out, and not at all old-fashioned, and who knew exactly what to do about Fergus and how to counter his tricks. Fiona positioned herself near Gloria as a shield so that she could be on the edge of things and peer at people around her. Gloria became her protectress and interpreter. Ralph – who thought himself a handsome man of the world and probably was – had pushed in alongside Gloria, although that meant his wife Chloe had to sit opposite him. It was Gloria who needed protection, because Ralph would keep putting his hand on her thigh, not caring whether anyone saw him, although it was obvious that she didn't like it, and kept pushing him away.

Chloe was a tall thin woman with a fine mane of fair hair and a long face. Fiona saw that she had spotted the movements opposite her and that she had pursed her mouth and raised herself. For a moment, seeing and recognising this remarkable gathering, Fiona thought that Chloe would whinny and snort, and then leap from her chair over the trestle table and bolt across the cafe and out into the cobbled road and away, mane flying, and that the others would follow, laughing and falling about. But Gloria saved the day – which was a pity – by excusing herself and then on her return sitting in another place, farther away. This not stop Ralph ogling her in a rather peculiar manner. It puzzled Fiona. Why did he do this when he had been married for some time and to a perfectly acceptable wife, given that she did sometimes look like a horse, which anyway was to her credit because horses looked very nice?

The school had succeeded in becoming impressive from a modest start. In origin it was a large Victorian manor house of uncertain architectural inheritance, being disproportionate with a large porticoed entrance and windows that had been enlarged to let in more light. The building, idiosyncratically, ran north–south and was enfolded in a deep hollow. It was shrouded to the east by a forest of protected beech and oak trees which cast it into permanent shade. Yet money had been found not only to improve the facilities but to extend them by additions on land to the north; and despite first appearances the school had now all the modern facilities it needed. It had aspired to and achieved high educational standards under a series of impressive Oxbridge headmistresses. It had become attractive to aspiring middle-class parents, and engaged their active and loyal support. Rachel approved of the school not only because as a Cambridge graduate she recognised and approved of high standards, but because it was a happy place for girls to be sustained in and encouraged.

The concert was held in the oak-panelled main hall which, if a little Gothic in dimension and atmosphere, and too small for much of its use, had fine acoustics. The gold-lettered panelled lists of pupils' names proclaimed the achievements of the school, but as important, they continued to advance the proposition that excellence mattered and was expected: pupils were successful and you too could be great. The weak might be intimidated by such an approach to life but girls at this school were selected, from the overwhelming number who applied to it for a place, from the doughty and the bold. As Fiona contemplated the performance to come she knew that Sophie would be a success. The very fact that she would stand there before them, in this place, was a kind of guarantee: unless, of course, by some act of God, she had an epileptic fit or something which threw her to the floor, and then that would not happen because she felt sure that God approved of the school as he was given such loving and obedient attention there.

As usual the Headmistress, Ms Girton, gave a short address. This speech was well-structured like Ms Girton herself, who stood straight, neat and unprepossessing before them, neither asserting her femininity nor betraying it. She spoke on all the public occasions at the school, and it was always the same speech. She told them that the days when girls were given a lesser educational consideration than boys were long since gone, and that their girls could be expected to pass through life with scholastic and worldly achievements second to none, and commensurate with their intelligence and talent. No less distinguished – one might dare to say more – than boys starting from similar privileges. They all clapped, believing it sincerely to be true.

The concert was to turn out the success that Fiona expected. Sophie performed after the break – which was a drag because you had to sit through everything – and once she had started it all seemed to go very well. Fiona sat to the left of her mother with the musician from London on her right. After a while, when it was becoming certain, she saw that her mother was crying. But the musician man with his mop of fine curly black hair was animated, moving with the music, counting, and saying 'Bravo' beneath his breath. At the end this man took her mother and Sophie aside, and although Fiona was not supposed to listen, she heard words like 'highly promising', 'scholarship', and 'studying in London', and on later inquiry she discovered what was being proposed. Sophie was being given a place to study at a music school near London. She would be leaving home. Fiona felt an immense pain. She gasped, and taking Gloria's hand she urged her away from the others and out of the hall.

Back home Sophie hugged her, knowing her departure would be grievous for Fiona; but already her eyes were looking away beyond her sister to another horizon of her own making, to a secret place where Fiona could not go. Gloria was the last of the party remaining, and she and Rachel were left talking in the lounge over coffee. Something intimate was going on between Gloria and her mother, Fiona knew that, and in a panic she hoped that she would not lose Gloria as well: Gloria was her friend too and she needed her fealty. She led Gloria by the hand to her bedroom and insisted on a bedtime story. She was too old for bedtime stories. She knew it, but Gloria did not mind. She enjoyed stories and had already started to read Fiona *The Jungle Book*. Fiona thought her problems could not be greater than those of the animals, and if it worked out well for them, why not her? She fell asleep while Gloria was reading.

So Fiona missed the adult chat that went on for some hours before the sound of Gloria's car crunching its way up the track to the road could be heard, startling the rabbits, disturbed in their own claimed territory and frozen in the car headlights.

Gloria loved driving in the country on empty roads in the dead of night, with the car lights picking out the night life ahead and to the side of her. It held for her a high sense of romance and unknown possibilities of joy and sadness. She had not wanted to leave but did not know how to stay. She had hoped that Rachel would have shown her how; that it would be for Rachel to take an initiative. They were close. It was romantic. Rachel had taken great care of her appearance that day. It had been an occasion. The two women, their heads and hearts close together, had looked a very pretty sight in the soft light of the lounge: Gloria with her fairness and animation and purity of intention, and Rachel in red velvet with the rarefied intensity of her auburn hair and her generosity of spirit. But Rachel was diverted by other thoughts; by the fineness and talent of her younger daughter, and her pride in her, and by her hopes of a better life for herself. Rachel had been thinking of Roger, who had lodged in her imagination, although she knew hardly anything about him.

At this time Roger was sleepless, and wandering aimlessly about his small abode, seeking solutions to his manifold problems in vain. Eventually he regained his bed and fell into a half-sleep, a reverie which took him into the realm of imagination, the only homeland he could occupy in safety. In his dream, in his boyhood, he entered the prefabricated building that was his local library. He was alone. He was alone in all these dreams. The coat of arms of his London local authority was on the wall, above the head of a decorous librarian, who smiled at him. And beneath the coat of arms were the words: 'Borrow – Discover – Connect'. He looked at her inquiringly, inviting her assistance: and she smiled and waved him into the library. The rows of shelves swam towards him, and their book spines, with gold and black lettering, seemed to float free as if to swamp him, pressing upon him, until screaming he woke.

Roger got up and busied himself. He remembered the library. It was a long walk to get there from home, and the choice of book was limited. He had made a start at school, so out of sequence he could read more of Forrester, Dickens, Buchan and Scott. Then he supposed there was no better method than to read alphabetically, punctuated only by author selection prompted by things heard of and which had aroused his imagination. In this way it had taken him two years to reach Yeats: but at fifteen he supposed himself to be the only schoolboy to have read the whole of Dornford Yates.

So he had borrowed a lot, but what had he discovered? Only nuggets of the unexpected: how to survive at sea as a cabin boy; escaping from your bedroom in the dead of night and crossing rooftops in the moonlight to detect spies; what it was like living in a nineteenth-century Indian village; catching a white whale; talking to wild animals, who proved to be better friends to you than humans and who helped you to discover treasure in the midst of the African jungle; and what it was like living in the Arctic zone, if you lived in an igloo and were a twin. And then something about adults and the absurd way they organised themselves and lived their lives: about ambition, power, war, exploitation, the world of work, and about sex – a lot about sex.

All this was very useful, but the real problem was one of connection. What had it all to do with him? And with what could he connect? At the age of fourteen, inflamed by the literature he was reading and then questioned, he had joined a Young Writers

Club, where books and the writings of its members were discussed. He wrote about connection. It seemed to him that human contact could not be entirely a matter of accident, but neither was it predestined. And as he looked from his bedroom window at the millions of stars, the fates of which were all joined up in some mysterious and dramatic manner, he imagined them as people linked by invisible threads, something like a spider's web, but with the spider hidden from view. This web might be broken, but then it could be mended again: the spider could repair it. All his life he had respected spider's webs, doing his best to avoid breaking them and enabling them, so far as he could, to be respun.

He imagined a vast web which somehow connected people wherever they were to be found, although in his imagination the web did not include oceans and jungles. In some way, which at that time he had not discovered, people would be able to meet and engage with each other by use of this web: but it was not inevitable, for the web might break and not be respun, and then there were the issues of timing and juxtaposition. You might miss the love of your life by being on the wrong side of the street to her when you passed because, say, you were in a crowd, or by leaving the store twenty seconds before her.

There were intellectual difficulties with his concept. How did you get into the web? How did you get started? He thought of levitation. You could lift yourself to it. This was no idle theory, for he had seen it done and later experienced it for himself. In the latter days of his soccer career, Tommy Lawton, the English international centre forward, and a peerless header of a ball, played for Leyton Orient. He had travelled to the ground with his dad especially to see the great man play. They positioned themselves behind the goal. The expected and dreamt-of moment arrived , the ball was crossed, and the great man rose majestically before them like a salmon. The cross was high and it seemed that his hero had risen too soon. The crowd around him drew breath, it sighed in anguish that the moment they had waited for would be unfulfilled. But he hovered there before them, their hero, waiting the ball's arrival. The Brylcreemed head, with its neat centre parting, glistened – and then with a swish the ball was in the net. He had tried this hovering at the peak of the jump himself, in private, and then on the football field, and thought he had succeeded. He could see that in the ultimate it was a matter of faith; but then why not? If you could believe in a virgin birth, the feeding of the five thousand, and making wine out of water, why not in levitation and transportation?

However, when he explored these thoughts at the Writers Club, people were polite but disengaged. He was discouraged and stopped attending. Perhaps he was a crank like Mr Jones next door, who had shyly told him one day that he had founded the 'inner cleanliness sect'; or like Simon Brown, who sat next to him in Geography, and insisted, even though the others laughed, that the earth was flat. But were they stranger, these half-formed beliefs of his, than say wild animals in the jungle speaking to you in your language or in a language of their own that you understood immediately without ever studying it?

Roger thought he had reached the nub of his problem. Why he was alone? Where was the connectedness? Why, he had built businesses employing hundreds of young people; he had belonged to political parties; and he had married twice and had produced two children. So why, now, were there so very few friends and little discernible family who spoke to him or were easy in his company? And why was it that he might die in his own bed in this ridiculous place and his death would not be discovered for days and days? Truth was your ally, he used to say, and self-pity an intellectual mistake. So what was the truth? He thought that it was not that he was not engaging in himself – he had plenty of evidence to the contrary – but rather that in any difficulty, any crisis, he relied only on himself, shutting out others; and while in business and political contexts he could compromise and mediate, in his personal life he could not, choosing to withdraw into himself and rely on no one but himself. And then he was obstinate. There was no one else, nothing, that could help him. Was that the truth?

He found himself laughing. No wonder they had all mocked his theory of connectedness. But at that time he had thought it all through. And we might surmise that if there were something to it, at that moment it might have meant something for Roger. He might have seen Esther using the last of the sunlight in Darien, Connecticut, at the point when the winter sun set on golden sand

and when the colours were elusive; and then seen her return to the warmth of her bedroom in the small hotel where, thanks to David's generosity, she had been resident for some weeks. He might have observed his principal adversary prowling his own space, or rather his mother's, safely back from bingo, and putting the details into place for his demise. He might have found Melissa gargling in the bathroom or proudly mounted on vast firmly formed pillows – better for breathing – in an immensely clean bedroom, with children sleeping uneasily elsewhere for confusion about what was expected of them and a certain dread of the next day.

If it was entertainment he was seeking, rather than bare truth, he might have observed the antics of Ralph and Chloe on their way home from the concert, a journey of two and a half hours. He would have seen something of what Fiona had observed without knowing its meaning: how Chloe railed at Ralph, even in the presence of his son Fergus – hands over ears and pretending to be asleep – about other women, and how he was always flirting with them, and in front of her; and the robust way in which Ralph had responded to Chloe's allegations. And then once Fergus was asleep, how they had engaged themselves once more in this row. And then to witness their emotions, provoked and coming to a high pitch; and to recognise and understand them to be a necessary preliminary to sex, with Ralph being aroused by them; and between them an unbearable tension only resolvable by congress. He might have recognised that for Chloe there could be no preliminaries, which she disliked heartedly, and that animal-like she wanted him to approach her fully aroused and then to take her, or she him, in a convulsive climax from which she would draw away into a deep sleep to wake in the relief of a storm passed. And if he had seen a little more, and understood it, he might have wondered whether it was what this couple meant by love; and he would question whether this necessary passion might burn itself out entirely and be replaced by mutual contempt, which in all the circumstances of their life would be insufficient to sustain them as a couple.

And then there was another adversary, Bob Churchill-Jones, who had fallen asleep in front of the television at the end of a day in which he had read and studied over twenty witness statements and made careful notes; and who later stumbled his way to bed, for tomorrow he needed to be afoot early for a busy day. After all if the mysteries of connectedness were anyone's game, so to speak, they were his: and until he had fallen asleep, they were what had occupied him.

CHAPTER 6

IT HAD BEEN accepted by Jenkins that some progress had been made with the case and Bob's team were left to get on with it. The two-week deadline for results had passed with no one referring to it. In truth there were larger fish to fry at the time, with a particularly nasty gang rape occupying media attention. But Bob was experienced and worldly wise enough to know that things could change very quickly: you were never safe with a case until it had been concluded, and even then the past had a nasty habit of coming back to haunt and persecute you.

Bob liked to work in an orderly fashion and always set aside time to review a case on a Monday morning: progress was reported, targets established for the week, and tasks allocated. Not everyone liked his methods. Some preferred a more excitable and creative approach to the work, with everyone taking their own initiatives and going about things in their own way. But Bob was insistent, and on this Monday morning it was report-back time as usual. All the initial witness statements had been taken and some further lines of inquiry were agreed upon. It was necessary to check some alibis for suspects around the times of the crimes, it being generally established now that there were three: the killing of Garth Droylsden, the Detroit shooting, and the burning down of the car port and damage to the car in Surrey. There was nothing to be done about the US killing which was being investigated by the Detroit Police Department, and the remaining two were under separate investigation.

Alec reported that their attempts to locate Esther Droylsden for a further interview had been unsuccessful. Her husband had received unaddressed post cards from her, the latest of which had been posted in New York; but for the moment only a routine enquiry had been made to the FBI for help in locating her, although if she attempted to leave the country she would be picked up.

Alec also reported on his interview with Ivor Bowen, who was emerging as a suspect since he had no credible alibi for his movements around the time of the crime, and freely admitted his presence in London on that day and his detestation of David Droylsden. Alec described the circumstances of Ivor's quarrel with David, and Ivor's allegations of David's wrongdoing. 'Not provable. None of it,' he said. It was agreed that Ivor's story and background should be thoroughly checked out and that he should be reinterviewed.

A house to house inquiry was being carried out around the scene of the car port fire, but nothing helpful had turned up. It was agreed to intensify these inquiries and to seek the evidence of CCTV cameras along the adjacent high street and at garages on the likely route that Roger Greer might have taken were he to have committed the crime. Nothing helpful at all had yet come out of the search of Roger's cottage: no one, but no one, was satisfied with that, and neighbourhood inquiries were continuing. The trawl of Roger's financial affairs had shown them to be in state of critical mess. 'No money there and no evidence of peculiar transactions. His main problem appears to be paying for the weekly groceries, not a hit man', said Alec, to a communal laugh. And last it was agreed that Roger's wife Melissa had to be a good source of information on him, and that they had failed so far to draw out much from her. She was to be interviewed again.

Neither Bob nor Alec revealed to their colleagues a vital piece of information: a check of Ivor's mobile telephone calls had revealed that he had telephoned Esther Droylsden a matter of minutes after the explosion at the Droylsdens' flat. Clearly the call had not been intended for her husband. A connection had been made. For the time being Esther was out of reach, but hopefully not Ivor.

Alec expressed his surprise at the implications of Ivor's telephone call. Impressed as he was by material wealth, Alec had been inclined to be admiring of Ivor's luxurious lifestyle, which searches of his bank statements and an examination of the accounts of his company had substantiated that he could afford. Ivor lived in a modern mock-Tudor house in a salubrious suburb of Chester, from which he sallied out by Mercedes to either his car dealership or the golf club, and in recent months more often the latter. He and his house were what the estate agents would describe as well-presented and desirable, but his plain, although well cared for, wife seemed to Alec not to fit the image, being a rather domesticated lady. Bob thought longingly of Gloria, and sighed. 'Appearances can be deceptive, Alec', he had commented. 'Never forget it.'

Ivor had not welcomed their first visit and had shown his discomfiture. It struck Bob as odd that a man of good standing such as Ivor would be greatly disturbed by a routine police enquiry. But he was absolutely straightforward in answering their questions, and disarmingly honest in not dissimulating in any way about being in London at the time of the explosion, and in not offering an alibi. Alec would have left it at that. 'A nice chap, what a very nice chap, and obviously upset by what has happened, even though he admits to hating Droylsden's guts', he remarked. Bob had muttered something to himself and insisted on a scrupulous check of everything. And lo and behold, they had it: a connection. So he could say, 'Evidence, Alec, don't forget it', without the possibility of a contradiction.

On the day of Bob and Alec's epiphany, Ivor spent time in his waterlogged garden in the morning creating things to do, then disappeared into Chester where he browsed in his favourite bookshop. Later he rang his office and gave certain instructions to Mrs Browning, his secretary for over twenty years. On the next day he gave his wife the news of an extended business trip which had come up rather urgently. Although surprised she didn't mind much, being used to it; indeed she rather welcomed it, as it would give her a chance to do her own things for a while without the complications of considering him. She helped him to pack everything he might need, which involved some last minute washing and ironing and a visit to the over-the-counter facilities of the local pharmacy. She waved him goodbye before leaving to stay with her daughter in Stoke, where she could be a granny for a few days. She would enjoy the journey, and he would not need her for a while.

When Alec rang Ivor's home to arrange a meeting he got the answerphone. He left a message. This pattern continued for a day or two before, tiring of it, he rang Ivor's company and encountered Mrs Browning. She told Alec that her boss was on holiday for a few days. He often took time off like this, and no, there was nothing strange in it at all. Mr Bowen did not like to be disturbed when on holiday. She didn't know where he was to be found, or his wife for that matter, and she did not expect to hear from them, that is, until they were ready to contact her. Of course, she would let them know if he rang in and how urgent it was that he contact them. But no, she really did not expect it.

Bob was furious with himself. All his police career he had been meticulous in method, in process, and now to be held up for the simple oversight of not warning a suspect that he should not leave town without telling them. His routine was breaking down. He was losing it. He took it out on Alec, who received it in good grace.

Routine did pay off in Bungay, however, for an enquiry at the local hardware store had established that the rather large spare petrol can in Roger's car had been bought by him there a mere two days before the fire in Surrey. The suspicion arose that Roger had been planning a long journey and wished to avoid stopping at a petrol station where he might have been picked up on a CCTV camera. When asked to explain, Roger's reply was robust: he had so little money that he was often in danger of running out of petrol without the means to pay for more. Finding himself temporarily with cash, he had taken the precaution of filling up a spare can. Why so big a can? Well, it was a long way to London to see his kids. 'We couldn't hang him on evidence like this', said Alec, and no one disagreed.

Around this time Bob, who was a lapsed Catholic, began to go to church. Almost by accident he found St Ethelreda's, tucked away in a side-street off Piccadilly, and hardly more than a hole in the wall, with a seating capacity for no more than sixty souls. It was a place of peace and tranquillity, and richly endowed. On his first visit he had been troubled without an obvious cause, and sitting there in this church on a shining, sweet-scented pew before the emblazoned gold and marble altar, with the saints looking down upon him, he reached a kind of peace with himself. He began to go there often, and even regularly, neither praying nor seeking counsel, but communing nevertheless. Sometimes there were others sitting there on neighbouring pews, meditating quietly like himself; but usually he was alone. Each day it seemed that fresh flowers were arranged, although he had never seen anyone busy with the task; and he thought such dedication to decoration and the sparkling intensity of each and every object must be the result of early morning devotions. He had never in all the times of his attendance seen a priest, so he came to regard his haven as having been dropped from heaven especially for troubled souls like him, without the mediation of an earthly body. At first it was enough for him to find solace, but later he began to seek meaning. He supposed his distress, and perhaps God's mercy, had brought him there; but whatever, and he knew that he was never going to be a theologian, he needed what he understood to be God's grace. He began to pray to God, and his prayer was that he be not forgotten. After some time he would join Gloria to his entreaty.

The consequences of buying a petrol can were the least of Roger's worries. The vengeance of others and their necessary retribution was upon him. He had believed his consultancy assignment with one of Britain's largest companies was as safe as houses; at least that was what Nigel, his friend and the controller of the research budget, had assured him. But now an embarrassed Nigel was on the phone saying he was obliged to bring the assignment to an end. He couldn't explain. He begged Roger's forgiveness. It was too awful. He had no alternative, having been got at. One day he would explain. Then Nigel made him an offer: if Roger would cooperate with him he would contrive to make him a single payment in lieu of breach of contract, but payable through a third party. Roger opened an account in Jersey in the name of a nominee to accommodate the payment.

Roger felt himself to be playing a game of high speed ping-pong. No matter how deftly a ball was returned, another appeared in its place. He was seeking to reach repayment terms with three main banks to which he owed large sums of money, and a host of smaller creditors, in order to avoid bankruptcy. He had made some progress. Now, out of the blue it seemed, things began to go wrong. A Swiss bank which had been helpful wrote out of context demanding payment in full within seven days of a debt of two hundred and fifty thousand pounds, and all his desperate calls to them went unanswered. The payment of his largest bank debt of a million pounds had yet to be resolved. He had a friend at court and had been quietly negotiating a way of dealing with the debt. But then he received a formal letter demanding payment, and on enquiry his friend told him that the Credit Committee had voted two to one to demand immediate payment. They were willing to meet, which suggested to him that there was still scope for negotiation.

On the train Roger worked out with care and foreboding, for it was a desperate matter, a deal he could live with and that he might be able to negotiate. The logic of the situation demanded a deal, but with banks you knew their logic to be perverse. There were far too few assets to pay all his debts, and a creditor pressing for payment through the courts would be likely to shoot himself in the foot and finish up with hardly anything, but that was not what his creditors believed. They thought a man like Roger Greer would have secret assets stacked away in foreign banks or property abroad, and they supposed that legal action of the right kind would reveal these assets, so they could grab them and get paid. Even if that were not true, or only partially so, they conjectured that if they were quickly out of the blocks they might force payment for themselves because of a debtor's fear and reluctance, for the shame of it, of being declared bankrupt. And then by a curious logic they took the view that if they could not realise the whole debt then they had no interest in a part of it: far better to press the issue on the probability of failure and the possibility of a surprising realisation, 'which was more common than you might think,' they said. Of course, the villains bunkered off abroad and avoided any payment; reappearing much later when the debts had been written off, and when the creditors might happily settle for less than ten per cent and call it a success; or if the going was good the villains ignored their debts altogether in the knowledge that they would never be asked to pay them. As for the genuine, like Roger, usually they had no hidden assets – or hardly any.

Roger sighed at his shortcomings. In everything he ventured upon he needed things to go wrong before he realised what was required for them to be wholly correct: and life was never a dress rehearsal but always the real thing. No doubt at the end of these dire financial dealings, if they could be distinguished in this way, he would become an expert; but in the meantime, it was a matter of groping his way forward.

The Bank's Debt Recovery Unit was located in the red-light district near King's Cross, which was a descent downhill from the station to a barrack-like building, with entry being effected through a side entrance, and then passage only after the consent of a security guard. No lush reception awaited him here, as it had done elsewhere in the bank in the good old days of recent memory, when it had been fashionable to urge loans on the provident and improvident alike. No money was to be wasted on the indigent. The building was dingy and badly lit, and you queued with other petitioners on an uncomfortable bench lined up before noisy stainless steel lifts. These lifts were to rattle you up to anonymous rooms; you would become a mobile corpse in a steel coffin hastening to your afterlife, to classification and disposal. Above, the atmosphere was antiseptic, and the practitioners of private greed busied themselves, armed with well-used thesauruses, and shielded by the law of the land, with the dissection of the assets and private lives of their customers.

He was received by two servants of the bank, a Mr Error and a Mr Fogg, young men in their late twenties dressed, Mormon-like, in dark suits and white shirts with close-cropped haircuts, so similar in appearance as to be indistinguishable on a dark winter's day. They removed their jackets, which they hung on the back of their chairs, so as to indicate their businesslike but accessible approach to dissection. On receiving their business cards he struggled not to laugh. He had always admired Dickens's use of names, and Mr Bounderby came immediately to mind, but with Dickens the name garnished the offering, whereas Error and Fogg, in the minor key, might be thought to be on lifelong quests to live up to, fulfil or deny the destiny of their names – or their fathers' names! This would not do. He concentrated and presented his proposition, detailing his case with carefully prepared documentation and evidence. They perused it and questioned him before leaning back carefully in their imitation leather chairs, looking at him and each other with grave and signifying eyes. Mr Fogg offered him a coffee from the vending machine, which seemed to be a good sign, and his hopes rose. Then like two judges in the Appeal Court they retired, having announced their need to consider his proposals in private. It was ten minutes before they returned. Mr Fogg said that with one exception his proposals had been accepted. Not an Error then, he thought, indelicately, but did not say. He agreed the change and they escorted him from the building. They would write. You could be certain that the judgement would be sent.

But what had he done? *Hast thou a wife and children?* He had done his best. His principal asset, his family's house, was to be sold, although the bank had no existing charge on it, and the proceeds given to the bank less twenty thousand pounds. The bank would permit the twenty thousand to be used as a deposit on a new family house, on which it would advance a mortgage. The mortgage would be in his name only, to which his wife would expressly need to agree, in return for the bank waiving all claims that it might have against her. The bank would have a charge on the new property, and in ten years' time, if it had not already been paid, a maximum sum of one hundred thousand pounds would become payable, which might then necessitate the sale of the property. So what had he done? He had given his family the possibility of a ten-year breathing space, but his wife would be denied any part of the capital value of the existing house, or any new property. In truth he had a poor hand. But had he played it as best he could?

Monty Wiseman said not, although what he really felt or thought was not obvious to others. His advice to Melissa Greer, or Browne as she was called now, was to grab what she could and in haste, before the others, and while there were some assets left. She pressed him a little, and his professional pride was engaged. He could see some merit from her point of view in the agreement with the bank. He spoke.

'If we agree to this we should also seek a property settlement with him to secure what maintenance and lump sums we can squeeze out.'

Melissa replied, 'Mathematics has never been my subject: but isn't a third of nothing, nothing?'

He didn't think it a laughing matter. 'Madam,' he said pompously, portentously, 'you would be surprised what the judicial process can reveal; what can be sucked out of the seemingly unappetising. We must squeeze him like an orange.' He demonstrated slowly but firmly before her. It was he who was worldly wise.

'I don't think so, but I suppose it's worth a try. Certainly, anything would be helpful', she said weakly.

'And remember,' he continued, 'we shall have the comfort of Legal Aid and can stay the course: admittedly not much of a course, but with my help – you can count on that. But he will have to finance himself, if I'm any judge of it.'

She warmed a little by the fire of his convictions and hoped that no one would be burnt.

Why had she gone to him? A political friend of her husband who surely should have stood off for knowledge of him? She didn't know. Would the thrust of cold steel from a friend mean more? A betrayal for a betrayal? Surely not. If she had but known, Monty Wiseman had been born Weizmann, a Polish Jew who had escaped from Warsaw in 1944 in the arms of his mother; through the sewers and into an hinterland where delinquent Polish youth were known to hunt you down in order to claim a reward from the Nazi occupiers. He had a deeply ingrained propensity to harbour grudges, and he remembered an occasion when Roger might, and logically should have, supported him politically, and hadn't. As worldly wise, he donned the robes of the gallant, the protector of women. He stood before them, this rounded and Capuchin-like figure, as pure unattached feminist champion. But was he really, and if so what sort of champion?

If Melissa had had the power to cast herself forward to the banqueting hall of Stationers School, to the memorial service there following Monty's premature death in his fifties, she would have seen a vast throng of people from many and diverse walks of life gathered there to remember him, if not with affection, then with gratitude. Why so many? To obtain this vast number did you not need to spread your life very thinly? Did this not presuppose, not just business, but a secret social life? What would have surprised her most was a wife and two teenage daughters mourning the death of a father with whom they had never lived and whom they had hardly ever seen, although he had financed their well-being for many a year; and to learn that no one present had known of them and all were as astonished as her. What would it have meant? Perhaps there were emotions here that belied a commonplace explanation, and coloured his thoughts and his judgements on the matters that crossed his desk?

So was cranked into motion the vast juggernaut of the law by which adjustments to people's lives could be effected; and a small army of bureaucrats and professionals busied themselves with the filling and checking of forms and with detailing the complementary and supplementary information needed. Complicated formulas permitted the calculation of sums due and allowances to be taken into account. Treasury officials added up the costs and determined whether they were within the guidelines. Solicitors consulted barristers, who asked for more information, which required adjustments to written statements and further documentation. Occasionally the fog cleared, and solicitors consulted each other as to whether the case might be settled, and if so, advised their clients on what was offered, on their rights, and on possible outcomes.

Notices were issued through the courts requesting information about this and the production of the other. Time was given, which was only reasonable in the circumstances. The welfare of the children was taken into account, and when it was apparent that all they wished for was a little peace from the adults in their lives and a chance to continue without disturbance, it was assumed, at least in most cases, that they would stay with their mothers and that the fathers would have visiting rights; and orders to this effect would be made in the full knowledge that if these rights were dishonoured there would be no way of enforcing them in the courts, given the unwillingness of the judges to act against the recalcitrance of mothers by fining or imprisoning them. Thus these custody orders sounded the death knell for many a relationship between father and child. And then these assessments of binary oppositions might be arbitrated, to the satisfaction of no one; a reasonable compromise being a situation where no one got what they wanted, even assuming that they were a judge of it in the first place. And adults who had set out with goodwill, whatever their anxieties and needs, not to exacerbate the matters at hand, found themselves thoroughly disgruntled and disturbed and in a variety of ways much the poorer; while their advisers, competent and incompetent alike, and the toiling servants of the legal process, found themselves not ungenerously rewarded.

Roger employed a local solicitor, Mr Morales, with a knowledge of the court where these matters were to be determined. He had read the papers and looked up, all worldly wise himself. He spoke. 'Remember, she is a woman, and probably an attractive one?' Roger nodded assent. 'And with dramatic gifts – potentialities – is that right?' It was. 'Then you've no chance in our court. A little care with her dress, revealing something but not too much, hair decorous, a touch of perfume, and then tears – copious but under control – and they'll grant her anything.'

'Excuse me, Mr Morales, this isn't a joke.' Roger was visibly annoyed. 'I've had a long and happy marriage, and although I'm in desperate financial straits I do wish to do the very best I can for my family under all the circumstances.'

Mr Morales was not put down. 'Of course you do, Roger, of course you do.' He was emollient now. 'And I'm going to help you. What we need to do is to discuss our options.'

Roger nodded. He could agree that.

'We have before us a claim for a property settlement and the payment of maintenance. As I see it there's no possibility of you being able to meet this claim, ignoring for a while its equity, and any attempt to do so would result in your bankruptcy, which would be self-defeating for both you and your wife. I consider there to be three options. You can give in, and if we decide you can't possibly win, that would be the best course – it saves money, time and tears. Secondly, you might fight it as hard as you can, and if this is your wish you must give me the dirt, and there will be tears, but not only your own. And thirdly, we could go for a draw, but in my opinion this might be difficult, and not achievable without some unpleasantness.'

Roger winced. 'Couldn't we play this down the straight and narrow and let the truth speak for itself? I've nothing to hide, and the truth about my finances is that I don't have two pennies to rub against each other, and my bank statements, chequebooks and bills will substantiate that: but I do wish to do all I can.'

Mr Morales leant back in his chair. This man was more stupid than he looked. 'You will do, you will', he said, pausing before continuing. 'How can I put this to you, while remaining civil? Well, Mr Greer, no one's going to believe you. Why, I'm not sure that I believe you. Until a short time ago you were an immensely rich man. Surely, they'll say, he has stacked something aside for a rainy day: a few unit trusts, PEPs or shares, perhaps not in his name, or cash in an overseas account. And if, as you tell me, you couldn't prove your income to the satisfaction of the Legal Aid Board for the purpose of getting Legal Aid, how do you think you can persuade the court? Yes, yes, I know, we'll sign an affidavit stating that you have no other assets or bank accounts, and the other side won't believe us. What's more important is that the judge won't believe us. He'll think, here's this very clever chap Roger Greer, resourceful and a proven survivor, and there's this very charming lady, bringing up two children on her own and unable to pay her bills. "Would you like to borrow a handkerchief, my dear, and we can break for a few minutes if you wish to compose yourself?" And there you are. One minute you're in a very difficult position and the next you're up a creek without a paddle.'

There was a pregnant pause. They agreed to think about the issues for a few days. Roger hoped that Mr Morales was as poor a soothsayer as he appeared to be a solicitor; while Mr Morales turned his thoughts to other things, the world being full of fools.

CHAPTER 7

GLORIA, FEELING MORE confident, decided to take the initiative, and invited Rachel to go to London with her to see an exhibition of late Renaissance Italian paintings, including several Titians, for which she had obtained tickets well in advance. She was late for the train and Rachel, positioning herself in an open carriage door, waved her on as she sprinted the last few yards along the platform, hair looser now and blowing in the wind, and jumping on board just at the last moment, excited, pale and flushed at the same time, laughing at the escape and looking wholly delicious. Rachel hugged and kissed her.

Choosing her moment, Gloria told Rachel that she had arranged for Bob to join them at Fortnum and Mason for afternoon tea. She chattered on about Bob for a while, seeming to be pleased that they were to meet him, with Rachel questioning her about him with a certain persistence and thoroughness. Rachel remarked that Bob seemed to be a very reliable and nice man. Did she think him dull for this?

'Dull? No, not dull.' She seemed surprised by the question. 'Bob's really interesting and unpredictable – well, sometimes, in some ways.'

Gradually, for the recounting was not easy for her, Gloria had drawn from Rachel something of her past history. She had married young while a student of English at Cambridge, to Alistair, a young and dreamy archaeologist she had met there, and without parental approval. Then having produced one daughter and while she was pregnant with another, he had upped and joined an important dig in Egypt, for which it had been an honour to be chosen. The party had only just been landed and settled in when Alistair fell ill with a virulent form of meningitis from which he died within forty-eight hours. On his death she discovered his impor- tance to her; she had loved him dearly and was distraught by his loss. The only positive outcome from this tragic happening was that it reunited Rachel with her family as a kind of collective response to the fates, who had acted against them, with a form of punishment which dismayed them, and which they felt as a warn- ing for them all. Her father, blessed with wealth from a long-estab- lished family publishing business, had responded by seeking to look after her, providing her with the money for a new house and endowing her with a plentiful and liberally managed trust fund. All of which was comforting: but her father was even then, as he had always been, remote from her, wanting to embrace her and to share the loss which he felt through her, but finding the necessary emotions to be beyond his reach.

What had she done to merit this blow? She knew not, so could not repent and change her ways. It was pleasant to drift in easy contentment with her children and her friends, not asking too much of them or of herself. In and among the driftwood of this life she had encountered Ralph, who had amused her with the effrontery of his advances and a disarmingly boyish charm. A minor fling might do wonders for her self-esteem, or so she thought: but then in her wantonness she had become careless, became pregnant again. Although it was not wanted, she carried the baby through. Ralph married her out of guilt. Later when Ralph remarried, and with Rachel not really caring in her own disgust, she had let him have the custody of Fergus, thinking in some strange way that they deserved each other and that it made a sort of sense of what had happened.

As she told Gloria this tale she hung her head and blushed, for it shamed her, this not loving, and the dreadfulness of conceiv- ing a child that could not be loved. Gloria had hushed her, whis- pering, telling her that she must have been disturbed at this time, and that a life realised, whatever the problems, was the giving of a precious gift.

Rachel had wanted to speak to her about Roger, to whom she had chatted on several occasions in the inn, and about her party, to which he had been invited; but whenever she ventured upon it, the words dried up and she held back. For the moment, and a precious and delicate moment it was to her, it was Gloria who held centre stage. Rachel gazed into the iridescent welcoming green pools of Gloria's eyes, sparkling in the early morning sunshine, and for the moment it was enough for her and she forgot her troubles.

In relation to Gloria, Rachel felt not only the taller but the senior, although Gloria was some four years older, and much as an elder sister with the duty of care for a younger. This was not all. At her girls' boarding school, the girls had often developed crushes, sometimes for the younger teachers, of whom they were in awe, and occasionally for another girl. For some this was little more than a giggle, a diversion, but for others, and for her too, it had sometimes been more. And then later, although she had given that up and had thought it not needed and even wrong for her, women friends had sensed something, and had tested her; and sometimes she had responded to them, although in her own mind she did not want or seek what it had become. When Rachel looked at Gloria, she knew that she loved her: that she desired her, hugely enjoying the moments they shared together, and trembling with the imagination of her. She did not wish to be labelled for these feelings; she knew that what she felt was not a dwelling place; and she feared that other signals would move them both on, that other emotions would tear them asunder.

The exhibition left them both breathless and excited. For the first time in living memory there was an opportunity to see many of Titian's paintings together in one place, representative of every stage of his life and development of technique, then to compare these paintings with representative paintings of his contemporaries. Titian's nudes seemed to be so real, and so delectable, that you wished to reach out beyond the rope barrier to embrace and caress them. And these nudes reached out for you also, so that even when you left them, to circulate and admire others, you felt their allure; calling you back, heavy with their desires and ecstatic in your presence. You felt the divine and the pure, yet you saw and experienced at the same moment the profane: the one bleeding into and caressing the other, as part of the same presence and being.

Rachel said, 'It's thought that Titian made love to all his models, and that it was only through the intensity of lovemaking that this wonderful sensuality could be captured on canvas.'

'Surely not all', Gloria responded. 'There's an awful lot of cherubs.'

They shouldn't have giggled, it was very hushed and earnest in the gallery. Rachel continued, 'Don't you think they look rather profane and joining in?'

They blinked and lurched a little, staggering arm in arm, as they regained the daylight, a little drunk with the exhaustion of it, as you would be at the end of, say, *A Long Day's Journey* or an Eisenstein film: out and away from the daze and darkness of a Renaissance bravura performance to the light grey of the world outside. And then into the gold and green, and the buzz of the tea room where you could stretch your limbs and clink your cup in an English normality, and where Bob was awaiting them.

Conscious of the occasion and the company of two attractive women who he imagined would cause heads to turn, Bob had made an effort not to let them down. He was proud of them, to be with them. When Gloria looked, she saw with a start that he looked different. She exclaimed, 'Bob what have you done? Where are your pinstripes? What have you been doing with yourself? You look different.'

He brushed it aside. He had 'gone Italian' with soft colours and a younger more 'with it' style. She teased him, while Rachel looked amused. 'There must be a woman behind this. Tell me.' She felt proprietorial, and although gentle, was insistent.

He brushed it aside, changed the subject, admired Rachel, which was easy for him and taken in good grace. There was a woman behind it. He did not quite know how it had happened. It was only a few weeks ago that he had sat in Gloria's car, proclaiming to himself that he would wait for her for ever and believing it. And it was still true, of course it was. But then the ownership of his favourite delicatessen, across the road from his flat and which he frequented regularly, had changed. He had become friendly, and then familiar, with a lively dark-haired Italian lady, Andrea, who made no secret of the fact that she liked him, favoured him, and then had invited him to the opera. And it had gone on from there: she had taken him in hand and he found himself enjoying and responding to her attention. You could not say she had stolen up on him, for it was all direct and challenging and left nothing to doubt.

He was embarrassed. He realised that the episode in the car with Gloria had been a high point, and had been reached without him recognising it; and without his understanding that emotions could not be arrested at such a point, but would inevitably recede. Now that he was seated with Gloria, and could observe the closeness of another and stranger emotional world, he felt awkward and redundant: wanting really to withdraw, but politely maintaining these necessary moments to their natural conclusion.

When Rachel retired for a few moments, Gloria asked him, and it seemed important to her, 'Well, what do you think of Rachel, now you've had a chance to meet her properly?'

He paused, wishing to be fair-minded, and not wanting to cause offence: 'Impressive. Very attractive. Clever....' He paused again.

'Yes.' Impatient with him, and valuing his judgement. 'Go on.'

'Cerebral: but at this moment, perhaps, out of gear with her emotions.'

'Interesting. Go on.'

'I'm not sure that I can.'

'Of course you can. Try harder.'

'Well, it seems to me, and I have some experience of it, that this is a very emotional girl who has been disturbed in some way that I can only guess at, but who's recovering; and who will be happiest, perhaps only truly happy, when her mind – and a very fine mind I think she must have, for she's a clever girl – is back in natural control.'

She leant over the table and kissed him on the cheek. 'Clever boy. How dare anyone say that you're not *the* detective? You're the greatest.'

Gloria was impressed, admiring his acuteness, but thinking that she would be the person who would bring everything together. What then would happen to Bob? She was uneasy, and felt a sharp pang of regret and fear, which lifted as she saw Rachel picking her way towards her and the turning of heads.

In the train home she clasped arms with Rachel and got close. She needed to know. 'Tell me, what did you think of Bob?

'I liked him. He was a little different from your description, if I understood it properly. More literate, worldly wise, which is reassuring, isn't it?' – so answering her own question. She paused and then said, 'Be careful, Gloria. Obviously he's very fond of you still, after everything. But some clever woman will swallow him up, if you don't move quickly. He's been very patient.' She beseeched Gloria, eyes and shoulders widening and showing the palms of her hands.

Gloria moved back and away. This was not the answer she wanted. This answer could spoil her day, and she was determined that it wouldn't.

Bob paid the bill and walked home, because it was a fine day. He was melancholy but enjoying himself, basking in it somewhat, at ease with himself despite it. Nevertheless, there were serious matters to consider. Andrea. He should cool it, he thought; it was complicating, and now he had the perfect excuse, for it was only that very morning that the Assistant Commissioner had called him in to review the Droylsden case, and it had been decided that Bob and Alec should travel to the States to interview Esther Droylsden, whose whereabouts had become known once she had signed up as a student at the Stamford Art College in Connecticut. The commissioner had expressed his disappointment at the progress being made with the investigation, which had been downgraded in importance, with a loss of personnel. 'Pull your socks up', was his enjoinder. Bob was in no mood to pull up his socks, he had more enticing matters to reflect on – and more pleasurable.

Alec had never been to the United States and was excited, talkative and full of himself when they boarded a British Airways flight to New York on a cold and rainy Monday morning; at a time which had demanded undue concentration for Bob so early in the week. Andrea had taken it well when he explained the necessary pause. 'No problem,' she had said, confident in her charms and powers and on the certainty of future joys. As they sipped their first whiskies of the trip, their well-being might well have been disturbed if they had been aware that winging towards them, on a PanAm flight, Ivor Bowen was enjoying a similar relaxation to their own, his task having been completed.

Arriving in New York some five days previously, Ivor's detection had been made simpler by the postcard from Esther, which he had taken out and read repeatedly on the outward flight until he knew its message by heart. Thus his task of discovery was straightforward, as knowing her address in Darien, he could reach it in his rented car without hassle or difficulty.

Although he was welcomed by Esther, this reunion, if it could be called that, was inevitably strained. Esther felt that the death of a son was against the natural order of life in which parents preceded their offspring; to say nothing about their responsibility for the events that had led up to her son's death. In some way, she thought, you almost always felt responsible for the death of someone close to you: might not you have done something, visited or written, been there, even on the other end of telephone; and when there to have listened, really listened, and to have been kinder, knowing that we all need the encouragement of others and especially of those we love? Even when the death was sudden or the result of an accident you were not absolved: you, yes, you, might have persuaded him to stop smoking, exercise more, and not to embark on a long journey when tired or when the roads were icy. And you didn't. You didn't care enough, being so wrapped up in yourself. And so for Esther to have been involved in a deeper way in the death of her son was an intolerable and dreadful weight on her soul, and even if it were to be judged a minor sin by others, at the very least she might have refused Garth the car keys if she had not been so absorbed in herself.

Esther would not let Ivor stay with her at her comfortable small hotel, although there was room, and he had to find another resting place; and then the meal itself was elsewhere, at a modest diner, which was all she would allow. He had done his best to be presentable and pleasing to her and had attracted favourable attention while he waited, as his formal manners and accent had delineated him as a Brit; but she had done very little, having slipped into the more casual manners of this small town and in anticipation of resuming her role as a student. He felt odd: a fish too large and exotic for the small bowl available, which is how she wanted him to feel: that it was no special occasion for her, and any expectation of his was unwarranted and unrealisable.

This was not a diner where the clientele lingered over their meals, so the duration of their stay attracted attention. They were a little too intense; their voices were rarely above a whisper, although at times they reached a noticeable pitch above the buzz and clatter of the diner. Once she started back, hand over mouth, suppressing a scream before drinking deeply from a glass that needed constant refilling. A casual diner might have surmised them to be boss and secretary, or master and mistress; say, lover and spurned, caught out, the two of them, at a moment of crisis and distress: but very few, even in this country large in criminality, would have guessed that they were co-conspirators plotting or harbouring a crime.

They parted without touching, having arranged to meet the next day. He thought then that she looked older and uncared for as they strolled along the beach and stared out at the slate-grey sea and lowering clouds before taking shelter from a drifting rain growing in intensity. They lay up in a small beach bar arranged and disposed for sunnier and happier days; but today experienced by them as a refuge. Desire had ebbed away. They drank coffee, silent for a while. Then Esther, breaking the barrier, was adamant and direct and waving her arms in emphasis. He said very little, taking it, accepting it with his head dropping lower as she spoke. Then he stood up suddenly, leaving her there and walking quickly away. When he reached his hotel, he packed up without delay, paid his dues and drove off, heading inland away from the false promises of the sea and the sand; far from the resort, with its constant idle chatter and allure. For three days he did very little before, almost of its own volition, the car changed direction to the west, to New York, and he could take the plane back home.

Bob and Alec, travelling in the opposite direction, knew nothing of what for them would have been a fascinating exchange. Bob wanted to sleep but Alec, ignoring hints, was talkative. Alec sought to assure Bob that all was well with this case and that it would come out right in the end. Really this American trip could be crucial and could provide just the information, the links, to solve it. He wanted Bob to know that he, Alec, had confidence in him to bring it off, to solve it, just as he had done with other crimes. Everyone said what a fine detective Bob was; everyone really in their hearts knew this to be true. Being en route to the States, Bob thought of Barry Goldwater, the controversial Presidential candidate. What was his slogan? Oh yes, 'In your heart you know I'm right', and look what happened to him! He didn't say anything to Alec, other than 'You're very kind. Do you mind if I sleep?'

But Alec didn't stay quiet. Idly Bob began to work out what his amiable and well-meaning companion and colleague was really saying to him, and bearing in mind as he did it that the road to hell was paved with good intentions.

Alec was worried. The case was not going well. To be frank it was in a mess, though it was true that persistence and a little good luck could turn a poor case round overnight. Alec had a career to defend, and he would stick with the case so as to avoid any black marks. It would have been said to him, 'Look, Bob's a very fine detective. He's capable of solving this crime, but does he want to? Is his heart really in it? Or does he have other things on his mind? There's his marriage, you know, on the rocks. He's taken that hard. Less than five years to pensionable safety, but will he make it?' Doubts would have been sown in Alec's mind.

Bob smiled to himself. Alec would not be the only person with doubts. He could borrow some if he wished. There were plenty to go round. He half remembered the saying of a nineteenth-century Austrian general reporting back to headquarters: 'You ask me now for my position. My right wing has collapsed after a cavalry charge supported by infantry; my left wing has been in general retreat for some time; consequently my centre is under severe pressure on three sides. All is well. I am counter-attacking.' He liked Alec and recognised that some good fellowship had been created by them working together on this case over several weeks; some bonding had gone on, to echo the sociologists. Was that what they were called? He thought of Andrea, which made him laugh. All was not lost. 'Well done, Alec,' he said, 'you're a good fellow. I appreciate it, I really do. But do shut up. We'll have plenty of time to get our act together.'

They did have plenty of time, for very little was to be taken up by the FBI, who had forgotten they were coming; or in their words, 'that they would be coming so soon'. The death by shooting of Bill Palfreyman was, they thought, a street crime. They were listening out. Detroit was a dangerous place, they reminded Bob and Alec; lots of people got shot, sometimes by accident but usually not, and then on some street in no man's land. But they were listening out. They would hear something, and as soon as they heard it – this something – Bob and Alec would be told. They could be sure of that. They had a few drinks together, compared notes, and told a few jokes which, Bob noted with distress, were the same on both sides of the pond. Soon the memory of these officers and what they had said would fade. Why, they could feel it fading in front of them as they spoke.

They proceeded to Darien and found their suspect startled to see them. In the hotel's coffee bar, for this was the only place she would favour them with, she answered their questions.

'What is your relationship with Ivor Bowen?'

'I haven't one. I did have one over ten years ago, when he was my husband's partner. In the sense that we met from time to time on social occasions, the four of us, with Dorothy, his wife. We all got on well.'

'How well?'

'Well enough to go on holiday together. Nothing more.'

She was vague about the business break up and its causes, other than expressing the belief that it had been a nasty affair, but even then not ascribing blame; and staying loyal to her husband. And what since? Had she seen Ivor since the business breakdown? They thought that she hesitated.

'Three or four times, when he was in London.' She paused, not wanting to say more, although more was expected. 'We remained friends, that was all, friends.'

They looked sceptical. She continued, 'You know, friends, you have them, and enjoy chatting over old times, and what's been happening to you and to them.'

She wouldn't say any more. They played their trump card. How did she explain the fact that Ivor had telephoned her a few minutes after the explosion?

She was sarcastic again. 'I don't explain. I didn't know about it. If you're any kind of a detective you'll know that I didn't take any call. The telephone records will show this, won't they?'

'Why was he calling?' they persisted.

'Who knows? Perhaps he was in London and wanted a friendly chat.'

'And why your mobile number? Isn't it a rather personal thing to give your mobile number to someone?'

'You must be joking. Are you on this planet? Do either of you have a wife or children? Get yourself a life.' She was sarcastic again, but in the knowledge that she had never previously been called on her mobile by him, it having been agreed between them that he wouldn't.

With the consent of the manageress, a plump and watchful woman of middle age, Alec had been busy questioning the hotel staff. Had Mrs Droylsden received any visitors? No one had seen a caller, but then, they complained, what could you expect with them being understaffed and overworked? For the moment it had to be left.

Nevertheless, Bob did not think the journey wasted. Esther was to stay in the States for a while and they wondered about that. Bob did not believe her. 'Something going on there', he remarked. 'But what? Connections, Alec, that's what we need. Between her and Ivor Bowen, and then how does it link back to Dublin?'

Alec agreed. He had been very agreeable throughout this journey, and Bob wondered about that.

David Droylsden knew nothing about their trip or the interview with his wife. Things had not been going too well with Orbis, the new company, and he was on his way to a special board meeting to discuss the early operating results at the offices of Westminster Investments, which had put up the money to acquire the old company and where the real power lay. Westminster Investments had no connection with Westminster and never had. Its offices were in Clerkenwell in a blue glass skyscraper, prematurely cut off in height because of planning restrictions which limited the number of stories; a building which jutted upwards amid stunted, mean yellow-bricked Victorian two-story buildings well past their sell-by date. David thought, like the one good tooth in the ancient jaw of a very old lady, who however well tarted up would fail to please.

They were displeased with the business results and perhaps him, these men around the table, for they had relied on him and put their faith in his acumen and business skills. Yet somehow, in a way they did not recognise or understand, the business had shrunk in size, revenue and activity, while the costs, although lower, remained obstinately high. Some staff had split off to run an activity in competition with the new company, while the loss of key staff elsewhere had caused a cessation of activity in what had been an important growth business area. The main business activity was traded but no growth had been achieved, with some clients clearly disgruntled about Roger Greer's departure and not anxious to continue joint investment activity with the new owners, and so putting the future into contention. The pygmies had come out of the company undergrowth, and while voluble, there was no evidence anywhere that they had even an inkling of how to grow a successful business. David remembered some words addressed to him by Roger Greer, which he had believed at the time to be a disgruntled jibe, that he David, 'could no doubt add up, and would be able to compute the numbers correctly as the business became smaller and unprofitable'. Now he thought uneasily that there might be some truth in it.

Around this table were seated four representatives of the venture capital business and David. The chairman of their gathering was a man called Anthony Valentine, a smooth young man in his late twenties with a good degree and a London MBA. David admired his style, although it was unlike his own, even though it made him feel uncomfortable. The venture capital business was a ruthless affair with a high failure rate for new investments: the key to success was to get behind the winners, and to detect the losers very early on and drop them like a bomb. Anthony had already told David in private that he suspected that this business was going to be a loser, and that he hoped that David would prove him wrong. He blamed David for a lack of concentrated effort, and maybe some foresight, and he looked to him to show the right motivation and drive. Now he told the others this too.

CHAPTER 8

D AVID FELT THAT the allegations made against him by
Anthony Valentine contained some truth, but there
would be time to put the situation right. He had asked
for time and believed he had been given it. In truth, since he was
being asked to deal in it, he had spent much of his time in pursuing inquiries into the death of his son. He had received a second
report from his own private investigator, and this had led him to
Dublin. There he sought out and endeavoured to talk to all of
Roger Greer's former Irish employees, and he succeeded in
doing so with all but one. From his discussions he got very little,
but as Sherlock Holmes might have said, 'The significance, my
dear Watson, was the dog that didn't bark in the night.' The missing person was a Gerry O'Callaghan, a man who it was
rumoured had been a leading member of the provisional IRA,
and who had disappeared without trace, or so it was said.

Should he believe it, this disappearance? Not really. There
appeared to be no relatives or close friends, and his mother, who
it was said had been widowed, had left Dublin some years ago
and no one knew where she had gone. Even this information
might be thought suspect, containing as it did some detectable
malice and glee. These Irish, he thought, were an untrustworthy
lot, wrapping you up with the sheer volume of their words and
drowning you with the liquid of their generous hospitality.

Bob found that in his absence in the States, David Droylsden had
passed this information about Gerry O'Callaghan to the
Commissioner, then as a thunderclap from above it reached

David Jenkins, an Assistant Commissioner, and his boss. He was not amused, complaining that he had been made a fool of, and that this information could and should have been detected by themselves. It was a tense confrontation, and the effects of it took some time to pass.

David Jenkins listened to their verbal report on the trip to the States. It seemed to please him, and the atmosphere became at first possible, then encouraging. He spoke. Good could come out of these things. There were clear lines of enquiry which he could report upwards. Bob looked at the ceiling in search of divine intervention and found there none. Jenkins smiled at them encouragingly. They were to take down his instructions; and Alec duly recorded them in his notebook. The team had shrunk to four, but the good news of endorsement from above was reported back and celebrated in the pub. Bob excused himself.

Now was the time for Bob to power on, but he could not find the energy to do so, or the resolve and commitment expected of him. He was tired and elsewhere, and so without notice he absented himself, spent time at St Ethelreda's, wandered into a teashop, did some shopping of his own and wound his way back to the flat. He had asked God the question that bothered him. How could he find his way back to Gloria? He knew this was what his heart desired. It was right. He loved her and wished to be true to the solemn marriage vows he had made all those years ago. And Gloria loved him, of this he was sure; but for her there was no matching desire to meet him halfway. As time passed her inability to resolve the matter was becoming a permanency to him, although she had held out to him an olive branch of her own gathering and wet with her tears.

He thought of Andrea and felt a somewhat different desire. How simple it seemed for her. 'You been separate for two years. You poor man. And all this time you no have any woman. How could you, and you so very nice. So no one take care of you, look to you, it's not right.' And then she had kissed him warmly. Would God grant him this comfort , this pleasure, if he were to be honest with God? But hadn't God granted him Gloria, and kept this path to her open? He waited for a reply to his prayer. God said nothing, leaving it to him. The others, when they suspected something going on, had said, 'Go to it. Life is short.'

And he had thought, but judgement is long, which was something he thought they would not understand or feel. He felt his
weakness. Andrea was filling a space, or more than just a space,
perhaps a void; and she would engulf him, fill it up completely,
and make all these painful considerations redundant. And then
where would he be? Would this long wait for Gloria , the
heartache and despair, have been in vain? Would it be a defeat?
Was he about to go down in defeat?

Dwelling on it was not for him. A telephone call to Chester
established that Ivor Bowen had returned from his holiday break,
and this time it was off to Chester and to Ivor's Mercedes showroom. Any doubts that Alec might have developed were dissipated: this was very 'luxious' as his girlfriend was apt to say. He
muttered, 'Well, he must be doing something right.'

'Or wrong', responded Bob.

Ivor had worked out his alibi for the trip to the States to the last
detail. He gave them the dates and venues, the name of the business colleagues with whom he had stayed, the hotel in Darien,
and his purpose in being there at all. This entire story would
check out. He was sure of it. And when later they did check it
out, it held up as secure as a drum.

They asked him about the telephone call to Esther at the time
of the explosion. He coolly glanced it away as just something he
did. He was in London from time to time and it was his habit to
call on past friends. It was nice to stay in touch with them.

Bob was unhappy and unbelieving. It was all too glib – too
perfect – and he decided to put a colleague full time on checking
Ivor out. Was there an Irish connection? That would be the thing.

The Assistant Commissioner had wanted them to interview
Melissa again, being dissatisfied with the witness statement.
'She must know more than she's saying. Probe her more on
Ireland and this fellow Gerry O'Callaghan. Does she know
him? Has she been to Ireland, and recently? What's her relationship with the Droylsdens? Sloppy work, Bob, I'm surprised
at you.' It was unfair. But if he was honest, perhaps by his own
standards it was a little bit loose. He could admit it to himself.
He should do better – wanted to do better, really. Alec was
embarrassed, and gritting his teeth, determined not to go under
on this job.

They interviewed Melissa again. It was difficult going. They knew the questions but it appeared that she didn't have any answers. Indeed, she was very vague on the matters of interest to them. She did have answers, and gave them; but not to their questions. Bob had encountered it before. It seemed to him that life offered a choice. You could develop either a good set of questions, that weathered well and could be used in most situations, or a good set of answers. Any correspondence between the two, in his experience, was entirely coincidental. His mind wandered off, as it was prone to do these days. For example, politicians, lawyers and social workers – and detectives, of course – had good sets of questions – and villains, answers. Really honest people ambled about in their own worlds.

He jerked back to the present. She was saying she had never heard of a Gerry O'Callaghan and couldn't remember the names of any of Roger's former colleagues, although she had met one, the managing director, who had stayed with them once. She remembered him as being very rude, going off on his own to a disco after an evening meal with them, and arriving back as drunk as a coot in the middle of the night. 'A person of no originality', she said. What on earth did that mean?

She said she had only been to Ireland on two occasions: once to perform at the Gaiety Theatre and the other for a cottage holiday with the family which was not a success, the accommodation being awful and it raining every single day. Bob thought that it was probably an honest statement because in his experience it did rain every single day in Ireland. As to David Droylsden, she had met him once at a monopoly party. At what? A party where everyone played *Monopoly*. David Droylsden had made an ass of himself by his addiction to defensive strategies and people made very rude remarks about him, which he must have heard, but which didn't affect his playing tactics. There was not an ounce of anti-Semitism in her, she protested, but she could understand how they'd felt. It was so silly in the circumstances.

Was there anything else? Quite a lot. But not relevant.

'She seems quite loyal to Roger', said Alec dwelling on the thought and thinking of his girlfriend.

'Under all these circumstances', said Bob, thinking of other things.

That was the trouble really, Bob thought. These days I'm always thinking of other things. He thought of Gloria, then Andrea, then Gloria again. He thought of sin, redemption and forgiveness. He truly forgave Gloria, with all his heart. Might he do something wrong, confess it and seek redemption? After all he had been so very good for so long. Well not absolutely perfect, for that would be too much to claim, but pretty good under the circumstances. He thought of Andrea. Did he in some sense deserve a little wrongdoing?

He knew these thoughts to be foolish, and did not need to be a Catholic to reach the conclusion. All those addicts maintaining that they took just a little alcohol or were occasional users of drugs, and thus protesting they were in control: exercises in foolish self-deception. And there was he on the same slippery slope. How was he to persuade Andrea that it would be only a little dalliance, the occasional relaxation, just a very little fun? Andrea had been to his flat. He had seen her eyeing it all, working out the changes she would make, admiring this and rejecting the other: changing it for the better, not realising, as all those women around her did not apprehend, that a man's taste, the things that might make him comfortable in his own place, might be vastly different from her own. After all it was only now, after two years in it on his own, that the flat was the place that he chose it to be. He could hear her tut-tutting. What was he complaining about? He would learn to love these changes, these differences, as he would come to desire and admire her, the two being indissoluble.

Andrea was difficult to stop. When it happened there was not a single moment when he was in command. She took him over without any conversation, mutual purpose or preliminaries. It was all perfectly acceptable, passionate, vigorous and complete. She announced herself to be very satisfied; and her surprise that they had they waited so long. He had passed her test. She did not suppose for a moment that he might have preferences of his own, and he wondered whether they could ever be expressed with her. Then he had to stop her, in full flight, assuming that they were becoming a couple. He explained once again about Gloria and that things between them had not been resolved. She did not understand, writing off his explanation, his hesitation, these niceties, as peculiar; as being an English sexual and family deviance from the human norm, only partly compensated for by niceness and decency.

This moment of surrender had not helped him. He was disconsolate. He rang his daughter to find her out. It troubled him to an absurd degree; to have someone missing when he needed them. He rang Gloria. He must have it out with her now. It had all reached a ridiculous point where no one quite knew where they stood. She was too busy to take his call.

He gazed round his living room, which had sheltered him these past years. Was it his fate that Andrea would soon be rearranging his dear possessions? Would the pictures come down and the silver gilt family photographs be disappearing into drawers, to be replaced by dark-haired smiling faces of people yet unknown to him, and who he might not like? And then would the precious memories be secreted into black plastic bin liners and dumped before he had time to save them? All these special mementos were finely placed. From where he sat he could see a slim gilt frame which held three small pictures of his mother's. When she had lain dying in the corner of a hospital ward, as she withered away, this picture frame was on her bedside table. He had sat there for some hours holding her hand as she slept. The people in the frame were those most important to her in her life, and at that moment, the moment of her death, they were her only hold on the past and now to life itself. He wondered about it: her mother, her father and her husband, now deceased. The three children? Nowhere to be seen. What did it mean? Was it that she had reverted to some earlier time, before children complicated her emotions; no longer accepting responsibility for the consequences of children and grandchildren? And then wakening for a moment she had said to him, 'Bob, what are you doing here? I can't help you any more, dear. Give my love to Gloria.' She closed her eyes again before he could say anything and these words were the last she had spoken to him.

He shook his head, muttering to himself that he should pull himself together, and that he must be turning senile. What would people say? His doctor would pronounce him of sane mind, at least he hoped he would. He would tell his char, Mrs Frost. She would lean across the bus gangway to her neighbour and whisper in an agitated way, to someone he had never met, that he had been tested and wasn't suffering from senile dementia. There would be thumbs up by people he didn't know in places he had never visited. And some would think that regular check-ups would be advisable. 'Don't you think so, dear?' they would say.

This was ridiculous. He made himself a cup of tea. If it went on like this he would have to go out and get himself something stronger. He watched a chat show on the television. He was a man of the people, he said to himself, and could watch such a show with the best of them – or was it the worst of them? Snob. The truth was that he could watch it for only ten minutes at a stretch.

He rang Alec. A girl called Nicki answered him, giggled, and said that Alec was otherwise engaged, if he could grasp her meaning. She had heard of Bob and would pass on his message, although it might be best for him to expect a delayed response. Damn cheek. He gave up and went to bed with a very dull book and was soon asleep despite himself.

While he slept Andrea lay wide awake planning his future. It had all gone very well. Not that she liked taking initiatives. In Italy … but then she wasn't in Italy. He was very nice and everything could be smartened up. She knew what to do. Style, Italian style, was the key to a modern future for them both. He would like it once she had explained.

Gloria had not been able to take Bob's call because she had been waylaid by Lucy, persistent as ever. Lucy had insisted that she come round to the inn, waiting for Gloria to become free and sitting with her in the most secure and private place they could command. Despite herself Gloria had become flustered. She had excused herself from the restaurant and had spent time preparing herself for the encounter, while continuing to protest to herself, and now to Lucy, that she had no interest. But Lucy saw that this was not so, that Gloria was succumbing a little to her charms. She had made an effort to look her best, and she had succeeded in looking very tasty. Lucy loved these moments. The closing in of the hunt, the thrill of the chase over, and the moment of fulfil-ment becoming nearer and soon to become inevitable. But not this time. The sous-chef had a moment of crisis and Gloria was summoned to the kitchen. The magic spell was broken, and from there she was able to make her way back to her bedroom and to safety.

In the security of her small bedroom she sat herself down. She was trembling. She couldn't stop it. Should she go down again and find Lucy before it was too late? Some time, surely, Lucy would give her up and find fresh pastures. Was that what she wanted? Slowly she recovered, then taking off her clothes she made her way to the bathroom shower to cool herself down, for she remained hot and flustered. Later, back in the bedroom, in the full-length bedroom mirror, she saw herself, and admired herself for what she had become in naked form. What was she saving this for, this thwarted passion, the unrealised emotions, the unfulfilled longings – and for whom? These splendours, these charms, would surely fade, for Bob, for Rachel, for everyone.

These problems were not for Roger. He had difficulties of his own. He had made his way home, a few miles from Gloria, from London, where he had spent the day with his children. He was tired. These days he became tired very easily, the type of fatigue that you could not easily shake off by sleep. It was etched into him now, this tiredness, so that even strangers could see it ingrained, and would hesitate, wondering whether they should approach him to ascertain whether they could help.

He had left a son, Adam, ten years old, angry in his bed, smelling the freshly painted wall and hating it: not the wall as such, or the new – or rather old – house that needed the decoration in the first place, but that his father had painted it – or to be strictly accurate had repainted it, finding Adam's efforts to be inadequate. Whose room was it anyway? It was lack of money that had brought them to this house, and it was not their fault and his mother was doing her best. So much was certain. But when his father came now, even to this house, there were arguments which ended with his mother in tears; and then later, when he had gone, a retiring to bed with one of her migraines. It made him so angry and really he did not want to see his father at all now, except that his mother said he must. His father had no rights so why was he repainting his wall and then telling a lie? 'Perhaps it needs another coat', was what he'd said. Liar. What he meant was that *his* efforts weren't good enough. And what about his father's efforts then? Had they been adequate? Some joke. He didn't mind the house, not really, or the room. His sister Faith had a bigger room, of course; trust her, she always got the best of it and his consideration came last. But it made him feel like a wasp in a jam jar: the confinement in this small room would make him buzz with anger and frustration. He used to do it in the old garden: catch wasps in jam jars and then put them in the shed, waiting to the last moment before releasing them, and sometimes forgetting. It was cruel, Faith said so, but it was not unfair because wasps could sting you and they would have their chance, just for a second or two – it was you or them. And now he knew how they felt. He tried it, the buzzing. He would go on buzzing, making them hear him until he could get out.

Roger had to face up to a difficult ten days. To avoid bank-ruptcy, which David Droylsden's actions with his creditors had threatened, he needed to enter into an arrangement with them. He required a court order, and after consultation with Mr Morales he had appointed a local firm of accountants to act for him. Action had to be taken right away, as the time for any manoeuvre by him was reduced to a few days: and to be successful required him to achieve seventy-five percent by value of the creditors voting. Roger had explained to Melissa that he would be hard pressed to bring this action to a successful conclusion, and that he had taken certain steps, which he had not told her about previously, to ensure that the house would be excluded from any arrangement with creditors. She cried a little, certain in her own mind that the house would be lost – hadn't her solicitor been right from the very beginning? – and the children, seeing her tears and hearing the raised voices, had demanded reassurances which he was hard pressed to give. He explained it all to her until her eyes glazed over with the effort of it. It was a quagmire, that was what it was, and she was being asked to help him get out of it although it was all his fault in the first place that he was in it.

'Of course, of course', she said, 'if I can help I will. You know I will.' But now when she said these things he no longer trusted her, because there was no 'we' any more and he knew that she listened to other voices. Perhaps, she has always listened to other voices, he said to himself, ungenerously, knowing it to be only reasonable that she did so now, when anyone in their right mind would. In the end all he could say to her was that he would give it his best shot. As he left their eyes, three pairs of eyes now, had turned towards him in their mutual gaze. He imagined a common voice. The voice said to him 'Some shooter, eh. Some chance.'

There had been many moments like this one: lying in bed, tired but not able to sleep, summoning up his childhood net, his invisible communication system linking himself to his past and to all those people who frequented it, asking innumerable questions but rarely getting any answers. But when you started, there was always a thrill in it because you never knew for certain whom you would summon up and what they might say to you; whether they would answer you or not: and after all there were many ways of answering a question. He had a thousand ways of posing his questions and he was proud of the variety he had achieved. But it all boiled down to this in the end: what explained his misfortune? Mr Morales had looked grave when *he* answered. 'There's such a thing as misfortune: a series of set-backs, some of them life-threatening, one after another, seemingly without end. History is full of misfortunes and, at the risk of discouraging you, worse than that – disasters.' He rolled his Rs dramatically like an old Scottish ham actor, although he was nothing of the kind, enjoying the moment.

Morales' answers did not satisfy him; it was simply not good enough. Was it perhaps the issue of expectation? Were his expectations always too high, so high that there was no reasonable prospect of him realising them at all? Was that it? Making promises to himself and to others with no realistic prospect of their realisation? He knew that he had been abandoned by his colleagues and friends, and now he felt by his family, because they no longer believed his pledges about the future. He had failed them big time. It hurt him that his daughter Faith, on whom he had relied, now hesitated before him on important matters. He imagined that she'd said to herself, could she trust him? On what could she rely? Was he there in her future?

He remembered boarding a bus many years ago, a young man socially and geographically mobile and busy, and being greeted enthusiastically by a man he did not know although he recognised him. It would not be exaggerating to say that this man was joyous to find him again and anxious to tell him his news, the words tumbling out to fill the precious time they had available; to tell him as much as possible about himself and his family in the few minutes their schedule and the bus journey permitted. He did his very best to hide the fact that he could not remember this man's name or anything at all about what they had shared together: rack his mind as he did, desperately, he did not remember anything at all. He almost succeeded in dissembling, but at the very last moment failed. A look of frozen horror appeared on the face of his accidental travelling companion, as Roger pushed his way free to get off the bus. So what was that about? What had happened between them, and what promises of a mutual future had been made there? It came back to haunt him, for try as he might, as he did over months and years, he could not recall anything.

It was amazing how very easily you could deceive yourself, so that hardly anything at all was real. He remembered during his officer training that a sergeant, walking to his rear and catching up, had greeted him as a lost friend. He turned out to be a boy called Wardle from his school, not in his class and not even in his year, who talked to him enthusiastically despite the hesitations of presence and rank. As they parted, he said inconsequentially to Wardle that he was surprised to be recalled by him, immediately and without hesitation, after all these years, by a casual glance from the rear. Wardle had replied that he had had no difficulty because he recognised his, Roger's walk, and that in his experience he had never encountered anyone who had a walk like his. It had upset him, this remark, and he had remembered it. Of course if you were a man, a normal sort of man, you never did see your rear, and probably hardly ever considered the way you walked. A walk was a walk. Women were another matter because they seemed highly concerned about how they looked from behind, and had evolved mirrors that could be positioned so that their rears could be seen. And then women talked to each other about these things, got a second opinion. But a man? Of course not. So what did it mean? Instant recognition because of the way he walked, because of the impression he made when he walked!

As you got older, and he was feeling aged now, the falsities mounted: there were the accumulated effects of the past which weighed you down, a negativity about persons and situations that did not work out well for you. If he was going to be fair to himself, and why not, it could hardly be entirely his fault that he felt like it. Could it? This negativity. But he had to admit that in a world of consenting adults and the complexities of urban life everyone was at it, and self-confidence, or in the everyday jargon of today, a positive outlook, was regarded as a virtue and people would say of you, 'I do so like him because he has such a positive outlook on life and is so encouraging' – to me, our team, and so on. And then it was true that a positive, as opposed to a realistic, outlook did seem to work: people got on with things and they had more energy and drive to better the situation and themselves. Perhaps you couldn't win? The more positive you were and the more you did, the greater the number of mistakes you made and the more people there were to object to you.

It was all very difficult but he thought promises to better things might be thought to fall into two categories: there were political and business promises, a lot of those, but they might be thought of as being necessary deceptions, and the occupation of consenting adults; and then made in situations where the language was quickly decoded. Lovers' lies came into this category too, since promises of bliss for evermore were unlikely in the extreme to be realised, but not to make them would be cheating someone of a bliss they were entitled to enjoy, even for a moment. But the second category was a disaster area, a minefield, where mistakes were catastrophic: unwise promises and knowingly, or to be fairer predictably false, expectations made to family and friends. Was that the problem? Was it that the qualities required to succeed in worldly pursuits had carried over to his private life and he had been unable to differentiate? Was the problem, at the bottom of it all, in essence, a matter of false expectation: first of himself and then, inevitably in its overspill, to others?

He fell asleep.

CHAPTER 9

B ATTLE WAS WELL and truly joined. David Droylsden had a good head start as he had already persuaded several key creditors to act to make Roger bankrupt, hinting at hidden treasure, and their petition was before the local court. Roger now presented himself to Temples, a local firm of insolvency practitioners, accompanied by Mr Morales, to seek advice and urgent action. Disappointed by the faded gentility of Temples' offices, where a wall plaque informed them that the company was established in 1923, Roger was soon disabused of his prejudice by Temple himself, an ancient man of wisdom and experience who remained completely able to act decisively. They were to put their own petition into the court on the following day, and then the court would stay the petitioner's proceedings so giving him time to present his formal proposals for a voluntary arrangement at a later date. The details of this proposal were then to be circulated to all his creditors, who would need to vote on it either by post or at a meeting called for this purpose. It was important, Mr Temple told him, to list all his assets and liabilities.

Even Temple was surprised at the preliminary list of debtors. He drew breath and whistled at the profusion of debt, the paucity of assets, and the confusion of his financial affairs generally. 'Quite an achievement, Mr Greer.'

He proffered his judgement sarcastically, and Roger realised once again that in his new role of abject suitor he was fair game for anyone. Temple thought it of importance that the new family house be included in the available assets, as there was no equity in Roger's small cottage. Roger had to explain the complex ruse by which he had put his beneficial interest in the house into a deed of trust. He gave the name of the trust's beneficiary to Temple, who was of the opinion that the deed was unlikely to hold up in court if seriously challenged. Temple was reluctant, but in the end agreed to overlook the house for the moment.

As Temple knew how easily these matters deteriorated, came to grief, he stressed the importance to Roger of checking out with the individual creditors their attitude to the likely proposal. 'Not good, I expect, for this offer won't lead to a repayment of more than six pence in the pound. But you can try. Why not?' He was philosophical again. Then there was the little matter of the fee. To get this show on the road Roger needed to provide a front-end payment of not less than two thousand five hundred pounds. Roger swallowed hard and said, 'Of course.'

Leaving the premises Morales hissed at him, 'Mr Greer, no more surprises, please. These matters are very serious and you must tell me everything.' Over coffee Roger told him a bit more, but not much more, for he was not sure that Morales could handle the whole truth and nothing but the truth.

It could not fairly be said that Messrs Fogg and Error at the bank were hard and immoral men, for they were the purveyors of a distinctive ethic of their time, the creed of the modern money-lender: but their trade was as ancient as the hills, and it was from its history, its trials and tribulations, that they drew their strength. They had committed themselves on paper to an amnesty on any action against Mrs Greer, but nevertheless they thought she might have something. They posed the questions, did she have control over assets, and was there something they might grab? They had received letters from Mrs Greer's solicitors pressing them on this point, expressing her need, her anxiety, to have something in writing on behalf of their client. 'Methinks', they thought in their own way, 'the lady protests too much.' So they called her in.

And there she was before them: immaculately turned out, precise, glossy, and vulnerable. They were impressed. Fogg, who was a romantic, thought of the Scottish Widows advertisement and imagined her as the Widow, passing through the storm-wracked rose garden, and then mounting the steps of a lighthouse, to the very top, where the searching light would beam into the troubled night. Error, who was something of a music buff, having been known to listen to Classic FM, the station specialising in the provision of sentimental tracks to listeners with a limited ability to concentrate, with a restriction on time-span, had heard her sing and thought how small she seemed for the production of such a rich and large sound.

She told them her story, which she had rehearsed a thousand times, and which at this moment could be played with great certainty. It was a moving story, and on more than one occasion she paused to wipe away a tear. Like all classic stories it was accessible, with a beginning, a middle and an end. Its musical qualities were evident: it was finally tuned, there were reflective passages of magical sensitivities, and others of high passion – and it ended with a coda. Her lovely head had been bowed but as she concluded, and the music stopped, she slowly raised her pale translucent face to them; her beautiful tear-dimmed eyes confronting them in a mute appeal for a favourable verdict. She awaited her fate with patience and faith in a favourable audience reaction.

They were deeply moved. Error moved away to compose himself. He thought of what piece of paper he might produce for her autograph and vowed to become a regular Classic FM listener. Fogg coughed. There was a pause. She knew it. It was the pause of an audience before their applause. She was safe. Fogg coughed again and said, 'Well I'm glad we had this opportunity to hear your side of things. There shouldn't be a problem, and we can get a positive letter to your solicitor. Please don't worry about this any more.' He felt it to be a privilege to help this lady, and escorted her from the building.

Great performances can have unexpected results: their effects ripple out in unpredictable ways and benefit not only the audience but other bystanders, without them knowing it. Not that Roger on this particular day was dwelling on beneficial effects, for he had received notice of a possibility far more forbidding than anything he had been confronting when he woke. He was telephoned by a policeman, a Detective Constable Ernest Strive, who told him they had received a complaint from a former shareholder in his old company which raised the issue of a possible offence under the

Financial Services Act 1986. Would he come into the local police station to answer questions under caution on Friday morning, please? And it would be wise to be accompanied by a solicitor. Strive would not answer any further questions on the phone.

For some time Roger was overwhelmed by the enormity of it. A lifetime's desire for respectability and honesty was overwhelmed in a second by allegations which, while they must be baseless, activated no doubt by malice, would hold him by the throat for some time. He steadied himself. Suffocating in the house, he left it for his usual walk across the marshes. Out, out to the river, flowing fast after recent heavy rain, dirt-filled dark-grey with stained white tops where the river was at its fastest. He stared into the water, merging the dark-grey with the distant bank, feeling the surge of the river through and around him, filling his ears and eyes with its busy movement. He felt a hand on his arm and looking saw a perfect stranger.

'Hello, old chap. Don't I recognise you? Haven't I seen you on this pathway before?'

Meaningless words, for of course he hadn't seen this man, spoken to him or anyone like him on this pathway or anywhere else in this marsh. The man was leading him away from the river, across the marsh, back onto the roadway, and eventually back into the town: to the comfort and warmth of tourist cafe, a cup of tea and a flapjack and the hiss of an urn. This man was local. Perhaps he had seen other figures like Roger out along the river, or perhaps not, feeling lonely and in need of companionship. Roger never thought to ask. Now at least there was no consequence. The words flowed on. Someone recognised him and smiled. The chat was Norfolk: nothing threatening there.

Roger said, 'It's kind of you. Don't let me hold you up.'

'All the time in the world, dear chap, for you. All the time in the world.'

When they parted the stranger said, and Roger hadn't thought to ask his name, 'Funny thing, life. We never know its value, the value of a human life, until it's gone. Don't you think? Don't forget me. I'm often on the marsh and here in this cafe. And good luck. We all need it.' The stranger squeezed his arm gently.

Roger got himself back into the cottage. He rang a friend and chatted about the cricket. His friend went on about some difficulty of his own. Roger gave some advice and they had a laugh together. He felt normal again. Surely this was the bottom. What more could there be: business failure and financial ruin, murder suspect, divorce, loss of his home and family, bankruptcy, the malicious and knowing pursuit of an enemy?

Mr Morales, who proved to be a jack of all trades, although no specialist in criminal law, acted for him. He sat next to him in the police station while two policemen informed them of their rights and then began to produce innumerable documents not previously shown to Roger and about which he was grilled. Roger had no difficulty with these documents or their questions, although he could not always remember details and context under the pressure of relentless questioning. Time passed. The questions were asked again. Roger protested at needless repetition. There were further questions. More time passed. Strive said, 'That's all we can do today. We'll have to arrange another time, another day.'

Roger was adamant. 'Not on your Nellie. You should be able now to see that these allegations are baseless and malicious. Why do you wish to waste everyone's time?'

They demurred, pointing out that it was his opportunity to produce documents of his own and to consult with his solicitor. Strive said, 'We could always arrest you.'

Roger responded, 'Have you ever heard of wrongful arrest?'

They smiled, having heard it all before. Mr Morales hauled him back, mollifying them, whispering to Roger, urgently, to curb his impulsiveness. And they arranged another date. Mr Morales said to him 'It's much better to answer their questions. They go on and on until you do. There's no point in arguing with them.' It sounded to Roger to be the type of good advice that no one should act upon.

In the interval Roger made some inquiries of his own. He discovered that the complaint had originated with a director of his former company who was now safely ensconced in the new. She had been put up to it. He rang her. She seemed embarrassed to speak to him and refused to deny or confirm her involvement, asking him not to ring her again. He took legal advice, but not from Morales, because it seemed to him that a complaint from her, even assuming for a moment that it could be upheld, was like the pot calling the kettle black. The action complained of was a board matter, had been decided by the board acting as a whole and so included her. He was advised that he could argue that the board as a whole was involved and that all the directors could be held to be complicit. When Morales was told, he said unhelpfully but realistically, 'Cut-throat defence, dear boy, cut-throat defence', by which he meant that even if she were to be charged with anything her defence would be that she acted under pressure as a servant to him – and he could be certain that all his former friends and colleagues would do the same.

At his next meeting with Strive they quickly settled into the pattern of the former: the same questions were asked, either, he deduced, because they had got nothing first time or in the hope that he would contradict his earlier answers. Time passed and the day yawned before them. Morales seemed to be asleep. Roger's frustration reached boiling point. He started to get up and Morales, not asleep, pulled him back. Roger spluttered, 'I've had enough of this farce. I intend to make a short statement and then get on with my work, for as far as I can gather I'm the only person around this table earning nothing by sitting at it.'

It was not as spontaneous as it seemed, as he had prepared something. He read it aloud:

'I have been legally advised that there is no reasonable grounds on which the alleged offence can be pursued and that I should desist after answering reasonable questions to the best of my ability. I have done that. I am further advised that if it is proposed that I answer further questions that I shall only do so once witness statements are properly taken and shown to me in advance. I have been advised to tell you (and this wasn't true) that it is probable that anyone acting against me would be held to be acting in a conspiracy to pervert the course of justice, and that if I am arrested that action will be taken for wrongful arrest.'

Strive did not prevent him leaving, and Morales, moving in his slipstream and muttering, 'Unwise, most foolish', took up the rear.

Morales was right, of course. The police would not be deterred from their pursuit by his breaking off; they would regroup and come again when ready. But for the moment they had withdrawn from his battlefield, which was crowded enough with enemy forces. And even Mr Morales, while not convinced, was impressed when Roger named the QC, a friend of his, from whom he had taken the advice.

Roger's immediate task was to seek to persuade his creditors to vote for his proposed arrangement. He needed seventy-five per cent of the debts by value, and after a comprehensive haul of the creditors the arithmetic was not in his favour: some creditors always opposed arrangements as a matter of policy or principle, believing they should take every opportunity to recover their money whatever the impact on the debtor. This was a practice with a long and dishonourable tradition. Others were entirely pragmatic, and as the Inland Revenue had informed him, experience indicated to them that they got more by opposing, being entirely competent in the whole business of recovery. He did the rounds a number of times and however optimistically he rated the don't know/won't says, the 'yes' column never amounted to seventy-five per cent. He sweated and contrived, and to his wife Melissa he dissembled, and the deadline drew nearer.

Many of life's disasters and triumphs come to us electronically or magically, to the uninitiated, through the air waves: and there it was, on his fax machine, a proxy vote in his favour from Mr Fogg for a million pounds. Not the one hundred thousand pounds he had agreed to repay the bank, but a million pounds, almost all the original sum owed. And there was a note from Fogg, who appeared to be in the ascendant, stating that as the agreement so recently signed was in jeopardy through no fault of Roger's, he was prepared on behalf of the bank to vote the balance of the original sum owed in support of the arrangement.

It hadn't taken Fogg long to decide. He remembered Melissa sitting in front of him, in that very chair, and the tears, and how deeply it had affected Error and him: and his impulse to help her, which moved him still.

There was still the Meeting of Creditors to attend, but the burden of it was lifted by the knowledge that he had the votes. However proxies can be changed and you are never home until the fat lady sings; or put more decorously in Mr Temple's words, 'People can and do change their minds.' They gathered in the meeting room of the local Rotary Club. Just twelve true men forgoing the convenience of the post, scattered across the rows of chairs, reminiscent of a non-conformist religious gathering, where after a while the text would shift from godly to self-righteous. There were some unfriendly stares, which caused Roger to shuffle in his vantage point on a small raised dais; and there was an audible hissing when the proxy vote was announced and those who hoped that their votes would be decisive realised that their votes had counted for nothing in the end. There were shouts of 'shame' and 'disgraceful', and Roger was jostled and jeered at as he left. Temple had seen it all before, and bought Roger a whisky in the bar to stop his trembling ahead of what now would be a four-year haul to repay debts at the agreed percentage. Temple commented that a hundred years earlier this debt would have been repaid from a debtors' prison, and Roger thanked him for the reminder.

David Droylsden rung Mr Temple in his capacity as administrator to find out the result, and could hardly contain his fury when he knew it. Roger had escaped this trap, but he would not escape the next: and in the final issue if he would not allow himself to be ruined he would kill him. David was clear about it. Roger would be killed. David had started the planning as an act of fantasy, but after evaluating alternatives in a businesslike manner he had decided on the method of killing and disposal of the body. The task of disposing of Roger had became real to him, and alive and active in his consciousness.

Melissa had greeted the news of the success of his voluntary arrangement with joy; but then Roger had come to realise that when those who have abandoned you express joy at your news, it never has anything to do with you, and they are rejoicing for themselves. With whom could he enjoy his success? He thought of Gloria. This evening he would go to the inn for a celebratory drink and tell Gloria. He was very fond of Gloria, in a brotherly sort of way, and there was no one better than her at listening. He found her quite stunning, and in the beginning had thought of trying to persuade her to something else, more intimate, but whenever he drew a little nearer she withdrew, and he had come to respect her for it. Her policeman husband, Bob, was still to be seen in the inn from time to time, and the investigation was continuing: but damn it, he was not going to lose one of his few resting places because of Bob. As it meant nothing to Gloria, why should it mean anything to him? He felt sure that her discretion was absolute.

Then, he might see Rachel at the inn. He thought of the coming party. Rachel was something other: if Gloria was stunning in a sunny afternoon, ice-creamy sort of way, which might be unfair to her, then for Rachel you might move the earth itself and all its planets, for she....What was she? The thinking man's idea of feminine rarity, a uniquely beautiful – what exactly? Something indescribably – what? He could not find the words. If Rachel were there he might tell her his news. It pleased him that she might be there, and that he was thinking of her in this way for the first time.

Gloria was there, but not Rachel. He told Gloria about his day, and she shone with her pleasure for him, excused herself from duties in the restaurant and sat privately with him in the restaurant lounge drinking champagne – and at her expense. He found the words to tell her how much he liked her, and how he wished that they might be closer, although he knew that they couldn't be, and how glad he was that they were friends. She was pleased because she liked him, and because having listened to him she felt that she could now tell him about her feelings for Rachel. She told him everything: that she did not want to lose Bob; that she had never had a relationship, that sort of a relationship, with another woman; that she was surprised that Lucy was persistent in wanting to be a friend; and that ... and how slowly the words escaped, that she had the strongest feelings for Rachel but that Rachel did not respond to them, or so she thought. But how could she be sure, make sure, without making a complete fool of herself?

Roger could not cope. He felt a dreadful ache for a lost future. He got his question out. 'Is Rachel like that – you know, other women?'

'Not really', was the response. 'You know, a few girly things, but don't all those girls, the posh sort at their boarding schools, have a few meaningless flings?'

He didn't know. He supposed so. He hoped not with Rachel. He said, 'You must be brave and ask her. Tell her how you feel.

If she says not, ask yourself whether you would want Lucy.' And then again, 'What would Bob say? Could you lose him by getting involved with either of them?'

It was good advice, and she knew it, but perhaps not for her. She said, 'I am involved with Rachel. It frightens me what I feel and where these feelings might lead me.'

It frightened Roger too, and entirely ruined his evening. He left as soon as he could without being rude to Gloria. She did not think him rude, being grateful to him, and relieved that there was at least someone that she could talk to about these strange and overwhelming feelings; at least one person she could trust absolutely.

Rachel had a slow bath that evening after a busy day during which, as a dutiful mother of two lively and demanding girls, she had hardly thought of herself at all. Sophie, her youngest child, had returned home for this weekend from her music college moody and withdrawn; and then, under loving pressure, tearful. It was all too much for her: the hours of practice, the expectations, and missing them – oh, how she missed them. Pent-up feelings broke as the waters of a mighty dam, but thereafter subsided to a peaceful flow and were then removed from sight, lost subterraneously in sleep. Fiona, as befitted the senior, was supportive and helpful and then at the last succumbed to her own needs and demanded bedtime consolation and reassurance.

Rachel addressed herself languidly, releasing the day, and the pressure of others, in a very hot bath which after a while would weaken her further. It was all very well living for others, living out your emotions in and for children, but in the end they would not thank you. What did she need for herself? If your children, ultimately, would let you down, they had to go, make their own life, of course they did, how could you rely on them, living through them? Not that she didn't love them desperately, to little pieces. And what of the alternative, letting adults close to you? What after all did adults all too frequently do to each other? They could be very cruel. Especially men. Still.... She thought of Roger.

CHAPTER 10

ROGER DID NOT feel his success as a triumph, for he knew only that he had edged ahead in one round, that there were many ahead of him, and the probability that at some point he would suffer a knock-down from which he would not recover. After several days of restlessness and disturbed sleep, and after checking his depleted resources at the bank, he decided to get away for a few days in order to recover. Since his car had been returned to him he was able to fill the fuel tank, and on a fine spring day he pointed the car towards the west, it seeming to be a long way from him, and set out on a journey without any known destination.

In so doing he broke the habits of a lifetime, for he told no one where he was going and left his mobile phone switched off in the attic, which now served him as a makeshift office, with no message to any caller. It pleased him. Of course, there were fewer people now who would want to contact him, and those who did, for the most part, were not those he would welcome: organisations still seeking payment although, the arrangement should have stilled them, and harbingers of troubles to come, and to hell with them. But he had made promises which he was now breaking: to Melissa who, anxious, had told him always to be contactable for the children's sake as they would worry if they could not speak to him when they had a need (and whose tone of voice had told him she would worry too); to two policeman, Churchill-Jones and Strive; and to Morales and Temple, guardians not only for him but now, with the majesty of the law on their side, for others. Well, he could always call in, assuming he could only define what being 'in' meant for him these days.

He made steady progress out towards the coast at Kings Lynn before hitting heavy traffic, vehicles with commerce in mind crossing to the very heart of England before turning north, while he, empty of purpose, would edge west taking minor roads whenever they were offered. If life was without purpose, meaningless really, a sort of game, he was out of it. If the question was, 'What's your game, guvnor?', what was his reply? 'Oh, nothing, nothing at all. No offence intended, ...' Fill in the gap where appropriate: sir, your honour, Melissa, detective. And if none of the above apply, please write in your reasons. He laughed. Writing in your reasons should be avoided, wherever possible. But it couldn't be. He thought of all those lectures on risk management he had given where he would say something like this, 'It is commonly supposed that given the prevalence of risk in activity, in the taking of decisions, the lowest risk profile must be associated with inactivity, in limiting the number of decisions taken. But this is far from the truth because to take no action, not to take a decision, is in fact to take one – that is, a decision not to take one, which may, in all the circumstances known to you at the time, be a very poor decision to take. The issue is not one of quantity but quality: take decisions when they are needed and make good ones; and then build in a method for change so that if it seems that a decision is not working out you can alter course with the minimum of collateral damage.' Easy to say, but how do you go about improving the quality of your decisions in life? That was the real issue. But then that was a different lecture.

So should he be taking decisions about his life and not simply reacting to these disastrous events? He supposed, yes, and he thought, no: there was a case to be made for either. At the moment he thought his state of mind to be so poor that any important decisions – and wasn't he surrounded by the need for them? – would be badly taken. Sufficient unto the hour is the evil thereof, he told himself. The decisions ahead of him were straightforward enough. Did he turn left or right or go straight on? It would help if he knew his destination. Somewhere on the coast, he thought, and then, Newquay on the Cornish coast which he had not visited since his student days. It cheered him now that there was somewhere to go. But Newquay was too far to make in a single day and would require a stopover. Here his indecision would not be helpful: he had left it too late to find accommodation and the hotels he tried were fully booked. It was very late and far out on the wilderness of the A30 when at last he found a small hotel willing to take him. Too late for the meal service, withdrawn at nine pm; too remote a location for a quick hamburger or fish and chips; and too near a main road to guarantee a quiet night. He replenished himself on the instant coffee and biscuits provided in his room and made the best of it.

He lay on the bed, eyes fixed on the ceiling, observing the fine cracks and discoloration, which denoted for him economies in maintenance that, while probably necessary, would work out badly for the owner. It would be better for the proprietor to do it himself, find the time, set an example: but the owner was now a corporation and couldn't do that, and the employees would say, if asked, that it wasn't their job. All his life he had been immediate about these things. If he were the manager he would do it, he would paint the ceilings. But other decisions in life were more difficult than painting ceilings.

As he thought about it, he accepted that there must be some reason, some commonality, why decisions of his went so disastrously wrong. It must be a character fault. But what, exactly? In Shakespearean tragedy it became obvious to the audience. Before your very eyes the cracks in character became visible; at first fine, but gradually opening up before you until the fissures became terrifying and fatal; great oak trees, immortal entities broke up and crashed to the stage as you wondered and watched. He got up and looked in the mirror. Where were the fine lines of his destruction?

These questions were not to be answered, if at all, on this day, and he fell asleep. The next day was better. He had a purpose and a fine sunny day to go with it. Newquay was as he remembered it, spread out around its generous bays and sandy beaches, basking and colourful, bustling and contented even in this early season; a postcard mixture of seaside colours, and the salty smell of the sea, which returned him to the rare days of holiday magic he had enjoyed as a child. And high above the sweep of surf-driven Fistral Bay he made his way to the Headland Hotel which, although having experienced better days, remained imposing and grand even in its shabbiness, and which offered him – after a brisk negotiation which for a moment restored his self-belief in his business acumen – a large friendly room which looked out at an angle to the beach below.

Roger sat down at a small table in the window bay and gazed on the moving panorama of life in the outside world. Opening the windows, he could hear the sounds he had come for: children at play competing for territory, the raised voices of the occasional reproving adult, and the persistent swish of the sea itself. When the hardly to be remembered coffee order was fulfilled, he could stretch his legs, close his eyes, and for the moment feel himself safe and at peace.

He had booked for seven days but thought he might stay longer, as long as was needed. At first he did very little, conscious of his convalescence; strolling around the town, sitting in cafes, and armed with sandwich lunches from the hotel, eating and dreaming on the grassy uplands; but later he got up early to go out with the fishing boats and to play the undemanding golf course, setting himself a target improvement programme but not minding when he fell short. Then, buying some unlined notebooks in the town, he began to write. Could he by writing come into a greater understanding of what had happened to him? Was writing a way of dealing with trauma, shapeless and without merit and purpose, no doubt, but nevertheless helping him, as painting might help others? He didn't know. He found it thrilling to be confronted each time he attempted to write with a virgin-white blank sheet.

Of course he knew that if you were serious, wished to be creative and to do it well, you had to plan something out. His English teacher had said you had to have a beginning, a middle and an end. That was no longer true, assuming it ever was, for he knew that no one wrote like that now. Still there had to be a start, you always had to begin, shivering in the anticipation of what that might mean; and, there was always a last word, in the end you ran out of space. He had always thought that in some novels the writer just stopped because the publisher had told him enough was enough; there were too many words, and to publish that number would be uneconomic. Always, as he looked at his blank sheet, he had doubts. If he was to go forward with this, writing things out, he had to accept his limitations. He needed to establish markers, signifiers, so that when he got lost he could go back to them and work out where he had come from. That was the thing to do, he concluded, and thus armed he began.

After ten days he felt better, and thought he would go back and face the music. As he drew nearer home he felt unwell with severe chest pains, and stopping in a lay-by he got out of the car and gulped in fresh air until the pain abated; but it resumed when he entered his cottage, and stabbed at him as he bent to pick up the post, and during his sifting out of the missives, which he divided between those he could open and those that must wait, to be dribbled out later when he was strong enough. When he had paused a little he summoned up his telephone messages, to be astounded by the various voices seeking him from the deep.

There was his daughter Faith, fitful and querying at first but demanding at last, with Melissa chipping in on her behalf. He rang and received a lecture on his untrustworthiness. Hadn't he always been told to leave a message, an address, wherever, whenever? 'Yes, yes, of course you're right. But what's the problem?' This was followed with more reproof, and in the end he found out. Faith was ill, had developed a fever, a lassitude, and had had a blood test which suggested a rare illness. Melissa was uncertain about the exact description, and further tests would be needed, but his help was required. He was so good at these things finding out and steadying everything and working out what was needed. Yes, wasn't he? It was true, he was very good at these moments, and of course he would help. He arranged to come down, he would speak to the GP. Then he spoke to his daughter, making her laugh and feel better.

Finding out and doing the right thing was to occupy a great deal of his time over the coming months. He felt Faith's condition as his own: it lodged in the interstices of his mind and imagination, and he wanted it to be there. Her illness was thought to be a type of degenerative disease affecting the mind, but as this was very rare, especially in twelve year old girls, there was no medical consensus about the diagnosis and therefore considerable doubt about the best treatment. The illness could be fatal, but then people survived it; there was no common ground on the best treatment and the medication, if not prescribable through the National Health Service, would be expensive.

Roger did some research which revealed that a Swiss clinic seemed to offer a distinctive and successful treatment for the condition. He rang them. They would take Faith in, find room for her, and quoted their fees for her care. Where would he get money of this order? He despaired. Then he discussed his findings with Melissa. Roger would do hardly anything for Melissa, and she would do nothing for him, but what united them was Faith. Together they had fashioned their daughter, and drawing from their happier times, in a conspiracy of remembered love, they were both prepared to conspire to do the right thing for her. They agreed to try to raise the money, she in her way and he in his. Four weeks later they were to meet and discuss the matter again.

For Roger it turned out to be easier than he had imagined. Out of the blue an old business acquaintance of his, a sort of friend, someone who might in some circumstances be a true friend, who had made money from the flotation of Roger's company and then got out in good time, invited Roger to lunch at the Savoy Grill. These days such an invitation was rare, and Roger relaxed into the plain luxury of his surroundings and of good food and drink. He told his friend of Faith's illness and the result of his research, and how unfortunately he did not have the money to pay for this treatment. They had been drinking, and fine wine fermented their impulses. Was Roger actually asking for help? Was he admitting he could not deal with his problem? His friend leant back and asked, eyebrows raised, 'How much can you raise?'

Roger quoted a modest sum.

'That all?' His friend tested him.

'At this moment, yes.'

His friend felt sporting. 'Look, I've made quite a lot of money out of you, and for the moment I'm flush. For every pound you can raise I shall treble it, up to....' He quoted a rather large sum. 'Not a loan, you understand. I never lend money, on principle. A gift. I know something about illness and I'll help.'

They shook hands on it.

Melissa's opportunities were somewhat different. A woman friend, without being asked, gave her a sum of money from her precious savings, saying that one day, perhaps, Melissa might repay it, but she really did not mind whether it was repaid or not. It should be regarded as a gift. It was not enough. She thought of her admirers and dwelt on one Luigi Ambrotti, an impresario from Milan. For some time Luigi had laid gentle but persistent siege to her, but since he was Italian she had assumed these attentions to be a reflexive characteristic, an automatic reaction of his when confronted with any attractive woman – or unattractive if the need was there. Thinking of him now, she thought she might be unfair. When Roger's company had collapsed, discovering through others that she was in financial difficulties he had rung her and offered help in a natural and friendly way, and she had refused him with regret, not willing to be compromised, for she had needed the money. Hesitating no longer, she rang him, and finding that he would be in London shortly, allowed herself to be invited to lunch.

And there she was, doing what she had tried to avoid for so long, having a very expensive lunch at the Dorchester with an attractive and sophisticated Italian womaniser; at a very expensive hotel, with the knowledge that a hotel room was booked in his name, and her needing money – a lot of money. She had discussed this situation in advance with a woman friend at the opera company. Donna was amused, for Luigi had a reputation. Melissa was indignant. 'It's not a joke, it's not a laughing matter.'

'Of course not.' Donna while continuing to laugh quietened down. She gave advice. 'Luigi's all right. He loves women and – so I'm told – he's very good in the sack.'

Melissa objected again.

'Well, ask for a lot of money. You need it and he's got it.' She continued to laugh. 'And you know what they say about Italian lovers: they're like Italian cars, very noisy and lively but they don't last long. He'll soon forget you when a new model comes along. Live for today for tomorrow we die, and all that.'

So there she was telling her story. Luigi's eyes, brown and spaniel-like, filled with tears. He held her hands in his across the table. She liked his hands, soft but firm and caressing her own. And then very close, and leaning towards her, he said, 'Dear woman, this is tragic, very terrible.' And then, a little later,

'Melissa, my love, how can Luigi help you?' She swallowed hard and asked for money. Luigi did not flinch. He reached into the inside pocket of his expensive Armani jacket and drew out a large chequebook, and an equally large golden fountain pen, and wrote her a cheque with a fine Roman flourish for the sum she had asked for. He rose, expressed his apology for being short of time on this occasion, kissed her on both cheeks and departed.

Donna would never believe this. And when she was told, Donna said, 'Well done. I guess you owe him one.' Melissa wondered if Luigi had been disinterested, genuine, and whether anything else would come of it, and whether she wished that something might, that she might well want to return the favour, if he requested it.

So when the two conspirators met to pool their money the sums raised were sufficient, assuming that Roger's business pal was as good as his word in his willingness to top him up three-fold. He was. He didn't blink either and paid his promised sum, though it was greater than he had expected, and without demur. Within ten days Melissa was able to take Faith to the clinic in Switzerland, and the diagnosis and treatment could begin. Roger saw them both off at Heathrow airport, and they kissed and hugged each other there in the departure lounge like any other loving family.

Temple had left Roger a message, and when he responded delivered a severe homily. Now that Roger had been delivered up to his administration, the roles had been reversed. Roger had to understand that it was Temple's duty to deliver as much as possible to Roger's creditors; he needed him to understand that the figure proposed by the court was to be regarded as a minimum; and he was concerned that Roger's present income prospects were not good. Roger must understand that any failure on his part to pay the minimum monthly payment would result in him, Temple, going back to court to discharge the administration, and a complete bankruptcy would follow. Holidays were just not part of the scheme. Temple had a point. Roger admitted it to himself with trepidation, for with the loss of his consultancy assignment he needed to find alternative employment, and quickly.

Morales was next: two messages from him. The date for the court hearing on his financial means had been set, and would

Roger kindly get in touch with him without delay as there was a lot of work needed to be done if they were to be properly prepared. How quickly the illusion of Melissa's solidarity and common purpose had been exposed, disavowed, as lawyers on their behalf joined the lists in full battle cry. Roger groaned. He would do his best but he knew he was not going to be believed.

Bob Churchill-Jones's message was a surprise. 'Would you kindly get in touch with me. Nothing formal – even official – really. I'm staying at the inn, Gloria's place, next weekend, and I wondered whether we could have a chat. Off the record, over a pint.' He left a telephone number. Later Roger rang and arranged to meet him.

And then a message from Rachel, which he hadn't expected, giving him the date of her long-postponed party. He rang her back, although there was no need to do so. They chatted for the first time. Roger asked her if she would have a drink with him some time, and she accepted on the condition that it would need to be a coffee over the weekend, during a morning, as for the immediate future her evenings were too occupied.

Roger smartened himself up for this encounter. He dry-cleaned his best casual clothes and polished his most wearable shoes, which he hadn't done for several months, and as the moment arrived he was very excited, arriving much too early and, as his mother would have said, 'in a state', like a teenager on a first date. But he would have been extremely unbelieving of Rachel's preparations. Rachel had carefully set her boundaries for this encounter. She had told no one. The time allowable, which her emotions permitted, was formally set out in her mind, together with the necessary excuses, which were rehearsed. Rachel spent a great deal of time at her hairdresser and in considering what to wear. So when she arrived at last, having kept Roger waiting and wondering whether he was right about the time, she succeeded in looking both casual and elegant – and entirely spontaneous. The gold rings in unusual places were gone, and at considerable expense, the red hair streaks had been eliminated. The jeans had been abandoned and the black trousers which replaced them were tailored. Rachel glowed, burnished and pale. He thought the blouse to be white but frilly, and he saw that she was wearing what seemed to be, but wasn't, an ethnic embroidered top. He got up from his seat. He stammered, which he hadn't done since a small child, and she smiled at him encouragingly, knowing her preparations to have been a success.

Rachel had the social gift of being able to draw people out. But more than this: she was genuinely interested in people, and at this moment in Roger. He began to tell her the most intimate personal details about his life. Rachel gently steered and prompted him, opening up new ways of considering his past, without any presumption on her part. Roger realised that she had the most wonderful mind, sinuous but stringent, and great personal warmth, so that though the subject matter was difficult for him, traumatic, he was never fearful or hesitant. Her warmth and sympathy buoyed him up through the dark passages and sustained him so that he could continue.

Rachel loved it. Learning about him, listening to him, working out how she could help – she was sure she could. Roger was aghast. A great deal of time had passed and he had asked her almost nothing about herself; and now, panicking, it was too late, for she showed signs of leaving, she would be distracted, and he would not be able to ask her anything of importance.

Rachel reached across the table and held his arm. She asked him, 'Roger, what at this moment is the most practical thing you could do to deal with all your problems?'

'Earn a regular income.' His reply was immediate.

It surprised her. She asked, 'With all your experience, Roger, and I suppose your contacts, can't you start afresh? Get some high paid job or start a new business venture?'

He was rueful. ' So many reasons. My age, I'm too old; loss of reputation, fatal in my business, and accepting that really I'm an entrepreneur; and immediacy, I can't invest in myself because I have dependants clamouring for my support and bills to pay.'

She was thoughtful while digesting his response, and then tentative in her suggestion. 'I don't know whether you know, but my father owns a substantial publishing company. And he's a sweetie. If I ask him he would give you a job. Nothing very elevated, but perhaps suitable for you: local, and with flexibility on working hours, so you can attend to your very many concerns. Would you mind me helping you in this way?'

He said, 'Yes. That is, no. I wouldn't mind. I'd be very grateful.'

'Good. How much do you need to earn? Be realistic and don't put it too low.' He told her and she wrote it down.

He was embarrassed. He had spent all this precious time bleating on about his problems. But she disarmed him. He looked. Beyond this delight, this pleasure in looking, and in being observed, was a keeper of rare pleasures. Rachel stood as if before a gate, a barrier which she had erected, now slightly open, but not at this moment for passage. Roger knew himself to be privileged. He was immensely impressed. Tongue-tied. He had paid and they were standing outside, on the pavement. Panic swept him. She was leaving, would be lost to him. Rachel continued to hold his arm. Then she said, 'Roger, be calm. It's a beginning. I'm very pleased to have met you and I know that in the end, perhaps not too far in the future, everything will work itself out for the best. Think of me as a friend. You have my goodwill. You will always have it, whatever, from now on.' She kissed him gently on both cheeks, and walked away from him without looking back.

Rachel lived up to her word. He was offered a job as a regional book salesman selling to bookshops and libraries in the eastern counties. The hours were flexible, he would be trained, but as her father's sales manager had said, 'An experienced businessman like you will have no problem', and the salary was exactly what he had asked for and needed.

The last message on the tape had stunned him. 'This is David Droylsden. Don't hang up. I think we should talk, and if you call me back we can arrange a time.' Roger had agonised over his reply. He felt sure that it was naught for his comfort and even dangerous. If he went, the choice of venue would be important. Should he be accompanied by a friend or a solicitor? The conversation would need to be taped. Roger agitated himself about it, but in the event curiosity got the better of him, and after carefully outlining to David what he would need to have attended to in order to ensure his safety, he arranged to meet him at the venture capital company; at Anthony Valentine's office in Clerkenwell, the viper's nest, where he had been badly bitten and given up for dead some months earlier.

CHAPTER 11

I N THE OCCASIONAL clash between financial interest and morality, as David Droylsden saw and understood it, there was never any doubt as to outcome. Despite all the difficulties of proof, of the necessary evidence, he had no doubt that in some way Roger Greer was responsible for the death of his son, and that the transgression had to be punished. But now he had to deal with him in another way. Enough time had elapsed for the new owners of what was essentially Roger's old company to conclude that it was not going to be a success: it was not going to yield the return on investment that they were looking for, in the timely way they had categorised for it. The responsibility for action lay with Anthony Valentine, and he had summoned David to his presence and told him what he wanted him to do. David was to explore whether, and in what way, Roger might be persuaded to assist the new company to move forward. David had been told that if possible Roger's ideas should be extracted from him without fees or commitment, for people like him, intellectual and enthusiastic, could usually be tempted to sound off and to be indiscreet in some way.

'Why me? I'm the last person he's likely to talk to about such things.'

'You're wrong about that. You are the depository of most of what he feels about us. If he's to talk to anyone, it is to you.'

Anthony was adamant. David was reluctant. Anthony spelt out the alternative options and David agreed to do his best. So against his will and better judgement he had extended the invitation to Roger, and had prepared for the meeting.

Roger was ushered into a meeting room, complete and curiously unused, and David made an entry. There was no handshake but hands were shaking. It was a striking contrast: David self-made, dark haired but greying, florid in manner and dress, with Savile Row suit and hand-made shoes and an abundance of gold ornamentation; and Roger neat and contained, young-looking and charming when relaxed, in Marks and Spencer clothes and with no ornamentation whatsoever: the first demanding that you stayed out of his way, while the other invited your interest. The sophisticated young receptionist who provided the tea was expeditious in serving David, and took too long, appealed too much, in serving Roger.

David's anger, painful, rising as a mist and confusing him, robbing him of his usual bearings, was almost too much for him. For some moments he said nothing. He stared at Roger, discomfiting him, until Roger, unable to avert his eyes, felt obliged to speak first. 'I'm here as you requested. What do you want to say to me?'

He was brusque. 'I have a business proposition for you. Not mine but Anthony Valentine's. Orbit isn't going too well and Anthony offers you a chance to make a contribution. I'd like to discuss some issues with you and get your input; then, if Anthony's convinced, we could offer you a consultancy assignment to implement some matters. I'm sure you wouldn't wish to see the efforts you've made over twenty years go down the drain.' David paused and Roger was silent. 'But before we continue I'd like you to answer a plain question. Did you have anything to do with my son's death?'

Roger remained silent.

'For if you were involved, in any way, and assuming the police can't prove a case, I'd need to make sure you were punished for it.' He meant that he would have Roger killed, but as Roger was recording the conversation he felt the need to constrain himself.

Roger looked at him with something like contempt. 'Is that it? Is that what you want to talk to me about?' He began to rise, and David beckoned as if to stop him. Roger sat down again and responded. 'Twenty years as a consultant, David. Here's the first principle: to define a client's problem will cost nothing, but to provide an answer will cost him. But first you pose a question to yourself. Would I work for such a client as Anthony Valentine? And my answer to you is no.' He continued, 'As for your son, naturally I'm sorry he died. Anyone who knows anything about me knows that I wouldn't hurt a fly. Thankfully I'm not answerable in any way to you.'

He got up again. David restrained him once more, standing between Roger and the door. 'At least discuss it with Anthony. Money may not be everything, but what it isn't it can buy.'

He laughed at his own joke. But Roger, not sharing his sense of humour, disregarded the suggestion and left.

David composed himself a little, for his relationship with Anthony did not permit setbacks, and he had to contrive a more acceptable position. He made some notes, inventing Roger's responses to the unanswered questions so that his thoughts might carry the authority and novelty of being passed off as Roger's. For the moment this would suffice. As for his son's murder, he assumed Roger guilty; a refusal to answer, the refuge of silence, implying guilt.

Roger was amused and pleased the company was in trouble. He had a job and they could stuff their money. But he knew that David did not believe him, and his pleasure did not outlast the thought.

David was not often downcast, and in the jargon, thinking of himself as a winner, he was hardly capable of dealing with failure. He had put a brave face on it but as he sat there inventing his draft for Anthony, he was cast down by an overwhelming desolation and not to be moved on by any act of abnegation. He was adrift on a sea of doubt without his usual means of rescue. Desperately he tried to keep the discordancies at bay, but reason, his sense of rationality, which had always served him well, as a dyke breached, could not hold the darkness from flooding in. There had been no time for grief: for a son, suddenly and brutally removed from this life; and for a wife, lost to him, somewhere unknown to him, a place where he had no right of abode. Others, perhaps his daughter, knew where Esther was to be found but they did not care to tell him; and he was too proud, mulish, to persist in his questions. All his life he had known how to define issues, to ask questions and recognise the correct answers; and now the only questions that might be of use to him defied articulation, unformed words cast away by the fear of answers he had never contemplated.

The idea of killing had grown with him, firmly lodging itself, now irremovable: no longer a matter of fantasy and horror, but a thrilling reality, akin to a sexual adventure which you had promised yourself and now anticipated. He shook his head but the thought could not be dislodged. At some time he surmised this idea, grub-like, would work its rotten way to a surface and become obvious to everyone. When he woke in the mornings, his desires had spawned in the night, and had become in the absence of other certainties, the dynamic that moved him, got him on his way, and became the justification for his time and motion. The object of this passion had stood before him, in flesh and blood: but the exposure of notions to human reality had not served to disturb his passion, but to feed it. He disliked the man who had stood before him, despising with all his heart what he thought of as privilege and the conceit of intellect and learning. He was annoyed by what he perceived as a unseasoned softness: by the absence of any hardening by experience of life on the streets. All his life he had thrived on a contempt of otherness, and he resented the need to compromise it. But what disturbed him most at this moment of setback was his self-judgement, his feelings about himself: he was no longer able to contain his feelings, his rage at otherness, and the inadequacy of his responses to it.

Living without Esther. Perhaps dealing with these foreign passions without Esther, not the fact of Garth's death alone, was his problem. The need to mourn for her without any reality of closure. The pain was acute and the loss suffocating. For some time he had felt her near him, still part of his life, his consciousness of it. He would see her in doorways, in places they had visited together; he had stopped perfect strangers in the street and endured the discomfort of false identity; and once when he had left the radio on in the kitchen he could have sworn that coming to it, she was there, that the sounds and smells were Esther's.

When he had completed his invention, typing it himself, and had passed the copy on, he felt normality had been restored. But what he had to discover, and ultimately, to do, was self-absorbing and crowded out other preoccupations. He decided to request an informal meeting with Bob Churchill-Jones. To his surprise, Bob had agreed to meet him later that evening, away from the office, and in the informality of a pub of David's choosing.

Meeting this policeman in pub surroundings did not inhibit David. He was resolute, determined to get to the bottom of the police investigation, and to form a better judgement of whether their enquiries would get anywhere. Bob had a purpose of his own: to find out more about David's enemies, to get him loosened up, inveigle him to say things under the influence of a little alcohol that would not otherwise have found a voice.

By normal rules of engagement Bob should have been accompanied. Alec would have been the natural choice. But he decided to go on his own, for increasingly he did not wish to be bound by police rules, feeling them tighten against him. But there was more to his growing independence than that: he no longer wished to be in pursuit, in any hunt whatsoever, preferring to lope away to pastures new, where if the inquiry had any priority for him at all, it would have found a natural and random place. Nevertheless old habits died hard with Bob, and he stirred himself to his task.

He had to tell David, in the best of all possible ways, that the various lines of enquiry had led nowhere. It was true that the identification of Gerry O'Callaghan, the IRA Provo, as a former employee of Roger Greer was promising; but all their inquiries, and the efforts of the Irish Garda and Interpol, had so far led to nothing. Gerry O'Callaghan had disappeared from the face of the earth, indeed he might literally have met that fate, being underground so to speak.

David thought policemen should avoid making jokes; they were usually uncalled for, and invariably of very poor quality. David was told not to concern himself, for wanted people turned up all the time at ports of entry and at random moments in their lives when officialdom became involved. If O'Callaghan turned up, Bob would make sure that David was informed.

After the starter of a stiff whisky, David had stuck to orange juice, and didn't loosen up. And after the initial fascination, for the unknown appealed to him, Bob quickly lost interest in David. Disliking him, and with his addiction to duty in a process of rehab, Bob's questions were desultory. He began to think of other things. He thought of Andrea and whether it might be fun to learn Italian, and what actions he could take to slow her down without discouraging her absolutely. He had no concern, at that moment at least, for the contradictory nature of these thoughts. Gloria had called him, on the excuse of talking about their daughter, their surviving mutual interest, to express surprise that he had not visited her recently; and then admitting to him quietly and with conviction, so that he believed it, that she missed him. She had a way of telling him these things at key moments when he was in a state of volition, and they had always been charged with the power to arrest him. But he had become conscious of her powers, and he wondered in a perfectly straightforward way whether she could be believed any more; and indeed whether she should ever have been believed.

While these thoughts were consuming for Bob, his attention to them was annoying to David, who soon tired of the vacuum they created. Without the usual acceptable courtesies of closure, David drew the discussion to a halt, rose abruptly, and left the pub. He fumed. What rubbish the Metropolitan Police had become. Honest citizens were reduced to tackling crime and criminals themselves. That was what it boiled down to in the end.

Bob accepted Gloria's invitation; then, emboldened, he rang an astonished Roger and left the message for him which led to their meeting at the inn. He shouldn't have done this. It was maverick behaviour, which in earlier days he would have reprimanded a subordinate for; but there was an exhilaration in it, this ignoring of the rules, and on his journey east he felt himself to be riding away to the blue hills of Montana and to its sinking roseate sun, and he found himself singing the 'lonesome blues'.

Gloria was very nice to him. She looked wonderful. Every time he said this to himself, and always he truly meant it. And every time, or so it seemed to him, she was more delectable. When living with her he had not felt this way about her, and perhaps, he ruminated, she hadn't been quite so alluring to him. Although he was tired and had been drinking a little, Gloria had shared her bed with him on the Friday evening. She prepared for going to bed and he saw that in her mind she had given consideration to certain erotic effects. Lovemaking was different. Now in these intimacies, Gloria took the initiative and remained in control throughout. In their long married life it had not been like that: Bob was used to being in command, as a strict adherent to the missionary position. It had been good. He was sure of it. Gloria had never complained.

The change of tactics was not entirely satisfactory to him, even assuming that it might be something he could get used to. In some ways he felt that Gloria was experimenting, that it was a rehearsal for something. He preferred to think of it in this way, for if not, she had surely learnt it in ways that were more disturbing to him; a contingency he dreaded to contemplate. Of course, she might have picked it up from women's magazines. He sometimes stole a look at these magazines, and in between the articles about the latest cooking recipes and the agony aunts (which he always read), they were full of advice on sex. All those housewives reading about 'how to please your man in bed' and 'one hundred and one ways to turn your man into a sex slave'. Were the women of England putting this advice into practice? Your mind boggled. Had Gloria been reading these articles? It was not that Bob was complaining. The advice, and in his case the sex, were very good. Of course it was. But somehow it had nothing to do with him.

He knew that these encounters could be worse. There was his experience with Andrea. Making love to Andrea required a higher level of fitness than he had reached for some time. It was an assault too on the senses which owed nothing to articles in *Cosmopolitan*. Vroom. She was on top of you demanding action from the start, urging you on, laughing and talking to encourage you, and then proceeding at a rising pitch, like a jet engine, to the triumph of take-off. On the first occasion, he thought he had been raped, and it had taken several days before he recovered. Even now, when he had succeeded in persuading her of the desirability of a change in the ground rules, he approached these encounters with a sense of foreboding. He thought that experimentation with Andrea could lead in his weakened circumstances to a premature death.

Over this weekend he was to discover that for Gloria, once was enough. Though he had timidly sought a further encounter, Gloria showed no interest. It appeared that she had re-staked her claim to Bob to her own satisfaction, and that nothing further was needed or to be encouraged. These thoughts of Gloria's motives were not entirely fair or generous. At least she had enjoyed the sex, and had emerged from the event flushed, and even ecstatic; but there was more on Gloria's mind than Bob, important though he was to her, and her imagination dwelt elsewhere.

Bob approached the meeting with Roger in a more relaxed state of mind. Gloria joined them at the outset, using what he detected as new social skills and an acquired ease in relating. He observed that Gloria greeted Roger with an affectionate familiarity, and that they enjoyed each other's company. He half-wondered, but only to dismiss the thought, that there might be something physical between them; but quickly concluded it to be no more than friendship and enjoyment of each other's company, although goodness, he thought, how important were these qualities given the naughty world of his daytime hours.

Gloria moved away and left them to it. There was an awkwardness between them at the beginning, a stiffness on his part and a diffidence in Roger: but soon they were easier, finding neutral ground that engaged them both. Then, warmed by the surroundings and the beer, they found a certain empathy: so that Gloria, observing them from afar, could relax, seeing them in animated and friendly conversation.

Roger allowed himself to be encouraged to talk about his children, and Bob saw how deeply he cared about them, how keen was his sense of loss, and how painful it was for him to be deprived of their company. Later Bob, although hesitant, found himself talking about his religious beliefs and how consoling and helpful it was for him to be able to pray quietly in such a beautiful and ancient place of worship as St Ethelreda's, where the walls themselves seemed to have absorbed the prayers and entreaties of the troubled over many centuries; and where it was not to fanciful to imagine that the very place had in some strange way embedded God's answers. Bob was embarrassed, never having spoken this way to any other human being, and Roger was quick to signal his sympathy, and in some way his support. Then Bob, reversing the role he had imagined and rehearsed for this engagement, spoke about Gloria; how very much he had missed her, grieved for her, and his doubts about his strength to go on in this way – hoping beyond hope.

Gloria, approaching them in order to pass, saw Roger hold Bob's arm, and the image of it remained with her, so that on her passage back she ruffled his hair and kissed the nape of Bob's neck.

Roger gave ground, in fairness, in his awareness that he had said too little. Prompted by Bob's concern with what might be considered to be the good, he ventured a discussion of what might be assayed as evil. He spoke of David Droylsden and the way he had managed to seize control of his company. It was a comprehensive account, for there was something about Bob that encouraged factual and detailed statements. Without understanding all the technical, financial and regulatory considerations involved in Roger's account, but by asking sensible questions out of his ignorance, Bob succeeded in getting a clear understanding of the events that had led to Roger's ousting from the company. Bob thought that for most people, and certainly in the courts, there was a tendency to regard truth as a matter of perception: and how tired he was of having to repeat his maxim that where the courts were concerned it was never primarily a matter of the truth of a proposition, but the plausibility of the evidence, and of course the final trip-wire – the law of the land.

Over his lifetime Bob had seen many crooks. If he was pressed to a judgement, he would conclude that David Droylsden was a natural but careful villain and that Roger was an honest man. But although honest, he might have broken the law. That was the point really. Honest men, under intolerable pressures or through carelessness, did break the law, and they had to be arraigned for it: the prisons were full of honest men who had fallen foul of their emotions and the law, and it was his duty to shuffle them forward – although, thank God, not to judge them.

They were well cooked now. Bob looked at his new-found friend with an earnest intensity. He found words. 'Roger, I think you're all right.' He stared at him, peculiarly, seeking expression for emotions that were strange to him, with only the familiar words at his disposal. 'You should tell me. Tell me now.'

Roger was amused, but conscious that this was not a time to weaken in resolve or to abandon reticence. He asked a question.

'Tell you what? If I can tell you anything, Bob, I will. I certainly will.'

Bob got the words out. 'This killing, this death of Garth Droylsden. Tell me. Tell me now. Did you have anything to do with it?'

Roger laughed, but not entirely convincingly. It was the second time in a few days that he had been asked this question. It must be catching. Although under the influence, he had the wit to answer carefully – still to chose his words. 'I can tell you, Bob, that I had nothing whatsoever to do with the killing of Garth Droylsden. Categoric. Nothing to do with his killing. I'm sorry about it. I certainly didn't wish to do him any harm.'

Bob heard him. He would have liked to believe him. Perhaps he did believe him: but in the end it was evidence that would count and not his belief.

Gloria was greatly relieved. The meeting could have gone disastrously wrong, and she had been worried about it. She supposed that these two men were the most important in her entire world at the moment, and she did not wish harm to come to either of them. Much about her new life greatly pleased Gloria, but she could not quite believe that it had turned out to be so good. So much was solid: but then there were shadows, presentiments of darker days, and a living on the edge of things. She could not bear the thought that bad things might happen to either of these men, and now that they were connected, and their fates in some way joined, she believed that they might both be harmed. But for the moment the meeting was a success, and she fussed over them both to show that she cared – and then made sure that her husband was put to his bed.

Roger drove carefully back to his cottage. He hated the thought that he was returning to an empty house. He tuned into a radio repeat of *Science Today*, to the middle of a programme on the significance of recent developments in quantum physics. He realised that this programme was pitched at a level at which he should be able to get something from it, that understanding it was not intended to be limited to boffins. He concentrated, straining his drink-befuddled senses. From the discussion he gathered that a concentration on atoms alone had given way to the consideration of the behaviour of waves, and that the behaviour of these waves was unpredictable, leading to doubts about the exact nature, as previously understood, of matter and time, and adding to the historic difficulty of proving the second law of thermodynamics. At least it was something like that, he thought, and perhaps they would repeat it again when he was fully sober. But what he thought he understood greatly cheered him.

Since his disgrace, or disgraces if he was going to be wholly honest, and after listening to Bob, he realised the importance of having an aspiration. He had revisited Freud. Now these two mighty illuminations were shining in the same direction – he adjusted the steering and slowed down after coming a little too close to the ditch by the side of the road – throwing new light on the human condition, on his circumstances. You could no longer think of people as hard and impenetrable objects, like atoms: it was all much more fluid than that. People did not bump into each other. 'How strange it is to bump into you', they would say to each other. But in the wider sense they were wrong. It wasn't like that at all. People leaked into each other. He was really cheered by the notion. There was Bob who, despite being a policeman, was a really nice and loving man, more loving, a better person than Gloria; and his goodness leaked into her and Gloria became a better person for it. No wonder she could not entirely give him up.

Rachel's goodness leaked into her children, he felt sure of it, and he supposed that Melissa's did also with their own: perhaps all good mothers had that capacity, to leak goodness into their children. Of course, it must work the other way around: evil leaked also, badness could flow. He couldn't think of an example. He was getting really fuddled now, but was anxious to persevere. Was he suffering from the Manichean heresy: that is, the belief that good and evil actually exist in the world, that they are physical entities at war with each other for the possession of human souls? No. He didn't mean that. And how could a non-theological person be guilty of heretical belief, anyway? Heresy was for believers. What he meant was not that 'goodness' and 'evil' in the world were absolutes but that they were catchable qualities that flowed between people. He was back now and hurrying to bed. Soon he would be asleep and the half-captured truths of a drunken state would be lost. He tried to summarise his position before his senses were lost. People leaked into each other. This characteristic of human relationships was more manageable than the collision of atoms, more hopeful, and could be a matter for rejoicing. There must be laws for it, explanations, decipherable truths – but lost to him now.

CHAPTER 12

MORALES AND WISEMAN had been hard at it. Notices had been served and motions for discovery sought, some of which had been opposed and had required court hearings and subsequent orders, which had time limits to be kept. Affidavits had been sworn, and solemn undertakings had been given that the information contained in them was the whole truth. When asked by Roger, who had expressed his amazement at the material produced by his opponent, Morales indicated that the petitioner was producing very solid evidence of hardship and that he, Morales, feared for his client, whose evidence seemed shaky. Morales did not doubt Roger's penury, for his client's slowness in paying his bills, despite verbal and written exhortations, was eloquent enough evidence for him; but no evidence at all, alas, for a court.

All the hopes and best intentions of the parties had been swept away now that the contest had been joined: and whatever reticences and inhibitions they may have had at the outset were now to be set aside in the excitement of conflict. Not that it was their excitement, for now as they gathered in the court waiting room, carefully corralled against each other with a praetorian guard mounted to ensure no fraternisation, they were quite downcast. The hearing was held in a judge's chamber, which while giving a superficial appearance of informality, with the parties seated on opposite sides of a long table and a judge at its apex, lacked the one essential feature of a fair trial: without the presence of the public, justice could not be seen to be done, and a vital safeguard of judicial proceedings had been removed. It was also a feature of these proceedings in the Family Court that an appeal against a judgement was increasingly difficult, and even if obtained was curtailed in scope and grounds. Moreover this was not the type of disputation in which historical precedent and case law were given much weight, the 'silver vein of discretion' being the rule. Thus when these features and the adversarial nature of the proceedings were taken into account, great power lay with the judge: and a moment of error made by a litigant, or incompetence on behalf of a lawyer, could be disastrous and without the possibility of remedy.

Roger looked along and across his table. Beside him sat Morales, whom he had learnt to respect as an honest journeyman, but a journeyman at that. Opposite sat his wife, her solicitor and his assistant, and Counsel. She had brought Counsel with her – it was news to him – a small and officious practitioner called Doughty, who from the very beginning was cracking insider jokes with the judge, who seemed to appreciate them as being a pleasant discourse between fellow and learned members of the same fraternity.

Roger admired his wife's outfit. Attuned to the need for performance, her appearance had been judged to a nicety. She was dressed in a sober black suit which succeeded in looking a little shabby and well-worn while not detracting from a certain elegance. The suit was buttoned down to reveal a crisp and modestly embroidered white blouse which revealed a little, just a little, of two full and shapely breasts. Later when she became agitated these modest jewels rose and fell so as to command attention and sympathy. Roger thought that they had always commandeered his attention, so why not the focus of the judge? Her hair was drawn back in a becoming and glossy bob. Eva Peron, the Madonna version, he thought: is she going to sing? He wasn't sure. She might; he really thought she might.

She avoided his gaze, eyes drawn down to her papers with which she fiddled. How sad it all was, he thought. For many years he had loved this woman with what he had always recognised as a rare romanticism. Of course, all true romanticism ends in sadness, and this one had certainly dribbled to a terrible halt. At the same time, he and this woman before him had been able to stay together, act in harmony, to save their daughter by acts of imagination and courage. They had hugged each other for that, and for a moment had renewed their unspoken alliance; a solidarity of the spirit, which recalled high-days and happiness. How quickly it had all been dissipated. She knew from that sobering experience they had shared, she must know, that he had no money and poor prospects: but here she was, in all solemnity, steeling herself to argue, or to have argued for her, the contrary view.

As he looked he remembered a holiday in Portugal, after a period of considerable personal strain, day after day of glorious sunshine with an aquamarine sea as far as the eye could carry; and how she had been thought of as Portuguese so that local people chattered away to her in their own tongue, sometimes not realising her otherness at all. Towards the end she had told him she was pregnant. Those were the days when they had been able to find a sheltered place in the dunes and make love in celebration. Seeing him continue to look, she glanced up and smiled at him. She knew what he was thinking about, and when she cared enough to consider it, she had always known.

'If the sun is in your eyes, Mrs Greer, we can draw the blind.' The judge intervened. She nodded. 'Would you help us with that?' He spoke to Doughty, who obliged.

Doughty presented Melissa's case at considerable length. As Morales had indicated, the evidence of her poverty was overwhelming. There were her bills, the majority of which she had great difficulty in paying, and all so reasonable. There was evidence of her income, all so carefully prepared by responsible accountants and with neat computations of the tax due, which, alas, had not been paid for reasons of penury. There were statements of monies lent to Roger at moments of financial need: precious monies, from her deceased mother's estate, the repayment of which was long overdue, and in all probability these monies were lost forever. Wiseman, acting with the benefit of Legal Aid, but in practice putting in far more time than could be recovered from the Lord Chancellor, had identified and quantified all these sums.

The judge took careful notes and was interested in the figures, which he seemed to be adding up. Morales took more general notes and muttered to Roger from time to time. Roger fumed.

Morales was shaken. The court could observe it, for his hands were trembling and his voice unsteady. It was worse than Morales had imagined, and was prepared for, or could deal with now. Morales asked some clarifying questions which seemed to be inconsequential. The judge fidgeted, wanting to get on with it. Roger scribbled a note and thrust it before Morales who, half-looking, ill-comprehending, changed ground.

Was it not true, asked Morales, that over a period of twenty years Roger had generously supported her and the children, giving them by his own efforts a very high standard of living, providing the best of education for the children, at the best of fee paying schools? And was it not true also that he had financed her through her very difficult profession, through periods of high expense and low income, and that no man could have done more for her?

It was true and it was admitted.

And was not marriage intended to be support in good times and bad, and that when the ship capsized, everyone went down with the ship?

Puzzlement was expressed by the other side. The judge was irritated, and could stand it no longer. 'Mr Morales, you should know better. These general statements about the past are no use to us now. What we have to do is to consider the responsibilities of the parties in the present . If you have no more relevant questions....' His voice tailed off.

'No more at this stage, sir.' said Morales. slumping down.

And what other stage could there be? thought Roger, knowing the answer.

Roger had to admit that from that moment of closure by Morales everything fell away for him. He did his very best to explain his financial circumstances: how being wrecked he had found himself clinging to the wreckage; that the exact financial position was not easy to explain. Yes, he admitted that the Inland Revenue had mounted an investigation into the tax he had paid over the last four years, although whatever their estimate, the payment of any agreed sum was caught up in his voluntary arrangement with creditors. He told the court about his new job and the basis of his remuneration.

As he went on it was obvious that he was not believed. Doughty asked him to reveal to the court all his undisclosed investments and bank accounts. There were none. Roger pointed out that he had made a declaration in an affidavit before the court. Doughty shrugged his shoulders. What was the worth of a declaration from a known liar such as Roger? On and on went Doughty. Did he have an account with Lloyds, with Barclays, with the Midland, in the Channel Islands, anywhere else abroad? The answer was always in the negative. Roger stated that his bank statements were before the court. Any unprejudiced person could see that these accounts showed considerable financial pressure. If it was, as Doughty maintained, that he had money elsewhere, wouldn't he have used some of this, transferring it into his account to ease the pressure? The judge did not bother to make a note. Roger pointed out to the court that his wife's income was greater than his own, and that he was paying the mortgage on the family house. The judge paused, as Roger watched him, before deciding not to write. The session ended on an unhopeful note, with Doughty expressing his contempt for Roger, without intervention by the judge, who stated calmly that he would give them his judgement on the following day.

Back in his own small cottage, prostrate on his bed, Roger exposed himself to his own judgement. Was he no longer honest? Had he deceived himself over all these years in believing himself to be so? Of course poverty was bad for the character, whatever anyone said to the contrary. Not that poverty would justify dishonest behaviour or the self-righteous reasoning which assumed that the world owed you a living, a certain standard of living, some unquantified expectation. But it was not that. Perhaps it was becoming a businessman, an activity which was at best amoral? Or was it narrower than this – selling? He had been obliged to develop selling ability as part of his job, which was contrary to the best in his nature, and he thought of others. Ordinary decent people hated sales techniques even when they were flattered by them. And if you started on that trail it was not easy to leave off when you left the office. He had seen the judge wince at some of his answers, his longing for a straight yes or no. Of course, that was a conceit of the judge; the belief that complex issues could be reduced to such certainties. Looking back, would his life had been happier if there had been no dissimulation, no white lies? He thought of some of those moments, when the 'truth' might have been considered an issue, whether to tell the strict truth, 'the whole truth and nothing but the truth', even assuming that there was such a thing and you could articulate it. And if discourse was to be limited to subjects and statements when you could prove your assertions the world would fall into a God-almighty silence.

The truth, or rather what could be demonstrated according to the rules, was however an issue for Judge Bircham. He was not any judge, but a particular one. For twenty-five years he had served on this bench, his judgements not so profound as to merit promotion, even the filling of dead men's shoes, nor so perverse as to trigger the dreaded retribution from the Lord Chancellor's Office. In practice, no doubt for the most admirable of reasons, it was difficult to dismiss a judge. Bircham had become his own man, and with the passage of time this 'becoming' had rendered him brusque with time wasters. He was known to be short-tempered and to shout at people of whom he disapproved, and to bend the law in the direction of his temper – to give tempered judgements. He thought the truth did matter and he didn't believe Roger. Opening his judgement, which he had written out very carefully in his own hand, and in green ink, Bircham said that he found the evidence raised a number of important issues of some complexity, but that it would not help anyone if he spent time in dwelling on them, because in essence it all boiled down to whether the petitioner was to be believed or not.

Did it really, Roger thought? Was it as simple as that?

Bircham said that on the one hand he had listened to Mrs Greer, who had made a very favourable impression on him. Her evidence had been meticulously prepared and documented, and it revealed without any doubt that she was hard pressed financially, and that Mr Greer's financial incompetence, and he would leave it at that although more might be said, had left her in a parlous position. Moreover, she had stood loyally by her husband as his business position weakened, lending him money from her limited capital, perhaps unwisely, although out of care for her husband, which by his profligacy he had lost. Then on the other hand there was Mr Greer's evidence.

He paused. He had no doubt that Mr Greer had suffered considerable financial loss and that his agreement with creditors was proof of this. But was that the whole truth about his financial position? He thought not, and in this conviction he agreed with the petitioner. It was his opinion that Mr Greer was not wholly honest with the court and that his financial position was considerably better than he chose to reveal in these proceedings. Moreover, even if this were not the case, he regarded Mr Greer as being a survivor and not a castaway. In giving his evidence before him he had noted that Mr Greer displayed an impressive grasp of his position, and indeed of business generally. He had little doubt that despite his age he could come again, in contrast to Mrs Greer, whose singing career would necessarily be limited by her age. He took into account that Mr Greer had come to an accommodation with his creditors, but this agreement, in his judgement, had no bearing on the issues before him: again, if anything to the contrary, for the agreement acted to limit Mr Greer's future indebtedness.

The judge continued that Mr Greer had not helped his case by dissimulation under questioning and he would have been better advised to be strictly truthful and frank. Taking all these issues into account he had decided to award Mrs Greer a lump sum payment of thirty thousand pounds, and that costs would follow the action, which for Roger would amount to a further eighteen thousand pounds. As to the practicality of such a judgement Bircham had nothing to say, it not being his problem. He refused leave to appeal and gave three months to raise the money.

But Bircham did have more to add, although it was not anything they had chosen to bring to his attention. He had noted that the house occupied by Mrs Greer, and owned by Mr Greer, was omitted from the agreement with creditors, and that Mr Greer had produced a deed of assignment giving the beneficial ownership of this property to a third party, not named in the proceedings before him, on the argument that without this person's financial assistance the house could not have been bought. He expressed his astonishment at the inequity of this arrangement, and while he could not deal with the matter in the proceedings before him, he stated his willingness to do so if it was properly put at issue.

So there it was. Down, down, and down the slippery slope. Morales muttered about the procedure for applying for the right to appeal, and that Bircham's word was not the last word. But for the moment Roger had no words of his own.

Others were hanging on to know the outcome. Roger's children heard the result with relief, for life was getting threatening and Adam's expulsion from school for non-payment of fees was looming – and other unpleasant things too, no doubt. And then their mother was awfully depressed and worried. Faith thought that her father could raise the money somehow, he had a gift for it, and his son Adam thought he would have to do so and it served him right.

Gloria had rung and had listened patiently while he had told her everything, as she demanded of him. She had sighed, offering him her sympathy, and had asked him to come over, pleading with him. He made an excuse.

Rachel just came. She had thought about him constantly for two days and finally, despairing of what she assumed, rightly, to be the worst, she came to see him, filling his sitting room for the first time.

Rachel held his hands in hers as he told his story again. She kissed him gently, this time with full lips which, while seeking him, held something back. He kissed her. They fell silent, then at her suggestion they took a very long walk together, during which they continued to hold each other while saying nothing more. Finding it cold, they sought shelter in a local pub where no one was interested in them at all; and they snuggled up to each other, pleading the cold in mitigation.

Rachel asked him, 'Do you have any chance of raising this money?'

He responded, 'No, I think not. I shall think about it, of course, but I really don't believe so.'

Rachel spoke very carefully 'Roger, don't be offended, but I want to help. Don't be too proud. I'm very rich you know, not by my own efforts, I can't say that, but because of the family. We're all very rich in our family. Let me give you the money. I shan't miss it and you need it. Let me do this for you.'

He could not be gracious. 'Rachel, it's a lot of money. It's very kind, but I could never pay it back.' Then, ruefully, 'And why, anyway, would you want to help someone like me whom you hardly know?'

'Look, Roger, you can be straight with me. You know why I'd do this for you, and you shouldn't ask me to spell it out for you. Look at it this way. To refuse me would be unkind because of the enormous pleasure it would give me to help. And you'd remain entirely free of any obligation. I'd just hate it to be otherwise.' Rachel leant across the small table with its smell of the decaying past, the cigarette ends and the spilt beer, and kissed him again, holding his head between her two elegant hands, which caressed and reached out for him, so that in the intensity of the moment there was nothing left in him that wished to resist her.

But that was all. For the moment there was nothing else. She got up to go, leaving him drained but without desperation. They stood together in the doorway. He knew that it was actually happening. That it was more than a start. 'Think of it', she said, 'as an act of goodwill.'

Roger told Morales that there was no question in his mind of an appeal and that for the moment he would do nothing other than to try to raise the money. He concentrated on his new job, determined to make a success of it, and being a talented and versatile salesman he did well and beyond the call of duty, for his ideas and comments, sometimes carefully quantified, were invariably shrewd and helpful to those above him. So when Melissa's father enquired of his progress he received back glowing reports.

Roger had a long conversation with his daughter Faith, his son being unwilling to talk to him, and succeeded in making her feel better about herself. Melissa witnessed her daughter's happiness and thought better of him for his efforts, although wondering about how he could summon the cheerfulness, and was grateful to him. Melissa decided to do nothing about the ownership of the house she occupied, despite pressure from Wiseman, who insisted that she had a very strong case. Wiseman argued that she was unwise, and that this was a moment when it was essential for her to take a hard line, where she should look to the future. He made a diary note to call her in a few weeks time when he hoped that by then she would have seen sense.

Later that week Melissa received a short note from her friend Luigi – for that is how she viewed him now – posted from Venice with a picture of the Opera House, and with a cheque for ten thousand pounds, which made her feel better about her financial future. She considered sending it back, not wishing to be compromised in any way, but then ten thousand pounds was not so large a sum that she would feel under an obligation, which she apprehended was very clever and knowing of him.

Wiseman informed Morales that his client had not yet decided to take any further action on the ownership of the house, but when he heard this Roger rang Melissa, and she told him she had decided against action. Morales, hearing it from Roger, rang Wiseman for clarification, and reluctantly Wiseman confessed that his client had decided to do nothing. Morales asked to receive this undertaking in writing, and Wiseman duly gave it. Roger was able to tell Melissa, to her very great relief and surprise, that he had been able to raise the money to pay the court settlement together with the costs. She did not ask him how he had achieved it, and he did not volunteer the information. Roger then paid Morales the fees he owed him with a promptitude which surprised him. These legal matters being so simply resolved, Morales was able to agree Wiseman's costs, and the Legal Aid Board promptly paid Wiseman. Thus flowing on from Rachel's love and goodwill, and the monies so shrewdly earned and preserved within her family for over a hundred years, all the matters before the principals involved, and which had engaged them so vociferously, were settled. Life could continue as before. Faith, pinning down Adam, on the phone said, 'There you are. I told you Daddy could do it.'

Roger told Gloria over the bar at the inn that he had been able to raise the money. She wondered about it, but delicately refused to press him on the details. She was just pleased for him – very pleased. But when she had wanted to talk about Rachel, thinking of him as a confidant, he shied away, and she was puzzled about this also. She wondered whether she had made a mistake with Roger. There was the problem with men that if you resisted an advance they took umbrage, their pride being involved. It might be that. Or he might not have liked the way she spoke about her feelings for another woman. God only knew it was a difficult subject. She grew agitated in thinking about it herself, and wondered about her audacity in raising this subject with Roger in the first place. She had not seen much of Rachel in recent weeks, and Rachel had not always returned her telephone calls.

But then the party was coming up and there was an opportunity to dress up and enjoy oneself. It thrilled her to think of it. She thought of what to wear and how she wanted to look, and quite forgot Roger.

But although it was the party that filled her imagination, the horizon was not cloud-free. There was Bob. Her daughter Susan, at their last meeting, had brought up the subject of Andrea. She had said, referring to a weekend she had stayed at his flat, 'It was nice to see that Dad's not entirely on his own.'

Gloria was quick, a feeling of alarm overwhelming her. 'What d'you mean, not on his own?'

'He has this friend, Andrea, a pretty and lively Italian lady from the delicatessen across the road. They're seeing each other. She's very good for him, takes him out of himself. Gets him going again.'

'Is it serious?'

' I really don't know. I only met her once. She was taking Dad to Convent Garden, to the Opera. Can you imagine that, dad at the Opera?'

She laughed happily, pleased for her father, so Gloria thought that the information might have been given without guile, that the intention was innocent and that Susan was unaware of the seismic tremor her words had set off.

Deprived of the chance to talk about Rachel, her first and favoured topic of conversation, Gloria took the first opportunity to talk to Roger about Bob. She found that talking about him helped her to articulate what she really felt: and then Roger was so helpful and constructive in how he led you on with these thoughts, showing sympathy and insight. Gloria told him about Bob seeing another woman, about Andrea, and that her daughter Susan approved of her.

'That's good isn't it? And that Susan approves.' Then, recovering from a bad start, 'And how do you feel about that? I had rather hoped that you two might get back together. I like Bob – not bad for a policeman!'

Gloria said she could not make her mind up. He mustn't misunderstand her, she loved her husband – and words in a similar vein.

Roger was unimpressed. 'It looks as if you'll have to make your mind up. If you really want him back you must get a move on.'

Gloria said 'Yes', and 'I suppose so. I should try harder to sort things out. He's been so very good to me.' But she meant that try though she might at this moment, in the present and as far as she could see ahead, she couldn't; and sadly, she could no longer tell Bob the reason.

Roger tried out his leaking theory. 'The very best characteristic of Bob's is his human generosity. He has a superabundance of goodness, so much so that it leaks from him into others. You're a better person for knowing someone like Bob. Amazing isn't it, me speaking like this about a policeman?'

She said to him that she knew it to be true.

CHAPTER 13

THE PARTY HAD been long postponed. In Rachel's mind it had been an idea. No more than to celebrate the ending of what had been a successful barn conversion, and a chance to consider with which few of her friends she might best enjoy the occasion. But she was reluctant to accept an end because this presupposed a new beginning. Of what? Consequently, she refused a finality by refining her vision of what the project was intended to fulfil, and delayed the ending of it by finding new things to do, so that it was never quite complete, never quite perfect – until her mother intervened to call a halt.

Mrs Janet Jackson was a formidable lady, well educated, lucid and forceful. Now in her late fifties, she remained an elegant well turned out female of the species. She was a 'county lady', riding to the local hunt and the chairwoman of many charitable organisations, all of which were pleased to have her and benefited from her extraordinary energy and organising power. Though she might have become one of those highly successful Conservative ladies that ornament local politics, she had the presence of mind and the confidence of a person of distinctive appeal; and so she dominated the political scene as an Independent, a person of influence who was not beholden to anybody.

Janet Jackson's idea of a modest celebration was somewhat different from her daughter's. Under her direction a large marquee had sprouted in the grounds and the variety and number of guests invited had grown. There were relatives and friends from disparate and far-flown places, which raised the issue of how they should be accommodated overnight; and a spreading out into the local community, partly because of the tradition of such social occasions, but also because of votes – as she would say, 'never underestimate the powers of patronage'.

At first Rachel protested, seeing her occasion vanish beneath the weight of something indifferent or even hostile to it; but relieved by the loss of her own problem of identity and purpose in this life, she allowed her mother her head, to the relief and pleasure of a great many people who would have thought very little of her ideas. Rachel's interventions, being few, were invariably accepted, and through the back door the local village jazz band made an entry, and a parade of nineteenth-century costumes and carriages was organised by Mrs Frewin, the local school history teacher, with the assistance of a Mr Carter who owned some rather smart stables a few miles away.

Her mother had been sniffy about Rachel's list of personal friends. 'Racy women,' she thought, 'without pedigree, but with plenty of pretension.' But she said nothing. She was curious about Roger, having heard something of him from her husband, and insisted on meeting him. Roger was invited to tea at the Grange, a pleasant Georgian country mansion which had been a family jewel for over a hundred years. Mr Jackson, Rachel's father, was on one of his frequent overseas trip to a book fair – there certainly seemed a lot of them – and so Janet had to perform her usual role as a general duty host.

Janet liked Roger and he was not indifferent to her. Janet was tempted to think that if it worked out that Rachel was not serious about this very handsome man, she might take an interest in him herself and invite him to lunch. She blushed at the thought of it, and for surprising herself. Her husband, Henry Jackson, while not entirely lacking in appeal and in the performance stakes, no longer saw his wife as an object of sexual passion, much as he liked her, and had acquired an eye for creatures more exotic and less overpowering. Being a wealthy and pleasant man, he was often able to command the attention he needed. As she stood beside this new man in Rachel's life, and as he paid her polite and careful attention, Janet felt a familiar if seldom used stirring, which to her relief signalled to her that she was not dead. Like many powerful people she assumed, quite wrongly in this instance, that her companion of the moment would share these feelings. Rachel, knowing these follies of her mother well, smiled at them both, and teased Roger about his appeal for older women. He disarmed her, glad that he had been a hit, and recognising the importance of achieving a good standing.

As Janet stood on the veranda steps of Rachel's very desirable residence, and looked across the verdant and manicured lawn, observing the first of the many visitors to arrive, disarmed by their very evident excitement and goodwill, she knew the occasion would be a success. She was glad of it, for not everything in her daughter's life had been outstanding. She was a very clever girl but had the most dreadful taste in men. The first husband had been very charming and all that, and had been helpful in producing two very desirable grandchildren, but what irresponsibility: wandering off to some God-almighty continent and contracting some dreadful disease, and then dying before anyone could do anything about it. As for the second, words failed her. What a monstrosity – and poor Fergus! And as for the current crowd of her friends! Well, all she could say was that you could do so much better, although one or two had their good points. It was so nice to see the children, very prettily dressed on this fine summer day, already trying out the stalls and queuing for ice cream, racing around these lawns enjoying themselves. If only grown ups could do that still.

Janet saw Rachel greeting people outside the marquee where the sounds of the jazz men practising could be heard. It was a long time since she had dressed so well: presenting herself at her best, in what she knew to be a very fashionable and befitting dress, becoming the attractive woman she had always promised to be. Janet noticed. It must be Roger. She felt a keen pang of jealousy about that, and reprimanded herself immediately to keep on top of the emotion.

At this very same time, Gloria looked out of a second-floor window at the lively and colourful scene beneath. She enjoyed this feeling, of being outside looking in, and she had read somewhere that this was the position of the artist in society. When she was very small, and had wanted to be noticed, she thought of herself as inside-out, but exposure to the antics of the Metropolitan Police over a very long time had changed all that. She had been dragged upstairs by Rachel's two daughters, Fiona and

Sophie, who had squealed with amazement when they saw how incredible Gloria looked. For someone who wanted to hide, it was unnecessarily splendid; for Gloria was wearing the most expensive designer dress she had ever purchased in a beautiful shade of violet, with hat and shoes to match. As the two girls claimed her, dragging her into the house, Rachel's Uncle George in passing said, 'Ooh la la', and pinched her bottom, which alarmed her for fear that unwanted dirty fingers might have stained her creation. But it hadn't, and the girls reassured her. Sophie played the violin for her and, although not an expert, Gloria could hear and feel the improvement in her playing. Sophie was at that tantalising stage when her playing might lead on to greatness, or stay on some entirely acceptable plateau of the very good musician. Greatness was all very well, thought Gloria, but it would mean a loss of Sophie to so many people who cared about her, who would be denied her presence in exchange for her playing – for her sound. Then Fergus came and busted it all up, and so they retired to this window and the sight below.

There were two types of force at work beneath them: a centripetal force which attracted people, mainly the oldies, into the marquee where they circulated in ever smaller circles; while a centrifugal force pushed people outwards to the stands, the house, the *Doctor Who* mobile toilets, and the bushes. In the centre, the conversation was of schools and ever-mounting fees, house prices, and whether Duncan's son would get back safely from the Gulf. The elderly stood helplessly on the surrounds, trying in vain to make themselves heard above the sounds of the jazz, while others moved steadily towards the food and the drink trays. Uncle Harry had designs on a small dark-haired plump waitress of tender years, whom he unwisely considered had given him the eye. He sought to manoeuvre her into a corner, but she was too agile for him and kept slipping away. 'Damn it,' he kept exclaiming, 'where is that girl, the saucy rascal?'

The racy women knew no overwhelming force, and moved towards the action wherever they could find it: but action was rare, and they rarely broke sweat. In the bushes ten year old Edna May earned twenty pence a turn for taking down her knickers and showing her bottom, but the small boys soon got tired of it and she didn't earn much. Simon, a gay friend of Rachel's, who considered himself an artist, would draw you for five pounds, and he attracted some gay friends who larked about on the edge of his booth and made jokes, sniggering behind their hands at some of the takers; although it was all very harmless and you couldn't really object.

From the second-floor window the shadows of the giant oak trees began to spread their fingers across the entire scene and the sounds of the delicious absurdity of people at play wafted in the air towards them as if signalling, beckoning them down to be part of it. But still they waited, secure in their heaven, part of it all although above it. Then hunger got to them and they joined the throng.

The horses and carriages had been lined up in a field at the bottom of Rachel's generous grounds where with the consent of her farming neighbour they could be displayed. It was a small display but in its way quite grand. The highly decorated carriages and the horses in special harness, with brasses and prize rosettes, were immaculately presented. But they were not inhibiting, and small children were encouraged to mount and to be given free rides around the field. These carriages had been winkled out of stables across the county, as they were on many a festive occasion, and represented something of a precious archive. Mrs Oldbury, who kept the local post office, although well into her eighties, who was admiring two mighty farm horses long since reprieved from work in the fields and specially groomed for the display, could be heard to exclaim that these horses and their accoutrements were better cared for than the humans who admired them, which was a turn in their fortunes; and a glance around at the older villagers present in the field gave substance to her theory.

Roger held his own in the marquee. Being a working-class lad in origin, he had experienced problems in adjustment to middle-class values and chit chat. Essentially, he wished to be direct and straightforward, and disliked the conventions of never quite saying what you meant and the elaborate codes that existed for achieving obliquity: but he had learnt to live with the conventions. And then there was the actual difficulty of his position: of explaining what had happened to him and what he was doing about it. As he was seen by some as becoming attached to Rachel, of being the man in her life, he came under an intense scrutiny from which he could not emerge entirely unscathed. It helped that Janet thought something of him, but as he circulated and she saw him not always at ease, she had her doubts. The unstated issue was, 'Is he one of us?', the answer to which could be, 'Who cares these days?' or 'Pity, perhaps not.' But he did his best, at a distance from Rachel, and in an effort to make nothing of it.

The Jackson family were High Anglican and the local vicar had been invited. The concordat between family and church was well established and critical to both parties. Church attendance was frequent although irregular; successive generations were baptised, confirmed and, it being ancient and sweet, married in the church. The family headed any appeal for funds, supported any church event, and sustained any incumbent: and for its part the church, through its incumbents, took a liberal view of family misdemeanours. The task before the vicar now was to assess the delinquencies that Roger, as a putative family member, might bring with him. Rachel, seeing his difficulties, had risen to the challenge and diverted the vicar with the urgent needs of another of his parishioners, although out of the corner of his eye Roger, breaking cover and out of the marquee, could see that the examination had been but postponed.

He decided to seek out Gloria, having seen an inviting glimpse of her earlier in the afternoon. At least you could talk to Gloria. And sure enough he found her on the veranda in close proximity to an engaging dark-haired girl with what appeared to be a genuine nineteen-twenties bob. Lucy smiled at him but edged her way at an angle to Gloria, implying a territorial claim, and an invitation to him to depart. He blithely ignored this by taking Gloria by the arm and leading her down into the garden.

She looked relieved.

'Are you all right?' he enquired, seeking an explanation.

'Oh yes, I'm all right'. She hesitated before him, wondering whether to confide, before deciding to offer an explanation. 'She's interested in me. And won't take no for an answer.'

He didn't know what to say, and then replied lamely, 'Of course she is. Any living person in their right mind would be.'

As they laughed together, the tension was diffused. But he wondered about it, thinking of Bob – and then of Rachel.

Later he caught up with Rachel over a cup of tea and a watercress sandwich. He told Rachel what he believed had happened. She did not seem disconcerted. 'Just like Lucy.'

'What do you mean?'

'Well, she's a very happily married woman, really, but she does so love a little excitement.'

'With other women?'

She was on dangerous ground now. 'It's safer with women – presupposing the need for excitement – you know, I'm sure you do – sexual restlessness.' She hesitated, blushing while she waited his response.

'And you? When you're restless, and need an adventure – some excitement – what do you do?'

'I don't need excitement in that way.' She was emphatic. At that moment she could be. And he half-believed her as she allowed herself to be swept away. She had escaped this time.

Their conversation was not the only indiscreet exchange to be heard, to be on view, that sunny afternoon as alcohol, sunshine and the presence of company loosened inhibitions. Rachel, observing the goings on, just hoped that this event, her event, would not be held responsible for the shenanigans: and when they all got home – and she was very fond of a lot of them – and had the chance to develop second thoughts, the pieces would come back into position. Of course men could be such fools. Surely Roger knew that if he wanted her there would be no others. But she wasn't worried about that, for she had every confidence that if this was going to happen she could very quickly reassure Roger about a lot of things, including her fidelity.

Around six o'clock people began to drift away, and the makeshift car park began to empty: young children were reaching their bedtime and the elderly, missing their afternoon naps, and tired by moving around in blessed sunshine, required their rest. Some of the relatives and the party goers, however, had hardly started: they shifted to the house, encouraging the jazz band – now well oiled – to follow suit. Soon there was a younger set rocking and rolling and generally enjoying themselves in the main hall of the barn. While Rachel continued to host the relatives, Roger and Gloria joined in the dancing: but not for too long undisturbed. Hurtling down the stairs and jigging his way across the dance floor, Fergus pulled at Roger's arms. His eyes shone with excitement and alarm.

'You must come – quickly – there's a naked man dancing in mummy's bedroom.' He was almost bursting. 'In her nightie. He's in her nightie.'

Roger glanced across the room where Rachel was speaking to her mother. At least, he thought he's not dancing with Rachel – and then recognising it to be an unworthy thought, he moved quickly up the stairs and others, overhearing the exchange, were quick to follow.

Fergus was right. Simon, the blond fortune teller, was dancing with a friend in Rachel's very best nightie. He wore a fetching pair of red boots with pointed toes in which he had come that day, and which up to now had engendered no excitement. He had used some of Rachel's make-up to good effect. Even Roger thought him rather fetching. Others cheered him on, wanting in some way to join in, but not knowing quite how, and then settling for dancing themselves and taking turns in dancing with him.

Roger saw Lucy stretched out on a chaise longue over two of the dancers' friends, pouring the remains of a champagne bottle into one of their glasses. Soon, very soon, this would all get out of hand. He began to tidy it all up, shooing the movers and shakers out of the bedroom and then grabbing the dancing pixie and pushing him into the bathroom. He locked the door, while he sorted out the pixie's discarded clothes. Shouts of 'Spoilsport' could be heard on the floor below, but acting quickly, he was able to shove the slowcoaches downstairs where they regaled the others with the stories of orgies on the upper floors.

By the time Rachel found herself upstairs, Roger had restored order. Janet's protestations were then difficult to maintain, because whatever it had turned out to be it was now no more. Still it confirmed her thoughts about the unreliability of Rachel's friends, and warmed her to Roger – she did so like a man to be in charge, to take over things. The event confirmed her in the belief that Roger was a man for the hour.

After these excitements it was not the same again – and of course it couldn't be – and the party began to break up. Ralph and Chloe, with a long journey ahead of them, needed to find Fergus, but he was nowhere to be seen. The girls denied all knowledge of his whereabouts. Fiona said that she was sure that he was all right, and when pressed, that she might have seen him go over the field down to the river. Sophie offered to go and find him, and sloped off with Fiona. They were a long time returning, and then without him. Tempers became strained, and Chloe began to shout and then to cry that she must get back. The adults conferred, and it was agreed that Fergus should stay on for a while, and that Rachel would return him in a few days' time. Roger and Chloe's silver sports car nosed its way out of the drive. Within minutes of their disappearance, Fergus manifested himself with a large grin and twigs, dirt and leaves all over him.

Fiona whispered to Roger, 'He was up a tree. Please, please talk to him and then talk to Mummy.'

'What about? What do you want me to talk to him about?'

'Roger and Chloe, they're just horrid to him. Get him to tell you. He'll tell you, and then tell mummy.'

Roger took Fergus to the bathroom and talked to him at length. There was no problem about talking and Fergus was difficult to stop. It just poured out of him. And it was a thoughtful Roger who tucked him up in bed and then found a tired Rachel on the veranda with fresh coffee for them both. It was a story of punishments, of being locked up in his bedroom for long periods of time; of being left on his own overnight, sometimes without warning or a message; of violence within the family and of the strange adult reconciliations that followed it. Fergus had told Roger that he did not want to go back; that he wasn't going back. Rachel went to see Fergus, to find him asleep.

On return she was livid. 'I shan't send him back.' She was white with rage. 'I was always wrong to abandon him, to give him to that man. Help me, Roger, help me.' She sobbed uncontrollably, with her head on his shoulder.

Of course he would help her. He stroked her hair and kissed her wet cheeks time and time again until she stopped crying, and they could kiss each other gently without the tears.

While all this excitement occupied Roger and Rachel, Gloria had become a spectator. She waited, all dressed up and with nowhere to go. Lucy sought her out and contriving a private place, kissed her, and when pushed away, returned and kissed her again until Gloria relented and kissed her back. Lucy had found a way of arousing her, by caressing her from behind, and despite herself Gloria found herself responding. She was in a state of rage and frustration. All this day she had waited for Rachel, for a time to be alone with her. And now at the end of this day, because of the antics of others, among whom she included Lucy, who had played her part, and now Fergus, she had found herself excluded until it was too late.

Gloria thought that she had never looked better, that she had never been better equipped, more prepared for a new adventure: that it had all led up to this moment, and now there was nothing but a dreadful anti-climax. And then there was Lucy doing strange things; and she heard herself moaning and then moving away with Lucy and receiving instructions from her. Lucy wanted them both to use her car, but Gloria hesitated. Some instinct for self-preservation, earned the hard way over the years, inclined her to leave in her own vehicle – and then if a car was left at Rachel's it would require an explanation for being there. Lucy gave way, urging Gloria to follow close behind. The two cars made their way down to the main road, and to a T junction. Lucy turned right. Gloria waited for a vehicle to pass by and then turned – left. She accelerated down the road in the wrong direction as fast as her dimmed wits permitted, back to the inn, up to her room, behind locked doors, with the telephone off the hook, her mobile turned off – and to safety.

It was a long time before Roger left. Rachel was distraught. Over all these years she had been unable to talk to anyone about her decision to give up Fergus, to give him to Ralph of all people. Even now she didn't know why she had done it. Perhaps she would never know. There was the unexpressed resentment at the loss of her first husband, for leaving her alone to bring up two girls; and the sheer effort of doing so. To love and care for these girls was something that might have been easy for many women, but not for her, it had been a mountain to climb. Roger reassured her about the girls: they were lovely, just wonderful and anyone could see what a tremendous success she had made of bringing them up. Yes. Yes. She knew it. But there was nothing left over for Fergus. And she cried some more. And there was her guilt at a loveless marriage with Ralph and the suppressed anger against his infidelities – for the stupidities of his behaviour. Afterwards she had been unable to love anything to do with Ralph; and to look at Fergus was to see Ralph, to remind her of the inglorious – her stupidity. Rachel talked and cried herself out, falling asleep at last in his arms, and allowing herself to be put into bed by him, and accepting his assurances of help.

Roger was as good as his word. He had never had any difficulty in acting, and he did so now, without delay. He arranged to see a surprised Ralph at his place of work – on Ralph's home ground – on the very next day. He explained to Ralph what had happened and what had been said, confronting the inevitable denials with brutality and contempt. He brought Ralph to a silence. Then, experiencing some evasion, he threatened him. Unless Ralph agreed to give Fergus up to Rachel, and to confirm this with the appropriate legal agreement, he would reveal all the sordid goings-on to Ralph's business partners and would report him to the Social Services Department of his local authority and to the NSPCC.

Ralph did not need to be threatened. He was going through the motions, with a decent display of self-pride. A man had to put up a good show. In his heart he was ashamed of what was going on. It was true. Fergus would be better off with Rachel and the girls. And if Fergus wanted it, why not? And so he agreed.

So Roger became a hero to Rachel and her three children. Maybe a flawed hero, and time would prove just how flawed; but in any event their hero – the only hero they had at that time. Rachel knew that there would be hard days ahead with Fergus. The past would not be lightly shrugged off, disposed of, but it was a beginning of something better. She had not exactly made amends for the sins of her past in relation to her son, but she had repented, and now – thanks to Roger – she could start to make amends.

As for Roger, he recognised that he had reached a moment in relating to Rachel when it was desirable to be completely honest with her; and then that it was more than a desirability; it was an essential prerequisite. He told her about the two police investigations to which he remained vulnerable. His confessions quietened her, and he feared that it might be too much – for her, for them – at this very delicate moment. But in the end she embraced him in a long hug, so that he knew it would be all right between them, and that it had been right to tell her everything – or almost everything.

Rachel said she would think about what was happening to him, and that she might have something to suggest. He knew her well enough to recognise that her strength of mind, her powers of imagination, might well prove to be decisive; and he was more than content to have such a true ally and friend.

CHAPTER 14

THE FUTURE SEEMED brighter to Roger. He had this wonderful girl as a friend, and perhaps in time something else: but in his lightening sky the dark clouds of the imminent legal proceedings against him loomed black, large and threatening. And like the weather it seemed that nothing could be done by him to alter events. He said to himself, he repeated it at all those times of weakness and doubt that assailed him, that he should concentrate on the immediate. He knew it was important to do all he could for his daughter: not to lose her by any carelessness or neglect, assuming Faith, languishing in a Swiss clinic, could be saved at all. The time was drawing near when he would go to the clinic to be told the results of the tests that had been conducted. As for Adam, his angrily buzzing son, all he could do was to hang on in there. Wasn't that what all parents had to do?

There was his work to occupy him, and this gave him the excuse, if one was needed, to spend time with Rachel, who had helpfully provided him with office space in the barn, with the most up to date computer and communications facilities. After a while the barn became home to him, and the direction that his car nosed out for him come high weather and foul. These two people had stolen up on each other, while remaining hesitant to become more than very good friends.

For Rachel it was a time to become closer to Fergus, to show him love, to give him the love she had so heartlessly denied him. She did nothing to excuse herself, and to Roger, at least, she could describe the impenetrable carapace that had enveloped her when the relationship with Ralph had degenerated into accusation and resentment. She wondered whether her repentance and Roger's help, which was genuine and wholehearted, would be enough to heal the wounds. She did not expect it to be easy, and perhaps Fergus would never wholly forgive her.

There was more to Rachel's reticence than concern for Fergus. She knew her relationships with her gay friends caused Roger some concern. He wasn't sure about her sexual orientation, and having been badly hurt himself he hesitated about her, not daring for fear of loss to question her deeply, and troubled by what she might tell him. It troubled her too. She liked her friends. They demanded nothing from her, were honest about matters that heterosexual couples lied to each other about, and they amused her. But then there was Gloria. She seemed to demand something, for the moment unspoken between them; and Roger knew something of that, although she did not know what, exactly. Rachel loved Gloria. She was her closest friend; loyal and understanding, witty and accomplished in her own way, which was a very comforting and loving way. But she was more than a friend. Why should she not say it to herself? She wished to be intimate with Gloria, finding the shape of her, the smell of her, her very essence, enticing and irresistible. There, she had said it. It frightened her.

Gloria felt inadequate. All her hesitant advances had met with no response from Rachel, and no indication that it might be otherwise. Now when she rang Rachel the talk was of Roger, and it was obvious to her that something very special was developing between the two of them. And she understood it. It would be so good for the two of them to be really close, and for the children. Gloria really liked Roger. When Roger had made tentative advances to her, she had been very tempted, and her retreat from him had been hesitant and not without regret. But what about her –what about her, what about her?

She could bear it no longer. One evening, without announcing herself in advance, she called on Rachel. She had prepared herself so that she was difficult to resist. And she was lucky for on that particular evening Roger was in the east Midlands on a sales trip, and Fiona had already retired to the stables where only the rising sun would disturb her.

Rachel was lonely. Already she missed Roger if he was not there in the evening. Rachel made them some food in the kitchen, and they talked over a bottle of wine, as they had done on many an evening. They went on talking as the two very good friends they had become. They became tired, and a tension grew between them. It became clear to them both that Gloria was going to stay. When Rachel got up from the table and moved away Gloria followed her, and taking an initiative put her arms around her, swivelling Rachel around to face her, obliging her to look into her eyes, inviting her to deny her if she dared. Gloria's green eyes shone with excitement and Rachel had no wish to deny her – quite the contrary.

Taking her by the hand Rachel led her slowly upstairs to her bedroom, inviting her to use the bathroom. Gloria, excited beyond words, could hardly remove her clothing fast enough, and in her haste delayed herself by clumsiness. She took a very quick shower and hastily dried herself and brushed out her hair. She took a very deep breath and then, satisfied and ready, for she had dreamt about this scene on many an occasion, entered the bedroom.

Rachel was lying on her back on the bed. Her hair spread itself on the pillow in burnished gold. She was long and slim and her body, used as it was to the outside and to exercise, was without fat and lightly muscular: lithe, wonderfully lithe, thought Gloria, her heart pumping. Gloria, by contrast, and in Rachel's eyes, was like a particularly delectable nymph at the Titian expedition they had visited together in London. Rachel laughed in her joy of Gloria. She made room on the bed for her, turning over and kissing her, at first gently and then with passion, so that Gloria slipped on to her back. Gloria felt that she was melting, that the boundaries of any possible resistance or inhibition had disappeared. Rachel was kissing her, caressing her, her hand gently moving over a very willing thigh, and then both thighs, which Gloria began to open in anticipation, feeling the urgency of it. And then Rachel's long fingers were cupped about her, gently moving and caressing. There was no possible prospect of Gloria holding back and the climax when it came, longed for over several months, devastated her. She cried out. Tears coursed down her face. Her body moved of its own volition – and without notice, she fell deeply asleep.

When she woke early the next morning Rachel was not there. Gloria was deeply disappointed. She had longed to show Rachel her love, and look what a foolish thing had happened. Hardly anything – but overwhelming for her.

Rachel brought her breakfast. She smiled and kissed Gloria. It was all right. Gloria apologised but it was not necessary. They held hands and talked, as they had always talked. Rachel suggested that they have a shower together. Now Gloria could be free. They kissed and soaped each other and Gloria for the first time could caress Rachel, kiss her very shapely breasts with nipples firm and bright as berries, and arouse her in a way which delighted them both. Gloria was in no doubt. Nothing that she had ever experienced, and there had been other men than Bob in her life, was to be compared with this delight: an enjoyment of equals and the loving play of innocents.

Gloria had to leave early, for Fiona would soon be astir. At the door, on parting, Rachel put her hand on Gloria's shoulder and gently pushed her away – to her car, to the drive and roadway, to her own home. Afterwards when Gloria looked back on that moment, she was left with this image – of a hand, a blessed hand, gently pushing her away.

Gloria was ecstatic and in the inn they teased her about her appearance, remarking that this newly-found glow was caused by love – that she had fallen in love. She had loved Rachel since their first meeting so it was not that: Gloria rejoiced not only in being in love but in freeing herself from the inhibition of expressing it. Now she wanted to go on. But soon she discovered that all was not well. Rachel did not answer her calls or reply to her messages, and there was a reluctance to answer her entreaties for a meeting. When at last they did meet it was on neutral ground, and there was an awkwardness between them. They faced each other across a coffee-room table in a bar which at that time of the day was empty, signifying that there was no audience for this conversation. Gloria was nervous.

'Is it all right between us? And say, yes.'

'Of course it is – and, no.'

'What do you mean? I love you, and now I know that you love me in the same way.'

'Yes, but no.' Rachel had thought it through and she explained.

'It's difficult to explain this, but I'll try. I want to commit myself to Roger. He hasn't asked me as such to commit to him, but I know he will; and I shall say "yes" to him. He may need me to reassure him about other people and my women friends, and I'll tell him that nothing's going on and nothing will go on in the future. And that's what I want. If Roger wants me I don't need anyone else.'

'I don't believe you. If it's Roger you want, why did you encourage me?'

There was a bitterness in Gloria now, but Rachel had antici-pated it. 'That's very simple.' She leant towards Gloria. She engaged her with her own eyes, tearful but resolute. 'Because I love you – completely. I needed to respond to tell you this. That to me you are part of me, that you're in my soul, and in my waking and in my sleeping. It was the best way to tell you this.'

Gloria was moved. She kissed Rachel, taking in the taste and smell of her. 'So, why then?'

'The children. Your Susan is on her way in life, but mine – there's many a mile to go. They need a man in the house, and I need one too – otherwise I'll fail. I'll be too weak, and I'll fail them.'

Gloria knew there was no answer to this – she too was a mother – but she tried. 'I love your children, and I think they love me.'

'Yes, of course you do, and I hope you'll continue to spend time with them. They'd be very hurt if you didn't.' Rachel was plead-ing with her. 'But it's not the same. They – and to be entirely honest with you, I – need a man. To be precise I need Roger. I love him more than I can say. And he needs me. He needs the goodwill of us all right now, and he's won mine.' She hesitated. 'It's more than that, really. Roger, without meaning to, has taught me some-thing of great importance. To survive his troubles he's had to learn to forgive himself and others. And when this became clear to me, I knew that this was important for me too. I have so much to forgive. We started with Fergus – and how precious that has been to me. You know what he did for me. How important it is. What it's done for me. So I've started to forgive myself for the terrible wrong I did to Fergus – and to forgive myself and Ralph....' She was incoherent, and came to a halt in tears.

Gloria was distraught and not in entire control of herself either. She cried out, 'I've helped Roger too. You're not the only one. I've always liked him and he likes me.' Somehow she felt this might square the circle. She explained to Rachel how she had helped. Rachel listened intently and without comment until she had quite finished.

Rachel kissed her, putting an arm awkwardly around her.

'It was very good of you, Gloria, very helpful to him, and very generous of you. But no more than might be expected of someone as good as you. She stopped. There was a need suddenly to be very careful about words. 'He may need your help in the future. If you love me I hope you'll continue – I hope you'll be willing to help him again.'

She was thinking about Bob, and she spoke about him. 'Don't you think you should do something about Bob? You're so lucky to have such a tolerant and kindly man as a husband. But unless you're very quick and determined you'll lose him.'

Gloria knew Rachel was right about Bob, but this was not the moment to think about him. 'Will I see you again, soon?'

Rachel was firm. 'Let's leave it for a while, Gloria. It's much too raw for us both at the moment.'

When Gloria was back in her dear little room again she was able to collapse. Weakness overcame her, and having made her way to bed she was unable to leave it. Life, which had opened up before her, completing and fulfilling her, now drained away, leaving her empty and without a will to continue. She made her excuses to Fred for the next few days, and kept to her bed until she could compose herself and think her way forward. Fred thought, lovers' tiff.

Gloria had agitated about it for so long: was she or was she not lesbian? And, if so, what did it mean to be one? Lucy had said she enjoyed men and women equally, and supposed herself to be bisexual – and that she believed this to be the natural state for everyone, before they started to spoil things by so-called moral laws and judgements. But other people said this was a cop-out, you were either one or the other and should have the courage of your convictions. Gloria had always liked men: not just Bob, but a great many men really, although she hadn't done much about most of them. If she had put her mind to it she would have encouraged Roger, for she certainly felt something for him. But she hadn't, and not just because of Bob or Rachel. Now she had got herself into a muddle, for she loved Bob and was holding him off, and for what? For love, of course, not just for sex or experimenting with women. She couldn't resolve any of these issues, answer any of these questions, because the truth was that she had fallen in love with Rachel. She might tell herself she had been foolish to fall in love; but since when was falling in love a matter of reason? And then you couldn't be in love, and perhaps stay in love, without possession. Or could you? She was tempted to call Lucy, because she had offered sex and wholehearted enjoyment without strings of any kind. That would be one way of answering a question. But no. She couldn't do that. It was a pity really but she was not interested in sex without love or possession, without commitment – there, she was getting muddled again. But Lucy deserved a reward of some kind for her persistence. She was so very engaging and pretty and probably very good in bed. Gloria blushed, enjoying the fantasy. But no, she couldn't do it.

To her surprise Gloria recovered very quickly from her setback. The main lesson of the past months was that life became better through self-improvement. She had become very good at her job and had met some very interesting people. She had met a venture capitalist on a weekend business course who, between bouts of admiring her, had asked whether she had ever thought of setting up in business on her own. She had scoffed at the idea at the time – mainly because she thought he was trying to flatter her – but on reflection she thought it an interesting suggestion, and began to put together a business plan for a venture of her own. One needed to be realistic: there was a limit as to what Fred could sensibly do at the inn, and perhaps there would be a time when it would be right to move on.

And then there was Bob. Now that Rachel had added her voice to Susan's in warning her of potential loss, she thought it might be wise to work out with him whether there was something they might do together. She began to call him more often, and found him disengaged and showing reluctance to accept her invitations to come down. She was not daunted. If Mohammed would not come to the mountain then the mountain must go to Mohammed.

She decided to call on him unannounced, and on one sunny Saturday afternoon she arrived at the former matrimonial home, and finding him out and the flat empty, let herself in with the latch key she had retained.

She drew a deep breath. It was different. It took her time to work out in what ways. The curtains, rugs and cushions had been changed. Some of the old furniture had disappeared. She remembered Susan had told her that her father had asked whether some pieces might be helpful to her. They had been replaced by some very stylish modern tables in rosewood and glass and contemporary chairs of quality. Very nice. Italian, she thought.

The kitchen looked lived in, with new utensils, a flowered apron, and cupboards and fridge bursting with much more than simple food; with the constituents for very tasty dishes indeed. Some serious cooking was conducted here. It made her increasingly nervous to apprehend these signs. She opened their bedroom door. God almighty, what a revelation. The bed linen had been changed to a snowy white kingdom with some attractive red cushions casually but perfectly placed on the duvet cover. There were mirrors and a large painting of a voluptuous nude over the bedhead. The oriental rugs were new. Shaken, she retired to the lounge and seated herself in one of the new Italian chairs. Comfortable as well as stylish, she thought.

She stirred herself. Bob was not the only detective in the family, or necessarily the best. She tried the bathroom. It confirmed her first impressions. There were soaps and bottles here that were for the use of women only; the medicine cabinet when opened abruptly led to the tumbling into sight of an advanced vibrator; while the washing basket revealed some very fetching black satin panties and a matching bra. She retired back to the fashionable chair and paused for breath, and to still a thumping heart. What was this? What was its meaning?

Written records and the spoken word were what she needed. Being a woman, and having no shame, she rifled through the sideboard drawers and sifted out his papers. There were thank you cards with roses signed by people whose handwriting she could not read. The answerphone was arresting. There were two messages for him. Someone called Kate said, in a very low and sexy voice, how much she had enjoyed their dinner on the previous night, and that she hoped he would call her soon; and someone calling herself his 'flopsy bunny' said, 'Wow! Call me.'

Suddenly she thought that she hated this place and didn't care to know its meaning, for whatever it was, it had nothing to do with her. But game to the last, she wrote him a note. It read, '*Bob dearest, sorry to miss you. See you soon. Love from your original flopsy bunny, Gloria. PS Call me for a delicious country lettuce.*' She hoped he would have the decency to blush when he read it – and left him her key to his flat.

He did blush, he did call her, and he did arrange to come down in two weeks' time. And he decided to make a confession at St Ethelreda's. Afterwards, a priest he had encountered before stopped beside him as he prayed at a stall, and when he was ready spoke gently to him, introducing himself as Father Matthew:

'Bob – it is Bob, isn't it? Can I help you?'

Bob explained his predicament: the personal problems he had laboured under over these past three years, and how inadequate he felt to deal with them. They were placed beneath a painting of Peter, replete with beard and the received wisdom of the Renaissance. Bob said, 'I suppose we should strive to be perfect like him. That should be our personal aspiration and the hope of us all – that we can be like him.'

The priest smiled. 'Forgive me, Bob, but tell me, how well do you know the Scriptures?'

'If I'm to be honest, very little.'

'And what do you do for a living? I've seen you here at many different times of the day.'

'I'm a policeman and a law unto myself, at least where time's concerned.'

Father Matthew delved into history. 'In olden days, Bob, when our diocese was a power in the land, the London police were forbidden to enter our church without prior written permission. You can see how liberal we've become; even policemen are welcome today.'

There was a pause. The priest filled the silence. 'Why not? Even a policeman can be honest if he chooses. Well, I imagine it to be possible.'

'Being honest, isn't very easy for anyone in my experience', Bob replied, retorted somewhat, feeling the strength of it.

'Tell me Bob, how do you suppose that you could be like an apostle, to know the future of peoples, even a single life, without Scriptural knowledge or the grace of God?'

Bob had no reply.

'Come to our evening Scripture classes, Bob. Wednesday evenings. They're a nice lot of people.' He moved away.

Rachel had said nothing to Roger about her escapade with Gloria, and never would. What she did do was to make Roger very welcome at her home, and encourage him to spend time with Fergus, who had responded to the added security of his new home by being very naughty and uncooperative, it being his way of testing their commitment. Would they send him back if he was naughty? There was too much at stake for him not to know. Fiona had encouraged him to spend time with her in the stables, which he loved, and threatened to throw him out if he behaved badly and distressed the horses. Roger took him fishing, and when he behaved well and had learnt some tricks of the trade, said he would take him on a night-time fishing adventure. They walked through a dark forest together where Fergus, hearing the movement of animals in the bracken and the hooting of a tawny owl, clutched Roger's hand very tightly. They pitched a tent by the side of the river, shining silver in the moonlight, and fished until two o'clock in the morning, when suddenly Fergus fell asleep and woke up in the tent at ten o'clock. They caught roach and perch. Roger told the others in a solemn convocation that Fergus was very good at fishing, and that although Roger had caught more, any fair-minded person could see that Fergus had caught the finer fish. And they had all nodded their concurrence.

In this way, and many others, Roger, Rachel and the three children had settled down together. But while the domesticity gave Roger much happiness, his sadness grew when the medical tests on his daughter Faith increased in number and complexity. The investigations ended with the two parents being summoned to hear a verdict in Switzerland. At the last moment Melissa called off as she was needed for an important professional engagement in Milan. Roger felt he could not object, because Melissa had already visited her daughter twice at the clinic, while all he had managed were some phone calls.

As his spotlessly clean Swissair 737 winged its way over the English Channel, Roger thought once more of his theory of parallels. Somewhere in these skies, travelling in a straight line, and he hoped at a different altitude, his former wife's BA flight was arrowing its way to Milan. Whether they would return in the same way, on the same day, he knew not and neither did she; but at this moment he was in no doubt that they were joined by their hopes and fears for their daughter. (Actually they were not, for Melissa was wondering how long she could keep Luigi at bay, and just how much she wanted to do so. But later they would be.)

Clinics in Switzerland (and more than this, hotels, lifts and public service buildings, high rise blocks, the homes of the bourgeoisie – everything really) had always unnerved him. They were so immaculately clean and disinfected that he had always felt the need for a face mask; and he had always been anxious not to breathe too deeply in Switzerland. The clinic at Caux was no exception. The staff were very precise with him, and thorough. They prided themselves on precision and comprehensiveness. Later when he had to relate these proceedings to others, he had difficulty in repeating what had been said to him. He supposed that the nub of it was that it appeared Faith was suffering from a rare form of adrenoleukodystrophy (ALD), a disease that led to the creation of long chains of fatty acids and to something called demyelination. It was a degenerative disease, which in time led to the breakdown of the nervous system and to death. But, they added, they could not be entirely sure, for this was a disease that boys not girls were prone to, and in some respects, which might be important, the tests did not entirely support the diagnosis.

Then they told him about a treatment, about Lorenzo's oil, which had a proven track record for arresting the disease, if not curing it, and if taken early in the disease – and it was early in Faith's case – could very often have the effect of enabling a person to live an entirely normal life and develop to their full capacity.

Roger was breathless and holding on. His questions tumbled out. The oil was freely available and could be prescribed by any general practitioner: they believed through the National Health Service – although he might be asked to make a contribution – and they would make enquiries for him. What he asked himself, unable to discard the business practices of a lifetime, was the bottom line? If these doctors were right – and they probably were – Faith could be saved. There would be a lifetime need of attendance to the disease unless a cure was developed – and the chances of a cure were not bad – but providing there was loving and dutiful care, Faith's life – her normal life – could be preserved.

Roger walked with his daughter through the clinic grounds, and they sat on a bench looking out across the still clean waters of a small lake. As they watched, a small rowing boat passed slowly from right to left. They played a game, recording and timing the boat's progress, calculating the distance and then the speed it was travelling at so as to determine a time of arrival on the other side, and all under a setting sun. He could reassure her that just like the boat, she would be all right. It would take time but that she would get there in the end. For the moment she would stay at the clinic while the arrangements for her future care were put in place, but soon she would be back home again. Faith hugged him. She knew – she had always known – that her father would sort it all out and that she could rely on him.

Rachel met him at Heathrow. In all the years of his international travel Melissa had never met him at airports – there were always excellent reasons why it never made sense to do so. Rachel had arrived early. Nervous for him, she waited where he was bound to see her, but she would see him first. He disembarked and passed through Customs. He had not expected her to be there, and if he had, the knowledge of it would have overwhelmed him. He could say nothing, and she asked nothing of him, until they were out of the traffic and away. Then he told her everything and she held on to him for a while.

Melissa had left a telephone number in Milan where she could be reached, and at the first opportunity he rang her. He did his best to explain and to answer questions. She always had more questions than him, and of the varieties incapable of answers. But her relief, and the warmth of her gratitude to him, and of their common love of Faith, were not to be disguised as they brought back the awareness of why they had loved each other to breaking point over so many years – a love that had produced Faith and which could now be drawn upon to sustain her.

The absurdity of his position was always before him. Here he was giving affection and comradeship to Fergus, a normality which this much abused small boy needed, while his own son, who had for years been a sweetness to him, was lost, buzzing his angry way through a diminishing world of his own. From time to time he rang Adam with ideas of what they might do together, things, events, happenings, suggested by Faith and Melissa as so tempting they might melt his resistance. But all to no avail. In a way he approved of Adam's defiance: it was original to him, and he accepted that in the end it was up to Adam whether he was to have a relationship with his father or not.

Rachel observed these things and waited on events of Roger's making, although she was not just waiting, because she was active in her own way. Now she put these things to one side while the drama of Faith unfolded. One blessing of the Jackson family was that it was incredibly well connected. She began to research the disease that Faith was diagnosed as suffering from, and then found a connection of her father's who was a neurological specialist and Nobel prize winner. With Roger's consent, she put this specialist in touch with the doctors in the Swiss clinic in Caux. These experts were pleased to talk to each other, to discuss the arcane mysteries of rare diseases, their causes and their cures; and their discussions had a number of highly practical outcomes. Rachel came up with some suggestions for Faith's programme of treatment which involved access and treatment in a London clinic. Roger and Melissa never quite discovered the reasons for this treatment being opened up for their daughter at a nominal cost. There was talk of a contribution from the National Health Service towards the cost of the drugs, a grant from a health foundation, public interest in rare diseases, and so on. All they really knew, and cared to acknowledge to themselves, was that the long-term medical care of their daughter had been provided for them at an affordable cost.

When Roger half-heartedly pressed Rachel about these arrangements, she laughed in an amused and happy way, exclaiming, 'What's the point of having really useful connections and a little money if you don't put them to good use?' She allowed herself the luxury of a really good hug and kiss. Before Rachel was a mountain to climb, before it would be safe to offer

Roger everything. The unfolding of events outside their control acted as a barrier between her and her hopes. But Rachel chose not to be entirely passive before the misfortunes that had yet to come upon them. She lay awake at night, thinking about their shape and imminency, and what she might do, in her own small way, to fend them off. So the intimacy which warmed them went no further than a comfortable friendship, although Rachel was as deeply in love as could be imagined, lost to herself while not available to him; while Roger was, through the pain of the veil of tears through which he moved, drawn to her and by her as the lode star by which he directed his way.

Friends and family were no more than bystanders, felt by him at various distances and intensity of light: some were like the children, aware that happenings mattered to them and wary about their effects, while others wondered and were fearful for them. Rachel's mother, while welcoming Roger as a potential force for good, muttered to herself, and to her husband when he was available, that it was so like Rachel to be attracted to difficult men with problems, and why could she not find a safe and predictable consort? Mr Jackson, heard to mutter back that there were no such men, earned a retort, 'Well, you should know.'

CHAPTER 15

ACCORDING TO ROGER'S law of unknown causes, in troubled times there were certain to be things going on. So he wasn't surprised when Morales said they had been asked to attend the local police station to answer additional questions on certain documents and statements accumulated by the police investigation into his supposed fraudulent behaviour. Roger was emphatic. 'Tell them to get lost. There is no case and they can never build one.'

Morales reminded him, 'If you don't go in they can arrest you.'

'Have you consulted Robinson?' Roger named the barrister recommended to him by Rachel.

'He said, "Go along and answer their questions."'

It took a day. There were a great many new documents and a large number of questions. Roger was patient and answered all of them. He had no difficulty in doing so. These documents were carelessly produced and the questions clumsy, almost as if these policemen were learning on the job. Then when the questions were answered, they started again with slight variations in form. Roger was less willing to respond, and pointed out – he hoped politely – that he had already answered these questions. They persisted and he declined, until the proceedings ground to a halt. The policemen were cross, and said he might have to come back in again because not all their questions had been answered.

'What questions haven't been answered?' asked Roger, becoming belligerent and ignoring Morales' tugs on his jacket.

They ignored him.

'Or do you mean that you go on asking me questions, despite my answers, until you get a response more in line with the politics of your situation?'

They brought the session to a halt and did not suggest another time.

Morales was cross with him. 'It does no good arguing with them. I've warned you about it.'

'It does me good', was the reply.

What was clear to both Roger and Morales was that the police had been mounting a major investigation. Morales, when questioned by Roger, said he was wrong in thinking the case being constructed against him lacked substance. He thought Roger was over-confident in himself and not giving sufficient credit to the efforts of others: comments which sobered him, for he knew it was a fault of his. Later Rachel listened to his account of the proceedings without comment. She looked thoughtful, and retired to make a phone call. She left it a day, until he had calmed down, before raising the subject again.

'I hope you don't mind, but I spoke to Patrick Robinson.'

He looked surprised.

She blushed. 'I didn't tell you, but he's my godfather – an old Cambridge chum of Daddy's. Well, you've spoken to him so you know how very good he is in these matters.'

'So what did he tell you?'

'His opinion is that you can do nothing at this stage. Most of these enquiries take a long time to evolve – two years or more, he said – and then the majority of cases fall by the wayside. They're very difficult to prove, apparently.'

'And if it doesn't fall, what then?'

'Then he can help, because he has an inside track.'

They decided to put the matter out of mind, and for a while they succeeded. Then out of the blue a summons was issued against Roger, requiring him to answer seven charges alleged under the Financial Services Act 1986 and the Theft Acts. An embarrassed looking policeman delivered them to Roger's cottage, together with two boxes of supporting documents.

Rachel took it very calmly, made some phone calls, and in a very few days Robinson called him and Morales to a meeting at his chambers in the Temple. Robinson was to the point. 'I've been through these papers. You've certainly been a little foolish, Roger, in putting some of the things complained about on paper, but I'm sure you're not a villain.' He looked over his glasses. 'Of course, I don't know you. You might be a villain for all I know. Are you? Don't worry, I don't want you to answer me. If Rachel thinks you're all right, I expect you are.'

Robinson said he thought the right course of action was to ask for a committal hearing and to demand all the documents, not just the ones the CPS wished them to see. 'You'd be amazed by the documents they hide. We'll smoke them out. Then if they still wish to proceed they have to appoint Counsel and I'll have a word with him. In the meantime don't worry. Be nice to Rachel – and leave it to me.'

Roger warmed to Robinson, and quite regained his good spirits. Morales retained his professional gloom and refused to look on the bright side of things.

'What I don't understand', said Roger, for he felt the need to say something, 'is why they do these things. They have a poor case. They spend hundreds of thousands of pounds on trying to obtain evidence, some of it dodgy. They meet together, presumably, agree the case is weak and then decide to bluff it into court.'

Morales was withering. 'You're much too sure of yourself. The reasoning's something like this. Taking action to enforce the law under these sections of the Financial Services Act is highly difficult – there is a high burden of proof. Naturally there's some reluctance in the CPS to bringing cases, expensive cases, that will get thrown out. But then the law must be upheld, and if the Act becomes redundant there's public criticism – all those Labour MPs sounding off about the establishment looking after itself. You know the sort of thing. So if an up and coming CPS solicitor gets the bit between his teeth, and wants to make a name for himself, he has a go when something comes up.'

Roger muttered that the whole thing was a public disgrace.

'Not at all. Of course it isn't – it's life. That's how it is.' Morales smiled to himself, weakening: 'Mind you, there is the Friday afternoon syndrome.'

'What's that?'

Morales continued, clearly knowing his facts from personal experience. 'They all meet together on a Friday – the police and

the CPS – to review all their cases. Not a glimmer of real light
with any of them. A certain number must come into the public
forum on a regular basis; there are statistical returns to be made,
inquiries to be brought to a conclusion, careers and promotion
are at stake. Then your case comes up and bingo, it's the lucky –
sorry, unlucky – number.'

'Careful,' said Roger, 'you're showing dangerous signs of
becoming human.'

Some time passed, for the wheels of the law turn slowly, but in
the end Morales received a pile of documents gathered by the
police, but which they were not proposing to use. Roger
collected a set from Morales, who although he had had them for
the better part of two weeks had not read them or communicated
their contents to his Counsel. But for Roger they were highly
entertaining, and the best read he had enjoyed for many a day.

He took notes. Amazingly he read that the principal Crown
witness, who had perjured himself in his witness statement, had
died. Two of his former colleagues, fearing the effects of their
evidence against themselves, whatever the assurances given by the
police, had been most reluctant to provide witness statements; and
six separate attempts had been made to persuade the last of them
to 'volunteer' a statement – and then it was given in a most mealy-
mouthed fashion. It appeared to Roger, not knowing much about
the law, that two of these witnesses had been caught out conspir-
ing to pervert the cause of justice. Computer tests carried out in
Roger's office confirmed that various warnings to individual
shareholders which he had authorised to be made by the company
had been suppressed by his former colleagues: all those surviving
directors and senior colleagues who were now lined up against
him. In summary it seemed to Roger, in his innocence, that there
could not possibly be a case to be answered.

A meeting had been arranged between the three of them, once
more in Counsel's chambers. Morales glanced at the papers on
the way down by train, but not for long, having other things on
his mind: Robinson found twenty minutes to peruse them in his
rooms ahead of their arrival, and squeezed out another twenty in
making two telephone calls – and by keeping them waiting.

When the meeting began, Roger provided them both with a
copy of his notes typed in double spacing and with highlights in

yellow and conclusions in red. Roger was excited; the others were cool. Robinson said, 'Well, well, interesting.' And read some more, although in truth he had already digested the documents and formed his own view as to their meaning. He continued, 'I've spoken to the CPS. They tell me they're very confident of their case but they're willing to drop the theft charges if you're willing to plead guilty to the charges under the Financial Services Act. What do you think about that?'

He looked at Roger quizzically over his spectacles.

'Tell them to get lost.'

But while Roger was emphatic, Morales urged caution, reminding Roger of the possible length of the jail sentence.

'Good man,' said Robinson. 'I thought you'd say that, so I've taken the liberty of telling them so.' He was enjoying himself. He continued, 'I've spoken to the Counsel they propose using. A sensible man. I know him well. We've reached an understanding. I've told him that in my opinion you're an honest man and this case won't hold up. He's promised he'll take an early look at these papers and if that's his opinion too he'll tell them it and the hounds will be called off.'

Robinson smiled beneficently, but Roger, not quite comprehending that an understanding had been reached and that there was nothing more to say, and unable to stop the engine of his indignation, went on about his notes and the importance of that matter and the significance of the other.

'Yes, yes, quite so. Very helpful. I think you're right there.' Robinson continued to beam. Then as they left, putting his arm around Roger's shoulders, he proffered a judgement. 'You're a very lucky fellow, Roger, if you've attracted Rachel's interest – and affection too, I dare say. Very lucky. She's a very remarkable girl – but of course you know that, I'm sure.'

Time passed. There seemed to be a lot of it. Roger sought refuge in his work, but there were few hiding places in his dreams. He dreamt of Newgate and the Marshalsea and all those poor souls who had cried out in their misery in the past: heaped up together and hopeless, as were the pieces of paper that denounced them for unpaid services and goods. Waking he checked, sweating, to see whether he had paid all *his* bills – as Dickens and Defoe before him must have checked their own: and sometimes he paid ahead of the due date in his anxiety to stay abreast.

Then he received the phone call he had dreaded and feared. Morales said, 'Good news, Roger.'

And he replied, 'Just a moment, I'm not programmed for good news.'

'Well, it's not all good news. It does need explaining.' He explained it. The CPS would not be proceeding with the case on the grounds of insufficient evidence. The summons would be struck out: but there would be a record of some sorts up on the police computer; that is, the record of the summons was not obliterated as such. Some people would be able to continue to say 'no smoke without fire', and were any small thing to come up in the future, the record of the past weeks would be accessible to the police.

'Of course that won't worry you, Roger. Nothing to worry about in that', said Morales. 'You're a lucky fellow and my best wishes to you.'

Roger was livid. 'You must be joking, Morales, and in bad taste. Tell me, please, in what sense am I lucky?'

Morales was mollifying. 'Well, not lucky, exactly, but you know what I mean.'

Roger was not easily flannelled by him. 'I hope I don't, Morales. I just hope I don't.'

'Come, come,' said Morales, 'let's not pick a quarrel. I'm genuinely pleased for you. Let's leave it at that.'

If Roger had stumbled into his 'crime', if that after all was what it was, David Droylsden was carefully planning his own – the obliteration of Roger Greer. For some time his intended killing had remained an active ingredient of his fantasy life, and he had obtained a kind of pleasure in it. But then inch by inch it had wormed its way into his consciousness, and out into the real world. All his hard-earned ground of legitimacy – of respectability – arrested the progress of his plan; but with him denuded of normalcy and the comfort of family life, the design grew independently of consciousness and common sense. Even then his criminality might have been of no practical outcome but for a coincidence – of fate – in meeting an old friend from his car-dealing days in a Manchester bar who, as his mother would have said, was 'no better than he need be'. This buddy had contacts, knew how to perform really horrible misdeeds, and what is more owed him a favour. So David explained, and his buddy said, 'No problem, David. Leave it with me and I'll get back to you.'

In no more than ten days his buddy was back in touch with him and they met up again. 'This is the deal', he said. 'The fee is two thousand pounds, half front end and the balance on completion.'

'OK. Who is it and is he reliable?'

'Hold your horses. You'll never know who he is and he won't be given your name. Everything goes through me.'

'Can I trust you?'

'David, how could you? Can you trust me indeed?' He threw his hands up in the air at the absurdity of the suggestion. 'He's very good. An experienced man. He won't let you down.'

'What do you mean, "experienced"? Is he some retired geriatric short of pocket money?'

'David, I'm surprised at you. Why do you insult me in this way? This man's one of the best.'

'OK, I trust you. When?'

'Whenever you like. Soon, if you wish. But you mustn't harass me about dates. He'll do it in his own time when he's worked out the safest way. Remember, he's a professional, and the first you'll know about it is when you read of it in the paper.'

They arranged for David to send a thousand pounds and a photograph of Roger and his address in a registered envelope, and he duly did so, with the anonymity of a typewritten script, and not on a computer of his own. The deed was done – well, almost done – arranged for and out of his hands. That night David slept well for the first time for many months.

Roger knew nothing of his proposed demise, but he knew he was not free of his own curse – crime! He thought about it – crime! What was crime? He knew there to be more of it by the day in Britain, and that the prison population, the greatest in any European country except Russia (was Russia in Europe?), grew every day. Were the British more criminal than every other European country – more than Germany, France, or Italy? He thought not. After his difficulties with the law, his divorce, the marriage settlement, his arrangement with creditors, the accusations of fraud, and now most serious of all the allegation of manslaughter, he knew that the problem was not his fellow citizens – it was the laws they lived under. There were too many laws and official regulations, and all with their sanctions in case of breach. A man was expected to sally forth into this world of bureaucratic rules and practices and to take great risks for material gain – and not only for himself – and the slightest mistake was pounced upon. Bang, that was the prison door behind you! If you got yourself caught up in the web of the legal system and the courts then sooner or later it was the end of you. And was that his case? As fast as he cleared himself of one jeopardy, it seemed he was swallowed up by another. Was that was how it was going to be for him?

He rang Rachel and discussed it with her. She thought not. 'One last push and you bound free', she said. But of course he couldn't push because his fate was in the hands of others.

These were questions that were asked by persecutors as well as victims. Bob remembered the words of Father Matthew, that nowadays even policemen might enter God's holy places, and he hoped devoutly that they were true. The shame of Gloria's discoveries and his own high jinks, which was how he described them to himself, lingered on. The trial subscription to the dating agency had not really been a success. Some of these ladies had been very dull, and seeking permanency and expecting it from him, while others, frankly, were after sex – which often was a prize that led on to something of an expectation. Actually he could take it or leave it – the sex, that is – and he was not seeking permanency at all, at least he thought not.

Then there was Gloria. What was he going to do about Gloria? Now that she was showing some real desire to put things right with him, he would have to make this long postponed decision whether to resume, and if so where, how and when. And in the wings there was Andrea, devoutly to be desired – but by him? He sighed. And he decided to join the Bible Study class at St Ethelreda's. As Father Matthew said, you met a nice kind of person at the church. Not that this would save him, necessarily.

So far as the Garth Droylsden case was concerned, it was fast becoming the joke of the Met. No sooner was a lead revealed than it vanished, so to speak, in their hands. No decent copper wanted to work on the case, and those that did became the butt of the best jokes. From time to time Bob and Alec were summoned to account by Assistant Superintendent Jenkins. Suggestions were made. Strategy was re-evaluated; tactics were altered; alternatives were reconsidered. And all in vain. Surely, they all thought, now was the time to call it off and to get on to other things; but expectation and fear of criticism for an unsolved crime kept them going.

Then out of the blue, but no more than might be expected, said the old hands, they got a break. Gerry O'Callaghan, their IRA suspect, was arrested when trying to leave the United States. The FBI rang them. If they wanted to question him they had best get their butts over the pond quickly, as they had limited powers to hold this guy and would have to let him go. Bob and Alec looked forward to it, another US 'bunbury' and a chance to catch up with their American buddies. But alas for them. Assistant Superintendent Jenkins decided otherwise. Now was the time for kudos, for the decisive intervention – for his intervention. He would undertake this task himself, and by doing so demonstrate to his superiors his overwhelming attention to duty and his determination and commitment to clear-up rates – a resolve which marked out the investigations under his command from the pack. He would lead from the front.

Mrs Jenkins was less committed. Had he forgotten her niece's wedding? For God's sake, she had written it in his diary herself. And considerable care and expense had been devoted to turn-out. Just how many chances did a woman have to dress up these days, especially if she was married to a policeman? And he was not to go missing during preparations. It wasn't fair, being a question of moral support. These objections being many and strongly argued, he reluctantly put off the trip for three days to a convenient time for them all, which did not absolve him from criticism, because he had willed his absence from the very beginning. Thus the wedding had gone on, from his family perspective, with something less than his whole-hearted enthusiasm and joy – for which he was blamed.

His colleagues looked on in amazement and with glee. 'Who wears the pants in your house,' they declaimed in their own uncertaincies, 'man or mouse?' Eventually, having ignored the advice of his colleagues at the FBI, who wondered at his dilatoriness, the Assistant Commissioner took to the air, to be met by the news on arrival that the cock had flown the coop. Had he not been warned, they told him, that in the States people had rights: you couldn't hold them very long without charging them with something? What nothing? And then this high-class criminal lawyer arrives with a court writ for Gerry's release, and off they go over the horizon, probably not to be seen again together – ever. Didn't he realise that in the States the IRA commanded big bucks, and wasn't it all political in the end?

But it was not all gloom and despair. They had interviewed this guy and gathered some data on him, to which Jenkins was welcome. And escorting him to his hotel they left him with his jet lag, the report and to his own devices. After two hours of sleep he was wide awake and ready for the report, which was a good deal more interesting than he had dared to hope.

Roger's laws of parallel coincidences would have led him to believe that a complementary movement from west to east would coincide with the Assistant Commissioner's transatlantic crossing – and so it turned out. High above him, blown east by powerful air currents, Esther Droylsden was returning to England, where she proposed to set up, at least initially, at the University of East London where her paintings were already greatly admired. She proposed to teach there for a while, and endeavour to find the level that her bold feminist-inspired female nudes merited – or alternatively, as some of her detractors were known to remark (and didn't fame and the courage of the avant-garde always bring out the critics?), more than merited.

Her husband would have had some difficulty in recognising her. Gone was the immaculately groomed and coiffured slim beauty so painfully maintained under his governance. Now she had put on weight and the jeans showed a sight too many rolls of flesh. Her hair had greyed, and she was quite without make-up. Now she had the courage of her convictions, and could be heard some rows away freely giving them. This was a woman hard to ignore, and if so, by someone who would need to be reckoned with. But this would be in a future which at this moment did not concern her. She was returning not to the marital home in fashionable Bayswater but to another place, a rented flat in Hackney in East London, the poorest of the London boroughs, close to the University of East London, where she was to teach a course in the History of Art as a visiting lecturer. And if you followed her discourse on the plane, you would have begun to learn something of her vantage point, her perspective, in her approach to the subject. A literate observer might have concluded that she was new to the philosophy of art, that her polemic was in a stage of development, and that her speech was something of a rehearsal for an event to come. But it was interesting enough, nevertheless, in its analysis of the neglect of women as artists throughout time and the historical causes of their subordinate position. You might have concluded that this new philosophy could only have been developed and absorbed as a canon in the United States, but that if it had touched a white middle-class American male, it might have the power to challenge deeply held values. Its effect might be to dismantle men and rearrange their lives by altering the way they related to the other sex – and a shiver might have passed down any man's spine.

CHAPTER 16

A S HE LOOKED back over this period David became
conscious of the severe impact on him of the loss of
Esther, for with her departure all the obvious channels
of grief for the loss of his son had been closed off. It seemed to
him that he had been left alone with the burden of guilt, and that
he had responded, as he had always done, by immersion in work.

He did not accept his guilt. There was nothing he felt responsible for, and he refused to chase others with explanations he
knew would not satisfy them. He would serve them best – these
people – by remaining strong. Now he knew, but far too late, that
he had been wrong in believing that the practice of his true religion, his addiction to work, would be sufficient to deal with his
problems. For with the explosion his life had started to crack. At
first he was not conscious of it. These were hairline cracks not
discernible without very close examination, and his withdrawal
into the usual prepared defensive positions ensured that no one
got close enough to observe them. But then, he was obliged to
himself to admit, that these cracks had widened so that any close
observer could see them and wonder – and to conclude that
things were not right, and that it was necessary to keep a close
eye on him, for fear of the unexpected.

Thus Anthony Valentine, fearful of an investment loss for his
company, became increasingly worried about the progress of
Orbit, Roger's old company, and blamed David for almost all its
problems. Anthony had now concluded that there was no future
for Orbit, and that he should evolve a strategy which reduced or
eliminated his losses and so maintained investor good faith.

But for his state of mind, David would have felt threatened and, being acutely aware of the options open to him, would have tailored a survival strategy of his own. For some time Anthony had hinted that it was time David dug deep into his own pocket and put in new money. Now he demanded it. He had his boys come up with a revised business plan, which showed things coming right in two to three years' time, and which required new money to keep the company within acceptable borrowing limits. He suggested the new cash should be a bank condition for the continuation of existing banking facilities. And he pointed out that, given David's generous remuneration package, and the fact that he had been given twenty-five per cent of the equity without an investment of any kind, it was only right that he put in cash now. The plan specified his contribution as five hundred thousand pounds.

David saw in hindsight that the plan and its supporting figures and assertions were specious, that it was all garbage; but temporarily, in his distraction, he allowed himself to be swept along. The money would have to come from the children's trust fund – he winced as he used the plural – and this required both trustees, Esther as well as himself, to sign. He decided, in her absence, to forge her signature, and spent several days practising before he could get it right. And there he paused, despite promptings, temporarily paralysed and indecisive. It was at this time that he had a telephone call from his mother's doctor telling him that she had been admitted to Manchester Royal Liberty Hospital following a serious heart attack. David packed a bag, switched off his mobile, and caught the first train north.

Judith Droylsden was a tough old bird and was not going to quit this life without a struggle. The heart attack had been severe and the diagnosis was poor, but attended by friends and distant relations, and with the bedside attentions of her son, she entered her last battle. David settled into a new regime. He slept in Judith's flat and was at the hospital bedside by eight o'clock each morning where, with intervals for errands and the summoning of relations, he spent the day until nine at night. He worked his way through family memorabilia each evening, and brought her the family photo albums so they could recall happier – and not so happy – days gone by. He held her hand while she slept, and he acted as an usher and doorman for the visitors. It felt like a whole new way of life, but where every day might be the last.

Back in her flat he could see his handiwork everywhere. It was as if it was his flat, really, and only shared with her, which would be natural, and he counted the hours of his labour and multiplied them by his daily charge-out rate. What an effort he had made over the years. And was it all now to come to nothing? What would he do with it? As the nearest relative he could claim the tenancy as his own following her death, and then when the requisite number of waiting years were over he could buy and then sell it. There was a tidy profit to be made. Was that what he would do? He found her will, which left all her assets to him. He added up their value, and noted with satisfaction that it came to quite a sum. His mother had been very prudent in her lifetime. There were equities, and unit trusts and a life insurance policy. What on earth was she doing in continuing with a life insurance policy over all those years?

After a few days the number of messages left on his mobile, mostly from Anthony Valentine and his cohorts, were numerous and, he recognised reluctantly, necessitated replies. He felt curiously light-headed and reckless, comforted as he was by the thought that at worst he could always return to Manchester and live in the flat.

Every day he bought several national newspapers and scanned them for any news of Roger's proposed death: but in vain. He knew he had to be patient about this assassination, and schooled himself to do nothing but wait.

And then one day when he arrived at the hospital her bed was empty and she was gone for ever. When he got back to the flat he rang Anthony to tell him about his mother, and that the arrangements had been made to pay over the money. Later he used to say that if his mother had not died on that day he would never had made the investment; that he had acted when the balance of his mind had been disturbed. And that when it had happened, London had seemed a long way from Manchester and remote from him; and that he needed to remain in Manchester to make the funeral arrangements – and days had slipped by without him noticing what he had put in train.

David was staying only some thirty minutes by bus from the unknown assassin, who was now in an advanced state of preparation for the foul deed he had financed. Albert Finch, a quiet little man in his seventies, of nondescript appearance and poor health, might have been considered an unlikely hired killer. Not that he lacked a criminal past, far from it, because he had been a petty thief for many years, with several spells in prison to show for it. When real thuggery had become physically too much for him, he had turned to occasional jobs as a get-away driver; but this activity had become more and more difficult with the weakening of age. Needing money in his sixties, he had agreed to make a hit, and then five years later another. So he had acquired a reputation, but actually he believed himself to be retired now, feeling that he had lived an onerous and dangerous life with very little to show for it in the end. Contrary to public expectation, the life of most thieves and villains is not a prosperous one. It is not a life which leads to regular income or a company pension, and one of the results of retirement is a high degree of poverty, which Albert might have borne for himself, but did not wish for his wife, who had stood loyally by him over what seemed to her to be more than a lifetime.

Reputations in the criminal world have a nasty habit of outrunning the facts, so when opportunities came along from time to time as the result of his former villainy, which his flesh and nerve decried, it was tempting to take them on for the cash. And this is how it happened in this case. He was committed to killing Roger because he needed the cash.

Not that this killing would be easy to do, because Norfolk was a long journey by train from Manchester, and the necessary reconnoitring would take a great deal of time; and to add to the difficulties Roger Greer was not a man of regular habits, as his sales trips necessitated much travel away from home and at the most irregular of times. Albert had decided to shoot his target with a trusty revolver, without any record of purchase or ownership, which he kept in the shed on his local authority allotment. Nearer the chosen time he moved the revolver to the cistern of his outside lavatory for fear it might be stolen. Then when he was ready to go he was further delayed: he caught a severe cold, which as he neglected it in the fever of his planning and preparations, turned to a mild bronchitis which took time to clear. His doctor said, 'Well, what do you expect at your age?' So for one reason or another time passed and nothing was done.

But then a time came when the deed could be executed. Albert had decided to travel by car and to stay over a weekend at the King's Head, a small hotel in Bungay around the corner from Roger's cottage. He planned to follow Roger out on to the marshes when he took one of his regular early morning weekend walks. He posed as a tourist, complete with maps and tourist guides, by which he hoped to create an entirely anonymous impression. While at the bar he asked questions about local sites, and took the advice of the locals. In this subterfuge he was not entirely successful, as when questioned later by the police the hotel manager remembered him well, and remarked that he appeared a rather anxious type of fellow in need of some good care and rest.

Albert was lucky, for Roger was at home that weekend, and was due to take his early morning walk on the Saturday before going to Rachel's for lunch. Because Roger was an early riser, Albert had to make arrangements for an early breakfast in his room. He was a man who liked value for money, so ordered a full English breakfast. He slept badly and grappled with the thought that this killing was overdoing things: this chap Roger seemed a decent enough cove to him, and he was really too old for this kind of job – any type of job. Before starting on the fatty paradise before him, he experienced some indigestion problems, some pain, but he was reluctant to take notice of that, as he needed the comfort of what had been placed before him. He said to himself that there was nothing unusual about indigestion, for which a loving wife had given him some tablets, as he had endured these difficulties for some time. Recently he had found it more difficult to digest his food: sometimes it seemed to stick in his throat and on occasions he had to vomit it all up to avoid choking. Age, only old age, he thought, ignoring the good advice of his wife that he visit his doctor. He believed that the way to avoid this discomfiture was to eat slowly, bite small portions and chew them well before swallowing. But this morning he was too excited and tired from the efforts of not sleeping: time pressed upon him and he wanted to get the meal over and done with so as to get himself into position.

When he started to choke there was no one present to help him. He drank some tea but it was too hot and scalded him, and so didn't help. Then, panicking, he had swallowed some bread because he understood that this was sometimes helpful in clearing a blockage. Nothing worked. Albert choked to death on the floor of his hotel room, where he was found two hours later by the chambermaid.

Roger had a pleasant walk that morning, and on the way back his cheery companion from more desperate days waved to him from a neighbouring pathway.

News of a death by natural causes excites no national interest, but it was big news in Bungay, where the chambermaid regaled the press and her relatives with her story of finding the body, and became something of a celebrity for a while. There was continuing interest in attempts to identify the body. Albert had used a false name when signing the hotel register. He was not carrying any identification and his car, it turned out, had never in its history been licensed to any owner. As Albert's death was determined by the coroner as arising from natural causes, there was no immediate thought that there would be some police record of him – but might there not have been fingerprints on a police computer? A check was made, but it was a difficult task at that time given the sophistication of police computer software, which could not claim more than a seventy per cent success record. In the event no match was found. In normal circumstances, Albert's wife might have been expected to contact the police to report his disappearance; but it had long been established between husband and wife that there could be no follow up of an absence arising from a 'job'. So she did nothing, not knowing what to expect, and unable to grieve so long as there might be a turning of the latchkey. Albert had very few friends since the ageing process had carried them away; and no one was surprised or concerned by his prolonged absence. Indeed in his career being absent was the norm. So nothing was known or heard about Albert inside and outside of Norfolk, and he slipped out of this life relegating the planned attempt on Roger's life to a question of fiction and of diminishing importance to anyone. Only David was left with any question as to the outcome of Albert's little adventure, and when, growing impatient, he asked his buddy about it he received the reply that nothing was known other than the chap had disappeared – which he thought a promising sign. How, thought David, could you follow up on the outcome of such a contract?

David had his hands full with organising a funeral, which turned out to be a demanding few days for him: death was a taxing business for everyone. His mother had requested an orthodox Jewish funeral. It was her last gesture in this life. As she had not been a regular attender at the synagogue this required some patient negotiation with the rabbi. There were some conditions laid down, and the attendees had be reminded of how to dress and behave on the day. The funeral was poorly attended, and mostly by the elderly. Perhaps the surroundings persuaded some more distantly connected persons to stay away; and the weather was atrocious, with heavy rain and gusting winds. David realised with a sense of his own mortality that many of his mother's friends had preceded her to the other life. Whatever the causes, there were no more than two score to wish her well on her way.

He came out of the darkness of the synagogue into the light and stood on the steps. The traffic moved about him. He felt himself light-headed and to be floating: more than his mother had passed on, but he did not understand what had drifted away. For the moment he had to hurry on, for rather more people were to gather for a wake at his mother's flat than had appeared in the synagogue. Now he had to explain the absence of Esther, which was awkward, and which led on to his account of the explosion and the death of Garth. He felt their disquietude. To lose one member of his family was a misfortune; to lose two, a sort of carelessness and a presage, perhaps, of grief to come – didn't misfortunes come in threes? His cousin Ellie was persistent. It was almost if she believed he had disposed of his wife. After all it was surprising that he had no forwarding address: the estranged were usually keen to learn of your distress and subsequent misfortune, and have the mail forwarded. Where too was his daughter Naomi? In Israel, he said. Wasn't that an easy reply, and wasn't there a lack of circumstantial evidence? Where in Israel? What was she doing and where was she staying? When did she go and when would she return? Actually he didn't know where she was at all, as he hadn't been told. When she had graduated in the year after Garth's death she had upped and left, not leaving a forwarding address, and he hadn't heard from her since. He thought that he should take steps to find her now. But in the present how could he recount that to all these caring guardians of Jewish family life? Then there were those anxious to give him hospitality, mostly of the glutinous family variety, but also by maidens who were surprisingly bold in putting themselves forward. He thought their boldness in inverse proportion to their charms.

There was talk of Israel and the success of the Gulf War opening up new opportunities. 'God bless America', said Uncle Sam, who given his name had always had a special affection for what he was largely ignorant about; and there were others to say 'Hear, hear' and 'You can say that again.' David felt detached from these tribal concerns for the first time. He even gave nodding room to the thought that there was something imperialistic and even racist about the usual comments. Was there perhaps something to the contention that the Israelis were occupying other people's territory and justifying their claims to them on the Hitlerite proposition, of dubious historical legitimacy, of 'lost territories'? Not that he was going to enter into an argument with them, for he too contributed to the cause, and had believed in it with the same emotional certainties as them. But he was confused a little now. Something had happened to shift things around. Were the cries of righteousness a form of imperialism, somehow mixed up with the darkness of the synagogue and the mustiness of ancient claims? And what was one willing to do to hang on to these claims, to these territories? And how much suffering among the innocent bystanders were you prepared to tolerate? The desire to dominate and to possess took many forms. He knew it and had warmed himself by it: his family, now scattered and no more; his team, United of course; his tribe; and his own self-interest as he defined it. Most of it quite harmless: but not all of it.

But he survived his mother's death, and when he had a quiet moment to contemplate her passing, he recognised the bridge crossed. He had read about it elsewhere, and had hardly believed it: there flooded in a sense of freedom and release. He was no longer accountable to his past. There was no need anymore to fulfil her dreams of him, material or moral. He was answerable only to himself. But with whom could he share this moment? What was the point in passage through this life if an epiphany, a moment of significance and even joy, could not be shared with any other living creature?

And then he knew that he had to go back, and that there was no pleasure in the going. In these moments of revelation he could tell himself part of the truth. There was no need for his usual bravado, for his boasting of power and influence, which was his usual means of buoying up a fragile ego. No one was listening. There was no one to impress. He had taken on more than he could master. He was not the world's greatest line manager; he had placed himself in a pole position to direct a sophisticated service business, which he did not understand, a business where intuitive creativity was a necessary quality and one he lacked. In this new world his own powers of leadership had failed him: he was not recognised or liked, and deep though he dug, he would not be likely to earn even a grudging respect.

Then there was Esther. He had pretended to himself that she was not needed, and through pride had done nothing to find her, to comfort her in *her* distress, and probably he was too late now. Someone else would have comforted her, and all his efforts and sacrifices over the years would have been brought to naught.

He had the reassurance of Manchester. The familiar sounds and smells of his city closed around him with the comfort of an old and valued coat: not perhaps the high fashion of the right end of London but something, and more every day. Easier on the mind and without unnecessary pretension. He had always liked the warmth and directness of the north, if it could be called that, and he found himself greeting more, accepting more; and as he relaxed into it and hugged himself with it and was hugged by it, he became more cheerful. He found himself wondering whether he might try something new here in Manchester. As the idea grew, he began to quarry out information about businesses for sale, and was pleasantly surprised to find that there were opportunities. His investment in Orbit had taken up most of what had remained in the children's trust fund, but there was his mother's estate: not a fortune, but enough to fund the sort of investment which might open up for him in his own town.

David's daughter Naomi had known nothing of her grandmother's death, and would not have attended the funeral if she had. While a student she had met a nice gentile boy, training to be a dentist, and not wishing to be parted they had moved in together. He had taken up a trainee position in a private dentist's practice in Bognor Regis on the south coast, where he had made good progress. He was quick to learn, and since he was a friendly and chatty person the clients liked him. The early prognosis was encouraging. He was earning good money and everyone thought he would succeed. Perhaps he would become a partner at some time or even set up in business on his own.

They had found an unfurnished flat on the sea front and sparsely furnished it with the few pounds they possessed. For the moment she did not work, and spent her days thinking about what she might do, and not really caring, for she was as happy as a sandboy. She found herself thinking she might have a baby. She would just love to have one. They had spoken about it, and Nigel had urged caution. 'Wait a while until we're more secure,' he had pleaded, and 'Don't you think we should wait?', anxious to stop her. Naomi had stopped raising the subject. She did not think she wanted to wait. It would be better to take the tide at the flood. Now was the flood and now the time. As for marriage, there was no security there. That might wait. There might be a time for it. She thought she might cheat and stop taking the pill without telling him. After all she could say, 'The pill isn't entirely foolproof, you know, there's always some element of risk.'

She did not know where her mother was to be found and did not greatly care to think about it. As for her father – she shrugged when the question was posed, for she knew that he would not approve of her choice and that would mean disapproving of her now – she chose not to let him know her whereabouts. But that was not for ever: she knew she would tell him at some time.

Her mother was safely holed up in a sweet little flat in Hackney, and becoming a hit: something of a celebrity in East London. A weekend review had published an article on her as a rising artistic star in which serious remarks were made on the quality of her art and its significance to what was now called, without any trace of irony or history, the 'new woman.' Neither David or Naomi read weekend reviews, so the news of her fame had not reached them yet. Esther knew nothing of her mother-in-law's death, and like her daughter would not have been likely to attend the funeral had she known. She had never liked the demanding old matriarch who had competed with her for the precious few moments of her husband's leisure time. Whether, in the event, the solemnity and finality of death would have reached out to her and softened her resistance was never to be known. Sometimes she thought of David. Some time ... she thought some time ... there would be a meeting, but not yet. There was no need for it.

As for men generally, or particularly, Esther had lost much of her interest. While she had not ruled adventures out, being willing to be taken by surprise and accepting that under siege she might relent, she did not seem to be presented with acceptable opportunities. In her mind that was due to age, although she had to admit that a good deal of it went on at the university, and not much of it could be put down to age. Anyway, it was not important. Her painting was what was mattered now, and her energy and imagination was employed in advancing it.

On the train journey back to the 'smoke', David tried hard to sort out his confusions, but he thought it would be some time before his thinking was clearer. Train journeys were always helpful in a sifting-out process – unless of course fools were making needless noise or holding absurd conversations , which wasn't the case on this occasion. The ice flows were breaking up around him and he could feel and hear the groans of their movement. It was certainly painful. The metaphors were mixed. In one respect his mother had been a keystone and without her the entire edifice collapsed. In another way of thinking, she had been a kind of lodestar and once he knew where he was with her, he could place himself, and navigate his way forward. He supposed he might still do this, imagining what she would have thought or done or urged him to think.

He was conscious of a shift in his priorities. What did he care anymore about this rogue Roger Greer? He was fatalistic. If the gunman got him, *c'est la vie, c'est la guerre*, and if he didn't, so what? He would forget about it, it would be fate. He could hardly believe that he was saying these things to himself. As for Orbit and the Anthony Valentines of this world, they could go jump. Then he realised how ridiculous he was being about it. Of course

Orbit had to succeed, there was money and prestige at stake. And then in another way it was all in the laps of the gods. What did it matter really? Would it bring back Garth or Esther, or his mother if he succeeded? He thought not – and not with Esther. There was something to do about Esther. He was really confused now and half asleep. Something to do about Esther. What to do about Esther? The words ran round his head even when he was asleep.

But soon he would be back in the thick of it, at Orbis. The battlefield would be there and memories and nostalgia for lost pleasures would not help him in the fog of the only war he had ever felt comfortable to wage. He was not down and out yet, whatever anyone might say.

CHAPTER 17

WAKING AT THREE am with the effects of jet lag, Assistant Superintendent David Jenkins put in several hours of reading before breakfast. He was impressed with the professionalism of the FBI report, which to him was the result not only of the recovery of details on file in a computer, but of careful and meticulous police investigation. Whatever Gerry O'Callaghan might have been in the IRA when he was an employee of Roger Greer's, he was now a figure to be reckoned with. Was this the right Gerry O'Callaghan, he wondered? The report set out a skeleton of this man's history in the IRA, and detail was limited to his activity in the States over the last few years. In the States it was believed that he had been involved in the drug trade (and at the very top), in illegal gun running, and in the legitimate business of fundraising. When his activities were legitimate they were publicised, so he had built a public profile of respectability. He travelled frequently and without difficulty between the States and Ireland, and it was rumoured he was a member of the IRA Supreme Council.

When local officers of the FBI had arrested *their* Gerry O'Callaghan, acting on their own initiative and in an endeavour to help the Metropolitan Police in London, the officers concerned had come under intense pressure to release him from a very fancy and expensive US law firm. Some concern had been expressed by their superiors about their actions, and it seemed that political pressure had been brought to bear for O'Callaghan's release. They had had to let him go, and his whereabouts now was unknown.

It was a long way to travel for a good read of a police report in an hotel room, and being a sporty type of fellow, Jenkins determined to do a little investigation of his own. Hank Morrow at the FBI expressed his doubts about the wisdom of any such attempt:

'You must be joking. Where d'you think we'd find him? He could be anywhere in the States or across a border by now. This country ain't a whimsy, whimsy island like your own, y'know. And even if we could find him he's not going to say anything to a British policeman, or for that matter an FBI agent – not unless he's paying him and then only to get the amounts right. Joke, joke, for God's sake don't quote me.'

Jenkins persisted. 'I'd like to get a bit nearer him to satisfy myself that he's our man. Hang out where he hangs out and ask a few questions.'

'You'd be wasting your time and getting both of us in the shit.'

Jenkins was not put off, and argued his corner, and at last Hank agreed to accompany him to the IRA fundraising offices in New York, and to a few Irish bars where Gerry O'Callaghan might be known but not spoken about. He was warned that it would be dangerous. 'You must promise me you'll say nothing unless I give you the OK – and for God's sake try not to look like a limey policeman. It even gives me the creeps.'

David did his best but failed. Nevertheless Hank was entering into the spirit of things, and they worked their way down town. 'Twenty-first street,' said the yellow cab driver, 'is that in New York?' They wondered themselves, for the lively, garish bustle of the centre soon turned to the shabby detritus of a great city, where even close to the centre the roads were holed and rutted; and farther out the buildings displayed the tired overuse of an undistinguished past, and to wander too far from the highway was to court personal danger. Where they were going, the bustle and vigour of a trading community remained, but with the uncollected rubbish of the market; the tatter and tastelessness of a vigorous commerce where the profit incentive governed the cost and price of everything – including humanity itself.

The cab driver showed signs of nervousness, impatient to get paid and accelerate away. 'Keep close', ordered Hank, fingering his revolver, as other men in safer places rattle the coins in their pocket as a signal of comfort and for reassurance.

The Funds for Irish Freedom (FIR for short) offices were unpretentious from the outside, and an ancient lift took them to the reception on the third floor; but inside was another matter entirely, for there was to be found a measure of comfort and even opulence. The office furniture was new and stylish, the carpeting must have knocked them back a punt or two, and computers and ancillary equipment were of the latest marks and as up to date as could be. At first glance the people did not quite live up to the setting, for they were of the meanly constructed, hard done by variety, with the unfriendly defensiveness of the depressed and downtrodden – although David surmised they were probably neither.

Hank showed his card and asked the front desk occupant for Gerry O'Callaghan, to be told that he was not in.

'Is he ever in?' enquired Hank.

' It all depends on what you mean by in', said the girl, practising her evasiveness.

'Who d'you think you are? I suppose you think yourself a Harvard professor of philosophy, do you?' said Hank, asserting his authority. 'Let's have straight answers, shall we? When will he be in?'

'Who knows? He never tells anyone. He doesn't have to tell anyone, does he?' She was unabashed, and with the certainty of what she knew and didn't care to tell you. And looking at David Jenkins with a degree of contempt, 'Would you like to leave a message? Who shall I tell him was asking for him?'

'There you are. Useless. I told you so.' Hank just hated a rebuff of any kind.

They had to walk some distance to find an Irish bar which Gerry O'Callaghan might have been supposed to frequent. Paddy's Place had a pink and purple neon sign above an unmarked black entrance which failed to light up the second 'P', so succeeding in giving an entirely false image of possible sexual favours. It was down some steeply raked steps into a long rectangular room where the bar ran the full length, a place of serious drinking with none of the pleasantries of a Surrey pub. Even at that time of the day, late morning, it was busy. There was chatter but it stopped on their entry, as all eyes turned towards them.

'What can I get you?' The barman assumed the normal drinking courtesies.

'Gerry O'Callaghan?' replied Hank, observing courtesies of his own.

'I've always admired a good joker', said the barman, entering into the spirit of things.

'Do you know him, and is he in now, and if not when will he be – or most likely to be?' Hank was to the point.

'Well, you have a lot of fine questions. And how am I to answer you?' He paused.

'Quickly, to the point and accurately,' said Hank.

The barman laughed. 'I just love a man like you. Now let me see. Do I know a Gerry O'Callaghan? Indeed I do. I've known three of them in my lifetime and fine fellows they all were. And do I know one now? I do. But he may not be your man. And this man – the one I know – does come into the bar from time to time but he never tells me in advance – indeed, why should he? – and he never tells me anything at all about himself. In this bar a man can keep his secrets.'

They would get nowhere with him. So they bought a drink, found a corner table near the door, and passed the time of day with every back in the bar turned against them. And then a busy little man (a runner of some kind, was the thought that flashed through David Jenkins's mind) paused on his way out. 'If you want to see Gerry O'Callaghan you may find him there this evening.' He pushed a scrap of paper with the name of a bar written on it across the table. 'Not before ten.' And he was gone.

They arranged to meet at Jenkins's hotel at nine pm. On arrival there he had messages from his office. He was to ring back as a matter of urgency. Tiredness gripped him. He told reception he did not wish to be interrupted, and as for the calls, later would do. He fell asleep on the bed, to waken when darkness had fallen and the only time left was for hasty preparations for Hank's arrival. Tomorrow would do for the calls back home.

Hank was on time, and they made their way back out to Pinocchio's, the Irish bar suggested to them as a possibility. For Hank it had become something of a joke: showing this Englishman the seedier side of New York, sending the lamb to the slaughter, except because of him it wouldn't come to that: one for the memoirs. The bar was not quite what they expected. For a start the neighbourhood was salubrious, and the bar respectable, with plenty of plush leather; discreet lighting and a 'gold-plated' bar with barmen in uniform. There were cigarette girls in bunny outfits, scraped-up blonde hair, big breasts and long legs, and smoke haze and muzak. 'Looks after himself, does our Gerry', said Hank.

Nobody bothered them, and they could look around without attracting notice. Not for the most part 'made', thought Jenkins, but rather 'on the make', with the men on the young side trying to look executive-like and the girls too anxious to please. Jenkins didn't feel threatened: it would take more than people like them to threaten him. Hank was enjoying himself, pointing out a few people he knew, some of them villains and some not – or rather not known or nothing against their name yet – but supposed to be up to no good. And then out of the blue haze and standing in front of them was their 'runner' with an invitation to meet Gerry at the back and a 'Would they follow him?'

Afterwards Hank found it hard to explain his carelessness, he an experienced officer on his own patch. He thought his normal instincts for self-preservation were missing: dissipated by the beers and the warmth of the bar and by the presence of this Englishman, the innocent abroad. But he knew his behaviour was unforgivable. They moved out of the back door into an alley where Hank was immediately rendered unconscious by a severe blow to the head, from which he came round in an hospital bed some hours later. Two men pinioned Jenkins and thrust him into a large limousine, where he was trussed up like a chicken with a thick plastic bag over his head. He thought he might say later, assuming there was one, a later that is, 'four men and he hadn't a chance'. He heard words in an Irish-American accent: 'Don't struggle and we won't harm you.' He decided to be still. He remained a policeman, a detective, using skills acquired initially as a boy scout and honed at Hendon College. He began to count to himself, and noted from the starting direction the number of turnings, and which were to the right and which to the left. He timed the journey at twenty-five minutes, then concluded after calculating the road speed in busy traffic that he could not be more than six miles from the start and that they were now west of his starting point.

When he was bundled out of the car he thought from the echo of their footsteps and the length of their walk that they must be in an empty warehouse. He was bundled into a room and told he would be on his own for some time, there was nothing to fear, and there was food and drink. After he heard the door slam he was free to remove the bag. He was in a cell-like room without a window. A heavy steel door, with what appeared to be an impressive locking device, shut him in. An air vent above the door was the only opening for fresh air, and he could not see through it. The room had hardly any furniture: there were a desk and chair, a large commercial fridge and a camp bed on which two grey and musty blankets were folded, and on which a towel had been placed. He opened the fridge. It contained soft drinks, ready-made meals and fruit. Above the fridge was a bread basket with fresh bread. A door led into a dirty and uncared-for lavatory, smelling from the drains, but the loo flushed and there was loo paper. He sat down in the chair and swivelled around (he had never been able to resist swivel chairs). He examined the desk. It was empty, and someone had made sure that there were no incriminating scraps of paper to be found. He relaxed. These were not the preparations of people who wished to harm him. They had the hallmark of improvisation. Something was going on, but damn it, he was British, and it was unlikely that anyone would wish to do him down. If he had known all this he would have brought a book with him and some writing paper. He settled down to wait.

Back in the FBI office there was considerable annoyance and concern at these events. It was all most improper and unfortunate. Calls were made to Scotland Yard, but the right people were absent – they had gone home. Gone home! They could hardly believe it. In the end they contacted the Commissioner himself at his home and the air turned blue. 'Lost him, mislaid him, might have been disposed of, like any old rubbish!' He couldn't comprehend his FBI colleague who had permitted this monstrosity: but for that matter neither could the FBI. The Commissioner was told that everything in their power was being done to recover the missing man, and they would keep him constantly informed.

The matter was on the top of the Commissioner's action list on the next day as a matter of great concern. He thought it important to ensure that it was treated as highly confidential; information about the missing policeman was not to be disclosed to

anyone within or without the service. If at all possible an embarrassment such as this should be kept strictly to those with 'leave
to know'. Admittedly a number of policemen already knew
something was afoot, but they were quickly contacted and
silenced. Among those in the know, which did not include Bob
Churchill-Jones, it became a subject of great ribaldry and curiosity. After all it was only human. There was 'Mr Efficiency'
himself muscling in on a New York jamboree, involving himself
in the detail of a case he knew very little about, and what does he
do? Gets himself kidnapped.

Bob felt his reaction to the mystery of David Jenkins's plight
to be un-Christian; but then you could be too harsh on yourself.
That evening he was off to his Scripture class at St Ethelreda's
and he would have an opportunity to reflect and to behave better
about it. 'But come on', he told himself, and laughed some more.
Bob needed this Scripture class, for he felt that his highly
controlled behaviour of the past two years was coming apart, and
he was not truly himself any more. His attempts to make new
friends had not been limited to the Scripture class. There was the
introduction agency. Joining the Make New Friends club had
seemed like a good idea, for he was anxious to give himself some
alternatives to Andrea, and to be frank, to keep her at bay. Various contact names had been given him by the club secretary,
together with photographs and descriptions. Then there was a
section in the application form in which you set out what you
were looking for in a partner. Other people could read it. In filling out his own form he had described himself as single, which
was the first time he had done that for twenty years. He felt bad
about it and stupid, for he had patiently waited for Gloria, whom
he still thought of as his wife, for over two years now. And he
loved her, he felt sure he did. But somehow loving her was not
enough any more. He had lied to the agency and to the women
he had met about other details too: he told no one he was a
policeman, inventing new occupations for himself with caprice,
once he had some measure of the other parties. It was no way for
a Christian to behave. But who knew it?

The women he had met as a result of these introductions had
amazed him. It seemed to him that they were far more advanced
than him in escape from the past. With the exception of one very

nice and very shy lady, who had cried when she spoke about her former husband, and who had gone home early, these women were seeking adventure. They were all of what was called 'independent means', which they had either chiselled out from the remains of their former husbands or earned themselves from a variety of occupations. A nice fellow like Bob, reasonably well off with a central London flat, looked to them to be fair game. So to his mortification he had enjoyed sex with different women on three successive nights. If this was how the world was to become ordered, he thought, why would any man bother to get married? Of course, there was the procreation of children. But then they had already procreated, at least most of them, so it was not an issue for them any more. As for him, he had Mrs Frost who kept the house far cleaner than any wife would, wives thinking that kind of thing to be boring and a waste of time. But he liked a clean and orderly house. As for food, he had a fridge and a microwave and the best restaurants and snack bars in London within easy reach. You could get lonely. That was true enough, but then as he demonstrated to himself there were ways of getting around that.

This evening Father Matthew was talking about forgiveness and of Christ's teaching that we should love our enemies and forgive people who trespass against us. He said that if Jesus could forgive us, who – or at least our forebears – had crucified and killed him, then how much more willing should we be to forgive our friends and neighbours for their shortcomings? And yet he said we were all going on about our grievances when to be honest, and usually, we were complaining about nothing at all – and how boring it was of us. Father Matthew said that forgiving people was very good for the person doing the forgiving and that we did not always realise it: that forgiving released us from the negative energy of grievance and enabled us to move on as better people.

On the way home, Bob thought about forgiveness as it affected him and Gloria. Perhaps the glue was coming unstuck now because he had forgiven Gloria. Over the past two years he had stuck to her because he hadn't forgiven her – he had been seeking to persuade her to change her mind, to say that she was sorry, which she certainly had no intention of doing – whereas if he had truly forgiven her and himself they could both have moved on. Was that it? Was that what he had done?

In his 'prison cell' David Jenkins was getting impatient. There was nothing to do with his time, and the room was cold. It was nearly two days before his captors returned, with hoods over their heads so that he could not identify them. The procedure swung into reverse until with wheely-bin plastic on his head he was dumped out of the car. A captor said: 'You're gonna be dumped in Central Park. Keep this bag on your head for two minutes. Just don't remove it before. We've one of our men in the park and if he sees you removing the bag before we're out of sight he has orders to shoot you. D'you understand?'

He said that he did, and they dumped him, and he waited as they instructed. When at last he looked he did not see anyone waiting to shoot him, but who knows?

Jenkins made his way back to his hotel, where he had been booked out of his room, and the reception staff, seeing his dishevelled state and the two days of growth on his chin, were reluctant to re-book him until he had explained and a call to the FBI had confirmed his story.

The FBI called around, although no one he recognised, with Hank being in the hospital and the others fully engaged with other things. He was anxious to tell them his story, in particular the calculations he had made about the whereabouts of the building he had been held in, and his other observations, all of which he recognised as being helpful detail in capturing the persons involved in the crime. He was surprised to find they had very little interest in all that. They explained to him that his absence had created something of a transatlantic furore, and that hard words had been expressed on both sides. His bosses had told the FBI they simply could not understand how he had got into such a mix-up. He might think of something on the plane, the FBI said helpfully. And, no, they said to reception, Mr Jenkins doesn't need his room and we'll take care of the bill; and to Jenkins they said there was still time to get him on to an evening flight. They had a ticket for him and it was their duty to get him to the airport. So he found himself safely placed in a first-class cabin seat where he could shave himself and fall asleep, temporarily oblivious of the gathering storm ahead of him.

And gathering it was. The Commissioner had had an early morning call from the Permanent Secretary at the Home Office, who gave him some disturbing news about Gerry O'Callaghan. The Secretary expressed his displeasure at the activities of his Assistant Commissioner. There was some talk of two left feet and blundering in where he had no business to concern himself. Then there were other revelations about Gerry O'Callaghan which amazed and dumbfounded the Commissioner so he began to say things like, 'Quite. I do understand ... and most unfortunate.... I do see ... although we could not be expected to know that ... didn't know that to be precise. And ... of course we will ... I'll see to it personally and you can rely on me.'

When the Commissioner put the phone down he was livid, and as his secretary Ann Thomson was the only person within reach he took it out on her, reducing her to tears, actions which he immediately regretted, for he was very fond of her and she served him well.

This drama was played out above Bob's head, quite literally as the Commissioner's office was on a higher floor. While he might normally have been aware of the gathering drama, today he was not, for he had drama enough of his own. One of Bob's maxims which had served him well over the years was that if it's important, don't leave it to others. In the Roger Greer case he had left it to Alec to review all those CCTV cameras in garages on the route from Bungay to Surrey on the night of the blaze that had partly burnt down the property of one of Roger's former directors. It was a tedious job, and one he knew was not suitable for your younger man, impatient as he was to get on to greater things. Bob decided to go over these pictures himself in the hope of finding something overlooked by Alec.

It was a long and boring task which occupied him for most of six weeks. And then: *voila!* There it was: a clear impression of Roger's vehicle registration plate at a petrol station in the right place and at the right time.

Bob said nothing to Alec. He decided to say nothing to anyone until this business with Jenkins had unwound itself and everyone knew where they stood.

Jenkins arrived home in the early hours to a welter of messages from personages high and low. He was in poor shape. He might have pleaded post-traumatic shock and sought counselling or recovery in a long absence from work at cost to the taxpayer, but he did none of these things. He unplugged his telephone and went to bed, where he fell into the deepest of sleep, as one might say of a newly born baby.

He woke to the sound of his doorbell being rung repeatedly. On staggering to the door he found the Commissioner on his doorstep. It was a first: the Commissioner had never before visited Jenkins at his flat. The Commissioner was highly animated and allowed him only a precious few minutes to collect himself and to make them both a coffee to deal with the early morning shakes. The Commissioner explained that he, David Jenkins, had been responsible for stirring up a hornets' nest: not deliberately, he appreciated that, but as a result of highly irresponsible behaviour which frankly he had not expected of him of all people. Normally this sort of behaviour would be dealt with through the usual disciplinary procedures, but there were reasons in this instance for not wanting to take this route. The Commissioner explained these reasons, while Jenkins tried hard to prevent his chin from reaching his boots.

'Well, Commissioner.' Jenkins found his voice. 'How on earth did you expect me to know that?'

The Commissioner had the grace to interrupt his flow while Jenkins recognised he was in a stronger position than he had realised at the outset. He continued, gathering momentum, 'I'll take legal advice, you know, if any action's taken against me.'

The Commissioner held his fire. This could get dangerous for him. He quickly reviewed his position before resuming, 'I don't wish to be unreasonable. This is what I suggest. You take some paid leave for a while: say, four weeks. After all you've gone through, you need it. Go away to some remote island and get some sunshine and rest. I'll promise that nothing will happen in your absence, and that everything will be as normal when you return. In this time we can let the dust settle and see where we all are when it's at rest.'

They shook hands on it. David Jenkins went back to bed not believing a word of it, while the Commissioner, still in high dudgeon, returned to his official car muttering to himself. Would it all settle down as if nothing had happened? He thought not. And as for his promises, '*force majeure*', he said to himself.

CHAPTER 18

FAITH WAS TO be released from her sanatorium in Caux, and Melissa flew to Switzerland to collect her daughter. It was a solemn and joyous moment for them both. Faith had passed through an experience she would never forget. Later in life she had the greatest of difficulties in entering any hospital, regardless of whether as a patient or visitor. While black represents for most of us the colour of death, for Faith it was white; and while quietness, sunshine and the sounds of birdsong might be expected to convey peacefulness, for Faith it was the presage of a passing away. That was what happened at the clinic. Ill people came and after a while they died and their bodies were collected. You could meet other patients at the clinic and exchange hopes and fears with them, so that you started to care for these people, wishing them well. You were grateful to them for listening to you and raising your spirits. But then you hesitated – and it was really hateful – without the confidence to become real friends with anyone because at any time you might find them gone, passed away, and the skids would be back under you.

While her stay at the hospital was short, the experiences of being there had a rare intensity which affected Faith forever. For the first time she became aware of the reality of the transience of life, her own life, and she arrived at a view that life had to be lived and enjoyed in its immediacy. As an adult she never planned ahead. Her friends thought it charming that she could up and go anywhere, it seemed at the drop of a hat, whether a spontaneous visit to the theatre or a trip into the wilderness. She forwent savings and pension plans, whenever and wherever they were offered to her, never on her own account owned a property on a mortgage, and always preferred the short term to any long-term consideration. Her emotional attachments tended to be of limited duration, and she drew back at the point at which she might have to commit her emotions beyond the present.

The clinic had its own peculiar smells: a mixture of disease and decay and the chemicals that waged their unceasing war against the unseen enemy – and then, being in Switzerland, the overwhelming pungency of sheer cleanliness. These smells were to haunt her, and later even household cleaners were to plunge her back to the trauma of these times. Plunging herself amidst Melissa's smells, burying her face in the wool and fur of her topcoat, was an ecstasy of release for Faith. At that moment Melissa was the boundary: on one side lay death and defeat, and on the other life with all its hopes and illusions.

'Where's Daddy?' she asked, for there were other smells and she had missed them also.

'He's meeting us, darling, at the airport in London', Melissa replied. It was not necessary really, but he had insisted, and she had given way very readily. It was nice to be met at an airport.

Faith was quiet and tearful on the plane, and as they neared Heathrow she fell asleep and had to be awakened from the depths on arrival. And then there was Daddy, who was burying her with his hugs and sweeping her from the ground and whirling her round like a dervish. She was too big to be carried by him, but she insisted, and he held her aloft for a long time until at last it was too much even for him. As she clung to him her heart sank. He had some grey hairs. He was getting older and would not be around for ever. He was mortal. She wasn't having that, and vowed to speak to him about it. He could pluck these hairs out, as her mother sometimes did, although she would not admit to it, or dye his hair – that was it – so he didn't have any grey hairs at all. She would talk to him about it.

They had decided for Faith's sake to travel back by taxi, wincing at the thought of the expense. They joined a long queue. Heavy rain had turned the road surface greasy and treacherous, and while the rain had lessened, they all needed the shelter of Roger's accommodating large black umbrella. Faith was still being carried by him and Melissa, coming closer than she cared

to, took his arm. She had to look at him. Still an attractive and
kindly man despite his problems, which she would have seen,
were she able to look closely, had aged him. It was not so long
ago that clasping him like this would have awakened her desire
for him. Why, in their early days, when he rang, her body would
sing like the wind in the reeds; her knees would buckle, and she
would become moist in her longing for him. It was very different now. She saw that Faith had closed her eyes in complete
confidence that he would hold her safely and warmly. How easy
it was for him, she thought, a quick cuddle and then away leaving her with the tasks of bringing Faith up and nursing her
through this dreadful disease

She had read on the plane the very careful and comprehensive
notes the clinic had prepared on the care that Faith would need
and the routine she would have to follow. There was a section on
What To Tell: the patient, friends and family and carers. She
would have a lot to tell to a lot of people, and things between
them would never be normal and relaxed again: they would all
whisper about her daughter, giving her anxious glances if any
little thing were to seem to go wrong. A section on Diet made it
clear that there were a great many no-go areas: McDonald's and
quick-fix ready meals were definitely out. Medication stressed
the vital importance of the regular administration of a number of
remedies exactly on time, and the dangers of missing any of
them. Given her job, her schedule, she would have to rely on
others. And then there were Dangerous Symptoms. She was to
look out for any sudden fever, listlessness, headaches and diar-
rhoea. Considering all these things, and her own itinerant occupation, she understood that her daughter would never be out of
her mind, wherever she was, whatever she was doing and in
whatever time zone she was to be found. Tears came at the vexa-
tiousness of it, which she knew was absurd, because what she
mainly felt was an overwhelming relief that her daughter had
been reprieved.

There was a diversion on the way home to collect Adam, who
had been left overnight at the home of a school friend. He was in
no hurry to leave, and was resistant to the thought of sharing a
taxi with his father. This house he was in was a real home. The
man in it was the right age for a father and had a regular job: he

left at about eight, and sometimes he dropped his son off at school, and then he was back on the dot at six-thirty. This family had regular holidays they could all rely on, and in sensible places, Greece, Spain and Portugal. And they had a lot of money: his friend had many times more pocket money than him, and every week and not only when his parents had spare cash, and paid into his own bank account. His friend had a computer, with the latest games, and a television in his bedroom, where he was allowed to watch any programme and to put up any poster.

Adam was pushed into the taxi. It was very embarrassing. These adults were very good about his tantrums. They laughed about them, refusing to take offence; they behaved as if they were all perfectly normal and just something to be dealt with. Roger made jokes about it but Adam could see, to his satisfaction, that his friend's family were not deceived by these pleasantries and that their bonhomie was false. They knew Adam was unfairly treated. Adam was committed to making sure everyone knew of his plight.

They squeezed up to accommodate him. Adam thought his sister too pale. 'Are you still ill?' he asked, moving his face close and then wondering whether it was catching.

'Yes, I suppose so.'

'Are you going to die?' He thought it best to know exactly where the truth lay.

'Adam, shut up.' His mother was cross with him.

'Well, are you?' Adam persisted.

Faith was tearful. His father replied in his comprehensive sort of way which bored you to death in the end and which never answered your question. 'She is going to get better, Adam. It'll be a long fight and Faith will need all our care – that includes you – and in the end, God willing, she'll recover completely.'

'So does that mean she might not – get better, that is?'

They ignored him. He thought that if she died he might have her room because it was much bigger than his own. Not that he wished her to die, because he didn't, but then it would be a consequence; and he had never known anyone close who had died.

He whispered to his sister, 'What do you have for me, and is there a present?' You had to admit that one of the perks of his father's frequent overseas trips had been presents on his return, sometimes exotic or unexpected. Guilt money, but still.

'No.' She was definite.

'Are you sure?' Ill people were sometimes confused.

His mother, overhearing slightly, said, 'We saved you some things from the plane.'

He held them in his cupped hands: chocolates, small pots of jam, a strawberry and cream trifle. Nothing tradable here, nothing to boast about. Although not bad in themselves. 'Is that all? Are you joking?'

His mother said something to the effect that it was the thought that counted.

Back home Adam could see that his mother had taken great care to make his sister's room warm and welcoming. She had left the heat on although she could not really afford to do so. Adam thought it unfair really. All that consideration for her. What about him? He hoped that she would get well soon so equality of treatment could be restored.

Melissa put her daughter to bed. Faith clung to her, begging that her father stay. Just for one night, she pleaded. Her mother had not the heart to refuse her, so Roger was provided with the couch for the night, and with the children in bed, the chance to talk to Melissa about their daughter. Adam did not go willingly. He protested, not wanting his father to be there in the morning with his do's and don'ts.

Roger said he wanted to be as helpful as possible, and that included putting Faith up in his cottage. He would take off time from work to be with his daughter. Melissa said that this was impossible, and that given the delicacy of Faith's condition she would need to be cared for in her own home. Unfortunately staying overnight with him in a country cottage could not be considered an option in the near future. If he had money to spare to take time off, he could help best by contributing it to the cost of the domestic help that would be needed when she was working away from home.

Roger knew his daughter needed him – and he needed her. But what he was confronted with was the ultimatum that all he was good for was money. He had rights, rights of access to his daughter. But in the circumstances of her illness there was no way to enforce them. That was how things were, and that was how they would stay. And upstairs also was his 'angry wasp' of a son. If he could he would sting, my God he would.

Seeing his distress, Melissa did her best to reassure him. She would be as flexible as she could. They would talk regularly. Of course, his daughter needed him. She would make it possible for them to spend some time together. She wasn't setting out to be awkward. It was the situation, didn't he see? And so on, and so on.

Being reasonable, he said that of course it was the situation, and he was grateful to her and recognised that the main burden of care would fall upon her. He would be as accommodating as possible. After all, Faith should come first, and the last thing either of them wanted her to think was that her parents were at loggerheads about her welfare. And so on, and so on. But what he knew was that he would not be able to care for his daughter; and what he feared would come back to haunt him was that one day she would say, and it would be true, that he hadn't loved her enough when she needed him most; and it would be impossible to explain himself to her – and far too late, even supposing he could.

As he hit the road the following morning he felt the wet kiss of his daughter on his cheek. Her entreaties that he should come back very soon rang in his ears, like tinnitus, blocking out all other sounds. He was always overwhelmingly sad when he left his children. He knew it was a sense of loss. Of course it was, but it was something else as well. He was being punished for his shortcomings. It was his fault that there was loss. He had failed them and there was no way he could put that right. But although he had been defeated, it was only a battle; if you only fought the battles you could win, and attempted no worthwhile campaign for fear of failure in the end, there would be no life, nothing done and nothing achieved. Still, it was a sorry business.

Melissa was nowhere as severe about everything as Roger might have thought. She had to be realistic because she was at the sticky end of all this. Men were so unrealistic and vague but the years ahead – and wasn't this true in general of bringing up children? – were going to be governed by a complex routine: doing things on time, parallel lines, and trains running to precise times, and everyone knowing what was expected of them, and if not, wham! Disaster. Roger could not be fitted into the timetable:

it was just too complicated however you regarded it. But she saw his problem, she knew that his presence was important to her daughter, and she was not unsympathetic. She would do what she could. There might be room for the occasional excursion train if it ran in the off-peak and the passengers all knew in advance of the special conditions attaching to travel on such a train, and abided by the rules.

Roger was now in the habit of reporting to Rachel, and he did so as soon as he was back home. She worked out the timing of his journey and was in the cottage on his arrival. She had a key now, and was in the habit of slipping into his home at odd times, sometimes on her own and sometimes with Fiona, and doing things: making sure the cottage was clean and tidy, putting flowers in vases, airing the rooms, washing and ironing his clothes so that he looked smart in a clean shirt and slept between pristine sheets, and sometimes cooking him a meal and leaving it the oven for him. He told her she shouldn't but she ignored him.

Rachel shared the meal with him. He told her everything he knew about Faith's condition and passed over to her his copy of the clinic's handout. Rachel read quickly. It was much as she had thought, for she was impressively well informed. He realised that she had continued to do her research on the disease and its treatments. He told her about Melissa's thoughts and reactions and his fears that he would be able to do very little. And she listened. He loved her for it, and it amazed him: for most of the time he saw her as vulnerable and sometimes confused, and it moved him and he wished to protect her; but when there was a problem to be dealt with, which required intellect and good sense to address, she was formidable.

And she was now. Rachel understood Melissa's difficulties and hesitations, and she told him Melissa was right. It was necessary for him to show that Faith would be entirely safe in his care, and that Melissa would have no need to worry about her at all if she was left with him. At the moment he could not state that, so he must wait patiently until those conditions were created. In any event it was much too soon to know how Faith would react to the new treatment proposed for her. At the right time, and it was yet to come, she would talk to Melissa and they could work together on the problems, but for the moment it was not appropriate.

Roger had mentioned Rachel to Melissa, and she knew that Rachel had been helpful in setting up Faith's medical treatment; but beyond that nothing had been said, and nothing inferred. Roger sought to be helpful. Arrangements had to be made for Faith to see a consultant in London, and this turned out to involve a series of visits. The supervision of the treatment was to be carried out by Faith's GP, and Faith had to attend the surgery. In practice hybrid treatment, part private and part NHS, proved difficult to arrange and there were bureaucratic objections. The difficulties were overcome. Roger sought leave of absence to accompany his daughter on these occasions, and time was readily given; partly because he was becoming a valuable member of staff but also, he thought, being dimly aware of goings on, because his manager's ear had been commanded from above.

Faith thought it was all right. Daddy wasn't there all the time, which was better than him staying and then her parents rowing, but he could be summoned up by her, she thought like a genie in a lamp. She imagined she might have one, a magic lamp, and then it would not be necessary for anyone to call him on the phone: she could lie still in her bed and rub the lamp and summon him whenever she wanted But if she couldn't do that – for getting a magic lamp was not easy – she knew he would still be there for her if she asked.

She held hands with him on all these medical occasions, and he explained to her in advance what was going to happen and the results, so she began to understand what the battle was about and what was expected of her. It was reassuring to have Daddy on your side, for although Mummy was very doughty she did sometimes get things wrong, and then on occasions she was too busy to listen or to be there. So her spirits rose that she had two real champions and not one and a half.

Melissa was reassured. Faith's medical treatment had been put smoothly into place and everyone knew exactly what was expected of them. Early signs were good. Faith was back at school, and life seemed to be back on a level course after several months of dread and disaster. For this she thanked Roger: when it had come to it, he had been splendid and could be relied upon. Melissa was dimly aware that there was someone else pulling strings here, but she chose to remain ignorant of the details and accepting of Roger's cover story: it was Faith's life that was at stake and that was all that mattered.

Late one Friday, Roger returning to his cottage found that Rachel had been there before him and had left him a casserole with instructions. She had signed off the note with 'love Rachel'. It was the first time either of them had used the dreaded word 'love'. It was a much-abused word, he thought, and used much too carelessly: with some people it just tripped off their tongues all the time. But Rachel was not like them. She was careful with words. They had both been very careful.

For Rachel, loving Roger was like peeling an onion. You had to do it very carefully and expect to cry a lot. She saw these troubles of Roger's as stretching to a distant horizon, but one day they would be no more. It was her faith. She genuinely believed that one day his misfortunes would be no more. If she helped him deal with them, hopefully to get rid of them, she brought the day nearer when they could address each other as free spirits. That was what she wanted, a man alongside for her and for the children, but not just any man, she wanted Roger. And that was not an easy thing for her to want. When she had turned away from Gloria, she had not been quite as resolute as Gloria might have imagined. It was on balance that she had wanted him, but when she did, it was with all her heart and soul.

He went up to his attic where he could look out across the marshes in the dying light and think about what it meant. He hardly dare think about it at all. He loved these large Norfolk skies. At one moment they could be entirely clear but then as you looked you could see them change before you. Close to the sea the weather closed in quickly, whatever it was to be: suddenly a clear blue sky could darken to grey, and the stillness would be disturbed by a whipped-up wind that scattered the brightness before you and beyond. Ever since his company had failed, his misfortunes had come regularly like the clouds building before him, as if there were no end and he had triggered off some force of nature beyond his control. There was before him still the great threat of a criminal prosecution, of which Rachel knew so very little. There must be a limit to her willingness to help him. He did not wholly understand the reasons for her great generosity to him, which far outreached the warmth of so recent a friendship. Should he tell her everything? Dare he tell her of the threat that now beckoned, and could there be any expectation of surviving a rejection?

He was feverish now, afraid of the questions and possible answers. He had never been able to deal with these dilemmas to his satisfaction. Should you dissemble, keep the truth of happenings away from a beloved when there was no need to tell, when after all nothing might come of it? And by this reasoning, should he tell Rachel of this possible charge against himself? You heard of it all the time. The husband rushes home and confesses to his wife some treacherous act, and the very next moment he and his luggage are in the drive. If you lived with it, gave the offensive up, nothing might happen and you would live happily ever after. But he knew it was nothing like that in his case, and winced at his own crudeness. One by one these misfortunes had to be dealt with, and there could be no future with Rachel or anyone at all until they had passed; and if life was transitory, so must be misfortune. But his sins, if he could call them that, might have to be repented, and then perhaps when he had been punished for them, life could go on. It all sounded impossibly puritanical.

He came down from the attic suddenly impressed by the sense of the inevitable. He would turn his mind to more mundane tasks; and he did. But every now and again he picked up Rachel's note and read in her clear handwriting the words, 'love Rachel'. What would he do for the love of Rachel? Almost anything. Did he dare to confess? Before him lay a bar not of his making. He did not choose to love Rachel. But nothing could come of it, he felt quite sure, until he had told her everything and she had forgiven him, truly forgiven him. But whatever she might say, it might not be enough, for there could be no future for them if he was prosecuted: he would be too mortified, too humbled to seek anything at all from her or anyone. And then in advancing his own cause with her he would have caused her a much greater hurt than if he had remained silent. So he hesitated. Declaring the possibility would in some way make the offence tangible; while silence might limit the offence to nightmare rather than event.

CHAPTER 19

NOW THAT GLORIA had been obliged to abandon her hopes of Rachel, her mind and emotions turned elsewhere. Her Open University course in Effective Management took up much of her time, and as her marks were high she grew in confidence. Andrew Thorpe, the venture capitalist she had met on her course, seemed to want to lend her money, and had started to send her details of businesses to buy which he maintained were right for development. She had accumulated considerable savings of her own, which were sufficient to put down a deposit, which together with a commercial mortgage would be her financial contribution to any investment. She was able now to put together her own return on investment model, and into this she put some of the details Andrew had sent her, to find that several of them offered an attractive return. She told Andrew, and he told her to come and talk about it, and invited her to dinner in a plush restaurant at a nearby manor house, a place that had excited her interest for some time. She had seen it as a problem that he was interested in more than lending her money, but now she thought, why not?

As she prepared herself she engaged in the task of self-examination which had seized her imagination since she had left Bob. She thought she had never looked better than at this moment – but she imagined it to be her zenith. She was thirty-nine and already the men she liked, and might wish to date, were younger. Andrew was probably several years younger, although he did not look it. It might be time to make her mind up about what she wanted in life.

Andrew was very nice to her and made her feel comfortable. The restaurant catered for the comfortably-off and had a discreetness – and an opulence – which pleased her. The meal was superlative, and the wines far exceeded in quality anything she could afford to buy for the inn. He was attentive and engaging, and as the wine began to warm her, she began to like almost everything about him. She gazed at his mouth and found herself wanting to kiss it; and her knees were definitely weakening with the tension of it all. If he asks me, she thought, I shall say yes.

He had not been forthcoming with information about himself, though, and it became important to her to know whether he was married. So she asked him and he said, 'Yes. Does it matter? After all, aren't you?'

She replied, 'I suppose not. And yes, I'm married but we've been separated for over three years now.' Then, 'Do you live with your wife?'

'Yes, I do. But don't you think it deadly boring to be committed to one partner without relief of any kind?'

She didn't know what to say, although she disagreed with him and hated being thought of as just the relief.

He had booked a room, which she did not like because it made her seem easy meat; and then she felt the whole meal to be no more than his aperitif. Even then it might have been possible. But then, when she went to the bathroom to undress – or not quite, for she thought it sexy to retain her sheer silk blouse, open to the waist, and a very pretty bra – she came back to find he had got undressed and revealed himself naked on the bed. As she approached, hormones bouncing, he sat up, resting on one elbow. She stopped, seeing that his chest and back – a chest somewhat artificially inflated from the gym – were covered with coarse black hair. Andrew was transformed in her imagination to a sort of gorilla: a person dwelling on the animal/human border. It was horrible. The whole of his front looked like a door mat. Each woman to her preference. She had always hated hairy chests and backs. She laughed. She couldn't stop laughing at the incongruity of it. The last naked and quite wonderful body she had seen was Rachel's – and now this!

She was hysterical now. Then there was silence and a few tense moments. She apologised. She explained that it was his hair that was the difficulty: it was just not her thing. She thought, there must be other venture capitalists. Of course there are. As quickly as she could she scrambled into her clothes and fled.

She never heard from Andrew again. For some time she was haunted by the thought that all venture capitalists might have hairy chests; that their occupation might bring out the caveman in them. But of course in the end she found a completely normal and correct one, so far as she could ascertain.

When she thought about bodies she preferred Rachel's to anything she could imagine, infinitely preferred it; but when she thought of niceness and comfort, she thought of Bob. Good old Bob. She resolved at the weekend she had planned with Bob to have it all out with him and to give him a proper chance. This sort of new beginning would have been approved of at St. Ethelreda's, which had become so influential with Bob. And in his heart of hearts, Gloria knew – despite the evidence of her own eyes – that it was what he wanted. Indeed at that time it was what Bob believed he wanted.

But what Bob wanted was a mystery to him. For so long he had just wanted Gloria back. He would forgive her and life would resume as normal. But time had passed, and then there was Andrea. She was great – everyone said so – and smashing to have on your arm. All that warmth and spontaneity. Very, very flattering to him. His daughter Susan kept saying, 'You're a lucky man, Dad. Anyone would want Andrea', and 'She'll sort you out.' Then there was the dating agency. It had been a mistake. There had been several very bad moments, but on the other hand one or two of the introductions had been fun and one a real revelation. But at his age did he want to be sorted out, or to live in fear of new revelations? He sighed, feeling the burden of his sexuality.

There was more to life than sex and money. He was sure of it, and that was why he attended St Ethelreda's. He wanted to sharpen up what he apprehended as the life of the spirit, which he believed should transcend all those other things that took up so much of your time. A life of spiritual awareness required one to live a controlled and rational life, and to keep the passions in their proper place. That was what marriage was intended for: to keep the passions in their proper place. It sounded boring but he knew that dullness was not inevitable: and passions would never be in their proper place with Andrea!

And there were other important matters pressing in upon him: the police, for example. He disliked the police force now, and when you started to hate your place of work you should really get away from it altogether and do something else. He had been there too long, and it was wrong of him to stay. When he had joined he was full of enthusiasm and motivated by the wish to serve the community and to put something back into it. And if he was pressed he would still defend the service from the serious doubters; for most of his colleagues were like him, and only wanted to do their best. He didn't share Gloria's robust criticisms. It wasn't as bad as that, and men knew that boys had to be boys. His conclusions were his own. He had always been his own man.

Alec asked him what he would do when he was not a policeman. 'Or would you do nothing? Live on your early pension?' were his questions. He had thought about that, and what he might do that would use his police experience and the enjoyment he got from dealing with human problems; and he had begun to scan the papers for job opportunities. There was quite a lot that he could do and get enjoyment from, but no decision could be reached until he had sorted out with Gloria what the future might hold for them.

The weekend was unavoidable. Both Gloria and Bob approached it with trepidation. Bob had decided he wanted to be clear-headed – Gloria was so powerful and overwhelming these days – so he asked her to book him a separate room a long way from her at the Ship Inn. She was surprised by his request, but thought if that was how he wished to play it, so be it. Then he didn't want to spend his time in a crowded bar, and asked her nicely to take some time off so they could spend time out of doors. And she did arrange it. So far she was quiescent. But he could not ask her to look less than her best or to choose anything other than the perfume he preferred most. So he had to admit that she looked stunning, that she moved to a rhythm that was overwhelming, and smelt like the goddess of love herself; and he could not deny her a recognition that she was all those things that flatter and seduce men. In short she had done her very best, and it was some offering.

They walked around part of the North Norfolk coast. Coping with a brisk north-easterly wind did not enable Gloria to project herself at her very best, albeit her outdoor coat was very smart and appealing. The cold wind numbed and preoccupied them, and the physical struggle to stay upright made it difficult for them to hold any meaningful discussion. But after some fluffing about and avoiding the issues, Gloria decided to get to the point, and asked him whether he wished to resume his married life with her.

It shocked him, this directness, whereas some little while ago it would have thrilled him. He equivocated. He spoke of his police career coming to an end and his thoughts about alternative employment.

'Good,' she responded, 'good for you', and 'Excellent, that might work out well.' She made other encouraging remarks to show him she was on his side.

He spoke about the Garth Droylsden case, and how he would for neatness's sake like to bring it to a conclusion, without telling her what he knew. She said nothing. He spoke of Susan and the importance of knowing how she would react.

She was brusque. 'She'd think it up to us, don't you think?'

'Yes, but she's been very good about everything, and should be involved in any decision.' Then very weakly, 'In my opinion.'

She noted that he had not answered her question, and left it for a while. When the subject was resumed she teased him about what she called his extracurricular activities. He blushed, muttering that they had been mistakes. But she went on prodding. Was there someone else?

He muttered that there had been other women.

'Yes,' she said, pressing him a little, 'but did they lead to anything? Anything more than one-offs?'

'No.' He didn't want to talk about it.

'And Andrea, is that serious? Susan speaks very highly of her.' She was remorseless. If there was another woman she was determined to find it out right now.

'No.' He was reduced to monosyllables.

They left it and returned to the subject at dinner. This time the weather was no enemy, and Gloria looked ravishing. She was determined to get her man. But it was all very pleasant and they enjoyed themselves.

Then the moment came, and the issue was whether she was to be taken or not. Gloria coaxed him to look directly into her eyes, green pools of invitation and delight which always served her so well. He had always found them irresistible. He hesitated. She took his hand and put it on her breast. He was very weak now but managed the words, 'Can I make a condition?'

She looked surprised. 'Yes, what is it?'

'Can I take the initiatives?'

'What, forever, or just for now?' She laughed at him, genuinely amused.

'Well, starting now, and then we'll see.'

'Come on then, come and take an initiative.'

She wondered whether he was up to it. But he was up to it. Oh, my, she thought, there must be something to these dating clubs after all.

In the end it was Gloria who weakened. She had really enjoyed it and was quite blown out. 'Surprise, surprise', she said, and she fell asleep.

When Gloria awoke Bob was gone, not just to his bedroom, but from the inn. A note stated that he was so glad and would be in touch. She was surprised, and wondered whether her question had been answered in the affirmative.

Bob had bought time. He was flattered that after these hard times of trying, his very beautiful wife had seemed to conclude that he was adequate and that there might be a future for them. But what sort of future? She had done so extraordinarily well, and showed no signs of arresting her progress so that he could catch up. And then quite frankly, and it seemed churlish to recognise it, he had more pressing things on his mind. There was the case against Roger Greer, which might now be proved, stultified now not by him but by the mysterious absence of his boss David Jenkins. There was his retirement from the police force and the excitement of finding a new career, or perhaps no more than a job; and there was Andrea, who simply could not be ignored. He had hoped that St. Ethelreda's might help him find a way through this maze, but while the class he had joined there, and the people he had come to know, were a comfort and even an inspiration to him, he did not see how it all signified. Father Matthew had urged him to pray, and had suggested ways that he might make a start, the key being to ask nothing for yourself, other than understanding, and to look outside yourself, in the love of God, to the welfare of others. He tried. It did not seem to work for him, but as Father Matthew said, 'God works in mysterious ways his wonders to perform.' Fair enough.

His daughter Susan had made it a habit now to visit him at weekends, usually but not always accompanied by her boyfriend Philip. He rather liked Philip, an earnest and quiet lad with a dogged devotion to Susan. He reminded Bob of a professional cricketer: there was an outdoor feel to him, and he was as brown as a berry, with short and hairy forearms with the power you imagined to punch drives on both sides of the wicket. By the time they reached London, Philip was usually slightly phased out, as if he had fielded all day in the sunshine without the protection of a cap. Bob thought him a good and calming influence on his daughter, and felt protective towards him.

On this weekend Susan was quick to waylay him in the kitchen, where self-sufficient now, he was preparing an evening meal for them all.

'Dad! What have you been up to? Mum rang. She sounded over the moon.'

'What do you mean?' He decided to play it long.

'Don't play the innocent with me. You know what I mean. Mum was so complimentary about you. Said you had changed. Much more understanding and open to things, and about time too!' She could not avoid the dig.

'Well, that's good, isn't it? I hope you approve.'

'Of course I do. Naturally I told her that it was all my influence and that I'd been spending time with you.'

'What a tease.' He smiled at her, pleased that she was happy. 'And what did Gloria say?'

'She said that I flattered myself and that in some of the ways she meant the changes could have nothing to do with me.'

'And you said....'

'I said Andrea. That it was Andrea, and I described her to mum. And I'm right, aren't I? It's Andrea.'

He thought not, but he wasn't going to go into that with her, of all people. And he realised a little sadly that her good offices were not available to him at all. How simplistic he had been to think that his daughter would welcome a rapprochement between her parents. Emotionally she had already written that off, and the struggle had been a deep hurt to her. At first she had hoped beyond hope that she would wake up one day to find smiling faces and happy parents reunited, and that the noise of quarrels and bitter disputes were past; although to be fair to Bob, he had shielded her from much of that and had remained calm about Gloria abandoning him. Susan had built a stout wall within which she had buried her feelings, and the polarity of her parents' separate lives kept her edifice in place . The thought that the wall might come down was more than she could bear. While there were at least two sides to every story, and she knew that she would never understand the reasons for the separation of her parents, Susan blamed her mother for the rupture, and there was no arguing with her about it. Nothing would change her mind: there was no place for facts, and she was blind to new illuminations.

Susan thought of herself as fair minded. If he had suggested that she was not neutral she would have protested. Of course she was. But he recognised that the reality was that she had not the slightest wish for her parents to be reunited, which she would have thought bad for them both, and that in the crunch of the moment, and if pressed, his daughter would come down on his side.

Susan said, 'Come on dad, admit it: a passionate and sexy Italian lady who thinks you are the bee's knees and loves you to bits. It can't be bad.'

He protested his innocence and she threw the tea towel at him. He would say no more to his daughter although she teased and probed him; and then, weekend over, she forgot about it all and concentrated on the matters of overriding interest to her.

Gloria did not forget. She began to call Bob regularly, and to discuss with him what was in her mind: her thoughts about buying a business of her own, and then, as she saw the importance of what might be called 'career change' to him, what he was thinking of doing and where, what part of the country, that might take him. She was willing to compromise. If he would tell her where he might go, she would look for a business there. She told him the world was full of opportunities, and that she received a regular flow of information about businesses for sale and of interest to her throughout the British Isles.

He loved her voice. It was so gentle and rounded but precise. As he listened he saw her lips before him, full and naturally pink, well drawn and even on occasion firm and resolute. As she elucidated her position, he could imagine her teeth, white, whole, and regular, teeth which he recognised were the result of the expenditure of a small fortune in the very best of establishments. He recognised a relentlessness which had always been there, even in the very earliest days, and from time to time a vulnerability and even a desperation. But mostly he was charmed and seduced by her, and gradually, and against his resistance, he was cajoled into thinking of things from her point of view; and he found himself willing to be persuaded to do what she wanted of him.

Gloria was not content to rely on the telephone alone. She said that it was important for them both to see more of each other now that they were serious once again in planning a life together. He had never thought about it in that way, planning a life together. When he had met her he had been swept along by her magic, and there had not been much planned about it. But he did see the point of cool consideration, and a lot of difficulties in life, he knew, arose out of unpreparedness. It made sense, of course it did. So when she suggested lunch at a rather famous London restaurant, and at her expense, he agreed very readily.

Whereas he felt a trifle self-conscious lunching in this place where he had always thought you had to be a celebrity to gain entrance, he could see that Gloria was fully at her ease. As he looked about him he could see a number of faces he recognised, and some he guessed he might have done but didn't; and many pretty and well-turned-out women. And when he dared to look closely he saw that some of these fashionable women might well be described as beautiful; and when one of them boldly returned his gaze, he blushed and looked away. But none of these women, he thought to his own satisfaction, outshone his very alluring wife, who reigned there, with these other women, in perfect composure. While it pleased and diverted him, it also brought more intangible feelings of alarm. She had travelled a long, long way, and as he understood it she was not finished yet.

But he was disarmed and pleased. Gloria spoke to him so gently and frankly about her life and her regrets. She said how profoundly sorry she was for the rupture in their life, for which she blamed herself; how she saw things differently now; and though it was quite horrible to say so, that it was sometimes necessary for people to pass through a period of reassessment in a long relationship, and if they were lucky, they could forge a friendship which was stronger and deeper than ever before. She told him that she had suffered; and that her feelings for him, which had never died, were now stronger than ever. He knew about relationships. The career of a detective could be very illuminating. And then he had read articles, as she had done, so the language was familiar to him.

She asked him about other women again, for she was sure there was an influence at work here. He explained again about the dating agency, and they could laugh together now about his experiences. There was no threat here, and she could see that these contacts had done some good. She asked him again, 'And have you told me the whole truth about Andrea? Susan talks about her. She sounds fun.'

He groaned. 'I wish she wouldn't. It has been fun but it's in the past tense now.'

She had tuned in. 'You don't sound too sure. And if you aren't, don't you think you should find out, work it out of your system?'

He didn't have a system. 'There's nothing to work out. Trust me.'

'I do trust you. You're a very trustworthy person.' She meant, far more trustworthy than me.

In a moment she would lean forward. Her wonderful green eyes would widen, first engaging and then beguiling him, so he wouldn't care any more about the truth of it; the memory of the long lonely evenings when he had grieved and longed for her would slip away. He wanted to look. What man wouldn't?

Gloria asked very simply and sweetly whether they could share a hotel room, as she did not wish to go back to the flat. She remembered the last time she had been there. He started to agree, and then stopped. The strangest feelings had engulfed him, and he couldn't respond. He made his excuses. The meal had taken up more time than he had expected and he was wanted back at the Yard. He reassured her that the occasion had been of very great importance to him, and that it had been a delight; that it had been so good and necessary to talk about their feelings, and not just about plans. She let him go, but only when he had promised to visit her again, and they had fixed a date.

On the way back he cursed himself for his stupidity. It was only later that he realised there had been no talk of love.

Gloria travelled back by train with her own thoughts. She felt the encounter had been a success. Naturally it took time to mend a ruptured relationship, and you could not expect to perform miracles overnight. She liked the changes that had been wrought in Bob. He was presenting himself better, and seemed more relaxed and confident in himself. That was important. She thought she was not yet out of the woods with him. It was too much to hope for immediate and unconditional success. But she would get there. She thought he had not written off Andrea. There might be something to worry about there, and she needed a strategy for finishing her off. But there was nothing to be done at the moment. It was important to keep him engaged with her in bed. She could succeed in that, and to her surprise, she knew that it could now be pleasurable.

Bob had no particular engagement at the Yard. The case against Roger Greer had ground to a halt and he could do nothing more until David Jenkins returned to work. The Yard was awash with rumours about Jenkins, but the powers that be had imposed a wall of silence, and all that one could do was to speculate.

Back in his flat he had cooked himself an early meal. There was nothing worthwhile watching on the television. He was restless and wandered about the flat. There had been a phone message from Andrea. Would he like to come over for the evening? It wasn't a command, but he thought it sounded like it. Was he the victim of a growing paranoia? He laughed at himself, and wandered about a bit more. It usually started like this. Restlessness. And then he rang Liz, the liveliest of his new acquaintances, and broke the most recent of his new resolutions.

'Of course you can come over, and don't forget to bring your toothbrush.'

He knew now that he could have a comfortable and lazy evening with no questions asked, some food, too much to drink and some casual but satisfying sex. It was all so easy.

CHAPTER 20

RACHEL HAD HER doubts. She did not welcome them, and despised herself at the thought that she might be harbouring them: but they were niggling away despite her best intentions. This road she was treading with Roger was so long and so arduous. She wanted it to end – she needed it to come to an end – for she was not as strong or as invulnerable as she thought she must seem. Her mother, who was anxious to think well of Roger, gave her a warning that men were trouble on two legs, and that some of them bore their distress as a badge of honour. She was not saying that Roger was one of these men, but it was important not to let things drag out. But then Janet Jackson thought that there might be many good reasons a women might wish to drag things out with Roger Greer.

Not that in the sense that Janet imagined it, there was anything going on at all. Sometimes Rachel felt there must be something wrong with her, that Roger had never brought her feelings for him to the test. Or something wrong with him. Perhaps it was him? But whatever the cause they had never shared the same bed, nor had she wished it. Something had held them back. She wondered sometimes whether the sacrifices she had made for him, her long abstinence and the loss of some of her friends, were all in vain: for she enjoyed physical contact, she liked her body to be admired, and now she was left to dry up as an isolated spinster.

She knew that Roger was relieved that these friends of hers had disappeared, but he did not know that it was pain and no gain for her. On several occasions she had been hard pressed not to ring Gloria and to make it up with her, to ask her forgiveness, and to go on. There were consolations, of course, for Roger had allowed himself to become close to her, and she loved it when he did. They had started to reveal the most intimate things to each other. That was a beginning. But she needed it to go on. Oh, how much she wished that it would.

What she believed was that Roger was holding back on the complete truth of the criminal charges that were overhanging him; and because of this she did not wholly trust him. And for his part, she imagined that this something about which he hadn't spoken to her about was so horrible that he believed if he told her she would abandon him. Which she might. She could see that she might. But she needed to know, and now, because she had become desperate.

There was a family boat with a small outboard motor and a cabin that could accommodate up to four people. She was proficient in its use. She asked Roger to share it with her one weekend, which was difficult to arrange because of his close attention to his daughter's needs, and his desire to see her regularly at weekends. But she contrived it. They chugged out together on the Norfolk Broads, which she knew like the palms of her hands, and when they were safely remote she moored the boat and cooked a simple meal. They drank good coffee together, well wrapped up, and in the fading light. Rachel lit a lamp and they lingered in their darkening world. The only sounds were of the sighing winds, the hush of the long reeds and the last cries of the moorhens.

Rachel thought that truth would be best served by bluntness. They waited. At last she came to it. Was there any truth at all to the allegations made against him?

He flinched and hunched. The cries he heard were his own. She wanted a yes or no. He gave her the sort of reply his son Adam despaired of: hypothetical, long, detailed, equivocal. She began to think that he would make a very poor witness in his own cause. She started to withdraw from him, and he saw it.

Frightened, he started again. This time he was shorter. She saw that the answer was both yes and no, which she had not expected, and which dismayed her. She cried out against him. Despairing, he tried again. This time the answer was, no to the most serious allegation and yes to the minor. It sounded like the truth. She hoped it to be the truth; wrung out from him, and leaving him gasping as a fish out of water. She excused herself and went below, leaving him gazing out at the slowly moving gleam of the waters until he could bear it no longer and followed her.

Rachel was lying flat down on her bunk with eyes closed. He started to undress. His limbs felt too large and too heavy for him, and every action was too much. What might have been a romantic moment had become a spiritual and physical torpor. At last he could get into his own bunk. She was inches from him and he could have reached out to touch her. He could hear her shallow breathing like the wind in the reeds. At last after all his struggles he had been capsized. He sighed deeply and fell asleep.

Rachel had fallen into a trance-like slumber. Some hours later she woke, and seeing him sleeping got up and stole out to the deck, to a night sky full of the most brilliant stars. This was not how she had planned or wished it to be. But the relief was overwhelming. If this was all he had done. If this was all of it, and at that moment she felt that it was, she could live with it. Would live with it. And now he was asleep and she was getting cold on the deck and the moment she had wished for would soon disappear with a new dawn. Already she could hear the first wakenings.

Rachel went back below. She slowly removed all her clothes. It was cold and she shivered. She found her brush and slowly stroked her hair until it gleamed and burnished. She counted one hundred strokes, which she had been taught in her nursery to regard as the minimum. Carefully she removed Roger's blankets and unbuttoned and loosened him, but carefully, so as not to waken him. She stole in because the space was tight, and lay atop; but lightly and gently until she was in place. Roger stirred, but she shushed him as she would a child. She began to kiss him, brushing her lips against his skin, starting with his lips and exploring his face. As she cried the tears joined in, coursing, caressing his cheeks and moistening her kisses, so that he could taste them – so many kisses and so tender and sweet that he would remember them to the end of their time.

Usually he woke slowly, with a thick head, which took some time to clear; but now wakening was immediate and a moment of wonder. He wanted to respond but when she quietened him he was content. The gold of her hair was within his reach, and he claimed it with his fingers, spreading it over his face as a magic canopy. She continued to kiss him so that every part of his body relaxed; he glowed with the pleasure of her tongue, her lips, and of her body moving gently with his in harmony with the movement of the boat on an early morning swell. She held him back, slowing him down, shushing him; and when he entered her she held him tight and moved him slowly to a rhythm of her own. Slower and deeper it became, until she hardly moved at all, and she stopped him, pleading with him to trust her until, with hardly a movement at all, Roger felt joined to her. There was no outer or inner. Then his body floated away. There was no longer a him and a her. And above him, as the night sky above, he saw the blue-grey of her shining eyes fragment into a thousand pieces, and felt the deep shudder of her body – and then something explosive happened, which went on and on and which he felt might last forever.

It was a long time before they woke again. Rachel had prepared breakfast by the time Roger joined her, and they hugged each other as he imagined Livingstone might have embraced Stanley. They said very little. The day being fine they moved downstream and found a sheltered spot for lunch. Rachel produced an Italian white wine which she had chilled by dragging it astern, and they became a little drunk. The broad was not busy, but an occasional boat passed and they were hailed. They moved their pitch inland out of sight, and stretched some rugs out on the grass, covering themselves with a tarpaulin. It was raining softly, and raindrops dripped from the branches overhead and pattered above them as they lay. Rachel murmured that she should not have been so selfish. He kissed her. And she let him claim her. Time passed. Rachel had collapsed in his arms. Her mouth pleaded, no more; but with her eyes and breasts denying it, he came again to her until he could do no more.

All these months of waiting and wanting, the desperation of needing to belong, found their climax in those few hours. From this moment they were one; and when the boat turned around and headed home it was for them a common direction. They had no knowledge of what waited them there, but they knew it would wait for them both.

Now Rachel knew the danger. Not for her to wait like a turkey for Christmas. What was to be done? There was Gloria. The person to speak to, risky though it might be, was Gloria; and through Gloria to Bob. That was the route to safety. Fortune, it is said, favours the bold. Rachel lost no time. She rang a surprised Gloria and arranged to meet her at the inn.

Gloria's hopes were raised. As she waited she could hear the beating of her heart. In seconds of the meeting her hopes were dashed, for this was not the conversation she had expected or hoped for. She listened very attentively, and as Rachel finished she put her head in her hands and stayed in that position for some time. It's too much, she said to herself. She's asking too much of me.

When she lifted her hands and spoke her voice was shaky. 'I'll help if I can. But I'm not certain how much influence I have over Bob at the moment. I'm hopeful but I don't know.'

'But you will do it. You will do this for me.'

Rachel was using all her powers of persuasion, drawing on all that she could claim for herself. She saw Gloria hesitate. Her face was so very sensitive to mood. Rachel could see it on a turn before her.

Gloria looked up. She was disconsolate. She said, 'You're asking a lot of me at a very difficult time. If it were anyone but you....'

Rachel kissed her full on the mouth, and stayed kissing her for some time.

The transition to being a couple was delicate: there were two sets of children to consider, to say nothing of family and friends. Rachel thought it best to ease Roger in gradually. As he was working for her father's company, it was natural for him to set up, formally, a small office in a stable wing, and then from time to time he stayed over, but in a bedroom of his own. Rachel's children watched these goings on with amusement mixed in with a habitual wariness. They knew what was happening and didn't mind; they liked Roger and welcomed his presence. Rachel's parents, or to be more precise her mother, presented other and more than presentational problems. Her father, from his offices somewhere in the City, in the air, and in other remote places, conveyed to them a steady but relatively detached goodwill. Rachel decided to invite her mother to dinner, being the parent to work on; and she warned her in advance to behave herself and to give Roger a chance.

On the day of this event Janet had arrived home weary and in a bad humour. She eased off her shoes, regretting the decision not to wear flats: there were appearances to maintain. Women of her age, she considered, were unwise to let themselves go. Keeping up appearances was a bore, and she was tempted to get into something sensible and to forget the commitment ahead of her. But she knew she wouldn't. Her usual quick brandy and a long bath would work their restorative powers. Working through committees was a terrible strain. As chair of the County Finance Committee she called the shots, but most people were very foolish about money, whether their own or other people's. Most of her colleagues believed that you served on a council to 'do good works', to improve public services. It was not their task to minimise public expenditure and to wage war on waste, and of course she saw their point. You did wish to leave things better than you found them.

At least she had money: wisely passed down to her, and soundly grown and protected. It gave her choice, and she exercised it now in rummaging through her extensive and expensive wardrobe for just the right type of outfit. She did so dislike appearing matronly. It was all so easy for a woman to slip into the nanny and then granny roles as if she had no life of her own any more. She thought she had avoided that error. She selected what she had named as her updated Ingrid Bergman look: black silk trousers, slightly flared, which sashayed a little as you walked, and a satin flounced white blouse which nipped in at the waist. With the right accessories, and she had them, that would do the job. And no compromise about the shoes: you could not beat a fashionable black stiletto.

Janet favoured full length mirrors – it was so embarrassing if you got things wrong – and she moved about to see the effects. At least she could still move and look agreeable from every angle. As she made up carefully she thought of Roger Greer. It was too late in her life not to have a working philosophy. She applied it to Roger. She considered that there were three main tasks in life for any coherent adult, or perhaps four if you stretched a point. First there was the issue of power and position, and if you started badly, low down, you had to do something about this. Secondly there was the importance of family life, and the care required to sustain it. Thirdly, there was sex, and then you could add what the pompous might call the pursuit of knowledge, for she could see that it was important in the universities, seminaries, and laboratories and there were practical applications for the professionals, but it was not really her consideration. If something was to go wrong with a person you could be certain that it went wrong in one of those areas. There was a lot that had gone wrong in Roger's life, and from the little she had been told, he seemed to have fallen short in them all! She knew from her own experience that you couldn't be completely secure in all these areas all the time; at some times you had an insufficiency and you had to restore the balance. But there were rules and conventions, and things should not be taken too far. There were delicacies in life. She tucked herself in, patting herself to make sure, and was relieved to find that everything remained firm and in its place.

Roger had been warned by Rachel. Janet grilled him without mercy. She was blunt and to the point.

Rachel blushed. 'Oh mother, do have a heart. You can't expect Roger to answer that.'

'Why not? You don't mind, Roger, do you? There, you see he doesn't mind.'

'No, no, I don't mind...'

Roger found an answer. One of his political answers, long, convoluted and clever. Janet didn't mind. She was familiar with answers like these and even enjoyed deciphering them. She liked clever and subtle men, and was used to them.

In the kitchen, helping out, Janet was worldly wise with her daughter.

'Do you approve of him, mum?'

Bluntness ran in the family. Rachel thought it would be easier to conform to family expectations; but she would be damned if she did and damned if she didn't.

'I like him. He's obviously a very talented and amusing man. And your father has a very high view of him, which is important. But do you think you're up to it? He's made a number of dreadful mistakes, and to be frank he's ballsed up his life. What does that say about his judgement? Not that *you* can talk about other people's mistakes...' She was quieter, and tailed off, caring about what had happened to her daughter and what might happen now.

'Am I up to it? Are we up to it? Yes, I think so, because we've paid a very high price for our mistakes. But only, I think, because we have each other. I don't rate my chances very high without him, and I'm vain enough to think that he'll be safe with me. I'm more certain about these things than anything else in life.'

Janet was moved. She hugged her daughter. *Force majeure.* Better look on the bright side. What were his assets? Position and power: nothing, but then her husband and she could look after that for him, because he was talented. Family life: the children adored him and there seemed no problem there. Sex: she looked at her daughter, she could handle it; and the pursuit of knowledge, it needn't apply. As she left, and hugged her daughter, she made her a promise of support.

Janet said, 'You're a lucky man, Roger.'

'Of course I am – and to have you too as my friend.'

'Flatterer. Watch that, Rachel.' She claimed her right to a kiss. Hmm, very nice she thought, letting it linger a little. Well, why not? They saw her long elegant legs swish into her small green sports car. She waved and was gone.

'Some woman', said Roger.

Janet did want to look on the bright side. Her experience showed the merits of a positive approach to life: but she feared for her daughter, having seen it all before. She reiterated her objections. Her daughter had a penchant for the most difficult of men. Why could she not have found a solicitor or accountant or something: a solid fellow of limited imagination? And why this man with all his problems? Still, it would be very dull to be married to a solid and respectable citizen, assuming in reality they existed, which she doubted. And then it would not be her daughter that would do such a dull thing. She laughed. Of course it wouldn't.

Janet was as good as her promise. She continued to look after them. She had a word – several words – with her husband. He agreed. He usually agreed, but on this occasion it was not difficult. Roger was promoted to Area Manager. This new position gave him a higher salary and other benefits which went with the job. Now it was entirely appropriate and acceptable for him to work out of his office at Rachel's, and the new chain of command necessitated regular trips to the London office, which dovetailed nicely with Faith's many medical appointments. Roger thought that this was what others would call nepotism. 'Shacked up with the owner's daughter, you know', might be a response to his preferment. On the other hand, although he said it himself, he thought the promotion an inevitability. He was the best man for the job; and as he hadn't enjoyed much nepotism in the past he thought he was overdue for some.

Now that the domestic arrangements had changed, Rachel thought she might talk to Melissa about Faith. Roger was mandated to fully inform his former wife that his life had moved on. Melissa had mixed feelings about the news: after all it was one thing to discard a husband, and quite another to see him passed on to someone else. But she was good about the matter, and of course she agreed to talk to Rachel.

After an initial tension the two women understood each other perfectly. Rachel thought, and conveyed it, that Melissa was an intelligent, sensitive and caring mother leading a complex and difficult life, and that, she, Rachel could help; while Melissa recognised the care and thought that marked out Rachel's position, and the organising capacity that shaped her proposals, and was convinced their precious daughter would be in safe hands. With envy she realised that behind Rachel stood a small but effective establishment oiled by money and motivated by goodwill. She was immensely grateful for it, and thought, with a pang of jealousy, that Roger was a very fortunate man.

' Is Faith coming to stay?' asked Fiona.

'Yes. Short stays with us at first, and we must look after her very carefully.'

'And will it be soon?'

'Yes.'

'Oh, good.' And then to Roger, 'Does she like horses? She could sleep with me in the stables.' Then, her hand to her mouth, 'Oops, I shouldn't have said that. Mummy disapproves.'

Rachel chose not to hear.

Day by day Roger's life was returning to a state that might be described as normal. He had a regular job which utilised some of his talents and paid him a sensible wage; he was living with the woman of his dreams, who loved and cared for him; he was seeing something of his daughter, although not of his son; and there were fewer angry people sniping at him and an important modicum of happy and shining faces. But in his dreams the titanic struggles remained unresolved. He would wake in the belief that he was back in his own company, trading was difficult but the problems could be resolved. He would wake with a start and jump from his bed because he must not be late into the office: then foolishly, in the bathroom, he would come to the recognition that this office of his was a long time gone. And in the clear blue sky of his new-found life loomed a large black cloud ever nearer, ever more threatening, of the yet unresolved, which might at any time result in the engulfment of their brave small boat, or it being hurled onto the rocks and to destruction.

Rachel heard him call out at night, saw his agitation and confusion, and it caused her to wonder.

Roger felt it in his bones that if a man sinned he would be punished; that the sinner was not entitled to a good life until he had served his punishment, and then even then he must repent. His was not a great sin. On some days he thought he should confess to the authorities. He would be punished and that would be that. But then he knew he couldn't, for even in his reduced financial and emotional state there were too many people who looked to him and who would be devastated by his disgrace. It would be better to leave it to fate, or as Bob Churchill-Jones might say now, with the authority of St. Ethelreda's, to God's providence.

But Rachel and Gloria were made of sterner stuff. There was much to be said for action and for giving fate a nudge. Gloria had made a reluctant promise to Rachel, but she was going to honour it. Somehow her action had to be fitted into her campaign to get Bob back, which was proving to be more difficult than she had imagined. She used all her feminine wiles and stratagems to arouse him, but she knew that there were others in the field and that her charms, to her astonishment, were not unchallengeable.

She got close to him. When he cancelled the weekend arrangement to visit her, she arranged another. She bought theatre tickets and contrived to get him there. She remembered his birthday and sent him her gift with flowers; and she got him away to a luxury weekend tryst in an expensive seaside hotel on the ruse of a bargain package – Bob had always loved a bargain. She talked to him about his plans for the future and showed a tolerance and understanding he had not noticed in her before. She got him into bed. She did things with him that she had never done before, and they astonished each other. Above all, in his busy life she contrived to take up almost all his free time and ensured that he thought of her constantly. No woman could have done more, and few could have done it with such sophistication and wit.

And then having engaged him, it was her plan was to weaken him in resolve so that he missed her. She might even cause him to feel that she had changed her mind about a reconciliation. He should crave for her, pursue her, and demand the emotional security of a new understanding: and it was only at that point that she might help Rachel. Little by little she drew him closer, and he wondered at his fate. Little by little he became reconciled to her as a part of the fabric of his hopes for a happier future.

Ahead of Gloria loomed the weekend when all these matters would be brought to a head. The apprehension excited her, for not only were her hopes and fears at issue, but Rachel's and Roger's. She kept herself busy and there was much to be done; but as the time drew near she could hardly contain herself. She rang Rachel on the pretext of reporting on progress and of the deadline: but she did it to hear Rachel's voice and to know, that at least for the present, she remained connected.

CHAPTER 21

WHILE BOB OCCUPIED a large part of Gloria's imagination, there were other matters on her mind. Shrugging aside the fiasco of her first contact with a venture capitalist company, she found another. They were very polite to her and suggested that she submit a business plan. She had got better with practice and was good at it now. She based her figures on a restaurant complex in Northamptonshire for which she had received a prospectus in the post. She had been to the site for a guided tour, and had spent some time in the local planning department to ascertain how the site and its neighbouring land was designated for development purposes: and then in the Department of Transport in London, where she had found road usage figures and details of proposed new road developments. It was standard stuff really, but a year or so back it would have been double-Dutch to her.

The venture capital company was much impressed. They said that their investors were looking for ventures just such as this, and that they were keen to give women opportunities to submit investment propositions. They suggested that she take the proposal she had advanced a stage further. She explained that it had been put forward as an example, and there might be other and better propositions. They said they appreciated that, but the opportunity she had studied was very interesting to them, and in their opinion – and they saw a good many project proposals – of outstanding merit.

It became clear to her in the discussion that they had sent one of their own to the site to check it out. They suggested some possible changes to the scope of the project, and indicated to her the matters that seemed to them to warrant further research. She was surprised but agreed to their suggestions.

On the way home she realised that she had no copyright over her project proposal – for this was what it had become – and they might mug her. On arrival she rang them and expressed her concern that her ideas might be purloined. They were not surprised or offended. 'Quite right,' they said. 'Good point. But we can assure that we could have no interest in the project without your involvement. We'll write to you to confirm it.' They said that their reputation and the rule book of their professional association required fair dealing. So she took them at their written word, carried out the additional research, revised the project proposal, and wrote to them again. They asked her to make a formal proposal to a committee of three. She prepared very carefully, with some help from Roger, and it went very well. They made her an offer. Roger said it was a very generous offer, and recommended a good commercial lawyer specialising in these matters who was not too expensive. And with his help the contract was revised to her satisfaction and she signed it.

All this was very fine but there was a problem. She had promised Bob that she would be sensitive to his job search, and that the geographical location of any investment would be the subject of discussion between them. She had been swept away by her own enthusiasm and ambition.

The weekend arrived, and so did Bob. Gloria thought he looked fine. Andrea's taste in Armani suited him, and he looked thinner and graver. She thought, a successful man of the world and not at all like an off-duty policeman.

While he might be at his best, she was not. It was not her fault exactly, for it rose out of complexity. The running of the restaurant, so successful and even glossy to the outside world and the recipient of much praise and many awards, was not easy. There was always a staff problem; always a shortage to take account of and missing skills. This weekend was no exception and she found herself helping out and becoming an extra hand and voice. A steaming kitchen is not the best place for a carefully composed woman: make-up, hair, composure are all at risk. And at the beginning of this weekend that was how it was for her.

Gloria was tired. The preparation of a winning investment proposal is not something lightly thrown together, and the grilling by experts had extracted an emotional toll. Temporarily her usual sensitivities were missing and her antennae untuned. When she looked back on these moments with Bob and contemplated their outcome, that was how she thought about it: it was unfortunate but she had not been her usual self. All of this was hard on her, for it was no more than any man married to a successful and ambitious woman might expect. And then, when at last she was seated before him and had consumed her first gin and tonic, she seemed to him to be her usual charming self and he was joyous to be there.

She sweated later at the brash impetuousness of signing a contract before discussing it with him. But there was an explanation. She had been taught on her business course to give consideration to timing: the right move at the right time. It had dawned on her that it was the right time for her to move on. The restaurant had been a huge success and Fred had grown fat and secure on the profits. He had never imagined that he could become the proprietor and landlord of such an outstanding establishment. Fred had no doubt that its success was due, almost in its entirety, to Gloria. He was thrilled to have such an outstanding and thoroughly pleasant partner. A star, that was what she was, a wonderful lustrous star. She had done so well and he was right to prefer and trust her. He felt genuinely close to her, not in the sloppy way that he had responded to her in those early days, going to her bedroom and all that (he blushed at the thought), but in a grown-up and professional way.

But then he wondered sometimes – and was ashamed that he did – whether enough was enough. Take the issue of skilled staff, for example. Gloria said that to attract the right kind of staff you had to pay them more, and to incentivise them by providing a package that included staff accommodation. She had a plan to buy up some neighbouring farmland, for which she said planning permission for development could be obtained, and to build thirty new bedrooms, reserving some for staff. She said there would be grants and that she was sure the bank would support such a development. He wondered how she could be so sure about these matters. Gloria was always coming up with new ideas which involved fresh investment, which she said was a necessity for any business; apparently, at least to her, a business should never stand still, and if it did it would die. He wanted further investment to stop. No more risks. No more plans. And if as a result the business slipped back a little, so what? It would become a good deal simpler to run, and within his competencies.

It was not just his opinion. A plump little lady called Margaret, who had started in the kitchen and now managed bar food, agreed with him. She was no fool, no fool at all, and very reliable; and she said her opinion was that the business was getting too highfalutin' and would come a cropper one day. He could see how it might.

Gloria could see that the scenery would be changed for a new drama for which she was neither producer, director or impresario – and that the time had come. But she knew she had been unwise not to try to involve Bob in her future, which in a way could become his as well.

He smiled at her and ordered another drink.

Gloria started slowly. 'I've something to tell you about Roger Greer. It's not easy and I must ask you – and I'm sorry that I have to ask you – to keep it, at least for the time being, confidential.'

He looked serious and sought a distance from her. 'I can't do that. You of all people know that I can't. I'm a policeman. If you're going to tell me something about Greer – and I'm not asking you to – it can't be confidential.'

'Don't be a policeman then, be a human being. Be the compassionate Bob that I know and love.'

It surprised and pleased him that she had used the word. 'Well I can be both, can't I – compassionate and a policeman?'

'Not at the same time.'

'Checkmate and game over.'

She tried again. 'Well, tell me what you know so far. On the two aspects of the case: the explosion and the burning down of the car port.'

'The same rules apply. Anything I know is confidential and you, in a remote fashion I admit, are an interested party.'

'Bob, it's me, Gloria. Bend a little.'

He relented. 'Well, the burning of the car port. There are two pieces of evidence against him: we have his car on a petrol forecourt not far from the house, caught on a CCTV camera, and a sighting of a car like Roger's in the street where this director lives. Admittedly it's not from a very convincing witness.'

'That's not enough. I know enough about these matters – all those cases – to know a jury would never convict on that.'

'True, but we might get more.'

'And the bomb blast?'

He hesitated. She was dragging him too far in. 'We know there's a connection between Roger Greer and an IRA terrorist who used to work for him.'

'Is that all?'

'Yes. At this moment.'

'Suppose I could tell you who was involved in the bombing. Would you then give me your word, as a man of honour, that Roger would be cleared of everything?'

He blinked.

'Let me get this straight. You have information about a killing which you won't tell the police about unless I give you an assurance in advance that Roger would get off the hook. Is that right? Explain yourself.'

'Bob, stop it. I'm not saying that. Rachel and Roger, who are a couple now – I knew I'd surprise you – are my very dear friends. I don't want Rachel starting out in a new life with the threat against Roger unlifted.'

'Who gave you this information about Roger and the explosion?'

She sighed again. 'Please, Bob. Do stop it. I can tell you who did it. What I can't do is to betray my friends by resuming things with you, with the case against Roger unresolved.'

Bob recoiled, visibly annoyed. 'What are you saying? Are you trying to blackmail me? No relationship with me unless I promise you no action against Roger? It's not in my power to do it, even if I wanted to, which I don't.'

He let himself be kissed.

'No. Don't be mulish. I'm saying that I can tell you the truth of what happened. You can make an arrest but I have to have your word that nothing, absolutely nothing, will then be thrown at Roger. And unless you do give the undertaking I can't tell you, and I'd have great difficulty in cuddling up to you, which is what I want to do.'

He swallowed hard. 'Do I have your word? Will you shake on it?'

She put out her hand and he shook it. And then she told him.

The weekend was not to turn out as Gloria had hoped, but it was not for lack of trying on her part. She was anxious that Bob read her business plan and the correspondence from the venture capital company; and that he would think well of it and of her. Feigning tiredness, he took it with him to his own bedroom. They discussed it at breakfast.

Bob, when quizzed, said, 'Very, very, good. I'm really proud of you. What progress! You couldn't have done that three years ago. There's only one snag.'

'What? What snag?'

'I've applied for several jobs, and the one I'm most serious about – and they seem interested in me, and have offered me an interview – is in Newcastle. Four applications and one interview, and not a single one in Northamptonshire. It's a long way from Northamptonshire to Newcastle.'

Of course it was. He had thought of distance when he had applied for his job at the Met in London, and of how desperate he was to get away from sleepy Shropshire to the bustle of the 'smoke'; and how he hadn't told her until it was a fait accompli; and how she had missed her friends, the garden, and the uprooting of their daughter from an early and happy exposure to other children at a very friendly nursery school. Was this an act of revenge on her part? Was it a tit for tat? She knew he was thinking it, and wondered about it herself.

Of course there would be lots of suitable jobs in Northamptonshire. She was sure of it. And for a while one could commute. The transition might be awkward but they needed to think of the future. He knew all the arguments, but she hadn't cared enough. When it had come to a crunch they both knew that what happened to his work life hadn't been important enough to her. He knew it because of his own actions all those years ago. He hadn't told her about the job application to the Met, because he'd thought she'd object. She had objected, but it had been too late. He had had to do it. And now she had done exactly the same to him. So how could he object to it now?

She attempted to make amends and to mollify him, and he wanted her to succeed. As the weekend closed and the train moved away, he wanted a reconciliation quite desperately. They waved. She jumped up and down and waved her headscarf. He shouted something jolly. But they were quickly out of sight of each other.

He might be leaving the police force, he had his own reservations about it, but by golly he had always tried to live up to the best standards of the service. Was he to throw these standards away, to abandon the principles of a lifetime, these efforts of his, such as they were, thrown to the high winds? Then he remembered the joke about the Republican Senator addressing his constituents at an election meeting. The Senator made an impassioned speech setting out what he had done, and what he had stood for over the years in which he had served their interests. Then as his peroration he proclaimed, 'These principles, these values, ladies and gentlemen, are what I have stood for over all these years, and I can tell you, without any hesitation, that if at this time you do not like them, I shall change them.'

He laughed out loud. You could be too serious about yourself. Nevertheless... nevertheless... nevertheless... And he laughed some more. And then there was Spiro Agnew – what a name! – the former Vice President of the United States, who when drummed out of office on allegations of corrupt practice is said to have remarked, 'I didn't know they had changed the rules.' That surely was the point: you were brought into this world under the tutelage of one set of rules, and then if you lived any length of life at all, the rules changed; and the longer you lived, the more they changed, and if you were not careful you finished up with no anchorage at all. When he had first come into the Force the rules had been plain to see and he had approved of them. Things had not been perfect, but when they were not it was only a bad apple or two, and you could winkle them out of the tub. Now it was all politics and everyone knew that no principles other than self-interest and self-seeking were at stake. People like him were mere grit in the system, and when gradually they were retired anything they had come to stand for would disappear. It was not nice, although amusing to them, to be treated as some type of dinosaur.

Gloria's suggestion was seriously against the grain. He wanted badly to do what she had asked of him: to stand aside and let the culprits of a serious misdemeanour go scot free. He really did.

Sometimes he yearned to please her. But what he had been asked to do, in the most charming way – albeit in the form of blackmail – was to put human considerations first: his own and Gloria's, Roger and Rachel's. In his career he had been tempted many times to succumb to all sorts of special causes, but had never compromised with that sort of thing and that way of thinking – putting personal convenience or gain before duty. He was proud of his record.

He drifted into the Yard. The place – at least his part of it – was awash with rumours. What had happened to Jenkins? The Assistant Commissioner had not been seen since his return from the United States. An office memo had been circulated which stated that after an arduous spell of duty Jenkins was taking leave of absence, and responsibility for the cases he was involved in had been reassigned. To his dismay Bob found himself in charge of the Roger Greer case, as it had become known: no good hoping to shuffle matters over to Jenkins, he had to deal with it himself.

'For God's sake, Alec, what's happened to Jenkins? What does the grapevine tell us?'

'Nothing. A complete blackout. I've tried my FBI contacts and they say everything is incommunicado, shut down, discouraged. The lads are under pressure to shut up and get on, so you can bet it's juicy. Very juicy.'

'Alec, you're a detective. Find out for me. *Toute suite*, if not sooner.'

Alec said, 'You flatter me. I'll use my best efforts, as they say in the trade.' He grinned. He was enjoying this.

Alec rang Bob at home two days later. 'No need for further research, guv. The story is, Jenkins is back on duty next Monday. You can ask him yourself.'

Bob was anxious to get his story straight. He made some phone calls but they yielded nothing. He made a trip to Manchester but came back having achieved very little. Ignoring his colleagues, and acting strictly on his own and against the rules, he tried to make progress by calling in Esther Droylsden, now in the country again, and interviewed her in a City of London police station. She was represented by a solicitor. Esther was resistant and would say nothing.

Gloria rang him and pleaded her case once more. How much he would like to please her: and how wrong it was of her to put this pressure upon him. He prayed at St Ethelreda's but God had no answers on that day.

At the weekend he was distraught. He went to a football match on his own. Not much fun. On the Sunday he went to the cinema; but on reflection he could remember hardly anything of the film. A lesson here for a detective! You could go to a film and if asked later, remember nothing of it. He called his daughter, who was busy with her own life and distracted by the need to finish an essay. Not that he could discuss the case with her, anyway. Andrea rang, and he enjoyed himself for a time. He put her off. But they both knew, or thought that they knew, not for long – there would be a reckoning.

Bob resolved to do his duty. On the Monday morning he was about early. Gloria rang him again, and enticed him once more. He promised nothing. He was at his desk at the Yard very early. The place was empty. He liked it this way. He thought idly that if they were really doing their job and catching all the criminals it would always be like this. No crime, no police; no police, no crime. Nonsense, of course. But did Parkinson's Law apply here: did work expand to meet the need for it, or was it the other way round? There's a thought. He stopped himself from the contemplation of this rubbish and examined his notes, where he had worked out what to say.

The office filled up and the usual bustle was resumed. He took a cup of tea and a chocolate finger from the trolley. Alec filled him in on some inconsequential detail but he was not listening. There was a need to dash for the nearest lavatory. Time passed. He changed his mind and then changed it back again. He put it off. Started out and came back. He stared at the wall.

Then Alec was tugging at his arm. Gleefully, eyes glinting. 'Bob, come see. It's too amusing for words.'

'Where to? Where are we going?'

'Ask no questions. Just follow me.' Alec took him to Jenkins's office, which had attracted a small gathering. They were scanning a typed notice pinned to the door. It read:

'Gentleman and Colleagues (a fine distinction here, said one of the wags)

I have taken up a new appointment at Hendon College at rather short notice and, unfortunately, I have not been able to wish you well in the usual way.
Good luck (you will need it).
Regards,
David Jenkins

'If you can believe that you can believe, anything,' said one of the bystanders. 'He hasn't even signed it!'

Bob went very white in the face, and his knees buckled. Alec, noticing it, took him by the arm and walked with him back to his desk. Then, seeing his condition, he brought him in rapid succession black coffee, water and a couple of aspirins. He said, 'Don't take it so hard, Bob. We'll manage all right. We're up with our cases, or most of them.' And, 'You're over-doing it. Ease up, Father William. Do you think at your age it is wise?'

Enquiries revealed no named successor to Jenkins, although one no doubt was in the pipeline. Later Alec caught Bob in the corridor, excited again, and arranged to meet him in the pub at lunch time, by when he would have put in a transatlantic call.

They met as arranged. Alec could hardly contain himself. 'Look, Bob, this is really hush-hush. If it gets traced back to us we're for the chop. That might not worry you, but it scares the shit out of me. You remember that guy we met in New York, the FBI guy. Well, I've got something out of him about Jenkins. You're not going to believe this.'

'Get on with it. I can believe all sorts of things.'

'This IRA man – Gerry O'Callaghan – turned out to be a real hot shot, a big cat. Jenkins got his nose in too far and something happened to him.'

'What do you mean, something happened to him?'

'No one knows, quite, but there was some kind of incident and Jenkins was rushed out of the country.'

He paused. 'But – and this is the real point. And by God it's hot stuff. This guy O'Callaghan is thought to be an agent. He's being run by us!'

'God, I wish you hadn't told me. We could get shot for knowing information like this.'

'Of course we could. It's really big stuff. The story is that even the White House and number 10 were involved. If it gets out to the IRA that this guy is a traitor they'll chop his legs off, kaput and no nonsense.'

Bob, stunned and bewildered, said nothing. Alec continued with the 'child's guide to the universe'.

'Don't you see? If this is our guy, the chap who blew up David Droylsden – or ordered it more likely – there's no way the CPS could ever take him to court. It'd come out, the whole shebang, and governments themselves might be threatened. No chance now. This Roger Greer stuff is finished. It'll never get to court.'

Bob, was not so sure. He was stunned, but knowing far more than Alec, he thought there might be other ways of getting the matter to court. It was difficult, but it might be done.

For the moment he was able to respond to Gloria. He told her that at this time he was going to do nothing more about Roger Greer. It needed further thought. He would not say, never, but he thought it extremely unlikely that any case could ever be brought; and he loved her dearly and hoped a compromise between them might be reached.

Gloria said that she loved him too, most sincerely she did, and that she was over the moon that Roger was in the clear. And she wondered, as she said it, how she could best broach Fred with the matter of leaving the inn. She had postponed telling him too long. Her backers were getting impatient, the contracts had been signed, and whatever Bob said to her, the open road was beckoning.

CHAPTER 22

D AVID DROYLSDEN HAD in his time raped many groups of investors of their assets with never a qualm. In the late nineteen-seventies, when he was a young man, and following the example of Slater–Walker and similar groups, he had concentrated his attention on small manufacturing businesses rich in tangible assets, in buildings and plant, but which were underperforming. In these companies it was often the case that the quotable or negotiable value of the share capital of a business was much less than the value of its physical assets, which following acquisition could be sold off at a profit, and the business closed down. It was regrettable that businesses went out of production and as a consequence employees lost their jobs; but then, it was argued, these businesses had no real future at all and their ultimate demise would be inevitable. Acquisition had the effect of hastening the day, it was true, but prolonging poor and badly paid employment was in no man's interest. The effect of an acquisition would be to eliminate low return on investment and hasten the day when assets could be more gainfully employed.

Critics of this industrial vandalism pointed out that many of these businesses were worthwhile, and that with a little encouragement could modernise and improve, so keeping industrial activity and employment at a higher level than would otherwise be the case: to which it was answered that the market, although harsh, reallocated these assets better than human goodwill. Whether this was right or not, it was certainly true that acquisition activity was immensely profitable to some and ruinous to others.

In the nineteen-eighties the activity had shifted to service businesses, and to the acquisition of what was called intellectual assets. It was a more sophisticated activity, depending as it did on the evaluation of new technologies and the contribution of rare skills, of highly talented people, to the processes; and unfortunately people turned out to be harder to manage – especially the intellectual types – than bricks and mortar. But David thought, with commendable ebullience, that he was up to these new challenges, although, to be frank about it, he wasn't.

Thus as he travelled into work on one sunny morning it was very far from David's mind that instead of being part of the solution to the successful exploitation of new information technology in Orbit, Roger's renamed old company, actually he was part of the problem.

Anthony Valentine, holding the purse strings on behalf of the investors, blamed himself for slowness of reaction to the warning signs of failure; but now, thanks to the cash injection of David's five hundred thousand pounds, he was in a position to put that right. As David approached the offices on that fateful morning at the end of a calendar month, he was caught up in a throng of indignant and protesting employees who, recognising him and blaming him, shouted their demands to be paid their monthly wages. He knew nothing, and they gave him copies of the standard letter they had received that morning announcing the closure of the company, now placed in administration, and the statement that no further payments could be made to them. It angered them that they would not be paid at the end of the month, as some knew there were ample funds available at the bank to do so. The letter explained that it was for the administrators to determine what payments should be made, and whether the business could be sold on as a going proposition.

It may often take a man time to recognise his ruin, but not now: no contemplation of event was necessary. David was done down, he had been tricked, ruined; he was the victim of a perfidious act, and not the mere perpetrator of it; and the dupe of chicanery. And that was how it turned out. The business was broken up and sold off as best as possible; some employees found jobs with the new owners while others hit the streets; the Inland Revenue and Customs and Excise were paid every penny owed to them; and the shareholders, which now included David, were paid twenty pence in the pound. David's losses were four hundred thousand pounds in the round; a lost job, and most important of all, the loss of his reputation in the City, without which no one would invest a further penny with him.

David had several set-tos with Anthony Valentine over his trickery, and involved an expensive firm of solicitors in an attempt to challenge Anthony's actions and rescue his money. But having been there before, he was quick to recognise the fruitlessness of his challenges, and once satisfied that there was no mileage in them, he gave them up and accepted his ignominy. He was not quite done for yet; his misfortunes were localised in London, but in Manchester no one would have realised anything of his failure, and he resolved that it would be in Manchester that he must make his stand and stage his recovery. Now that his family were gone and the London flat no more than a repository of unpleasant memories, there was nothing to stop him moving on: and it amused him that he might mount a new life from his mother's flat, the fruit of good sense and governance over many years.

Esther, alarmed by the emergence of the Metropolitan Police in her life, had determined to bring to an end the disastrous road she had been treading, which had begun in a pleasant and nostalgic dalliance, and had resulted in death and diaspora, and goodness knew what else. This road had led to surprising destinations, and when she thought about them, she was astonished to be doing the things she did now: speaking out about her ideas of how things were, and writing them down to an increasingly admiring audience. When she looked at her drawings and paintings she knew that there was progress to record: the later works were more complex, more abstract, more thought-provoking. A critic had written that her work was coming to embody the very essence of feminine being as it had evolved in post-industrial Britain. Apparently she knew better than any other living artist the nature of a woman's body: a figure no longer represented by the flawed and partial imagery of the male voyeur, or even the emphatic artistic statements of the feminist movement. In the history of art she had progressed beyond partial visions to a concept of a body that could inspire both sexes – or what might be put more crudely, to a bisexual notion of how it was today.

Until these comments had been made, and had become dissolved in the academic debate about artistic form, Esther had not thought of her work in this way: she loved the human body in all its shapes and sizes, and simply wished to bow to the great masters, to learn what she could from them, and express her own love of the human figure on canvas. But now that the critics had spoken, she could see that her work had broken new ground, that it conceptualised something moving and profound about what it was to be a woman today. As time had passed she could see that female form in her paintings had become more abstract, in a sense more subtle and less obvious, and developed to a point when one artistic male traditionalist could remark that he was hard pressed to find any female body at all in her paintings. But of course he was missing the point – he was 'past it' and had lost the script.

She was becoming an icon, a celebrity in demand, and the price for her paintings – even the earlier primitive versions – soared; until it made little economic sense to her to occupy a regular teaching position, and more appropriate to appear in many places of artistic excellence around the world and in reach of a television audience. But it had to be said that none of this desirability was consistent with participation in a police witch hunt, and she was determined to put an end to the threat.

She thought that first she should talk to David. A telephone call to the Bayswater flat yielded the discontinued signal. A call to her daughter's mobile phone resulted in the information that the number had changed, but did not give her an alternative. She plucked up courage to ring David's mother's flat, to get the BT answer service. God, how life had changed: oversleep and no one could be found, and your place in the universe had been vacated. There was no option but to go to Manchester and find him, and she took the train there.

Unknown to her, but Roger's laws of parallel lines would have predicted it, David's journey to Manchester preceded her own by two days. He had hardly got his head on the pillow and around the transitional problems of being there when she was ringing his doorbell. It was an unpleasant surprise. First her being there at all, because he had accustomed himself to life without her, and had forgotten – perhaps lost – the feelings which had brought him pleasure from her before all the disasters had occurred. And secondly, because of how she looked, for although she had become an icon, what he saw was that the well-turned-out and comely vision of the past had been replaced by something more of the people – that the street might offer you – and without the accommodation of anything that you might think of as respectable or conventional, at least in Manchester.

She hadn't intended it but it was all to burst out. He was soon aware that nothing had changed. He was to blame for disasters that were entirely of his making, which could have been predicted, and which arose out of defects in his character: short-comings which, now unalloyed by any mitigating influence of her presence and good sense, would continue to dog his life and blight his future. He took it in surprisingly good humour:

'Why are you here?' he asked at last.

'To get up to date. To know what has happened – is happening.'

He told her about the failure of his new business venture, the loss of the money he had invested, and confessed to the forging of her signature to take money out of the children's trust fund; the death of his mother, and her will and testimony; taking on the tenancy of his mother's flat; the quitting of the London flat; the address of their daughter and the nature of her circumstances; and a decision, which he was about to make, to set up in business in Manchester. Recounting these disasters and events, without calculation of her interruptions, took him less than ten minutes.

He said nothing to her about his mission of revenge against Roger Greer and putting out a contract on his life. In the past two days in Manchester he had enquired about it of his friend, extracted from him the man's name and address, greatly against his wishes, and taken a taxi to the spot .The taxi driver said he would have 'No luck there, mate'. And he was right, for all the houses for several blocks around had been pulled down as part of an inner city redevelopment scheme. He had enquired at the Town Hall, and they had no record of any person of that name. Neither was Albert or his wife on the electoral register. He upbraided his friend, who said that the man might have been using a false name, but not to worry because 'bad eggs' usually turned up. David had decided to do nothing more. The fever to destroy Roger Greer, the overwhelming desire to hit back, was gone; and sanity had returned in its place. He thought that this experience must be common: that it must often be the case that capital crimes were committed under the duress of the stress of the moment, the emotions of which were unlikely to be repeated ever again.

Then Esther told him what had happened to her, a discourse which lasted nearly three hours with hardly any interruption, which was like her old self, he thought. He was interested. She could see that he was sincere. He told her how much he admired her achievements, and that he was sure that she should persist. It was not like his old self, and she thought that these disasters might have had some beneficial effect on him. She told him that she did want to go on and she was thinking of rebasing herself in Manchester, that creatively she needed to be closer to her roots.

Yes, he could understand that.

Then she told him that she had been disturbed by the police, and talked to him about the interview at the police station and the questions – some of them – the police had asked.

David's heart sank. It was not so easy to forget the sins of the past. The police! What could they want of her? And what did they know? He said, 'What did they ask you?' And then obvious questions. 'And where does the IRA come in here? What's the connection?'

She had not intended to tell him about Ivor, but now she answered that they kept asking her about Roger Greer and Ivor Bowen. She panicked. She had alarmed herself, for she had mentioned them both in the same breath. He was quick and would work it all out – all the connections.

And how did he reply? He was to the point. He was always to the point, and as bad as any policeman, or so she thought.

'No', she said. She had not seen Ivor recently, not for some years and then by accident. She wanted to probe him about Ivor, to find out whether he was on to him, but not to tell him anything; but she failed. When it had come to it she didn't know how to control what she felt. She wanted to tell him everything really, but she hadn't for so long a time, and she knew that she couldn't; events would whirl out of control and it would be worse than ever. But Esther could not prevent herself thinking about threats, and reflecting upon them; they brought her nearer to blurting out the truth. At some time she must come clear about everything.

They had supper together at a little French restaurant they had frequented in the past. It was a success. She was really pleased to see him, she had missed him, she really had missed him, or at least those parts of him she remembered with affection: and he for his part was able to forget the misery of the past months, to look past the feminist icon presented before him and to reminisce. She giggled a little at the good things, and he saw in her again his very own sweetheart. She told him that she was glad she had come, and he replied that they must do it again. They shook hands on it, each convinced that it was good to behave in a civilised grown-up sort of way, and that it did them both credit.

Nowadays Esther's feelings of goodwill to all men did not last long. She had arranged to meet Ivor Bowen the next day at a motel outside Chester, a venue of his choice, denoting for him a place of refuge close enough to home for him to retreat to it in an orderly fashion, and where he believed his presence would not be noticed.

Esther arrived early, and took a seat at a corner table from where she would be able to see Ivor enter. She felt all those emotions we would expect of her: anger and rage at the death of her son, and self-disgust that she was waiting in an hotel for a man who, by his own admission, had been instrumental in that death. But it was not all that she experienced at that moment, for there was a melange of other feelings: of excitement and dread in meeting him, as on a first date; and a tremulousness deep within her which arose from the need to engage with him. Her ire had not abated since the death of her son, but try as she might, she could not focus her fury entirely onto Ivor.

Esther reviewed once again the story Ivor had told her. He had told her that when he had heard of Roger's business downfall he had arranged to meet him in a pub. They had swapped stories, agreeing on the similarity of the methods used by David to secure control of their businesses. They considered at great length the details of each other's case history and grew indignant in the telling. Ivor emphasised to Esther that he was cast out of his mind by the recollection of the fearful and humiliating memories of his downfall and of the consequences for his family. He thought that Roger was in a similar state of mind. Jokingly Roger had told him he had half-thought of taking revenge, or more accurately, jolting David out of any composure he might feel by his victory. He told him a tale of a Catholic employee whom he saved from arrest by not insisting that he travel to Belfast on a consultancy assignment at a particularly sensitive stage of the troubles. To Roger's astonishment his employee had offered to return the favour, 'one good turn deserving another' at any time, in any place. Roger had drawn a card from his wallet with the man's name, address, and telephone number. He had kept it over all these years. He should not have done it, Ivor was in tears as he had told her, but he had asked for the number and had pleaded with Roger for a message from him so that the 'favour' could be taken up. And he had taken it up. But, and Ivor was emphatic as he said it, there was no intention on his part, and he believed it was so for Roger, to do anything more than give David a very nasty shock. The communication of this intent to an IRA operative on the ground had gone seriously wrong.

Esther thought it through once again. Who was responsible for the death of her son? Someone must be held to be responsible. Who or what should she blame? Was it the system that laid down the ground rules for capitalisic exploitation? She thought not, for there had to be one – a system – although perhaps changes and tighter controls might help. But whatever the system there would be powerful and cunning individuals who would subvert the rules and regulations for their own gains. So was David to blame, and the people with whom he associated? After all without David's activities, without his greed and ambition, and the willingness of investors to go along with him, there might – arguably – have been no ruin for either Ivor or Roger. *He* would argue that his interventions were legitimate, of course, permitted and within the law, and desirable in the broader economic interest. Were they? She didn't know. But even if legal were these actions moral? She thought not.

She was in no moral position to dwell on these niceties, for even if David had gone too far, what of her own behaviour? But for her, for what existed between her and Ivor – and hadn't she willed it?

– Ivor might never had been drawn back into the nightmare of his feelings about David. Ivor had been stupid to think that he could dally with the evil of the IRA, for even he must have realised that 'he who sups with the devil must use a long spoon'; but were we not all guilty of stupidities? And then a host of other thoughts crowded in, which she attempted to keep at bay. Might the IRA have checked out Ivor's phone call by calling Roger? Might Roger, and what a horrible thought, have stiffened it up to something more than a scare for David? Did Ivor and Roger conspire together – was that what the police would think? Or would the police pick one to pursue and use the other to give evidence against him? If so, who would be the fall guy? She would never know. What she hoped she knew were the new boundaries she had established for herself. The death of her son marked them out. She would have nothing to do with systems that brought about such evil, or with people who carelessly operated within them to the detriment and distress of others.

But when Esther saw Ivor pass through the door, saw him recognise and engage her, her heart skipped and painfully missed a beat. She had always been moved by Ivor. This occasion was no exception, despite her protestations to herself to the contrary. He was to her the most open of people, with a pleasing naiveté not successfully concealed by a lifetime's business career. It was just this quality that had made him, in the end, a victim of her husband David, because it opened up crevices of vulnerability to exploit: temptations that, to David, were irresistible. She supposed that this vulnerability had endeared him to her, made him accessible, and why, when things had gone so terribly wrong between her husband and Ivor, she had wanted to take Ivor's side.

That was how it had happened, a mutual empathy and a common cause in protection from her husband. At first he had misunderstood it, feeling her sympathy as much more than she wished, and advancing towards her like a puppy dog, a large and flamboyant one, but blessed with seeming innocence of purpose. Not that he was simple or unblessed with the acumen and hardness needed to succeed in business: but rather that in his personal life caution, which now he had in abundance, had been acquired the hard way and over a long time. She supposed that this innocence, combined with lean and gangly good looks, opened him up to women; that they found his moments of innocence beguiling, believing that they could get closer and enjoy a measure of harmless intimacy, not realising the dangers that innocence could bring upon you, and how devastating it might become for the unprepared. It was from the basis of this appeal that opportunities with women presented themselves, and as he enjoyed them, led him so frequently astray.

As Esther sat there, in this very ordinary hotel lounge, prepared for indignation and anxious to express it, she was overcome by the appeal of his disingenuous and inviting manner; by a spell which had always worked for her. He absorbed, charmed and enticed her, as he had always been able to do; turned her about, and then disarmed her in his own particular way. She was bewitched and acted upon, thrilled by his manner of being there before her, and by the magic it was always within his competence to effect, both before and after the widening chasm of her son's death. For Esther it was never whether he could disarm her, but when.

All of this did not help her, for her declared mission was to tell him of her interview with the police, and then to urge him to go, to quit the country and to leave her in peace.

It was not news he welcomed, or a conclusion he could readily accept. They argued, and the magic dimmed. She was adamant that he must leave the country. She cried, and could not be moved from her conclusion.

Would she tell on him? He hesitated. She pressed on. She was blunt, going to the very edge of her final appeal to him. She pressed him with something that felt like cold steel. If he cared for her, if what had happened between them had ever stood for anything good, then he must take her advice and go. He had to go.

Or what? The unspoken sentence. Or what? Do your worst, let them do their worst, he wanted to shout. But he didn't. He got up very slowly and kissed her. Not the lively sassy and quite beautiful girl he had fallen for all those years ago; but the American updated version, the enraged and wounded creature of mistaken passion. Should he pay? Did he really owe anything? He supposed he did and that he might. He muttered that he would think about it, about what she had said – and seriously, of course. He looked at her now with new eyes, as she was now, and he wondered at how it had happened. He thought that if he saw this woman as she was now, and for the first time, he would not even blink. And now he was going to have to pay a price of some kind, a very high one, an outrageously high one, and for services already consumed.

She caught hold of his arm, holding them both in a single frame, and pleading, with eyes that no longer held any appeal for him. He muttered something she did not hear, and left her.

She thought that she had said what she had to say; that was it, and as for the rest it was up to him. She remained at their table for some time after he had left. She ordered another coffee and twiddled her spoon. When she arose, it was slowly, and to the rest room, where she wiped away the tears and restored her face. It was an end and in willing it she had stayed within her new-found boundaries. She knew she had behaved badly towards him, but at least she had done her very best to save him.

Esther had intended to catch the evening train to London, but she decided to stay for a day or two. It had crossed her mind, although she was unresolved about it, that she might do her best work in Manchester. It might be argued that it was all too easy in London; after all there were liberated women everywhere in the capital, whereas it was harder in the north. Here women must arise from the grit and dust of a yet unreformed Industrial Revolution. In her own mind this struggle was being fought out before her. She felt that she embodied it, and with good fortune she could empower these new women, at least in artistic terms.

She spoke to her agent. 'Goodness,' he said, 'you must be psychic. We've just had an approach for you. Would you be interested in a two-week exhibition at the City Gallery in Manchester? Look them up while you're up there.' He gave her a name.

It was all very encouraging. At the gallery they were so enthusiastic about her paintings, and there was an element of local girl made good: they could claim her as their own, which would help in the marketing. Esther had just enough works of the required standard. They discussed prices and a split. The arithmetic worked out. It seemed a sign of some kind to her. She told her agent that it was all in the affirmative, and he agreed. It was very, very good: by far the most important exhibition since she had started. It had been a struggle, but now she had truly arrived. After all it was rare for a prophet(ess) to be honoured in his (her) own country. She would make money – perhaps a lot of money – and from there the world would be her oyster.

While that might have been thought to clinch the matter of whether she should resettle in Manchester, leaving her free to scuttle back to London, there remained two black clouds in the sky: there was David, and the issues of divorce or reconciliation, and then there was the protection of Ivor. All the good life, the life ahead of her, flowed from their resolution. Until she was clearer in her mind on consequences she couldn't catch the train.

Unlike his wife, David lacked a lynch pin. His abject business failure, and the death of his mother, had left him confused. He had resolved to buy a small car dealership, but he was fearful of error, and lacked the confidence to clinch a purchase. For the moment the assignation with Esther had acted as a restorative, and under pressure to conclude what he recognised as being a tidy buy, or what in other days he would have called 'a steal', he summoned up the courage to conclude a purchase. All of this he ascribed to the visit of his wife.

Anxious to celebrate, and to take further what appeared to him a genuine prospect of a reconciliation, he rang her at the hotel, to find her lingering there; and finding her receptive, invited her to another meal. He thought he would forgive her, and maybe Roger; that was, if the assassin had not performed his duties. In a way mysterious to him, the philosophy of an eye for an eye and a tooth for a tooth had died with his mother. He was curious, of course he was, to find out what had happened; maybe, when time permitted, he would go to Chester and seek out Ivor and confront him; but for the moment it was best to concentrate on his own survival.

The promise of the first meal was not confirmed or enhanced by the second. Although she had good news to impart about the exhibition, Esther was unwilling to share it fully with him, limiting herself to the possibility of it happening at some time: while David found that his optimism about his deal, and frankly his boasting about it as being 'a steal', was less overwhelming than he had thought. Esther groaned inwardly as she remembered the early days of second-hand car dealerships, with repossessions and auctions. For him what felt like progress was for her regression.

He pressed her for a commitment, or if not quite that, a promise that she would give the matter of their being together again her further thought. She dithered. He assumed it. She raised the issue of Ivor's dealership in Chester, fishing to see whether he might have been there. Did he think Ivor might be doing well?

David committed himself only to the comment that as he was a fool, an 'egg head', he doubted it.

If they were fishing, it was in different pools. Vaguely they said to each other that they would get in touch. David kissed his wife, but it did nothing for her. Even David could feel that.

For Esther this second meeting was enough. She hoped that she had done enough to save Ivor, and in doing so, saved herself. As she looked back, which she had avowed not to do, she blamed David: but for him she would have stayed a faithful and dutiful wife, and her son would still be alive. She didn't forgive him for that, but it was not a matter of forgiving him or not; these things had happened, time had passed with its bounty of distress, and it was time to go on. She had not been afraid of being on her own, and she wasn't now.

David thought that it was all a matter of proportion. He saw her wince when he spoke of the car dealership. Was it reasonable for her to expect him to sacrifice his business career, as he still thought of it, to satisfy the prejudices of a wife? No, he thought not, after all that had happened. But he felt calm about it. Lodged in his mind, however, was the question of Ivor's involvement, and although he told himself that he did not wish to pursue him, an envelope of venom was still there waiting to be reopened.

Some weeks later, finding himself in Chester on other business, he decided to pay Ivor a call. He admired the car showroom from across the road before venturing to enter. It was admirably well set up and equipped, and he was prepared to admit that a great deal of care and capital must have been committed to this business over the years to bring it to this prime condition. He began to estimate how much money. It was a habit of mind.

At the front desk the receptionist (whom he thought attractive but dumb, and how like Ivor that she should be) looked incredulous, and told him they didn't have an Ivor Bowen but they did have an Ivor Thomas, and was this who he wanted? He said, 'No' and could he have a word with the manager? The manager was out, the receptionist said, but the assistant manager would 'see to him'.

He waited. The assistant manager, who was in his mid-twenties, expressed his amazement. There wasn't an Ivor Bowen and to his knowledge there had never been one, although to be fair there might have been under the previous ownership, but he didn't know anything about that.

David asked, 'Who owns this business now?'

'New Ventures Limited.' The lad pointed to the brass plaque on the wall.

'And who for God's sake are they when they are at home?'

The lad thought him unnecessarily rude. 'The company's registered in the Cayman Islands, and that I suppose is home.'

David knew enough about the nature of the Cayman Islands as a tax haven to know that his chances of establishing ownership and details of sale were poor. He looked up Ivor in the telephone directory. Sure enough he was listed there, and buying a street directory and with a bit of hit and miss, David found the house. The sold notice had not been taken down. He spoke to the neighbours on either side and across the road. Nothing was known. He visited the estate agent who had sold the house, who said he could tell him nothing as the information was covered by the Data Protection Act and by industry 'best practice'.

David retired to a bar and gave the matter his best shot. If he put his mind and his wallet to it, Ivor could be found. Was that what he wanted to do? If he put his mind to it, Roger could be killed. But then he had stopped pursuing the contract, preferring to let fate take its course. He could put out another contract on Ivor. It was complicated because Ivor might be anywhere. Playing at being god was a terrible responsibility, for how could he be certain who had committed the crime, or who was responsible in any other sense? Perhaps, and he wasn't going to admit it, it was his fault. After all Esther was a sensible woman, and that was what she thought. And then he might do nothing at all. It was always the easiest decision to do nothing. Perhaps he had done enough in this life, or if not enough, perhaps sufficient for the moment. He muttered a family heresy that there were better things in life than the exaction of revenge.

CHAPTER 23

THE COMMISSIONER OF the Metropolitan Police made a special point of being present at Bob's leaving ceremony, which was an unusual honour for a detective chief inspector, and remarked upon at the time. There were some, but not many, who thought this to be an appropriate recognition of fine and long-standing service; others, who were in the majority, thought there was something rum about it and it reeked of guilty conscience, although there was no consensus about what exactly; and a very tiny number knew it was pure desperation on the part of the establishment to keep the Jenkins escapade under wraps with no hard feelings on Bob's account.

In a short speech the Commissioner reminded them that Bob had been a loyal servant of the police service over a working lifetime, and that his conduct and professionalism had borne the test of time. The Commissioner reminded them that Bob's approach to the policeman's job embodied precious values which the British public had learnt to respect and indeed expect in their police: good sense, fair play at the point of conflict and fair dealing with the consequences of crime. He only hoped that these mighty, and might he say British values, would not be lost with the passing out of the service of Bob and people like him. He made a joke about evidence (to audience laughter), and said that Bob's epigram on the importance of evidence ('It's evidence we need, evidence, evidence') was part of the folklore of the service: and how true it was.

They all sang 'For he's a jolly good fellow', and in the pub later on they toasted his health and drank at his expense. And the next day, for the most part, he and his contribution were largely forgotten.

Although he knew the brevity of his loss, Bob had been moved by his send-off: it was not everyone, after all, that was sent on his way by the Commissioner himself, and he was inclined to sign off with good grace. But being an honest policeman he was embarrassed that he did so with knowledge of crimes that he had not acted on, when others might conclude, if any of this evidence should see the light of day, that he should have done and had suppressed it for personal reasons.

So much for the eulogies. While the manslaughter was now out of reach, he did think, idly, that it might be possible and desirable to take some action against Roger Greer for burning down the car port. Admittedly it was a minor matter, but nevertheless he had done it; the consequences might have been terrible, and justice always needed to be done. But then who would thank him for persisting in it now? The game had moved on. But he didn't thank them for moving the goal posts, nor did he like it that it was Gloria of all people who had put him under pressure to step aside.

At this time Gloria had already taken action to tell Rachel the good news that Roger was in no danger of prosecution. He would not get a letter to that effect, but 'as sure as houses' the matter was dead. She needed to tell her in person, and they arranged to picnic at one of their old haunts.

Rachel, greatly relieved, was moved by Gloria's bravery and skill in taking on this vital task for her, and overjoyed at the outcome. Gloria could see that Rachel was changing, the unconventional was being teased out of her, and she was taking her colour from Roger. It was a more elegant Rachel, more relaxed, and a much happier person. Gloria could not help but be pleased; but with a pang of jealousy. She tested her. Had she, Gloria, been forgotten quite so quickly?

Rachel took the comment in complete seriousness, and needed to demonstrate that it was far from the truth. They kissed.

Gloria told Rachel for the first time of her plans for the future, the purchase of the leisure centre in Northamptonshire, and that soon she would be leaving. Rachel thought that despite this wonderful and testing project, and the sensitivities of taking Roger's position to Bob – and she questioned Gloria closely and earnestly about these – her special friend had protected her. She was moved by Gloria, and kissed her again. She wanted Gloria to understand that her feelings for her remained true and strong and for evermore. And then though they knew it was unwise, and that it could lead nowhere, nothing could come of it, they lay together until a gathering darkness obliged them to move.

Leaving the police service was a highly emotional occasion for Bob, and made him vulnerable. Soon he would be homeless unless he took action to rehouse himself. Personnel had reassured him that for the moment he was free to stay in his tied police flat, 'there was no rush', and that assurance had been repeated at the highest level; but all too soon there would be knocking on the door, and by then he needed to be on his way.

Andrea brought him a bottle of champagne and invited herself to the flat to help him drink it. She knew this to be her moment. There had been other women. He didn't dissemble very well, which was good, for she would always know when he was up to no good – that was, if he was so stupid. She had a very good sense of smell. When there had been some other woman she could smell the scent of her – she always could. Her sense of smell was a very useful gift.

While she understood that, having been hurt, he needed to rescue his masculinity, she was surprised, now that she was here, that he needed anything else but her. Men could be so difficult. For a woman rising forty she looked so good: a very tidy figure; nice well-cut black hair; well dressed; a great cook; a friendly person; and passionate, very passionate – none of her men friends had ever complained. But he was equivocating: on the one hand he might do this and on the other he might do that. How many hands did a man need?

She told him he didn't need any other people or to get a boring job in some English wilderness, he could have her, and they could do interesting things running businesses, if he liked, in London. Good fun and good money. She said she was all woman and that she would show him, remind him. She started to take off her clothes. There was a brief moment when he might have said no, but this was a night to celebrate and the champagne had got to his head, and to other places, and so he went along with her.

'So now what you think?' she said some minutes later.

'Wonderful,' said Bob, being less than truly generous, for his mind was elsewhere.

In the time remaining for her move, Gloria was anxious to involve Bob. As he showed some reluctance to travel to Norfolk, she came to London, and he met her outside Green Park station. They sat on a bench in the park and later, at her expense, had tea at the Ritz Hotel. He was so proud to be with such an elegant and attractive woman who could turn heads in any gathering: and she enjoyed his presence, for whenever he had been relaxed and himself she had always loved his company. Gloria was at pains to tell him everything, and many details had been clarified since they had last met. Now she had coloured brochures which showed how the leisure complex would look when it had been extended, and outline plans for everything. It would be quite a place when finished.

Gloria apologised to him so nicely for racing ahead with this investment without listening to him properly, without involving him, and at not listening to his thoughts about the future. But if he could forgive her and just look at the project on its merits, he would see what a splendid opportunity it would be for him too. Why, he could take up responsibility for security at the place because there was a need for his skills; but only until he had sorted out exactly what he wanted, of course. She felt sure there were opportunities in abundance in Northampton. They could live in the complex at the beginning, but if he would come with her at the very outset they could look for a house together – if that was what he would prefer.

On the way to Liverpool Street station she told him about Fred:

'You'll never believe this,' she said. 'Fred's going to marry Margaret.'

'What, little Fred? And who's Margaret?'

She explained. 'Margaret runs bar sales, but she was in the kitchen.'

'Oh, that Margaret.' He was surprised.

'She's a honey when you get to know her. Very nice and reliable. Fred's a lucky man.'

He thought it was nice thing to record a one-up for marriage amidst the disappointment of divorce and separation. Two, actually. 'You know young Alec, don't you?'

She did.

'The other day he came home from work to find his girlfriend had left him a note. One of those Dear John notes. And he'd had the philosophy, which he'd believed his girlfriend shared, of an open relationship: each partner doing exactly what they liked with other people and no questions asked.'

'Yes,' said Gloria, but she had always doubted it.

'The note went like this. *"Dear Alec, I've decided to get married to a man I met some time ago called Frank who, unlike you, really wants to get married and look after me. Girls do need looking after, you know, at least I do. I'm sorry about it but I did warn you. Love Sandra. PS If you have any sense you'll get rid of that Nicki of yours, she's a right snake in the grass."*'

'And did she warn him?'

'I don't know. Alec says not. But whether she did or not's beside the point. Alec's very cut up about it.'

Gloria thought, serves him right. She was silent for a while, remembering how Fred had told her his news. He had been so very pleased, crediting her with giving him the confidence to think he could win what he described as a good woman. He said that when he'd come to know her, Gloria, he realised that there were good women in the world. And Margaret was grateful to Gloria too, he'd said, for helping her in the kitchen and bringing her on. Then Margaret, glowing with the joy and pleasure of it, had thanked her too. She told them both that they had done all these good things at the inn themselves and they should give themselves the credit for it. And she had been so convincing in her praise that they had readily accepted her kind words. As she looked at them both, working in a quiet and determined togetherness, she thought that they would manage everything very well, and in their own way, and she was both proud of them and pleased.

On the station platform Gloria gave him a very warm hug, and told him she loved him. He said he loved her too, and always had done. She asked him whether it was all right between them, and he replied that he thought that it was. She was tearful on the train. What more could she do?

The day arrived when Gloria was to leave the inn. She had agreed with Bob that he would come down to the inn early in the morning, and that they would drive together in the van to the leisure centre. Gloria had prepared everything the day before, so it was only herself that had to be put into position. She was cheerful: a new adventure was to start. The one thing you knew about Bob for certainty was that he was punctual: it was a very considerable virtue.

When he was more than thirty minutes late she was gripped with feelings of foreboding. She rang his telephone at the flat: there was no reply. She rang his mobile, but it was switched off. She panicked and began to shake. She tried to still herself. She asked the van driver to take a break for an hour, and took coffee in her room. She tried his mobile again, to receive no answer. She sat on the bed feeling faint and having turned a deathly white.

Finally she could bear it no longer. She had been dumped. Retrieving the van driver, she started her journey. As they left she looked back at the inn, her refuge for so long, hoping that someone would be waving her goodbye. Fred was in the restaurant changing the menu cards with Margaret. There was no one there any more to wish her godspeed.

Bob had packed his clothes and a few of his personal possessions over the previous week. Later on he would have a formal removal of his furniture. He had been surprised there were so few things remaining. Gloria had taken her personal possessions, of course, and then there was Mrs Frost, his cleaner. She was a great one for charity, and every week, or so, it seemed, he was supplied with a new charity bag and the request to sort through the things he didn't want and put them in the bag. What could he do? It was important to her, which was important to him, and anyway he believed in good works. When he weakened she grew bolder and took initiatives of her own by putting objects in the bags without asking him first. And when he had the temerity to challenge her, she would say, 'Surely, Mr Churchill-Jones, you don't want to hang on to that old thing when there are people suffering out there.' He would reply, 'Of course not.' And gradually in her relentless pursuit she had denuded him.

On the night before he retired to bed early, for he knew he needed to make a prompt start in the morning. Early rising did not bother him, for he was used to it in the police service, and at his age you did not need so much sleep. Now he was tuned into the natural rhythm of the day, and rose once the light changed and the birds started up with their claims for territory; and went to bed when it grew dark. But this night he couldn't sleep. It was his practice to make the most of not sleeping. He would make himself comfortable in his big chair with a fine coffee and a good book. It would be a time to thumb through his classical record collection and play something long and dreamy. A lot of his reading and listening came to him this way. But this time he could not settle himself.

He knew himself to be disoriented, and was nervous of too many big changes coming at the one time. He had become cautious. He picked up the silver cup his colleagues had given him at his leaving ceremony. The inscription read, 'To a fine policeman and good pal.' Is that what he had been? Had it amounted to that? And then he had heard the sniggers when the Commissioner had spoken of the importance he, Bob, had attached to 'evidence'. What did they say: 'Truth was a matter of perception' and it was important to 'conceptualise', and only then could you hope to 'get to the bottom of it'? It seemed obvious to him that when you said that something was perceived, that you meant something more than that it had occurred. And if an event had actually happened then you could detect it, and it would become evidence.

So what was their problem? What was this something more that they insisted was so important? He thought this extra 'truth' that they argued for, that they brought into the argument, was a theory of knowledge: the idea that you had to start with a 'percept': that you collected propositions, most of which were related to dates of things occurring – and which therefore could be remembered – and then you asked what events could you infer from those 'percepts'. The answer to this question had always seemed to him to be obvious: not necessarily anything at all! Of course, you might, he could see that you might. What he thought, and it was of immense importance to him, was that any event or group of events was logically capable of standing alone, and therefore, that they were wrong in thinking a group of events could of itself provide demonstrative proof of anything.

Of course, they had a point: you could make this too personal, because if you confined inference to deduction, your known world was limited to the events in your own perception – even assuming you could accept the reliability of recall or memory. He recognised the limitations of his position; but on balance, and certainly when applied to crime and its punishment, he thought the deductive approach to be more real, and therefore human; and that they, and very often, were the victims of an idealism which in its own way was just as personal as his own approach. Bob sighed. Like most things there was no resolution to it, and you just had to act up to what you believed, no matter how many people sniggered at you. He was glad he was out of it.

As he looked around his flat he tried to remember the happy days he had shared with Gloria. They were right about history and remembrance. Without a good deal of prompting it was very hard to recall much; but that did not mean there was no importance to what had been forgotten. He remembered an affair of long ago. His friend, for that was what she had been, had on one occasion been so enamoured of him, moved by him, that although an experienced driver she had run her car, with him in the passenger seat, up the pavement and through the railings of the Tate Gallery. It was very embarrassing and for a long time he could not pass the Tate without searching for the exact spot and laughing. But ten years later he had come face to face with this lady in Harrods, and she had looked straight at him without a flicker of recognition. Did this amnesia denote that the events and emotions of that long hot summer were of no significance because she did not remember? Of course, she might have remembered and chosen not to reveal it. *C'est la vie. C'est la guerre.* No one should believe that detection is easy.

Andrea had been so sweet to him that he had felt it right to take her out and tell her of his plans. They had been to a cinema, and she had held his hand and kissed his earlobes in anticipation of delicacies to come. She had wanted to come straight back home, believing, for her at least, that eating out was a waste of time and money when you could produce a much better meal more cheaply in your own kitchen.

When at last he had found the courage to tell her, she had hardly been able to believe him. She felt his inadequate statement as a finale, and pushed him out. She shouted something in Italian at the shop front which he did not understand. Bob thought afterwards that his concern to tell her in the right way had been misplaced: it would have been better to send her a short note.

It was grey outside and soon the street lights would be extinguished. He looked across the road at Andrea's delicatessen with its shining surfaces. Soon she would be dressing her shelves and placing her delicacies in their time-honoured and familiar places. It would be ample. He would miss it.

He was restless now, and wandered about the flat as if pacing it out for the last rites. How easily were things lost. Once this flat had echoed to the sound of happy voices. He supposed that those days, when his daughter Susan had been young and he her hero, when he had whirled her about his head in this very room, and when sunny days had meant outings and picnics, had been the happiest days: nothing that was to come later would be comparable. Gone forever: as soon he would be gone. And those that followed would pull down the wallpaper and rip up his carpets: ugh, they would say, how hideous and old-fashioned, and they would replace them with hideous objects of their own desire, heedless of a past they did not share. And this desecration would be unknown by him. It was always so. But that did not stop you grieving about it.

He thought of Gloria. It was several years now since he had sat holding her hand in this room. How he had first loved her. He hadn't chosen her: she had burst into his heart claiming him as if 'she was the only girl in the world and he was the only boy'. Not that he had resisted. It had been breathless and as natural as an early summer day. He had once written in a birthday card to her, 'Shall I compare thee to a summer day?' Shakespeare always had the best words, and sometimes the only words. And in those days he was desperately short of words to shape his emotions and to tell her what he felt. These feelings for her had never diminished, even when his career took up almost all of his waking and sleeping hours. He had tried always to tell her that his love for her was constant, but then there had come a time when she wasn't listening; when he knocked on the door and there was no one present. And then she was gone. He had thought about it, God only knows how many times he had thought about it in this very same room: but he was as surprised and uncomprehending now as he had been when it had happened.

He thought about forgiveness and Father Matthew. He must have forgiven Gloria, for how else could he be sitting there with his bags packed? But was what had happened an apt subject for forgiveness? Was the act – if that was what it had been – of growing away from a loved person – of both of them growing away – the subject for forgiveness, or rather of mere understanding, acceptance and regret? Not that he did understand it, her leaving, for it had come upon him – that is, he had experienced it – as a massive avalanche which he had believed would bury him for ever. You could not see it coming, but when it hit you could hear and smell it, the sounds and fury filling your ears; and you remained rooted to the spot. Some time afterwards you might come up for air. He had. But what did it mean, this coming up, when the devastation was all around you? Nothing.

He looked at his watch. There was not much time if he was to catch the train. Not much time. And he hated to rush things. At this time he should have picked up his bags and walked to the taxi rank, as he had done a thousand times. But he didn't. He went for a stroll out into Regent's Park Road, and then into the park where he had wheeled a pram and kicked a ball, sat on a park bench by the lake and thrown breadcrumbs to the ducks, and carried his daughter on his shoulders. As he sat, he imagined the train clanking its way out of the station and gathering speed beyond the confines of the City and out through the Essex marshes and rolling Suffolk hills, greener and greener, flatter and flatter, until the sky merged with the sea. In spirit he was moving there. As a boy, innocent of purpose, on a jaunt; when the comic cards and the jolly pictures of sunny destinations above the carriage seats spoke of another world, a universe of fun and jollity, and the chatter and shrieks in the corridor were in anticipation of this world: of moments when their parents would tie handkerchiefs over their heads and roll up their trousers and skirts to paddle in the sea and make complete fools of themselves – and so could you, and without recrimination.

The trains were black, the sky was blue, the sands were golden, and so were you. Families, whole families streaming from the station, then out to a High Road of pink floss, cafe awnings striped in red and blue, and ice cream cones of yellow hue; out up onto an esplanade that looked like the Mall in pinkish tone, and must surely lead to a Palace dome – but which turned out to be an entertainment arcade with playing machines and dodgem cars. His father would say, 'Be careful, they're dodgy' as if this was the best joke in the world, and you laughed at it, even while you were groaning. And the day had an end. Sometimes early if it rained; and sometimes late in the dying evening light; when the human flow reversed itself, red and gritty, and depleted of food and drink, but loaded now with souvenirs and jollities – which everyone knew would not last a season. An ending where everyone had been redeemed, forgiven and tolerated; but where you knew that tomorrow would be different – but then it might happen all over again.

All those happy virginal days gone forever, he thought. Now he knew that something very serious had happened: he had missed the only train open to him going east on that day that could get him to the inn that morning. It couldn't be helped, it couldn't be helped, but the recognition gathered speed. He hauled himself to his feet, and legs leaden, made his way back. He took a diversion so as not to pass Andrea's delicatessen. He was back now in his room, in his big chair. He made another coffee to steady his nerves.

He rewalked his room. It was important not to forget anything. He could never vacate an hotel room without leaving something in a drawer or on the bedside table. He looked in the wardrobe, in her part of it which he had never filled. The wedding dress, sheer white in its original cellophane cover, and the white shoes in their box were still there: he had never thought to remove them, or Gloria to take them. He thought he would put them in the latest of Mrs Frost's white charity bags. He left them under their covers, taking very great care to fold the dress carefully. Someone was going to be thrilled. It was a very expensive and elegant dress, and he had never paid more for any pair of shoes. But this time surely not Mrs Frost, who without demeaning her could not be imagined wearing them. It was an unkind thought but sometimes he supposed that Mrs Frost and her family were the main beneficiaries of the charity bags. Perhaps a grand-daughter or a niece would wear the dress.

He sat at his small Edwardian writing desk and reread the letter offering him the position of Security Services Manager in a large and well-known industrial company in Newcastle. He had thought long and hard about this letter. It had remained there on the desk in full view even when he was disregarding it. He had not mentioned it to Gloria or to anyone else. The letter stated that he could join at any time of his choosing, but not later than one month from the time of writing. He rang the very pleasant Personnel Manager who had interviewed him for the job and written the letter. She said, 'Of course, we'll look forward to it.' He stamped the envelope and on the way out he posted it. He caught the first available train to Newcastle.

CHAPTER 24

RACHEL HAD TOLD Roger of the dropping of the case against him on the very evening of the day that Gloria had told her. While she was joyous, he could not help but observe that there was a sadness to her which he did not understand. When they discussed the matter he was nonplussed; for it was as difficult for them to live with a conclusion of 'not proven' as it was with a verdict of 'insufficient evidence to justify a prosecution'. A reasonable man might conclude from such outcomes of police enquiries that there was no smoke without fire. Roger felt unhappy and unsure of himself, because he did not feel wholly free, while Rachel had been left with a feeling of unease that the hydra beheaded might be capable of growing many more heads. But if there was a cloud and a shadow between them, and touching them both, it was soon dissipated by the growing awareness that the intimacy between them would not be interrupted.

The first beneficiaries of their confidence were the children. They found a moment when the children were gathered, to tell them that Roger was a permanent fixture and would be staying. 'Good,' said Fergus emphatically, 'can we go fishing then?' Sophie said nothing, resolving to steal up on her mother in a private moment, and then to ask all her questions when she had discovered them, worked out what they were; while Fiona came right out and asked whether they were going to get married. She thought it would be nice to have a conventional family that none of the other children made remarks about, even if they meant no harm.

'Not yet,' said Rachel, 'we haven't really thought about it.'

Fiona thought, why not, why haven't you thought about it? But as the others were laughing and breaking up, she didn't say anything.

While marriage in the past had brought happiness to them both, it had also brought grief. Philosophically one might recognise that so did life itself; and the thought that there could be some way or state of living that gave you one but not the other was absurd; life could not be absolutely perfect in any state of union. But at this moment they didn't need a theory, they just needed to get on with it; to enjoy their honeymoon period without the interruption of man or beast.

But there was not just the children to fend off, there was the undoubted weight of authority of Rachel's parents. Janet Jackson had a 'word', as she would call it, with her daughter, advising caution and the ultimate goal of a wedding, any sort of a wedding. She had already asked the Reverend whether he would marry these two divorced people, so she knew what she was talking about. Rachel resisted, appealing for time – 'Time alone will tell.' For the moment the line held. Then Janet wheeled in Henry Jackson and he had a 'word', a diffident word but potent in its own way. In the nicest possible way he asked Roger about his intentions towards his daughter; in effect, were his intentions honourable or dishonourable? Roger bit his lip to avoid making the Oscar Wilde quip that he didn't know he had a choice.

Honourable, of course, was the answer. But it was a troubling conversation, because for Roger and Henry Jackson there was no common grounding of values and conventions on which to base an exchange; and their footings were always on sinking ground. While emanating goodwill and professing that it was Rachel's interest that needed to be considered, to be in the foreground, they could keep going – but only to confuse and disturb each other.

Rachel rode to the rescue, taking her father away and telling him what she wanted, her judgement about herself – a preliminary conclusion – which left them all feeling none the better. She asked for remission; for them both to be left alone to sort themselves out; she urged upon them the belief that Roger could be trusted, that he was a good man; and she reminded them that marriage had been tried by them both in abundance and had not proved to be so wonderful, or so superior, as to make sacrifices for it as an institution a self-evident proposition. All of this, in its way, was not very satisfactory. But for the moment they claimed and received uncontested territory.

Roger was acutely conscious that but for the financial generosity of this family he would have gone under; it seemed that at every one of the disasters that had come upon him they had been there to save his fall into the pit. But it did not follow from their benificence that his freedom had been bought, and that lock, stock and barrel he was their own. He had never wished to be part of what in their very pleasant way he thought them to be, to represent: position, wealth and power. Although to be entirely frank, they had little enough of these: only a modest place; influence, not command; and a reliance on their abilities to persuade. The ladders of his own making had helped him up and among them. He had looked down, then as he fell, snake-like, to a place near the bottom they had but played him out a ladder so he could rise again. It would be his pride that prevented him grasping it. For the moment he was out of the snake pit and that was enough for him.

Rachel had wriggled free. She had no room for family considerations, but loving both her parents she had no wish to hurt or inconvenience them, confident that in time there would be harmony. She had hardly dared hope for it, but her patience had been rewarded, for now she had the man she had wanted for so long, and whom she knew she needed. She knew herself to be far from perfect, to be weak. She had shown such poor judgement in affairs of the heart, and when she drew near what she treasured most she had always been able, with unerring aim, to destroy it. Not now. She was determined to take this last chance: to absorb this man so that she saw the world through his eyes, claimed his values as her own, and joined herself to his physical presence – to have her weaknesses squeezed out by his strengths.

It was not a time for reflexion, and they decided to have none of it. Flushed by the promise of each other they took a villa in the north of Corfu with Rachel's children, with a pool of their own; and transported themselves to small shining coves, green hills and bustling tavernas; to laughter, the pleasures of their bodies, and the ease of being somewhere else, in a place where they were accountable to no one. And seeing the adults in their life happy, the children relaxed and the past could drift away. They had no wish to return: perhaps they could stay for ever, or if not that, for a very long time. They joked about it, more than halfway serious. But then there came the dreaded time to return, and they reappeared in the disguise of their old selves.

Roger was back among the books, now the trusted and competent Area Manager; and Rachel, with Roger's help, had devised a small business of her own. Roger had been greatly impressed with her ability to ornament, to embroider articles of women's clothing: blouses, scarves and handkerchiefs. She was highly imaginative and dextrous, and had a firm grip on the quickly changing fashion scene. She had already made a small breakthrough in supplying some expensive West End boutiques. He encouraged her to show samples to larger stores, who were willing to contract for the longer term and for higher volumes. Roger showed her how to set up a workshop on her property, and how to recruit those rare people who could work quickly and flexibly to her designs. Henry Jackson, highly amused, supplied the rest. Rachel was not entirely financially self-sufficient, for she continued to rely on a generous allowance from her father and an income from her trust fund, but as she progressed her very own business activity she grew more confident that she could stand on her own two feet.

Not that she found life easy; she never had done so. Sometimes she felt the need to wander off on her own to 'sort herself out', as she would say to herself, and to others if they pressed her about an absence. But now she never pressed her distress to the point where people worried about her presence and state of mind. Roger came to accept that the sun that shone on him would from time to time be hidden, but that that even then there was always the promise of better days to come.

Others, knowing Rachel well, might have supposed that the uncertainties that had always haunted her being would linger on in this her new life: and in some ways they were right, and in others emphatically wrong. Her parents continued to worry about her, and in their anxiety they extended their hospitality to both her and Roger. They breathed life on them, encouraging them to live and believe in the best of all possible futures.

Their good intentions sometimes succeeded in driving things to a brink. At dinner parties Henry Jackson was known to expound; after all, he was entitled to it. He would ask Roger, mischievously, such questions as 'You do agree, Roger, don't you, that the British Empire was a thoroughly good thing?' And, 'What, Roger, do you think about China? And, 'You do agree, Roger, don't you, that a Socialist government can't be expected to manage a capitalist society?'

Roger would answer as carefully as he could. 'Well, it all depends on what you define as a good thing. Good for whom?' And, 'Indeed, China remains a mystery and a potential force of both good and evil in the world.' And, 'Well, we aren't likely to have a socialist government in Britain, are we? No danger of that' (to which he was heard sometimes to mutter, more's the pity).

Henry Jackson found closer contact on common ground: industry, business and economics. But there were dangers here too, although diminished by Roger's increasing lack of combativeness.

All this, the common assumptions and values of another social class, was the thin ice on which they skated; but with dexterity they avoided serious falls. It was a strain but not as yet a disaster.

They were on more solid ground with the children. Janet Jackson admired Roger's sensitive and fatherly ways with the children, both Rachel's, and his own daughter Faith. She could see just how close they had all become, and the way he cared for them and the ways they respected him. A man, albeit an intellectual, who loved children and who was loved by them could never wholly be bad – and Janet thought, perhaps dogs as well. So she admired him for these qualities, and on the strength of them and her daughter's word and continued glow, she left them alone. She missed something. Janet, for all her acumen and worldly wisdom, failed to recognise that these two people were as close as any two souls could be: in mind, spirit and body.

Melissa, recognising the rarity of her own feelings, did not care to dwell on what might go wrong between Roger and Rachel. She knew herself to be the vulnerable party. Fond memories of past happinesses were of no use to her. Already the memories of all those moments of love had faded. A long time ago, she thought, remembering despite herself both the pain and the ecstasy. What she did care to recognise, and she was profoundly grateful for it, was their assistance with Faith. It was proving to be a long and expensive battle to save her daughter from the debilitating illness that had besieged her: a siege requiring rigorous attention to diet and frequent visits to hospitals and clinics. The drugs used were changed many times before the right combination was found, and they assumed that even this medication would not be the last. Through all this Roger had been a rock, and Melissa assumed Rachel was also. For Rachel would intervene if she thought it right with suggestions of her own, always sensible and sometimes very helpful, so that Melissa imagined that Rachel's dreams must be filled by Faith as if she was Rachel's own daughter – and loved her for it.

Doctors at the hospital believed that the tide had turned for Faith: not only had the disease been arrested, but there were signs of recovery. The future looked brighter for her, although the warning beacons would be out for the rest of her life. Faith loved her father, and now that progress had been recorded, she started to stay at the barn. Each time she urged her mother to let her stay for longer. Melissa's relief was tangible, for although as a mother she would sacrifice her own life for her child, it was a godsend to resume her life in something like its normal and expectant shape. If to perform was an agony, deprivation from doing so was a greater affliction. She began to resume some recitals, and then as her confidence grew, to accept engagements farther and farther afield. Whenever they were needed, Roger and Melissa were there, and although continuity of schooling was a problem, on the whole Faith's essential needs were attended to.

Luigi Ambroso had been put on the back burner, although his solicitations remained constant, and the adventures of Milan had become a distant memory. But he remained there in the background for her, with just a touch of expectation and mystery: her birthday was remembered with flowers, and when he was in London, if possible, they met. As she widened her net Luigi, sensing the change, suggested some recitals which placed her in his path once again: and when she performed them, there were always some pleasing happenings, which when examined led back to him. Melissa began to nurse the most pleasant thoughts about him.

As Luigi was well known in operatic circles throughout
Europe, Melissa could gather information about him. She
realised that creating a sense of mystery – for this was what she
recognised him as doing – served a number of purposes. It was a
marketing ploy which increased the value of any real exchange;
and it was a cover – but what was it a cover for? She discovered
that he was married, but not in any obvious way; and she read
somewhere that he was gay, but when asked, he laughed it away.
Often he was photographed with glamorous women on his arm,
but she knew that for an impresario this form of conspicuous
appearance was normal. She asked him in Milan to explain
himself, but he laughed, and then with the skill of a Jesuit turned
her away again.

After Milan, and his sexual exploits with her, she had expected
much more. But then there was Faith and her needs; and in his
respect for her position, there had been a distance. Recently,
though, there had been a change, and she had begun to want him,
to reach out for him and to find out if he was for real. There had
been a meal in Rome when he flew her out; and a visit to the
Cannes Film Festival, where he had put her up in a flat he owned
but where he did not stay; and where the press had caught him
out with another feminine jewel, but no more than a starlet glad
of his arm. She concluded that he was pleased that she was there:
he had been ubiquitous but fleeting. She wanted more than that.
She began to think him an angler, and her the fish: a master
angler who caught her with the right bait and slowly reeled her
in. It was not all linear progression: he reeled her in, she struggled, he let her out, he tickled her a little, encouraging her to
accept her fate and with him the master, played with her so that
she lost her sense of direction and purpose. And then – was there
a climax?

He invited her to the opera in Vienna and made her a proposition. Would she come to Milan, his home, and take a very nice
flat he had already bought for her, and … he was blunt about it,
become his mistress? It would be very, very pleasant. He was
devoted to her. There would be opportunities for her. She would
be one of his family, a very important member. Everyone would
love and respect her. She would be one of them. As for her children, they would be very welcome. Italians loved children. He

loved children. Why, already he loved her children. He would be a father to them. She was not to worry about money. Yes, he knew that she was proud, and he respected that, he too was proud. But he had a lot of money, a very great deal. Far too much really, and he would be glad to give her some.

She said there would have to be a formal agreement setting things down, so she would be protected. He waved his arms in agreement. She excused herself and went to the Ladies Room where she rang her solicitor, Wiseman, on his mobile. She told him and he said, 'No problem.' She returned to their table and said 'Yes.' And then she agreed to go to his hotel room and give him all that he desired and deserved. It surprised him. 'English ladies! Melting icebergs.' It was all so unexpected, but didn't displease him.

Melissa broached the possibility of going to live in Milan with her children. Faith said, 'No, no, I want to stay with daddy and Rachel.' It was rude of her but had the virtue of transparency. Adam said, 'Yes, please. What team does he support, and can I get a season ticket? And if it's Inter I want to get there before the season starts.' Which also was clear. Melissa was willing to give way. She asked Roger whether he would accept an informal arrangement so they could avoid the expense and delay of the courts. He said 'No.' He wanted custody of Faith, and was willing to seek an order from the court if she would promise not to oppose it; there would be reasonable access for her, with Faith able to see her at any time. Melissa said 'Yes.' Roger thought that it was quite amazing what could be agreed, and quickly, if there was a will to do so.

And in no time at all there was jubilation and whooping in both Milan and Norfolk at the outbreak of good sense and adult maturity. 'At last', said Fiona, dragging Faith off to the stables.

Was this the end of it: the long journey through a desert of humiliation and ignominy, the pathway Roger had been treading for longer than he could remember? Nothing more to be humiliated about and nothing more that could be rescued, with victims being cared for – admittedly – as far back on the track as you could see? It was not easy this side of the grave to bury truth. He had paid a heavy price for all that he had done wrong, for all the limitations and imperfections of his character: and he had repented his sins and asked for forgiveness. But was it quite all? Had he faced up to everything, and was there, perhaps, more to come? But did not everyone sweat upon things they had done that they ought not to have done; and were there not sins of commission and omission troubling the conscience of every man?

It had become a habit of Roger's to rise early when at home and to go into Rachel's unfinished walled garden. He would sit quietly on a bench there and look over the meadows. The neighbouring farmer would pass through his line of vision, shotgun under his arm and eager snuffling retriever at his heel, or suddenly dashing across the field out of vision. The farmer would wave, and he would signal back. He supposed that these salutations were as old as man himself. Soon the line of her stone wall would block out this view; but as Rachel said, you could see the surrounding countryside from almost everywhere else in the house and surrounding gardens. Nevertheless, it would constitute a kind of barricade, shutting out more than it contained within. What he loved most in the Norfolk countryside were the long lines of vision over open fields to a distant horizon. But he was in favour of the walled garden because he was in favour of her.

The work was being done by local gardeners and tradesmen, and at a very slow pace. Rachel said that any garden of value took ages to create, and that haste would achieve nothing. His labour was not really needed, but on many mornings he would do something. This morning he thought digging out a partly created bed would be the thing. Rachel had been persuaded to let him plant one of the beds. He thought, that if he did this carefully, it might constitute for him a brief claim on the attention of posterity. This issue of impermanency had always troubled him. What did life amount to, other than moments of brief pleasure; and so why not create a garden such as this? How long might it last? Rachel had been brusque and determinate: it will give us great satisfaction to create it, and who knows, bring pleasure to many others in years to come. That was sufficient justification for him; but then not every garden could be a Sissinghurst.

As he looked towards the house he thought that almost everything he loved – or that he was allowed to love, thinking of his son Adam – was within its walls. If she had not slept in the stables overnight Fiona would soon be stealing across the yard to them: but she would have no wish to find him, for he was not a part of this secret world. Rachel had stirred as he left her side, not wanting him to move, needing him even in sleep. Sometimes she preceded him. When Faith was fighting back some part of her shadow of disease Rachel slept by her side as a guardian angel holding her hand. He did not know how she had always known the times of Faith's need, but she did. And he thought that this solidarity was peculiar to women; that they could respond to these unspoken needs in ways blocked to men.

From the garden he would go to his office where he would fax out messages to his sales people and make early morning calls. He was fond of his sales people, and knowing their needs and weaknesses he would give late night consideration to them, and their particular problems, which for most of his working life had been his problems too. Lately he had taken time to bury himself away in his study to update a journal he had been keeping over the past few years. He attempted to write something every day, and if he missed a day or two he would leave blank pages and endeavour to catch up at the end of the week.

He thought wryly that if he became truly happy he might have nothing to write about. It was so much easier to write about being miserable. It was usually Rachel who found him there, hugging him from behind, kissing him, murmuring that she had missed him, and nudging him gently back into the flow of real life and the breakfast table. It was perverse of him not to know whether it pleased him that a loved one missed him: for on some occasions he was pleased and on others he wasn't, not being always able to shake off the feeling that it was unwise for any other person to be dependent on him, for he was not always to be relied upon. Rachel, knowing it, had always thought his responses to be highly silly: he was the most reliable man she had ever known.

Rachel knew that Roger had not told her all the truth about the tragic death of Garth Droylsden, even supposing that such a truth existed: and she didn't care one damn. Not that it wasn't a consideration. If she allowed herself to dwell on it, to ask him further questions about the past, to justify himself again to her, it would sour things between them. The real issue was whether she trusted him in relation to her, and to their life now. She did. There were necessary lies between people who were close, and the real issue was whether these lies, mostly little ones, mattered.

His dissembling did not matter to her. She was dimly aware that little lies heaped upon each other over time could amount to something more than a molehill – but that was not yet an issue between her and Roger, and hopefully would never amount to one. Then there were her own little lies. If she told Roger everything about her life, down to the slightest misdemeanour of her youth, she would achieve nothing. She might hurt him a little, and what point did it serve, this searing sort of truth? He knew, anyway. Not details. Not the prosaic but the essential truth about her. Sometimes she thought he knew more than she did. On occasions, when she was unwisely bleating something out, he would stop her; and if it was really silly, he would kiss her; and if she was tragically stupid he would – if the occasion permitted – take off all her clothes and make love to her. So she knew that what might be the whole truth was not required of her.

When they were freshly committed to each other, in the beginning, she had taken out a notebook, and having pondered, had written down the points she considered essential to keeping him – for she thought it a miracle that he loved her and that he was with her as an integral woven-in part of her life. She looked back, which she knew she should not, at the fading script, and wincing a little at her callowness, read it once again. She was to be a complete woman to him; she was to be faithful, putting him before any other – even her most dearest – because without him, without his love, she simply couldn't exist for anyone else; she was going to care for him down to the slightest thing, starting with his health and his food, his leisure and his dear ones, all of which was easy; she would listen to him and detect him, which she thought the key to success, developing her intelligence about him, even when he was in a distant land not of his choosing. She was going to be absolutely perfect or as damn well near perfect as anyone could be.

But for the moment this was all theoretical. For this day, a Saturday, they would be very busy. Fiona would be riding at a gymkhana in the afternoon and Roger had promised her that he would get her there in good shape, because she, Rachel, had to go into town to order the plants she had agreed with the gardener, who was fussy about these things; and then she had promised her mother she would drop in by lunch time, and take her on to see Fiona ride. And then there was Faith. Who was to take care of Faith? Faith had best stay with her, for it would be too much for Roger. It was all too much really, and far from perfect, but then what could you do?

CHAPTER 25

THREE YEARS HAD passed. Roger, Rachel and the children bumbled happily along, treating each new day as an adventure. Rachel's parents retained their reservations about the stability of their daughter's family arrangements but, loving her, they swallowed their doubts and did their very considerable best to support and sustain them all.

Gloria had made a considerable commercial success of the leisure complex, which had been developed beyond the original concept. The expansion required new capital and Gloria had to borrow large new sums of money to maintain her share of the venture. She could hardly afford the interest payments, and knew that at some time she would have to dilute her equity interest or sell out altogether. She had housed herself in a wing of the complex, in a spacious and luxuriously fitted apartment. She remained single, and to those who had known her before her success she was more beautiful than ever: but they thought a little melancholic from time to time, which since they liked her, saddened them as well. Inevitably there were rumours about her private life, which she attempted to keep to herself. Complex staff had noted comings and goings, and speculated upon them as being unusual; but then what did they know? Gloria continued to spend time with Roger, Rachel and the children; she came to stay in the school holidays and they spent time at the complex. They all remained very good friends.

From time to time Roger and Rachel found themselves at the Ship Inn. It continued to be a happy place to visit but a little shabbier. They thought that standards had slipped somewhat: the food service had been greatly simplified and there was no special joy in eating there any more. There was no getting away from the conclusion that the heyday of the inn was in the past.

Bob was perhaps the most fortunate of them all. He liked his new job, and living in Newcastle where people were open and friendly to him. Then, he thought quite out of the blue, he was summoned by the Personnel Officer who had appointed him in the first place, for what he thought would be a wigging. What had he done? This very attractive lady in her fifties then very diffidently offered him a date, which he accepted with alacrity. One thing led to another, and in no time at all they became engaged; and then seeing no profit in delay, they married. At this point she promptly retired, and with her leaving financial package, and with savings of Bob's, they bought an attractive period house in the suburbs and set up a perfectly charming home together, establishing household arrangements which were pleasing and a pleasure to them both.

David Droylsden lived on his own in Manchester. His business prospered in a minor sort of way and he was content with it. He bought his mother's council flat, and when the qualifying time had passed sold it at a profit and acquired a small modern house in a respectable suburb close to his golf club. There he lived in miniature the life he had looked to as a young man.

He maintained the keenest interest in his wife's artistic career. Early on he had bought several of Esther's paintings, and since then he had added to them from time to time. These paintings were not displayed in either of his properties, but remained well preserved in their original wrappings. They had all appreciated in value many times over, and when he would come to sell them, which at some time he had resolved to do, he would make a pretty penny; for his wife had achieved international acclaim, from a base in Manchester, as an avant garde painter of considerable potential. From time to time David read scandalous stories about his wife in magazines, but he had too much good sense to take them literally – and anyway, it meant nothing to him these days.

Melissa and Adam were happy in Milan. Melissa had developed a flourishing business activity as a voice coach, which although owing something to Luigi in conception, did no more than reflect her own prowess in doing the job. Adam began to find a place in a society that valued his good looks and singularity. He was caught up in a network of women who treated him kindly: aunts and cousins of Luigi's who fed and spoilt him, and nieces, younger girls, who even then were willing to flutter their eyelashes at him and to be coy.

Roger had spent time writing a book, and had sent the final chapters to the publisher in September. It was late in October before he had an acceptance. There were a few minor corrections and suggested alterations which he was expected to consider before the book could be printed; but he was so eager to put his mind at rest that he reacted to this final request immediately, and that very morning, when in town, he posted his agreement to all the suggested alterations – of everything. The young editor had written 'Absolutely Perfect' on the compliment slip in her childish copperplate writing, which was very nice of her: but he thought the writing much too close to life to be described in this way. Earlier in the year he had completed payments to creditors under his voluntary arrangement, and in the previous month he had at last received a court order stating it. What he hoped now was that he had wrought his own redemption in the writing of the book; or if not quite that, for it would be asking a lot, at least that in understanding better the disasters of his life he might have helped others who wondered about them still.

He dined with Rachel in celebration of his book completion with a very good vintage burgundy and they had retired early. They made love, which was infinitely preferred by them both to fine wine; and had slept soundly until the approach of dawn, when Roger woke suddenly. He lay there for a while, on watch for Rachel, keeping her safe. He admired the way she lay in her bed, stretched out and composed; an adult in apparent full control of her life rather than the shapeless lump of foetal mass he imagined for himself. He knew that if he placed his hand gently on her thigh, or caressed the nape of her neck, no matter how deeply asleep she would wake like a goddess from the depths of the sea; she would turn towards him, winding herself around; and she would melt into and become one with him. This morning he did not want to wake her; and gently kissing a breast he stole from the bed as she murmured his name.

He sat in the window-seat and looked over the gentle greensward which swept away to the distant beech trees protesting to a persistent breeze. He thought he heard their troubled and turbulent sighs rising within him, first singly and then as a chorus. Outside dark blue was turning to slate grey, sombre and disturbing; and soon the birds would join this chorus in an agitation to reclaim a territory which at that moment he shared with no other creature. He recalled childhood illnesses when he woke at these times and felt the greyness as a veil of pain which would abate with the light of day. If he were lucky the early autumn sunshine would play on the pillows behind him, turning the reddish-gold of her hair to the magical brilliance of a Renaissance painting. He twitched at the curtains in an endeavour to capture any early shafts of light by placing them at precisely the right angle to the rising sun.

Beyond the trees was the river. And then the land would race away from him on and on to the sea. As he leant forward he knew that he could cross to the other side; that it was possible for him now, and that in some mysterious way the whole of his life had brought him to this point. He was glad and at peace with himself. Soon the sky would turn roseate with the rising sun. It was even now turning colour. Then he saw a thin red band had formed, expanding and rising toward him as water on glass, turning everything red. Roger recalled that he had regretted this, the blotting-out of the view, the sea of red. He remembered also that he had called out to her and that he had heard no reply. But he did not fear the waters rising around him, for he knew at the last that he could sail on.

Rachel found him hunched on the window-seat with a hand splayed out before him on the windowpane. She cried out, placing her arms around him, not realising from the first moment that he had gone. Tears bathed his head, now bowed and helpless before her, as first the water had touched him; gathering him in the grace of her love, and the numbing pain of her loss, while her cries went unheeded. Later the doctor, meaning to be kind, said that Roger had experienced a massive heart attack which must have killed him immediately: Rachel must not reproach herself, as there would have been absolutely nothing she could have done to save him.

Roger was cremated and Rachel scattered his ashes from the boat in a Norfolk broad which to her marked the spot where it had really started. There was a memorial service which some twenty people attended. A number of people said kind things about Roger; but to Rachel's sorrow – and despite the urgings of the adults in his life – his son Adam was absent. Inter were playing a home match on that day.

Rachel kept a candle in the window of her bedroom at the exact spot at which Roger had died. When at home she lit it before sleep and snuffed it out upon waking. On the second anniversary of his death she snuffed out the candle for the last time and laid it to rest in the drawer of her bedside table.

DRAMATIS PERSONAE

(in rough order of appearance)

The Droylsden family

David Droylsden	husband and entrepreneur
Esther Droylsden	wife and artist
Garth Droylsden	son
Naomi Droylsden	daughter
Jacob Droylsden	David's father
Judith Droylsden	David's mother
Ivor Bowen	former partner of David and friend of Esther
Dorothy Bowen	Ivor's wife
Anthony Valentine	a director of Westminster Investments
Albert Finch	an assassin

The Greer family

Roger Greer	failed entrepreneur
Melissa Greer	wife and opera singer
Luigi Ambroso	friend of Melissa, opera lover and impresario
Faith Greer	daughter
Adam Greer	son
Sylvia Clarke	Roger's girl friend

The Churchill-Jones family

Bob Churchill-Jones	Detective Chief Inspector at Scotland Yard
Gloria Churchill-Jones	wife and friend to Rachel and Roger
Susan Churchill-Jones	daughter
Mrs Frost	Bob's cleaner
Alec Cook	police sergeant and assistant to Bob
Sandra Jones	Alec's long-term girl friend
Nicki	Alec's bit on the side
Fred Chateris	Landlord of the Ship Inn
Margaret Chateris	Fred's wife
Andrea	Bob's friend across the road

The Jackson family

Rachel Jackson	friend of Roger and Gloria
Janet Jackson	Rachel's mother
Henry Jackson	Rachel's father
Fiona	Rachel's daughter by first husband Alistair
Sophie	Rachel's daughter by Alistair
Fergus	Rachel's son by her second husband Ralph
Ralph Darcy	Rachel's second husband
Chloe Darcy	Ralph's second wife
Lucy Rogers	a friend of Rachel's

Others

(in random order)

Various bankers; clerics, a vicar and a priest; company directors; FBI agents; friends and relatives; a judge; policemen at Scotland Yard and in Norfolk; professional advisors, including an accountant, solicitors and barristers; secretaries and receptionists; staff of FIR, a fund raising organisation of the IRA; venture capitalists.